Dead Eye Hunt
A Post Apocalypse Adventure
Peter Meredith

Copyright 2019
Peter Meredith
Blah, blah, blah, lawyer speak,
lawyer speak, blah blah, blah.
Do we really need to go into this?
Here's the deal. Looky-no-touchy.
It's as simple as that.

Fictional works by Peter Meredith:
A Perfect America
Infinite Reality: Daggerland Online Novel 1
Infinite Assassins: Daggerland Online Novel 2
Dead Eye Hunt
Generation Z
Generation Z: The Queen of the Dead
Generation Z: The Queen of War
Generation Z: The Queen Unthroned
Generation Z: The Queen Enslaved
Generation Z: The Queen Unchained
The Sacrificial Daughter
The Apocalypse Crusade War of the Undead: Day One
The Apocalypse Crusade War of the Undead: Day Two
The Apocalypse Crusade War of the Undead Day Three
The Apocalypse Crusade War of the Undead Day Four
The Apocalypse Crusade War of the Undead Day Five
The Horror of the Shade: Trilogy of the Void 1
An Illusion of Hell: Trilogy of the Void 2
Hell Blade: Trilogy of the Void 3
The Punished
Sprite
The Blood Lure The Hidden Land Novel 1
The King's Trap The Hidden Land Novel 2
To Ensnare a Queen The Hidden Land Novel 3
The Apocalypse: The Undead World Novel 1
The Apocalypse Survivors: The Undead World Novel 2
The Apocalypse Outcasts: The Undead World Novel 3
The Apocalypse Fugitives: The Undead World Novel 4
The Apocalypse Renegades: The Undead World Novel 5
The Apocalypse Exile: The Undead World Novel 6
The Apocalypse War: The Undead World Novel 7
The Apocalypse Executioner: The Undead World Novel 8
The Apocalypse Revenge: The Undead World Novel 9
The Apocalypse Sacrifice: The Undead World 10
The Edge of Hell: Gods of the Undead Book One
The Edge of Temptation: Gods of the Undead Book Two
The Witch: Jillybean in the Undead World
Jillybean's First Adventure: An Undead World Expansion
Tales from the Butcher's Block

Chapter 1

Manhattan
June 3rd, 2161

The girl was trying to pass herself off as a vamp. The flesh of her throat and the high mounds of her partially exposed breasts were so white that he could see the blue veins pulsing beneath. She had midnight-black hair that sat piled on her head in braided coils. They wound in ever-tightening circles, a foot in height and made her seem taller than she was. Her teeth were unnaturally white. They were the sort of white that only money could buy.

Her clothes were expensive as well: the boots that went up to mid-thigh were real leather, and the bone corset was trimmed with ivory and silver. The long, elbow-length gloves: one snowy white, the other rich burgundy, were silk.

She even had the half-lidded, haughty, slightly bored-with-life gaze of a vamp.

But now that she was only inches away, Mack-D wasn't fooled. Beneath the smell of 5th Avenue gin wafting from her breath was the sharp odor of syn-mint, which was normal enough at street level, but down below where the sun's light could never reach, no self-respecting vampire would touch synthetic anything.

With difficulty, Mack-D kept his disappointment in check. Sucking the blood from a vamp was a Dead-eye's wet dream.

"Welcome to the outside world," he said, calmer now that he knew she wasn't real. A minute before, his heart had been pounding at the sight of her and his stomach was roaring louder than the music vibrating through the walls. Still, vamp or not, he had to fight the urge to latch onto her right there and drain her dry. He was hungry after all.

It was a mortal hunger, and endless pain that he would take to his grave.

"The outshide?" she replied, slurring in a gin-mumble. "Oh right. I was slummin' it. But now, I gotta go home. Where's the shtreet?" She had taken the wrong door out of the club and now she found herself in a piss-smelling alley, eyeing a slag. And a big slag at that. She had to pitch her head well back to look into his tattooed face. As she did, the first touch of fear began to burn its way through the gin.

Mack-D could smell fear rising off her. He sucked it in deep, his nostrils flaring, his brilliant blue eyes almost closing as his lust and excitement mounted again. The blood was richer when they were afraid, and the flesh sweeter. The animal in him could barely be contained by what was left of the thinking man he had been. He held back. His filthy nails dug into the flesh of his palm, but he held back.

"I can take you home," he blurted out. Her fear spiked at the unexpected and unwanted offer. Her fear smelled like shaved brass and, as he breathed it in, saliva flooded his mouth. *No!* He couldn't give in to temptation. If he killed her now, draining her, eating his way into her heart, he wouldn't be able to stop. He'd be seen and the damned taxmen would be called. He didn't care about the police, they were lazy and could be bribed to look away from anything. But if they called in a hunter, his only chance would be to flee over the wall. Hunters never stopped. Never.

"It's okay," he said to her, holding up his large, filthy hands palms out so that she wouldn't see the black blood beneath his nails. "You don't have to be afraid. I'm a thumper here. You know, a bouncer. We provide security."

"I ammm shecure. Just get outta my way, 'n I'll be fine."

She tried to push past and he took her by the arm. Now he smelled the cheap lye soap beneath her expensive perfume.

"Hold on a moment. Taking you home is part of the package. You know, the service we provide for our exclusive clients. You are exclusive, aren't you?" He was guessing that exclusive was the right word. Or should he have said premium? It had taken him hours to come up with this idea and to memorize his lines. Now, he waited, not sure what she would do, but fully prepared to crack her on the back of the head.

"Yeah. Yeah I'm 'sclusive. You got a limo or sumtin?"

Limo, limo, limo, he ran the word through his slowly disintegrating vocabulary and came up blank. "Uh, yeah. We have all sorts of limos. The best limos. My limo is *exclusive*."

"Really? But you're a slag."

Sudden fury swept Mack-D. *I ain't no slag!* he seethed inside, wishing he could chew her curled lip right off her face. It was true that he looked like the spitting image of a slag. His face was scrawled with tattoos in a desperate attempt to hide the pockmarks that were deep as small craters, and the scars that ran like ravines, and the strange snake-like scales that kept peeling from his throat. It was getting progressively worse, but he was no slag. Radiation poisoning wasn't his problem. In fact, other than his endless hunger, Mack-D would say he had no problems.

That was the best part about being a Dead-eye. Before he had been infected he had been nothing more than balding Michael McDonald, a complete nobody. The day he was infected was the day he stopped worrying about bills, and work, and the missus complaining about the apartment, or what the neighbors thought of his drinking. He didn't care if his kids had their indentured licenses sold to one of the horrible Mandarin sweat shops that worked them until their fingers bled or until the toxins built up in their systems so much that they slagged out and became no better than trogs.

He didn't even care about the fallout that filled the air or the industrial toxins in the water. None of that mattered because it couldn't hurt him now. Very little could hurt him any more and when he did get hurt, he healed in hours. They left scars but they were no consequence to Mack-D

But he couldn't exactly say that to the girl, could he? "It ain't my limo. It's the company's." He held his breath, hoping she wouldn't ask: which company? The company he worked for melted down trash and strained out the good parts. As far as he knew, there were no limos at the plant. There was only a horrible stench that made the real slags go green beneath their tattoos.

"Oh, ho-kay," she said, falling into him. It was another sign that she was a fake. Even drunk, a high-box vamp wouldn't touch a slag. "Where's the limo?"

"It's close," he said, pointing.

She didn't like what she saw of the alley: the trash, the long oily puddle that ran straight down the middle, the over-flowing dumpsters, the dingy, grey panel van. At least beyond the van was the street. The real street. Behind her the alley was shadow-black as it wormed into the warren of a mid-center block. There was no telling what was back there. Even in Manhattan, a mid-center block was dangerous for an unarmed girl who didn't belong.

Mack-D led her up the alley, his hand on her tightening as he neared the van; she would try to run. Drunk or not, she was not going to go quietly. God, how he wished he could let her go, so she could scream and run for her life. He never felt more alive than when they screamed. It was always so primal. It was at that moment that they truly became prey and he became the hunter. Everything before that, the tears as they lay trussed up in the van, the begging, the same insipid questions—*What are you going to do to me?* It was all just foreplay.

She edged away from the van as they came close, not wanting to get her clothes dirty. He stopped her. "Hold on." He wanted to add more, maybe a reason why she should wait calmly while he opened the side door, but no reason came to him, as he fumbled with the latch. It was such a simple thing: lift and pull, and yet his left hand was missing two fingers and had become less reliable as he gradually lost dexterity.

"Hey, what're you doing?" she whispered, fear beginning to cut through the gin. "This isn't a…" Mack-D finally got the door open. The back of the van was windowless and dark as sin. She surprised him by not screaming. "No," she whispered, sobering quickly. His grip on her arm was like steel. He was hulking and outrageously strong. She was thin and shaking.

"Yeah. Get in."

Before she knew it, she was pushed inside, barking her shin against something hard and unforgiving. Everything inside the van was like that. She was twisted about and pushed down onto an uneven layer of rigid metal. "Please, wait," she whispered. "I-I'm rich. My f-father will pay good money for me. Just don't hurt me, please."

He was already hurting her. Mack-D had bent her arms behind her back at a severe angle and held her pinned face-down on the metal as he struggled to get the length of nylon rope from his pocket. "Why would I want money? Can't very well take a trip, can I?" He pictured himself on a white sand beach, sipping some sort of fruity cocktail and turning grey in the sun.

"Then what are you going to do with me?" She sucked in a sharp breath as he began trussing her up, looping and knotting the rope. It seemed to go on forever. In her mind he was creating the most elaborate knot ever tied. In reality, he couldn't manage more than a series of granny-knots, though he made up for their simplicity by tying the knots as tight as he could.

"What I want to do is eat you. I'm going to hang you upside down and slit you wide open and drink straight from your throat." He was bent over her, drooling down her neck. His hot breath smelled like an open sewer. She screamed, and it was all he could do not to tear into her beautiful flesh. "But not yet," he said, balling a fist as he fought for control. The screams had to stop and the fist was a convenient tool. One shot to the back of the head and she went face-first into the scraps of rusting iron.

She woke sometime later, just as the van was slipping beneath the skin of the earth. She was too frightened to move. Like a child, she hoped that if she just lay there, he would forget about her. Then his groping hand found her thigh.

"Too skinny," he muttered, giving it a pinch and a poke, like someone assessing a piece of poultry.

Tears came then. Silent tears.

The van chugged out a trail of black smoke as it entered the labyrinth of tunnels below the city. It took too many turns to count, still the girl was hopeful she would recognize one of the reflective signs that sometimes hung across the top of the roadway. Hope died a quick death as Mack-D swung into one of the unlit passages that branched from the main road.

Down they went into unrelenting darkness. There were no signs down here, no traffic, no pedestrians hurrying home. The road narrowed until the van filled the shaft.

"We're almost there," Mack-D told her. "Fourth left. There's number three." He slowed, looking for the turn. It always came up so suddenly when driving. When he saw it, he let out a long breath. He took the turn and stopped in front of a wall of solid iron that was splashed with graffiti. It was then that the girl began to realize she would never see the sun again.

Although she had been calling herself Allegro Albarossa all night, her real name was Christina Grimmett, and she was most definitely not rich. The fancy clothes she had on were the cast-offs of her employer, Ashley Tinsley. *She* was a true vampire. She was so rich that she only wore an outfit once before having it burned. Were she to be seen in the same outfit twice she would likely hang herself, and donating her clothes was something she could not contemplate. What if, God forbid, some lesser creature was seen wearing *her* outfit?

Christina had stolen the outfit piece by piece and now realized it was wrong and that this was her punishment. She began to blubber which made him grin.

"You can scream if you want," Mack-D told her, as he slipped out of the van. They both knew screaming was useless now. The earth would swallow it just as it had swallowed her.

She struggled up, realizing that he had left the van running. Here was her chance—but to do what? He was working a heavy key into a slot, and the door or the gate or whatever it was, would be open in seconds. She would never be able to get the rope off her in time and even if she could, she didn't think she could back out of there without crashing.

Then a thought made its way through her rising panic: *Maybe I don't back out. Maybe I crash on purpose.* Her captor was framed between the headlights. All she had to do was get in the front seat, somehow get the van in gear, and slam on the gas. With her hands tied behind her back, it seemed impossible. Still, she had to try.

Squirming, she threw her torso into the passenger seat and then kicked her legs around to the driver's side. The plan failed at that point. Somehow, she got her crooked arm caught up on the gear shift jutting from the center console—and she couldn't get it off! To make matters worse, as she fought to free herself, her knee banged the horn and it let out a single tired honk, like a dying goose.

Mack-D reacted slowly to the sound. He turned and stared through the filmed-over windshield at Christina, his dulled mind unable to comprehend what she was doing. This gave her an extra few seconds to try to jerk her body off the gear shifter, but all she managed to do was mush the shifter into reverse. With a wailing shriek, the van ground backward against the tunnel wall. Desperately, Christina tried again, bucking as hard as she could.

The van jerked hard as it slipped into drive and then began to roll forward at an achingly slow pace. There should have been plenty of time for Mack-D to do something, but he only stared into the headlights as the van crawled up to him at a steady six-miles-an-hour. He seemed mesmerized by the lights, and to her amazement and grim satisfaction, the van crushed him into the iron wall. He let out a blast of air as his chest took the brunt of the blow and for a moment, he hung his head.

"Ha!" Christina shrieked. "That's what you get! That's what you..." What she saw when he lifted his chin choked her words off. At first, she thought one of his eyes had popped out and was sitting on the stunted hood of the van. Then she saw that it was only a contact lens and what she took for a gaping hole in his face was actually his real eye. It was black and wet as oil.

"No," she whispered, finally understanding what he was. "Dead-eye." It was one of them. One of the undead.

Her mind reeled. There hadn't been a zombie seen east of Jersey since before she was born, and yet here was one grinning at her, black blood dribbling from between its teeth.

She had to escape and not just from the beast, she had to get out of the city altogether. If people found out that there were zombies in New York, there'd be a panic. She'd be in a race for the harbor against ten million people. With a head start, she might beat most of them there, but could she beat the bombers or the missiles?

In Ottawa, it had taken only a pack of fourteen Dead-eyes for that city to be wiped off the map. That too was before Christina's time, but they say the city still glowed at night from all the radiation.

Desperation lent her strength. She heaved herself over the shifter but as she tried to roll over she nudged it with her hip and shoved it once more into reverse. Back went the van, freeing Mack-D. A scream built inside her as she watched his black grin grow wide as he walked around to the driver's window.

"Yes. Scream for me," he said, climbing in, his face dark with hideous pleasure.

She did more than scream and he loved every second of it.

Chapter 2

It was only four and already the day was growing dark, not that it had been all that bright to begin with. A sunny day in New York was a rarity and Cole didn't like them. They weren't natural. A sunny day made him feel exposed. No, Cole preferred the anonymity of a dismal wet day.

The ugly clouds had been pissing out rain since noon. Not in torrents as it sometimes did, but in spurts, and now the streets were slick with muck.

New York had its own brand of mud. For the most part it was made up of human shit and ash that drifted in from the cratered remains of Newark. There was also a good deal of rat turd in the muck, and industrial waste sometimes made it fancy with prisms of obscene-smelling rainbows. Finally, corpses added their own special tang to the mix—the "daily" pickups had ceased being daily when Cole was a boy, and now a body might sit in the gutter for days before anyone came by to dispose of it.

Cole hunched broad shoulders against the rain and watched his prey as he finally left the Mandarin joint off 6th. Cole had never been to one of these joints where lunch wasn't a ten minute, eat-while-you-stand affair. If he lingered any longer than that he always had some tiny, wrinkled raisin give him the stink-eye and tell him, "Go way. You order more food or go way."

But the sick bastard Cole was after had been in the joint for three hours. Cole absolutely hated waiting like that. It made him antsy. Standing around doing nothing made his muscles stiff. He liked to be loose and ready for anything. In New York you had to be ready, or you could very well end up as just another bloated corpse, stripped bare-ass, maggots doing the funky jive in your hair, and rats tunneling into your bowels.

In this case, the waiting was meaningful.

There was no way a Mandarin was going to let some slick hang out in his shop all afternoon unless a deal was being made. Cole just hoped it was his kind of deal. He wouldn't have blinked an eye if the slick was trying to move uptown ice, or mule that had been spun-up in a Rican's toilet. People threw away their lives all the livelong day and that was on them.

But if 'ol Santino was buying up large amounts of syn-ope, well that would be quite telling. Dead-eyes needed to be on downers twenty-four-seven or they'd go monster. Near-lethal doses of opioids kept their rage in check and dulled the hunger for blood.

As always, the question was whether Santino Grimmett was a Dead-eye at all. There was a depressingly good chance that he was just a run-of-the-mill murdering psychopath. Cole hoped to God he wasn't. There was no money in it. Putting down a Dead-eye would net him ten-large. Killing an un-convicted psycho could very well lead to a prison sentence. Cole's predecessor was turning dusty in some black hole in the ground because he had offed a human.

Cole had to run a fine line. If he was too quick on the trigger, he faced prison, if he wasn't quick enough, he would end up like so many hunters: recycled out of a rat's ass.

The career of a hunter was generally short and violent. Still, the money was good. It kept the lights on and the booze flowing...barely. Things had been tight for Cole, and he was probably the only person in the world who wanted Santino to be a Dead-eye.

As the slick moved into the crowd, Cole trailed after, watching him closely as he trudged north. In this light, Cole's hazel eyes were as grey as the rain, though it was hard to tell as they were at squints as he looked for the smallest clues. Santino moved slowly, almost aimlessly, while all around him the faceless crowds hurried to get home and dry. Was the syn-ope kicking in? Were his neurons black with the virus and his brains drowned in a sick goo?

Or was he depressed because he had stabbed his wife of twenty years, butchered her remains and stuffed her different parts in his freezer? Of course, it could have been that he was tripping balls. It was hard to tell. Judging a person from behind by the way he held his shoulders was far from an exact science. Still, something was wrong with him. Something made him stand out.

Unlike the hundreds of people pushing along with him, he didn't duck his head as he passed through a grey curtain of water falling from a second-level catwalk. And he didn't seem to care when he angled off the sidewalk and his foot came down in the ghastly muck that everyone else avoided. He was also the only person who didn't glance nervously around as he crossed the unmarked boundary into Red Dog territory.

Even Cole let his eyes slip off his mark. A half dozen young morons with poorly concealed handguns lounged on an awning-covered stoop. They thought they were tough. Cole thought they looked like targets.

The pedestrians went stiff as they passed, holding their heads straight, while canting their eyes far to the right. All except for Santino. He moved like a sleepwalker and passed by without a challenge.

Cole was a different story. As much as he tried, sometimes he didn't blend in. He not only had a certain air of danger about him, but he also stood a head taller than most of the people in the crowd. The poly-leather black coat that hung to mid-thigh might have been expensive; and maybe the narrow tie, a black stripe down his white shirt made him look like an office worker, and everyone knew they had money.

At the same time, his black boots were worn and he had the partially inked face of a man who was slowly becoming a slag.

Two of the braver toughs came off the stoop and strode into his way, wanting a closer look. "We got a sidewalk fee here," the taller of the two said, giving a what-can-you-do shrug. The Red Dogs claimed they were pure breed Irish but in reality, they let in any pasty-faced wanker as long as he had a freckle or two. This one had a spray of them across a girly little nose. "I'm afraid we're gon' hafta charge you ten."

They also affected an annoying Irish brogue. They weren't alone in this habit. The Rastas acted like they were from Jamaica instead of from Jamaica, Queens, the Ricans called everyone "Ese," and Cole couldn't go to an Italian restaurant with a slick without wanting to punch him in the face. Rigatoni became ri-gahTONEY. And the damned Mandarins acted like they were fresh off the boat but there wasn't a one of them whose family hadn't been here for six generations.

Normally, Cole had little patience for this sort of thing. Just then he had even less. "Ten?"

"Each. In cash, o' course." The bigger one cast a quick glance at his companion, who wasn't going to be a Red Dog much longer. Cole was tall enough to see the slag building up in his thinning, greased hair and behind his ear. His eyes were already a bit dull.

"I could do fifteen," Cole said, pulling back his coat, showing off the 10mm Crown on his belt. The aluminum alloy winked silver in the low light. The gun was literally worth any three of the Red Dogs, and they stared as if they were looking at a diamond of the same size. They blinked back into the moment when Cole dropped his big hand down on the grip.

The leader started to draw in a long breath, which would end with him going for his gun. Judging by the bulge beneath his brown corduroy jacket, Cole figured it was one of the ludicrous .44 caliber Eagle knock-offs that were all the rage. Because of its size, it wasn't a weapon designed for a quick draw.

"Maybe you should rethink this," Cole advised. "I'd hate to waste a bullet killing you."

"There's six of us," the Dog answered, losing his accent in his attempt to sound tough.

They were teens who probably hadn't ever fired more than five rounds with their over-sized guns. The damned things were made of composite plastic and had a habit of cracking after a few shots. After thirty they could explode.

To make matters worse, their eight-inch barrels were overly-light and with the rounds in the grip, the guns were completely unbalanced.

Cole wondered if any of them could hit the broadside of a barn. "I'm not too worried," he said. And he wasn't. The kid's right hand was frozen about a foot away from his body. When he tried to reach for his gun, it would be mechanically stiff and slow. His friend had been so cocksure that he had walked up with his hands behind his back. He might as well be handcuffed.

"You and your little puppy friend are the only ones I need to kill. Once you're stretched out, the others'll run inside crying for daddy."

"Maybe," the Dog said, trying to sound tough. "Or maybe there are a whole mess of us and one of us will get you."

Cole glanced up at the building. Like so much of New York, its windows were bricked over in an attempt to keep out the acid fog, the fallout, and what the previous governor had called "heavy particulate airflows." It was the PC way of saying industrial contamination that made the southern wind smell like metaled rot. When it came in thick, it turned the sky the color of an old bruise and had been known to asphyxiate infants in their cribs.

"But you'll still be dead," Cole said, flicking his eyes back at the Dog. He was about to go on when they heard a sharp whistle from up the street. Two stoops up, a gaggle of money-honeys pulled their skirts lower as they scurried inside.

"Taxmen," one of the Red Dogs warned in a hissing whisper.

The lead Dog pulled his coat tight around his meager chest, doing little to hide his gun as a patrol of four police officers came strolling up the block. Like all taxmen they were tall and strapping to begin with, but looked even bigger decked out in their body armor. Beneath the plates of grey metal, they wore urban camo, and in their hands, they carried the scaled-down Forino version of the old Colt M4. They looked more like soldiers than policemen.

"We already paid our taxes, officer," the lead Dog said, raising his hands. "We pay Manua every month, rain or shine."

"That's Lieutenant Manua to you," one of the officers shot back. "And those taxes only cover everyday activities. This doesn't seem all that conventional. It looks to me like you boys were about to throw down right in the middle of the street. You know the governor frowns on a dozen people getting gunned down in broad daylight. And when he frowns on it, I frown…holy shit."

Cole grimaced at being recognized. He knew this officer all too well. "Bruce, it's good to see you," he lied.

Sergeant Bruce Hamilton laughed. "Look fellas, it's the White Knight himself, Cole Younger. How's the back? Not bothering you too much, I hope." Four years earlier, they had been on the same squad right up until Hamilton had "accidentally" shot him in the back.

"Better than new. Look, I'd love to reminisce about old times…"

Hamilton spoke over him, "You turning slag on me?" He pointed with his rifle at Cole's tattoos. They were a cheap blue-green. The four on the left were stylized hammers; on the right were six skulls suggesting he was part of the "Sledge" gang. "If so, I can put you out of your misery. That last bullet was just a warning. We both know I could've killed you."

Cole didn't have time for Hamilton and his hooked nose and thin greasy blond hair. With every minute Santino was plodding further out of reach. And yet this was the first time Cole had seen Hamilton in those four years. "You act like shooting a friend in the back is some kind of accomplishment. If you had taken me on, face to face, I could understand that cocky smile of yours, *taxman*."

At the word, Hamilton sneered. "Keep telling yourself that, Cole. I warned you. I told you it was going to happen if you didn't play ball. It's something I never understood about you. All you needed to do was take a little here and a little there, and maybe turn a blind eye every once in a while. If you had you probably would've made lieutenant by now. Instead, you're one of the little people."

He laughed aloud, but then something caught his eye. Stepping closer, he used his rifle to push back Cole's trench coat. "And what's this? I thought you knew that packing heat out on the street is illegal. Got a license?"

There was no need to answer. One of the other police officers snatched the Crown while a third took his wallet. "Says here he's a bounty hunter. His license is up to date." The officer sounded disappointed. Bounty hunters held an odd position within society: not quite cop, not quite one of the little people that made up the masses. They couldn't be "taxed" while on the job.

"Ain't no bounty going to cover this," the other officer said, sighting down the length of the Crown, carelessly pointing it at a young woman who was hurrying by holding her child's hand in a crushing grip.

No *normal* bounty would ever cover the cost of the gun. So far, Cole's highest bounty had been fifty dollars for bringing in a serial rapist. The Dead-eyes were another story altogether, one that he couldn't ever mention.

The fact that they were in the city at all was deemed classified. If he mentioned them even in a drunken ramble, he would be liquidated. His body would be dissolved in a vat of acid and his name expunged from every record in the city. Each new recruit was given the same speech, the same warning, and had to watch the same video of some idiot who had talked. He had been lowered into the vat slowly, toes first. The grainy video ran for twenty-nine excruciating minutes.

"Some bounties pay better than others," Cole said, holding his hand out for the gun. "I doubt I'll get rich, but it's honest work, unlike what I used to do." The officer had been about to hand over the pistol, but stopped at the jab.

Hamilton laughed and slapped Cole on the back with stinging force. "As always, Cole, you're a damn hoot. That mouth of yours is going to get you killed some day, and hell, that day might just be today." He nodded to the other officers to give him back his belongings. As Cole holstered the Crown, Hamilton pointed up at the tenement. "Is your bounty up there? If so, have at it. You know I'd love to help you out but whoa, look at the time. Me and the boys are on our mandated break."

The gang of Red Dogs backed up a few steps suddenly looking uncomfortable and confused, not knowing whether they were about to be attacked or they were expected to attack a man with an entire squad of policemen watching.

Cole solved the problem for them. "Boys," he said with a nod to them, and then took off at a loping run. Behind him, Hamilton and his men shouted a few insults. Cole didn't care what they said. They were criminals themselves. It's what happened when no one policed the police.

Snagging Dead-eyes was far more important and far more honest—just as long as he didn't kill a human in the process.

After two blocks, the rain began to come down harder than before. It was a cold rain and tasted like dirty pennies. That was usually a bad sign. It meant it was coming in from the west. Cole slid his hood from the back of his coat and pulled it down in what was almost a useless gesture. A hood wasn't going to do jack if he was showering in radioactive water. "The sirens aren't going off," he told himself, and kept going, slowing down at every side street and alley he came to. If Santino took any one of them, he could disappear forever.

It was only after another couple of blocks that Cole realized where Santino was going. He was going home. For the last week, Santino had been hiding out in a flophouse in the village, but like so many criminals before him, he was drawn to the scene of his crime.

Santino's apartment was seven blocks away and Cole figured he could be there in minutes, only just then the klaxons started to sound.

"Shit!" he hissed. The klaxons were far worse than the sirens. It meant a Cat-2 radioactive cloud was coming in. "Or it's already here." The sensors set up on the Jersey side of the Hudson were always breaking down; the smart thing to do was to get inside as fast as he could. "But when am I ever smart," he muttered, pulling out a small emergency mask. He slapped it on and kept running straight down the street, which had gone from annoyingly crowded to deserted in seconds. Even the few taxi cabs that sometimes still prowled the streets were nowhere in sight.

It was like he was the last person left in the city. It was unnerving, but at least the empty streets made sprinting easier, and he ran like his life depended on it. By the time he made it to the building he was reeling from the run and from trying to suck air in through the mask.

Yanking it off, he laid it over the rail of the stairs, and then stood half-bent, gasping and staring around. The interior of the building was cleaner than most and as dim as all of them. Only the vamps could afford to properly light a stairwell or to run an elevator.

Santino lived on the seventh floor; a long climb after the run. Cole sucked in a deep breath and started up. His eyes had yet to get used to the dark and he kicked something after only the fourth step; and at eye level was another small lump. Although his mind immediately thought: *trash*, he hesitated. Trash was usually kicked to the side and these two objects were in the center of the staircase.

The first was a single high-heeled shoe, a spray of white plastic beads gleamed dully up at him from the toe. The other item was a purse. It hadn't been discarded, it had been dropped. He was just fishing the wallet from it, when he heard a thud, a scraping noise and a muffled shout. All of this came from below him.

Like practically every building, its foundation extended deep into the earth. There would be basements and subbasements. Sometimes there were proper tunnels that led to the subways. Other times there were hand-dug warrens and dens where squatting slags lived and died like roaches. They were dangerous places and frequently slumlords chose to brick off a shaft rather than trying to evict the poor creatures. It was efficient, but the smell of their rotting bodies would linger for months.

Cole did not relish the idea of going down to look and tried to tell himself that the thud and the dropped purse weren't necessarily connected. Only he knew better. Dead-eyes were vermin. They liked the dark, and they especially liked to feed in the dark.

Santino had probably surprised the woman who owned the purse. Caught alone, she would have been easy prey and maybe the temptation had been too much for him.

"Son of a bitch," Cole whispered, easing the Crown from its holster, and slipping down the stairwell, hurrying as fast as he dared. Syn-ope wasn't the only thing Santino might have picked up at the Mandarin Joint. Mandarins would sell a person anything as long as the price was right. Santino might be armed to the teeth.

The level below the street was made up of more apartments. Sub-gardens they were called, and Cole couldn't stand them. It was like living in a prison. The air in them never moved.

The next level down was where the darkness took on a physical quality. It sucked in around him. Cole carried a slide-light for the Crown and clicked it in place beneath the barrel. It gave off a timid light which the darkness greedily ate up after only a few yards. Still, it was enough to show him that the level had been designed for storage and at one time it had been filled with metal cages. The metal had been sold for scrap decades before and all that remained were rectangular rust outlines on the dusty floor.

Within the dust was a confusion of tracks. The shoeless prints stood out to Cole. They seemed so small, as if a child had been taken and not a woman.

Because the darkness was so thick, the subbasement had an endless quality to it and Cole suddenly felt the need to run to catch up with Santino and his victim. He raced along in their tracks and came up on them in a back corner, where they grappled together on a low mound just in front of a hand-dug tunnel that sloped away into an even deeper darkness.

"Let her go!" Cole bellowed.

Santino was a big man, almost as big as Cole, which made it a wonder that the woman hadn't already been dragged down into the hole. It was hard to describe her since all Cole saw of her was a wild mane of blonde hair whipping about as she fought like mad, clinging desperately to a gun they were both holding.

"I said drop it! I'll shoot if…"

Suddenly, Santino was flying at Cole with outstretched arms, his hands going for Cole's throat. With no idea where the woman was, Cole couldn't risk shooting. Instead, he threw himself backward, twisting his torso at the same time, so Santino passed over him, his nails scraping over Cole's poly-leather coat. They both fell and then got to their knees at the same time.

"Wait!" Santino hissed, holding out a hand that was dripping with black blood.

Seeing the blood was all the proof Cole needed. He fired twice from a distance of three feet, sending Santino's head back with such force that his neck broke. One shot struck just off the center line of his forehead and the next took out one of his dark eyes.

Cole wasn't taking any chances. In his line of work, he could never afford to take chances. He got to his feet and came to stand over the man and pumped two more into his head.

"That'll be ten-thousand dollars, please," he said, grinning. With a happy sigh, he spun his flashlight around at the darkened subbasement. "Ma'am? Are you okay? Hello?" She wasn't just gone. She was *infected* and gone. "Sad," Cole muttered.

He wasn't really sad. It was hard to be sad when he had just bagged a Dead-eye and had another on the hook. He'd let her stew in her juices for a day or two and then swing by and break the bad news. *No, that ain't the flu you got, girly. Sorry, but I got to pop you.*

Chapter 3

The free coffee wasn't worth the wait. The coffee beans were synthetic, meaning they weren't really beans at all, and the brew only tasted vaguely like coffee. Overall there was more of a tinny, bleach flavor and Cole made a face every time he took a sip.

The brown fluid kept him awake and that's all that mattered. He needed to babysit his bounties because *things* had a way of happening when the government was involved. Bodies got misplaced, paperwork was lost, and checks could come back missing a zero or two. He had spent his entire adult life working for the city government and there was always a mistake and never one in his favor.

For the tenth time that night, he glanced over his report, making sure the wording was correct. It was important that the woman had: "*…entered the building because of the alarm warning.*"

Hunters were supposed to keep to their own territories, however the big bosses cared little for nuance as long as the job got done. If word got out that the woman in his report lived in the building, Cole would have his hands full keeping the others away. That's why he added: "*Dropped purse appeared fancy, with steel or silver clasp.*"

In the dark, he hadn't noticed any clasp and guessed that it had been a button job. This area had been a middle-class neighborhood and the women couldn't afford metal clasps or even faux leather. He paused, trying to remember the feel of the purse when he'd picked it up. It had been heavier than expected and maybe a bit larger than average. But was it faux leather?

"Don't matter," he muttered, as he wrote in: "*Dropped faux-leather purse appeared fancy…*"

He was just thinking about embellishing the shoes when his boss came in looking more haggard than usual. This was saying something since he always looked haggard. Cole wondered, and not for the first time, if he had slipped out of his mom's puss tired and scraggy with little baby jowls and a pinched angry look. Right away, Cole noticed that he wasn't carrying one of the green envelopes that always held his check.

"What gives?"

"You fucked up, Cole. Get in here."

Lieutenant Joshua Lloyd's office was in a constant state of dishevelment. His desk creaked under a mound of reports, while along the wall, the drawers of his four filing cabinets were so stuffed with files that none of them could close. Even the lone couch across from his desk was upholstered in paper a foot deep. When Lloyd slipped behind his desk, he seemed to meld into the mess.

The only chair in the room, besides the one under Lloyd's wide rump, held another stack of papers, that were topped by an ancient *Air-o-lux* box fan that was older than Cole and Lloyd put together. It was held together by tape and wire.

Cole didn't want to sit. "I didn't fuck nothin' up. It's not my fault the skirt took off. And I don't blame her either. And yes, I went after her, but she went out in a Cat-2 for fuck's sake. You don't pay me enough to run out in the middle of a Cat-2."

"The girl isn't the problem. It's Santino." Out of habit, he glanced toward his door to make sure it was shut. "He wasn't a Dead-eye."

"What the hell are you talking about? Of course, he was. I saw the black blood, Lloyd."

"It was dark. You said so yourself. Blood looks black in the dark."

"It wasn't dark when the recovery team got there." Though it had been a two-hour wait and congealed blood did darken over time... "No, it was black. I saw it. Damn it, Lloyd! What kind of shit is this? I want to talk to the recovery team. I want to see their damned notes."

Lloyd sat back shaking his head, making his limp hair move more than the *Air-o-lux* ever did. "You know what their job is. They're there to destroy evidence, not to preserve it. Do you really want to bring them in on this? It's their man who ran the tests. All he's going to say is that Santino was a *human* and that you plugged him four times, twice execution style. Son, you're just lucky this happened out of sight."

Cole heard the threat and had to grind his teeth on an entire string of curses. "There was a girl. He took her down into that…"

"Yes, the recovery team saw the bare print. It's why you're not being charged. Santino was a murderer, we all know it. But God, Cole! If he'd been just a regular guy…" He shook his head again, letting Cole know he would have been strung up for killing him.

"If he was a murderer, wouldn't there be some sort of bounty?"

Lloyd muttered, "Unconvicted murderer. Look, I'm not trying to dick you on this one. Santino's in the morgue. You can see for yourself. What's left of his brain is as pink as my balls."

"I will look, thank you," Cole said stiffly, doing his best to rein in his anger. Ten-thousand had just gone out the fucking window. Twenty-thousand if he counted the girl. Furious he started to storm from the office and was halfway out the door when Lloyd called him back. "By the way, your paint's running. You should fix that."

Crap! One more expense he couldn't afford. His tats weren't real; they were squid-ink henna and usually lasted a few months if he was careful. The recovery team had been less than careful. Everything in the basement and the stairs leading down to it had been bleached and scrubbed, and that included Cole. Nine hours later and his clothes were still damp.

Without his tattoos, he looked exactly like a cop pretending he wasn't one. "This day just keeps getting better and better," he groused as he stomped down the stairs to the third subbasement. As always, the morgue was like a hothouse, and as always, the smell was enough to turn a hard man like Cole green beneath his smeared tattoos.

The morgue worked like a production line. The bodies were even placed on a conveyor belt. At the first station, they were stripped and any "valuables" placed in a single small bag. Those items not deemed valuable—a highly subjective term—were divvied up among the crew at the end of their shift. At the next stop, the body was printed. At the next, it was photographed from every possible angle. The actual autopsy came next. A difficult case might take all of five minutes. Santino probably took less than one. At the next stop, whatever notes that had been written were typed in triplicate.

After that, the body was sent to be mulched.

Cole caught up with Santino as he was rumbling down the line to the mulcher. He possessed no authority in the morgue except his voice, his steel fists and the fact that he would obviously use them if he had to. Three reasons that were good enough for the techs who got paid hourly and didn't mind the break, short as it was. There wasn't much reason to look any further than the holes in Santino's head. The brain was clean, as were his eyes.

"Fucking human," he whispered.

Mumbling more curses, Cole stormed from the morgue and then up out of the station, stopping on the crumbling steps outside. He thought about going back to his apartment, but it was a thirty-minute walk. He'd been planning to take a cab, but without the bounty he couldn't even afford to spring for the train, and that was seventy cents.

What was at home, anyway? Nothing. His apartment was cold and virtually empty. Other than a few old suits, a mattress and some bags of boil and eat ramen, he possessed next to nothing. Except pawn tickets that is. Over the last year he had collected enough of them to cover his walls. His phone was dead because he hadn't been able to pay the bill, and the electric would go any day.

His luck had been on a downward spiral and he hadn't picked up a decent bounty in months. And now he'd lost two in one night.

"I need a drink," he muttered, glancing around. There wasn't much to see. The sun was coming up in all its glory and somewhere people were enjoying it, they just weren't enjoying it in New York. The night mists were turning to a grey drizzle and the ghostly skyscrapers were beginning to solidify…more or less. Many of them weren't exactly solid. They were dying, crumbling monuments to an old world.

Cole was still staring up when someone pushed him.

"Get your ass off the steps, slag." It was a police officer, bringing in a stick-thin money-honey, in a see-through red dress that matched her contact lenses. She was twitchy, coming down from riding the Rican Mule. All in all she looked as though she had been pulled from a gutter.

Normally, Cole would have knocked the beat cop's teeth in and strolled away before he had the chance to come to, only just then, Cole was the one who felt beat down.

The cop and the honey swept by and he stared after them. If she hadn't already, she was going to lose the cash she had made that night from renting out her body. Cole didn't want to know what her daddy was going to do to her. New age pimps were rarely kind.

"But that's not my problem," Cole said, repeating the New York mantra. His problem was that damned slick. Cole couldn't get him out of his head and he knew that even if he went home, he wouldn't be able to sleep. There were too many loose ends, too many questions without answers. If Santino wasn't a Dead-eye, why on earth had he chopped up his wife and stuck her in a freezer?

"He could have buried her in the basement. It's what I would have done if I was just an everyday murderer. But why would an average killer take out her heart?" It was the wife's missing heart that had brought Cole in on the case. "I need to see the report on *her*," he decided, turning on his heel and following the cop.

Since computers had gone the way of the dinosaur a hundred years before Cole was born, every report generated in the police station was eventually sent to the "Hall of Records." If there had ever been an actual hall it had been buried under paper ages ago. Now the "hall" consisted of the top ten floors of the immense building.

It was a world unto its own.

The hall and the mole-like people who worked there had their own rules and worked on their own timeline. If a record took a week to be found, then it took a week, and no amount of bitching would ever move them along faster. If an officer was of a high enough rank, the moles could be threatened to produce reports quicker, and, like everyone else, they loved a bribe, and a good one could produce amazing results.

Cole had no money and less authority than anyone in the building, except maybe the honey.

He tried turning on the charm, however his smeared slag impersonation made his smile pathetic and the little person behind the counter—he couldn't tell if it was a man or a woman behind the thick spectacles—only turned up a sneer at the attempt, before squinting through the quarter-inch lenses.

"Hmm," he/she said. "A special? This early? It's going to be a while." The mole gestured to the waiting room, which was empty. It was always empty. A half day spent in the Records Hall waiting room was equivalent to six years on the outside. Still, there was a couch of sorts. It had been a cloth-neoprene mesh forty years before, now it was apparently made of tape. It could have been made of brick and Cole would have still slept on it.

Four hours passed in a blink and he was deep in a chaotic dream in which he was running through miles of barely lit tunnels when he heard: "Mr. Younger." Cole cracked an eye and found himself staring at the oldest person he had ever seen. It was a woman half his height, stooped, wrinkled and so dusty that her white hair looked grey. She wore a faded pale peach blouse from the turn of the century that was tucked into an equally faded blue skirt. Apparently, she used the waist band of the dress as a bra.

It was not a sight to wake up to.

He sat up, quickly, thinking that she might rap his knuckles with a ruler and admonish him for having his feet up on the couch. "Yes...ma'am. That's me. I'm Cole Younger."

"That wasn't in question. I know who you are. You're a bounty hunter." She sighed and shook her head. "Follow me."

Cole stood, noticing for the first time that the lights in the Records Hall had been dimmed and that the place looked deserted. As the building was windowless, there was no way to tell if it was night or day. He guessed it was night and was surprised that it wasn't even noon. "Where is everyone?"

"On a break," was all she said as she waddled along, watching her feet. He had to take achingly slow steps to stay abreast of her as they passed, with glacial slowness, through towering stacks of files each twice his height. They were so tall that he wondered how the diminutive clerks reached the higher ones. The moles hired their own people and it was obvious that men of Cole's stature need not apply. Or people of his age either, for that matter. The moles had an eternal quality to them. There was never a "new" person. Each of them looked as if they had always worked there and always would, long after Cole was mulched.

"In here." They had come to a door made of actual wood with a doorknob that was real brass. The knob was the only thing in the Records Hall that wasn't filmed with grey dust. It actually gleamed. The old woman reached out a spotted hand for it, again so slowly that Cole felt himself catching up to her in age.

"Let me." He opened the door, noting the stenciled name:

Joanna Niederer
Director

"Joanna or should I call you Director Niederer?" Unlike Lloyd's office, Joanna's was well lit and fastidiously clean. The walls were painted a stark white and empty of pictures. The floor was softly carpeted in white. The only real color was the desk and the two chairs that sat on either side of it. Again, they were of real wood and in perfect condition. Cole didn't feel clean enough to sit in the one on his side of the desk. What was more surprising than the wood and the cleanliness, was that there wasn't a single piece of paper in the room. He had expected her office to be a smaller, messier version of the Records Hall itself.

The director eased herself into her chair so slowly that she made all the sound of dust settling. "You can call me Jo."

He liked Director Niederer better. It seemed fitting. "Sure, Jo. Was something wrong with the form?" Other than maybe changing a lightbulb for her, it was the only reason he could think of why he was there.

"Of course, there was!" she snapped. "This is a special, and not just any special. It's a *special*, special." He wasn't following her and it showed on his face. "A special record usually involves a special person or a special case. You still don't get it, do you? Sorry to burst your bubble, but we're not all special. Yes, that talking butterfly my granddaughter watches on tv has got it all wrong."

Although she had the smell of a grandmother, Cole could not picture Jo ever being young enough to have a child herself.

"*Everyone* has a record, even the mega-rich douchebags you kids call Vampires. They are the special ones. If you're a famous person, or a mob boss, or a politician you're considered a special. But this is a *special* special. Your kind of special."

Cole only stared at her, refusing to acknowledge the obvious. She sighed tiredly and sat back. "Yes. I'm talking about a zombie. A Dead-eye." Jo pulled out a folder from her desk drawer and slid it over. "See the reference number. It starts with a 6. That means it's a special. The following 13 means it's either a *special* special, or it's tied to one. In this case, it's the latter."

"Tied to Mrs Grimmett?" Cole asked, sliding into the chair as he scanned the report. "She wasn't a…one of them. I don't see any sign of the infection. Her white count is within normal ranges. Was it changed?"

"No. She was only tied to the case. Take a look at her injuries."

Cole was still reading and said, almost absently, "Injuries? The cause of death was blunt trauma to the back of the head." When he glanced up, he found Jo had managed to summon the energy to cock a furry white eyebrow at him. Once more he felt as though she were about to rap his knuckles. His answer was incorrect. He looked again at the photos. "Her heart was taken out post-mortem. The lack of bleeding along the…wait."

He looked again at the notes. "Her blood volume was three ounces? Oh God. She was bled, wasn't she?" He saw it now. The jagged cut that took off her head had disguised the deep incisions on either side of her throat.

"Yes. It's a *special* special and you don't just come here demanding to see the notes on one of these. *You* of all people should know this. People talk, even my people, maybe even especially my people. I know it's hard to imagine, but this isn't the most exciting job and whenever any special comes up it becomes the stuff of gossip. And talk of actual specials is the last thing we need."

"I agree. May I take this?" he asked, holding up the file.

She scoffed, rolling her eyes. "Are you kidding me? No one takes my files."

It didn't matter. He had leads. Perhaps Santino wasn't a Dead-eye, but the blood he had taken from his wife was a lead. Had he sold it at the Mandarin joint? Or maybe at the flop house, or maybe…

He stood, his mind in a whirl and was about to leave when he stopped abruptly. "What did you mean by 'you of all people?' Did Lieutenant Lloyd say anything about me?"

"No. I've just read your file is all." From her drawer, she pulled another file, this one an inch and a half thick.

Cole grimaced at in disgust. There were probably horror stories about him in the file. The force needed to justify taking his meager pension and cutting his insurance off while he'd been recuperating in the hospital. "Don't believe everything you read," he told her.

Chapter 4

Unless you had a torture rack, a soundproof room and a lot of time to kill, breaking a Mandarin was next to impossible. Even the wrinkled-up grannies would only glare ferociously, cursing you and all your unborn children in every language they knew.

They could be bought, however. For the right price, they would sell out that very same granny. Unfortunately, Cole didn't have the money. He had just a few pawnable items left and only the Crown would get him anywhere near enough cash to move the Mandarin to give up info on a customer peddling blood. People bought and sold everything under the sun in New York, but blood was one of those items that raised flags, and for good reason.

Cole could see the reason from his apartment window when he raised his lead shutter. Jersey was a brown wasteland across the polluted waters of the Hudson. It was the edge of the *Zone* where a hundred million Dead-eyes had been incinerated a century and a half before. People had short memories for most things, but not with zombies. Everyone knew about their insatiable hunger for clean blood, and even a Mandarin would hesitate to sell it—unless the price was right.

With the smeared tats washed from his face and wearing his best long coat, Cole entered the Mandarin joint at just after one. He was immediately assaulted by the aroma of three-day old fish. Beneath that was the pervasive, cloying smell of fried food. Every Mandarin joint smelled like this.

There were fifteen or so customers; most at the standing tables in the center of the room. Two Mandarin families were sprawled out in a pair of booths in the back. They were all rather nondescript to Cole. It was another story with the wait-staff. They eyeballed a couple of almost-slags as if they were on the verge of becoming full-blown trogs in the middle of their Pho. The lone black man had it worse. The waiter wouldn't come near him. He passed in a wide circle around the man and when he dropped off his plate, he left it at the far end of the table.

To Cole's left was a counter where he could order seaweed noodles thirteen different ways, hot soup five ways, and "fish" either fried crispy or fried limp.

"We pay ah taxes, taxman," the lady behind the counter said, right away. "We pay on time." She spoke in the clipped tones of a recent immigrant. There was no such thing as a recent immigrant to New York. People paid good money to get smuggled out of the city, not into it.

"I'm not here to shake you down. I'm not even a cop. I'm here for a bite and maybe a chat. What's fresh?"

Because of the way Mandarins were, he judged her age to be somewhere between twenty and sixty. She wore her black hair short in front—razor sharp bangs sat high up on her forehead—and long in the back, reminding Cole of a silken mullet. Her eyes had been squinty to begin with, but at the mention of a "talk," they practically disappeared.

"It all fwesh." She cocked a thumb behind her at a filthy plexiglass aquarium where three fish of indeterminate species floated in some sort of fluid that was so grey and murky that Cole didn't know if it still qualified as actual water. As the fish weren't belly-up, he supposed that they weren't dead yet. Then again, they weren't alive like fish were meant to be; they only existed.

"You make insult, you go," the woman added.

"No one's insulting anyone. I'll have the number two." A quarter for soggy seaweed, a couple of old carrots and bits of "fish" bobbing about in the soup. He'd had worse. He ate slowly, ignoring the glaring counter girl. The black man had left, leaving Cole as public enemy number one.

It was an hour before a stunted little man slipped into the booth across from him. By his attire and the grease glazing his pockmarked face, he was a cook. By the way he studied Cole with dark, intelligent eyes, Cole knew he was much more than that. "You Uncle Wu?" The neon sign above the joint's door read *Uncle Wu's Happy Fish*.

"It's just Wu. You buyin' or sellin'?" He had no accent whatsoever.

"Buying. Syn-ope. I'm looking for maybe a kilogram." Moving a kilogram meant jail time and yet the man's expression didn't change.

"Twenty-two hundred, up front," he replied quickly, wasting no time. "Delivery: a quarter a day for four days."

It was too much. "Fifteen-hundred. All tonight. And I might need more tomorrow."

Wu's reaction, a tiny shift of his chin, was significant. He was interested. "Eighteen hundred for tonight. Short notice and all. If you give me more notice, I can shave some of that off for tomorrow."

"This is my notice. Thirty-two hundred for two kilos. I'll pay half tonight, half in the morning."

Instead of replying, Wu studied Cole for a long, uncomfortable minute. The entire time Cole was forced to sit there, a placid, simpleton's smile on his face. Finally, Wu said, "I need ID." Cole had never heard of a dealer asking for ID, and he sat back with what must have been a stunned expression on his face. Wu's flat, emotionless look had not changed since he had slid across from Cole. "I have friends on the force. I need to make sure you're legit."

In this case, "legit" meant being a criminal. To most of the police force, Cole was the worst sort of criminal. He slid over his ID. Wu took it and disappeared for a full hour. It took all of Cole's patience to sit in the sticky booth with the counter girl unrelentlessly sneering at him. The only time she took a break was when she sneered at a young girl with a bad case of slag who came slouching in. All the tattoos in the world weren't going to cover up the rot eating away her nose.

"The taxmen don't like you much," Wu said, coming to stand at the end of the table. He almost smiled. "That means I like you even more. Sixteen-hundred tonight. Order the number thirteen to go. Pay in cash and go. Simple." He didn't offer to shake hands.

"One other thing," Cole said just as Wu started to leave. "I need some clean blood." Wu's eyes narrowed slightly, otherwise his face might have been made out of wood for all it moved. "Not much. A few quarts every other day maybe."

"I don't move that stuff," Wu replied.

Now it was Cole's turn to remain still. He forced himself to count to forty in his head before speaking. "You will for the right price." Blood and Syn-ope; the implications were obvious.

"Maybe. Wait here."

Once again, he went into the backroom and once again Cole was kept waiting. He figured it would be another interminable wait but Wu was back in only fifteen minutes. "I have a call in," he told Cole.

"Will it be long?"

"No."

Then why did you come out? To keep an eye on me? Cole's eyes flicked to the counter girl. Her sneer was gone. She was standing very still. The stagnant, grease-stinking air had become thicker than it had been. Had the alley door been shut? Cole suddenly felt trapped, both in the booth and in the restaurant.

"Have a seat while you wait," Cole suggested.

Wu's head turned toward the back. "No, I have soup on the fire and I…" Cole's left hand was below the table, the flimsy, wobbly, light table. He heaved one end up and smashed it into Wu's surprised face. The Mandarin fell back as Cole leapt to his feet, his right hand sliding into the long black trench, going for his gun.

The counter girl was no poker player, but God she was fast. She reached beneath the register and hauled out a cheap scattergun. The tip of the sawed-off barrel struck the register, giving Cole a split second to drop down and to the left, close to where Wu was scrabbling out from beneath the table. The girl hesitated, afraid she'd hit both Cole and Wu.

In that split second, Cole had the Crown out and fired, aiming purposely to miss her. With the force looking for any reason to sink him, he'd be facing a murder charge if he actually shot her. He shot the aquarium instead. Three hundred gallons of brackish, toilet-stinking water exploded out, washing over the tiny slip of a girl and throwing her off her feet.

Her scattergun went off with a deafening roar, taking out two ceiling tiles and a light fixture. Before the glass was done raining down, Cole was flying out through the kitchen. A knife was thrown his way, missing his ear by inches. The cook who'd thrown it reached for a second, but then lifted his hands as Cole aimed his gun at his face. "Where's the back exit?" Then he saw it and raced on, glaring at a skinny teen with a wisp of black hair on his lip. He had picked up a bowl of near-boiling pho and had been thinking of throwing it at Cole. Instead it sloshed on his already stained wife-beater, making him shriek.

Cole slammed through the back door, sending a pack of rats squealing beneath the battered trashcans they'd been feeding from. Hard, cold rain slashed his face, momentarily blinding him and nearly sending him into the back of a delivery van that was up on blocks. In the next second, he was racing down the alley, the sound of police sirens cutting through the storm.

He took a quick right, then his first left, and immediately slowed, throwing his hood over his head to blend in with the rest of the afternoon crowd as it plodded dully about its business. Cole's business was staying out of jail long enough to figure out how Santino and Wu were connected.

As he walked, Cole ran over the timeline: Santino kills his wife and drains her dry. Sometime in the next few days, the wife is reported missing by a sister and Santino runs. Cole is given his ticket, tracks him to the flophouse and then to Wu's. Santino dies half an hour later in the basement of his building.

"He attacked the skirt to drain her," Cole muttered, "and right in his own building, too. Talk about stupid." He stopped in the middle of the sidewalk, trying to remember what Santino's slag numbers were. Sometimes the slag built up more on the inside than the outside, and every slag eventually turned into a moron.

An armored police car trundled slowly up from behind. Cole recognized it by the crunching sound its wire mesh tires made. "Shit," he whispered as it began to slow. When it pulled up abreast of him, he didn't wait for the window to be cranked down; he turned and raced to his right. There was no alley to duck into, there was only a series of stoops, each leading to its own tenement building.

With no time to be picky, he rushed for the nearest, taking the stairs three at a time.

"Stop!"

The one word was all the warning Cole could expect. The police could now legally shoot him if he failed to comply, something he had no intention of doing. He was through the door like a shot and found himself in a small vestibule that once held rows of mailboxes on either side of the front door. They were long gone. And so too was the door that led to the rest of the building. It and its frame had been stripped away, leaving a gaping hole that opened onto a long dim hall.

Running up one side of the hall was a flight of warped "poly-granite" stairs. There was no actual granite in the formed rubber, and neither were they very hard. Each step sagged under his weight as he went up at full speed. Behind him a cop had just charged into the building. He paused long enough to jerk out his .480 service piece, which fired a huge slug that could turn a man inside out. They could defeat body armor and car doors with ease, and it was said they could penetrate an engine block, if that was ever needed.

Cole felt his back tingle on the last few steps, expecting the bullet that would send his spinal column shooting out through his belly. The shot never came. He blended in so well with the darkened stairwell that the officer couldn't line up a good shot in the split second he had Cole in his sights.

The officer followed Cole up the stairs, losing ground with every step. He was carting around thirty pounds worth of body armor and another ten in equipment. The man was something of a juggernaut, built for power, not for speed. But he didn't need to be especially fast. All he had to do was get a clear shot and that would be that.

Cole wasn't going to allow the cop the opportunity. With his life on the line, he ran at a full sprint up a third flight before speeding down the hall. This hall was even darker than the ones below and Cole was only a distant shadow by the time the cop made it to the third floor.

Cole was only steps from the far end of the hall and another flight of stairs when thunder exploded behind him. It was followed immediately by a *crack!* as the bullet tore through the plaster wall in front of him. Then he was on the stairs, leaping down them seven, eight at a time. Down he went until he was at street level and, without pausing, he burst into the alley, knowing that if he was unlucky, he would charge right into one of the onrushing police cars he could hear screaming into the neighborhood.

He knew that he was hated, but when he saw a cruiser turn down the alley and plow into a slow-moving slag, he realized they weren't thinking about taking him alive.

The driver of the car stopped, rolled down his window and looked back at the slag bleeding in the street. Cole saw that it was Bruce Hamilton driving. "You heard the siren, didn't you?" Bruce yelled at the slag. "Next time, stay out of the damned street." By the time he turned back, Cole was across the alley and slipping between two buildings. There was barely room to move sideways and smack dab in the middle was a mound of trash, taller than he was.

There was no climbing it, but with the walls so close he was able to put his back to one and shimmy up and over. Dropping down on the other side, he froze. Not fifty feet away was another police car, shining a light through the driving rain. The narrow passage was shadowed to begin with, but with the rain, it seemed like night, and Cole slunk down low hoping to blend in.

The beam of light passed only a foot over the top of him and stopped. A curse was just taking shape in his mouth when he heard a low, hungry moan behind him. He cast a look over his shoulder and found himself staring at a grey…thing. It had made a burrow of sorts in the trash and was now emerging, flashing broken, yellowed teeth in black gums, and when the spotlight hit it, the angry moan became one of pain. Immediately, Cole's mind screamed: *Dead-eye!* and he dug for his gun.

Before he could get the gun from its holster, the creature hissed, "Go way," breathing the hideous stench of death over Cole, causing him to shudder.

It wasn't a Dead-eye. A Dead-eye as grey as this one would have attacked without hesitation. No, this was a trog. A trog was what happened to a person when the slag building up in them hit a runaway point. Half of its face had rotted away, as had four of its fingers. The rest of his body was covered in lesions and boils. There was no telling what sort of insidious tumors were growing inside him.

Trogs rarely ventured out of their pits beneath the earth where they lived out the remainder of their shortened lives. If the police hadn't been searching for Cole, they would have killed it without hesitation, citing a "quality of life" law that had been in place since the bombs fell.

Just then a trog was low priority and the light passed on. "Sorry," Cole said, backing away from the thing. He still had his hand on his gun and was thinking about using it if the trog came any closer. They carried every disease known to man. "I'm leaving, just relax."

"Go way." It pointed half a finger toward the street.

Cole backed away from it until he saw it crawl back into its mound. Then he turned and hurried on, glad for the rain washing down on him. When he got to the street, he saw a police car half a block down. Despite the short distance, he breathed a sigh of relief, glad to have gotten away from the trog without being touched. "I'd kill myself before I ever got that bad," he muttered, stuffing his hands down into his pockets and turning away from the police.

After five blocks Cole felt that he was in the clear and he cut across town to the only place he was likely to pick up any leads: Santino's apartment. The small lobby was just as dark as it had been the day before and this time, Cole wasn't going to take any chances. He had his gun tucked in his coat pocket as he mounted the stairs on cat's feet.

He took the seven stories slow, stopping only to ask the one woman he passed about Santino. The man's trench coat she wore hid whatever form she had, but Cole could see that she was well past her prime and crabby about it. The frown lines running down her cheeks were now permanent.

"Never heard of him," she muttered and tried to push past. Cole showed her a picture. "Nope," she said after barely a glance.

"Look again. It's important."

She jerked her wrist out of his grasp. "And so is getting my shopping done before another Cat-2 comes in. Now, get out of my way." She went stumping down the stairs in oversized boots that matched the coat.

Cursing her, he went up to the seventh floor and paused before stepping into a windowless hallway. Evenly spaced along the ceiling were nine light fixtures; only three were working and the light they emitted equaled to a few candles. They barely gave off enough light to form a shadow among the shadows. While he waited for his eyes to grow accustomed to the dark, he listened: two doors to his left a woman was nagging her husband about his job. In the apartment next to it, a baby was wailing while Station 3 played the annoying *Busy Bee* show. Another television was blaring some soap: "I've always loved you, Rhett!" A man's rasping snore could be heard from behind another door.

Once his eyes had adjusted to the near black, Cole crept past these doors and their living occupants and came to apartment 714. Out of habit, he put his ear to the door. It was eerily quiet inside. After giving the knob a single twist, he broke out his set of lock-picks. The lock in the door was ancient and the tumblers were practically begging to turn. The door opened into a cramped two-bedroom apartment that was almost as dark as the hallway. Light trickled in from a crack along the edge of a lead-shuttered window.

In front of him was a living room with two couches; one threadbare and the other still wrapped in plastic. They were canted toward a big box television that sprouted bunny antenna three feet long. Past the living room and to the right was a narrow dining room that held an eight-foot long table with four high-backed chairs. Although they appeared to be made of wood, they were hardened plastic.

A single door in the dining room led to the kitchen, while another in the living room went to the two bedrooms and the apartment's only bathroom. At first glance, there was nothing special about the place. There was no suggestion that a Dead-eye had ever lived there—or a murderer for that matter. He had expected there to be a smell of death in the apartment. Instead there was only stale air and a whiff of cologne, it was a scent he knew.

He sucked in his breath as a cold barrel touched the side of his neck.

"Sorry, Cole."

Chapter 5

"Sorry about what?" Cole asked, turning to face Aaron Reynolds, known widely as the Fox. "I'm the one who should be apologizing for the ass kicking I'm about to lay on you."

Aaron chuckled at this, his white smile, genuine. "Oh, please. I have the gun out for that very reason." He waved it up at Cole. Aaron was half a foot shorter than Cole and was as neat and trim as his nickname would suggest. His luxurious black hair that hung past his shoulders was decorated with tiny silver ornaments: crosses, bells, stars and the like. His goatee was meticulously trimmed and, as always, was an exact match to his eye color, which today was a sky blue.

The blue was also a match to his scarf and the fur trimming along his calf-high boots. These set off the two thin jackets he wore, one in silver, the other simple grey.

"Besides, why would you want to kick my darling little ass?"

Cole advanced on the slight man, looking down at him, completely ignoring the gun even though it was the latest model Crown with glints of gold on the tips of the emblem and the sights. With anyone else, Cole would've figured it was paint. With Aaron it was likely real gold, and the silver doodads in his hair weren't plastic. Aaron was the most successful bounty hunter in the Referral Program. He'd bagged four stiffs a year for the past decade and didn't look like he was slowing down at all.

He was smart, devious and unscrupulous.

"Because you're standing in the middle of my territory, hunting my Dead-eye," Cole answered.

"Please, Cole, I've done you a favor. The trail has turned cold. There's no sign that a Dead-eye ever lived here. No empty dope bottles. No animal bones. No flour makeup. And we both know what the autopsy said about Santino."

"You were down in the morgue?" Cole demanded, grinding his teeth.

Aaron flashed his smile even wider, before turning away and sauntering around the far end of the ratty couch. "Of course, I was. But not for this little mistake of yours. I have my own cases. I was just curious as to why you're out here shooting random humans."

My ass you're just curious, Cole thought. "Maybe I think it's fun."

"Or maybe you sniffed something out. So, what did our dead friend pick up at Wu's?"

Cole tried and failed to keep his face blank. His report hadn't mentioned Wu or the Mandarin joint. "Who the hell are you bribing?" Cole asked, taking a step closer to the couch.

"Ah, hold up there, big and tasty." Aaron raised his gun a little higher. "I bribe the right people, and catching onto this Wu thing didn't take more than a few dollars. Really, bribes are something you should consider doing if you plan on sticking around any longer. If the police don't get you first. I hope you know you're all over the police band. They say you were trying to buy blood. Damn it, Cole, that's a class 1 felony."

"I was only trying to find out if Wu moved that sort of thing. Anyone with half a brain knows I can't afford blood even if I wanted it. By Wu's reaction, I'd say he doesn't move it. I honestly don't know what Santino was after."

Aaron gave him a long stare before saying, "And I guess we will never know now that he's dead."

"Fuck you, muncher," Cole growled.

The tips of Aaron's goatee lifted as he smiled again. "You wish, sweetie." He let out a big theatrical breath and said, "I guess there's nothing here for me now. If you'll move those ridiculously broad shoulders out of the doorway, I'll be on my way." Cole wanted nothing more than for him to get out of his territory as fast as possible, but Aaron stopped as he passed. "That girl you rescued. Is this her?"

He held up a picture of a young woman with jet black hair, a high nose and dark eyes. She was young and vivaciously pretty. "No. Who is she?"

Aaron had been staring intently up at Cole, looking for any sign of recognition. "No one, I guess. Have a good day, Cole. Try to stay out of trouble. I'd hate to see anything happen to you. I mean that." He left, only to stick his head back into the doorway. "And Cole, don't call a muncher, a muncher. It's rude. And dull. Only a muncher can call a muncher, a muncher. Understand?"

In response, Cole slammed the door on him. "Fucking ass-munchers," he grumbled, looking around at the dark room. He tried the light switch and was pleasantly surprised when the overhead blinked on. Normally, the landlord would cut the power and water to an apartment as quickly as they could when there was a death.

Cole's first stop was the kitchen. It was missing the refrigerator, the dishes, and all food stuffs. Everything else had a faint bleach smell to it. The recovery team had been there and had done its best to destroy any evidence that a Dead-eye might have ever lived there. "And left me with nothing to go on."

The bathroom was in the same condition as the kitchen: uselessly sterile. Everything from the soap to the towels had been taken. The master was the same way. Other than a few pictures hanging on the walls, a stripped bed, an empty dresser and an old *True Time* clock radio, there was basically nothing left.

"Freaking jackals." Recovery Teams had a tendency to "over-recover," and made a tidy sum reselling items on the black market. On the off chance he'd turn up something that had been missed, Cole lifted the mattress and checked the boxspring. He pulled out the drawers of the dressers and checked beneath them. He used his flashlight to check for seams in the closet where a false door might be hidden.

Nothing.

Feeling like Aaron had been right and that this was a dead end, he went to the spare bedroom, still grumbling under his breath. Like the master, it had been stripped so completely that it looked like it had been vacant at the time of the wife's murder. Still, Cole went through the same steps: bed, closet, dresser. It was when he was pulling out one of the drawers and checking beneath it that he heard the faintest *clink*.

Looking down, he saw a hoop earring. It winked gold at him. He knew it wasn't real. Santino had been straight middle class all the way. There was no way he could afford a real gold earring, not when gold was running north of $9,000 an ounce. "Iron, sure. Maybe he could afford aluminum, but not gold." He bounced the earring in his hand; it had heft, and he thought it was more likely iron than aluminum. Which would make it cheaper as well.

Pocketing it, he inspected the drawer from which it fell and found nothing special in it except a single long black hair. "The girl in the picture! Fucking Aaron!"

He dashed back into the master bedroom and inspected the pictures on the walls. There was Santino smiling, his arm around the woman he'd killed. She had been an ash-blonde with short hair. She had that same high nose. "Did Santino have a daughter?"

There were four empty frames on the walls. There was no way the recovery team would bother taking a picture without the frame. It had to have been Aaron, trying to erase Santino's daughter from history. "There are always records," he said, heading back into the kitchen where he'd seen a Basic Bell telephone hanging on the wall. "Come on," he whispered and lifted the handset. The dial tone buzzed angrily in his ear.

"Yes! Now I just need ol' Jo to be still at work."

He whisked the rotary around eight times and listened to the phone ring for two minutes before a dry husk of a voice answered, "Hall of Records."

"I need information on a special," he said right away, speaking quickly and with as much authority as he could muster. "Case number 613-3651-9-1. I can save you the trouble in locating it, the *Director* had it as of this morning."

On the other end of the line, the clerk sighed in the ageless way that government workers did. "Regardless of who has it, you have to go through the proper channels. Please file the requisition form three-six-nine…"

"There's no time for that!" Cole barked. "Lives are at stake here. Tell the Director that Cole Younger is on the line. Go." Technically, the only life that was at stake was his own. He had no idea if Santino's daughter was in any danger whatsoever. She could be off in Brooklyn safe and sound.

The clerk sighed again; this one even slower than the first. "She's in a meeting. The best I can do is to tell her you called, and maybe she'll call you back. What's your number?" Cole gave her the number printed on the center of the dial. The woman hung up on him the millisecond he gave her the last number.

Cole began pacing. Then he snooped some more, not finding much except more of the long black hairs. Each felt like some sort of vindication on his part. He doubted that Joanna Niederer would see them as any more than hair.

After going through the entire apartment, he flicked off the lights and settled down on the plastic-wrapped couch. For a few moments, he considered turning on the television just for the sound. He had grown up with the chaos of an orphanage as his backdrop. Silence made him lonely. Still, the manic, overly-happy shows that played around the clock would be out of place in an apartment where someone had been murdered.

I'll just rest my eyes while I wait, he thought right before he fell asleep. He dreamed of rain and very black tunnels. His sleep was so deep that the pick scraping in the lock didn't penetrate and if it hadn't been for the Cat-1 siren suddenly blaring he might have been strangled in his sleep. He woke, bleary and confused, thinking: *I have to get the shutters down.* The fear of turning into a slag got him off the couch faster than anything else could have.

It was only when he was standing that he remember where he was. The lead shutters were already closed, so where was the breath of air coming from? Turning, he saw the front door was open and that there was a shadow crouched in the doorway.

On its own, Cole's hand shot to his holstered Crown and it was out before his eyes focused on the shadow; it was very small. The size of a woman or a little man.

"Miss Grimmett?"

She hesitated on the threshold as if trying to decide whether to run away or answer. "That's me. Who are you?"

"My name is Cole Younger. I-I'm an investigator looking into the death of your mother." That was so much better than saying: I'm the man who killed your dad because I thought he was a zombie. Sorry about that.

"Yes," was all she said as she shut the door. She didn't turn on the light.

Goosebumps flashed across Cole's arms as he took a step back. What young woman wouldn't turn on the lights in this situation? "You're not her," he said, bringing the Crown up.

"I am. I am her."

She advanced on Cole, her heels clicking on the floor. He backed up, brandishing the gun. She couldn't miss it, just as he couldn't miss the fact that she wasn't frightened in the least. *Was this a dream?* he wondered. The situation had more of a nightmare feel to it. He went around one side of the ratty couch while she went around the other. She was stalking him!

"Look, miss, I'm a city-licensed investigator. And I'm armed," he added after a second. His backside hit the dining room table, and now there was nothing between them but stale air. *She's going to attack me,* he thought. It was insane on the face of things unless...

To his left was the chandelier switch and he slapped it up just as she launched herself at him. The light was harsh white with a blue-grey tint. It wasn't particularly brilliant and yet it stopped the woman in her tracks. She flinched back from it, her face cringing in sudden pain. This wasn't

Santino's daughter. Yes, her hair was long and dark and her eyes deep brown, but her nose was small and narrow.

And she was also a Dead-eye.

The reaction to the light was one give away, the fact that she showed no fear of his gun was another.

What didn't make sense was the deep-blue velvet pantsuit that she wore. It was stylish and Dead-eyes generally stopped caring about such things quickly after being infected. The woman also had perfect, unblemished skin, which was again a rarity. These little things made him second guess himself. Maybe she was a drug-addled vamp. It was possible and Cole couldn't afford another human death on his hands.

"Your mother loves you," he said, quickly. It was one of the Empath statements he used when testing his targets. A normal human reaction was a nod, some sort of agreement or a bitter laugh, depending on the person. A Dead-eye had to *think* about what the proper reaction to the statement was. There would be a pause and then a cold smile, followed by a brief acknowledgement of the "fact."

The woman hesitated. "Yes," she said. Had this been a real test, she would have failed the question. Five more failures and he would've been legally allowed to ask for a blood sample.

Cole didn't have time for all that. He shot her just off the centerline of her breastbone. The force of the impact staggered her. Her shoulders did a wobbly dance before she collapsed to one knee. There was no scream, no tears, and no begging for her life. She only glared up at Cole as he lined up the Crown for the coup de grâce.

It was at that exact moment that Santino's phone rang. He glanced at it, thinking that it would be Joanna Niederer. That one thought took a fraction of a second, and in that brief time, the woman launched herself at him. Her left hand locked onto his right wrist while her right grabbed his coat near his shoulder. Despite the hole in her chest, she drove him, the dining room table, and all of the chairs back until the table crashed against the far wall.

Like he was a child, she bent him back over the table and then stretched her jaws wide to take a chunk of flesh out of his face.

She was viciously strong for her size, but she was still not much more than a hundred pounds. His left hand was free and he grabbed her by the throat, lifted her bodily up and threw her off of him. She landed on the floor, and because she still had the painfully tight grip on his wrist, he was dragged down with her. They rolled, flailing back and forth, both fighting for the gun.

At some point his head was slammed against the floor. The gun went flying as she pried back his fingers with wild demonic strength. Before he knew it, she clawed her way on top of him, and it took everything he had to keep from having his throat torn out as her perfect white teeth came closer and closer. When her ghoul's breath washed over him, true panic began to flood through him. In desperation, he lashed out, heaving and kicking.

One of his booted feet caught the cord of the telephone and stopped the shrill ringing that had been in the background of the fight.

"Cole! This is Jo Niederer…"

"Jo," he said in a squeak. The Dead-eye had hold of his tie with one hand and was pulling it up like a noose.

"…you have to get out of there. The police are on the way. Cole? Can you hear me? That case number has been flagged and the…" Police sirens could now be heard blaring over the warble of the Cat-1 alarm. "…the file's been removed…"

Both Cole and the woman were frozen, listening to police come closer. After a second, she leapt off him and dashed from the kitchen, heading for the door. There was no way Cole was going to go after her without his gun. He scrambled after it, pausing only long enough to grab the phone. "Jo!" he practically shouted into it. "I'll call you later. Thanks."

"But…"

He hung up before she could spit out another word. In two seconds, he was out the door and caught sight of the

Dead-eye flying down the hall. Her speed was inhuman and even as he brought the gun up, she darted into the stairwell. Cole was no slouch when it came to running, and yet she was four floors down by the time he got to the stairs, and when he got to the bottom, she had vanished.

Cole stopped in the doorway of the building as red and blue lights lashed the night from both directions.

The police were coming for him.

Chapter 6

The sirens were coming from all directions. They were trapping him now, making sure he couldn't slip through their fingers as he had earlier. Cole locked the door to the building and then backed away from it, pausing at the stairs leading up, thinking that he might be able to go from rooftop to rooftop...but for how long? The block only stretched so far, and by the sounds of it the police were bookending it. In minutes, every entrance to every building would be blocked.

If up was out of the question, that only left going down.

Cole did not hurry. There was a better than even chance that the Dead-eye was heading for the tunnels as well. He attached his under-barrel light to the Crown and went down, treading carefully, making sure to check around every corner before moving on. Above him, the front door was smashed in with a ram and the lobby was flooded with officers.

By then, Cole was on the second level and walking towards the tunnel, swiveling his light left and right to make sure he wouldn't be surprised. Nothing came for him.

When he reached the little mound around the hole, he paused. The smell coming from it made him want to turn around and try to fight his way out. There was death down in that tunnel. The obscene stench of it made his head swim. A gunshot and a long wailing scream from above decided things for him. The police were not playing around. Somehow he had kicked over a hornet's nest.

"Or Santino had." Maybe the blonde skirt hadn't been a victim at all. Maybe she had been out to kill Santino. "Dead-eye skirts being used as assassins. What the hell is this world coming to?"

Cole eased down into the tunnel, needing to squat low until it leveled out and came to an intersection. Visually, left or right didn't seem to matter. In either direction the tunnel was dark and wet, and was maybe three feet wide and six feet in height. He could walk with a bit of a stoop.

Here and there along the passage were small alcoves carved into the dirt walls. Most were the size of deep closets and were uninhabited. A few of them were sunk down a few feet and smelled ghastly; they were undoubtedly subterranean outhouses. As he passed these alcoves, he shone his light down into them, regretting it every time.

The first person he found was a trog that smelled worse than one of the outhouses. One of its arms ended in a black and rotting stump. Its face had nearly disintegrated. Ears, nose, lips were gone. Its mouth was a bleeding gash surrounded by grey mold. "Turn off that fuckin' light," it groaned when Cole glanced into its pit. "Turn it off! Turn it off!"

"Sorry," Cole muttered.

The next people he ran into were a trio of slags sleeping like worms beneath a single blanket. At least two of them were naked, their flesh covered in boils and lesions.

He hurried by before they could wake up and scream at him, as well. He passed two more sickening little pits and a side tunnel, and was just wondering how far he had gotten when he ran into a girl who was not quite into her teens, but who was already showing slag on her cheek and neck. Her eyes were dim, like slow pools of grey mud. They were mostly hidden behind heavy lids. "Hey baby. One dollar. What do you think?" she asked, her words came slurring out of a mouth that still held most of her teeth.

She had a mass of green hair that she decorated with strips of multicolored yarn. It was longer on the slag side, but was tucked behind one small ear. The rest of her was hidden beneath mismatching clothes: A long purple scarf that looked as though she let the ends drag in the mud, red polyester pants that hung off her skinny hips and were tied in place with a phone cord, and a dull tan shift that looked like it belonged to someone a foot taller than her.

"Are you kidding me?" Cole said, pulling her hands from him. She had been trying to urge him into the closest alcove. "You need to get up top and find a damned shelter, for goodness sakes."

"What about fitty-cent? Huh? I know you got fitty-cent. I'll do anything you want if you got fitty-cent."

Cole pushed her away. "I said no. Now get out of here." He walked away, muttering curses under his breath and wiping his hands on the dirt of the ceiling, figuring it was the cleanest part of the tunnels. Some of his anger stemmed from guilt at having left the girl. She wasn't exactly a honey-bunny as the child whores were called, but she was damn close. Still, he knew better than to try and "rescue" her. She was riding the Mule and nothing he could do would get her off it.

He was just rationalizing that the creatures below the earth weren't really human at all, when he saw a white light ahead of him. Quickly, he turned off his own and ran back to an alcove he'd just passed.

Peering out, he saw a pair of cops come down one of the side tunnels. In their armor and helmets they filled the passage, blocking it completely. Since there was no profit in trying to shake down the trogs, the police rarely went down into the tunnels.

"But here they are," Cole whispered, wondering what the hell he had done to warrant this.

He really didn't have any chance to run away. The dirt passage was too straight and he knew he'd be shot in the back before he could make it ten feet. "I'm going to have to shoot my way out." And then keep running, forever. People who shot cops did not have trials, they did not get lawyers, or a phone call. They got a bullet to the guts and a long, slow death in a dark, dank cell.

Cole took a deep breath, readying himself to kill two men in cold blood, only just then, he heard the clank of tin and a loud, all too familiar hissing. When he looked back up the passage, he saw a red glow on the ground ten feet away with what looked like smoke coming from it. But it was not smoke. The police did not use smoke or tear gas.

No, this was neuro-tech gas and just a whiff of it would have a person seeing double. It worked on contact as well, which was why the two officers didn't bother putting on their masks. They had thrown the "can" as it was called and were already running up the passage leading back to whatever building loomed twenty stories above them.

Turning the under-barrel light back on, Cole ran back the way he came, racing for the closest side passage. He knew the police would be trying to box him in and he would be lucky if he had even a minute to get out of their box before it was too late.

Neuro-tech gas was used for crowd control. Above ground, where it infused into open air, a single can could put a thousand people into a day-long coma. Below ground, the gas could be deadly. If a person was left lying in it for too long, the toxins would shut down their respiratory system. They'd turn blue and die.

There was no telling how many slags and trogs were beneath the city block with Cole. Though, if truth be told, Cole didn't care a whit about them. The gas would be a mercy to the trogs, painlessly putting them out of their living hell. With the slags, it was different, but not by much. At a certain point, they became the New York version of an untouchable. Eventually, they would be practically un-hirable except for the most dangerous or disgusting work, which frequently resulted with them being exposed to even more radioactive or polluted waste. Inevitably, they would spiral into trogs and live out the remainder of their hated lives in the dark, slowly rotting into nothing.

Despite this, Cole would've saved all of them strictly out of principle, but there was no time. The gas was filling the tunnel from behind and as he raced back the way he came, his light picked out the grey haze of another cloud. Twenty feet in front of it was the side passage he had passed. He sprinted for it, thinking that if it ran straight and he was quick enough, he might get away.

He had just made his turn when he caught sight of a shadow against the grey backdrop. It was the skinny, little runt of a girl! Bounding off the dirt wall, he ran back.

"Hey baby. One dollar. I do anything..."

She looked confused as he snatched her hand and pulled her back from the cloud. "It's a dollar, mister. You got a dollar, right? I do anything for a dollar." The fact that he was dragging her along the passage didn't faze her a bit. "Hey, there's a spot," she said, as they passed an alcove. "There was a spot back there."

"Shut up!" Cole snapped. Louder, he shouted, "Everyone out! Everyone out of the tunnels!"

No one so much as poked their head from their little alcoves. "Idiots," he seethed, and then stumbled. The passage had angled up over a rocky point and the girl had tripped, falling into his legs.

They fell together, Cole throwing himself down first so she wouldn't plow her face into the dirt. When he rolled over, she blinked and asked. "Done already?That's cool. Where's my dollar? I bet it was good, baby."

Cole yanked her to her feet and kept going up and over the rise. At the top, he shown his light down into a pooling green-grey cloud. "Back! We have to go back the other way. Do you know the way out? Hey! Look at me. Focus. Do you know the way out?"

She tottered in place, gazing blearily back and forth. "Out of where?"

"Never mind." He hauled her back the way they came, pointing his light into every alcove until he found one that had a very narrow tunnel running from it. Cole had to turn sideways to squeeze through. It ran at a decline and soon they were slogging knee-deep through a bog of urine and shit-stinking mud.

These are my best shoes, Cole thought, his anger growing into a rage.

Thankfully, the muck ran for only twenty yards or so before the tunnel leveled out. Cole was so busy kicking the muck off his feet that he didn't see the first tendrils of cloud wafting along the dirt passage until his feet were in it. The stinking layer of mud protected their lower legs, which was all well and good, but he saw that the cloud was quickly filling the passage ahead of them.

They were almost entirely trapped. Their only hope was to make it to a branching tunnel that wasn't far in front of them. Of course, it was even then being covered by the cloud. "Hold this," Cole said, pushing the flashlight into the girl's hands. She gazed at it without recognizing what it was. While she was busy trying to figure it out, he grabbed his emergency mask and shoved it down over her face.

"Hey!" she cried.

"Leave it on," Cole barked at her. He took the flashlight from her and then hauled her even faster toward the gas. She wasn't afraid, but should have been because once the gas hit her flesh, it began to sting like needles. The girl jumped and screamed...and then stumbled. The toxins stung for only a moment, then it began to numb the flesh and muscles beneath.

With his suit and long trench coat, Cole was better protected than the girl. Her clothes were loose on her skinny little body and in seconds she almost fell. Cole grabbed her and flung her over one shoulder, took a deep breath and charged through the cloud, his eyes at squints. Immediately his hands, face and neck began to burn.

Although he was in the cloud for only seconds, the entire right side of his face was completely numb. His right hand felt like someone had sewn a corpse's hand to his wrist.

"Suh-a-itch," he gasped when they were through the cloud and into the branching tunnel. His jaw wasn't working properly and neither was his right eye; it stared down and to the side and no matter how hard he tried, he couldn't get it to blink.

He tried to set the girl down, however neither of her legs were working—she was just starting to become afraid. Knowing that more danger could be in front of them, he picked her back up and trudged on, constantly looking for a sloping passage that would bring them to the surface.

After a long way, he found a passage that was half-filled with water. He would've ignored it except he saw that the water was rising higher. "Ih aining," he told the girl and pointed up. It was raining on the surface and if they could follow the running water they could make it to safety.

She was still light in his arms, and he was able to splash through the passage until he came to a sloping shaft that had water gushing down it like a raging river. The passage was slick and at first neither could gain any traction and they kept sliding down. Very quickly Cole was soaked from head to toe, and as much as he wanted to grouse about what the muck and the rain water was doing to his suit, it was also washing away the neuro-tech gas.

Soon their muscles were working like they should, and the two were able to climb to the surface, where they found that it wasn't just raining. It was a grey deluge and it was wonderful. They stood near the side of a machine shop where a downspout provided them with a gushing shower.

Cole used the water to wash his clothing, going so far as to hold his fancy shoes up to the stream.

"Where's my dollar?" the girl asked. Her eyes were clearer now and her belly emptier.

"I should be charging you. I saved your hash, not the other way around." Of course, he had been the one who had put them all in danger in the first place—something he thought best not to bring up.

The mule was bucking her off and her head was beginning to hurt. She would need more soon or the come down would leave her with a migraine that would make a spike through the head feel like a kiss on the cheek.

"Come on, man, you promised. You can't just bang a girl and then not pay. That ain't fair."

"We didn't have sex, so forget it. Now shut up. I have to figure some shit out." He needed to get to a phone to call Joanna Niederer. He needed a change of clothes. He needed cash, and he needed to keep out of the reach of the police until he could straighten things out with his boss.

What he didn't need was to babysit a honey. "Why don't you go find your daddy and leave me alone?"

"I ain't got one. Daddies are useless. You pay them to protect you from getting smacked around, but they smack their girls around more'n anyone. I seen it a ton."

"Then go home."

"Ain't got one."

"You got any kinda parents? Brothers?" She shook her head. He wasn't about to ask her about friends. People riding the mule didn't have friends. "Then go play in traffic. Alright? Get lost."

She crossed her arms across the nubs of her breasts. "Not til I get my money. I had stuff, you know. Good stuff. It's all ruined now because of you. All that down there was your fault. I know it. Do you think a girl on her own can just set up shop anywhere? No way, buster. You're into me for way more'n a dollar."

"I'll give you two just to go away."

The cold water, the neuro-toxin, and the fright of the whole thing had set her mind straight better than a three-day dry spell. Her wheels were turning well enough for her to know that the big guy was one of those rare marks who'd fall for the poor, helpless bunny look that an old honey had taught her years before.

Step one was to make a connection. She stuck out a hand—her left one. "My name's Corrina Marie, but you should call me Corrina because that's what everyone calls me. What's yours?"

He rolled his eyes and ignored the hand. "Cole. Now, come on. I owe you a bed for the night, but that's about it." He was already walking away.

"I had food down there, you know. So, you gotta throw in breakfast as well. That's only fair. And lunch of course. I had lots of food stashed away. You know what a larder is? I had one of those just packed with stuff. You ever have cheese from a cow? I had some in there."

Cole didn't think she'd had a real meal in a month. He highly doubted she'd ever seen cow cheese in her life. It was damn expensive stuff. "Sure you did."

"Honest. I had cow cheese and Charlotte bread. I betcha never ate Charlotte bread. And I had a Georgia ham…" Corrina went on to list every fancy dish she could think of and in the process forgot exactly why she had started talking about food in the first place.

It hardly mattered since Cole wasn't listening. At first, he'd been trying to formulate some sort of game plan. He couldn't go home. The police were undoubtedly watching his place, and when they couldn't find his dead body in the tunnels, they'd double the watch. Finding a motel was also out of the question; he only had four dollars to his name and even a crappy little flophouse would cost him fifty cents, and that would be with sharing a bed with some stiff. Perhaps worse than all of that was the fact that Joanna was probably compromised by now. Director or not, her phone would be tapped and the Hall of Records watched.

All of these were tomorrow's problems.

He wasn't listening to Corrina because he was too busy watching a cruiser that had just turned onto the street they were walking down. It was only a block away, rolling slowly along, shining its spotlight down every alley. There were a few other people on the street hurrying through the rain. As each passed the cruiser, the light blazed into their faces for a moment.

It was too late to run.

"Take my hand."

"Huh?" She looked up at him a little taken aback, thinking that maybe she was wrong that he was a pushover. "I guess, but it's still a dollar and you still owe me for the rest."

He took her hand and pulled her close, undecided whether to pretend to be a kiddie-perv or a protective dad. His own instinct said go with dad, reality suggested that perv would be more believable. As the cruiser pulled alongside him, Cole ran his hand down her back and leered down at her.

The light was harsh and blinding, making him grimace. Corrina held up one hand to shield her eyes and with the other she flipped off the cruiser. "I'm working here, taxman!" she snapped. The light burned into her for a brief moment and then washed past. "Ah, my fuckin' head. Damn, Cole. I'm gonna hafta charge you double. You know, because of the cops and all. I'm sure you understand."

"Seems only fair. What's two times zip?" When he saw her trying to puzzle out the math involved, he said, "I'm not sleeping with you, so I'm not paying you. But I will set you up for the night if I can. Maybe."

"Maybe? Look Cole, I just saved your bacon. I can call them taxmen right back if I wanna. What do you think about that? Huh? Is that what you want?"

"I'm getting you a room. You should be happy with that."

Her head was beginning to bang the gong and she muttered, "I can't eat a fuckin' room, can I?" She couldn't smoke it either and just then she wanted to climb back up on the 'Rican Mule and forget the world.

She closed her eyes and tried to capture the infinite calm she always felt when she was riding the mule. It wouldn't come. Harsh reality kept creeping in. She was cold and wet. The inside of her head was on fire. Her shrunken belly ached for food, while at the same time it kept turning over, wanting to hurl out whatever green juice was sloshing around at the bottom.

They crossed the street and stole up another, gradually losing themselves in the city. She walked hunched in on herself, hating this part of her life. Being clean, even for an hour, meant being miserable.

"Here. Take this." Cole pulled off his trench and slung it around the girl's shoulders. She eyed him suspiciously. "The proper response is, thank you."

"Oh, yeah. Thanks bunches for ruinin' my life." He glared and cursed, and considered taking the coat back. While he wasted his breath, she searched his pockets, finding the flashlight and a pair of handcuffs, but no cash.

She dangled the cuffs in front of her face. "I thought only taxmen had these sorta things. You ain't a taxman, are ya?"

"Bounty hunter," he said, snatching them from her hands.

"That sounds like a taxman to me. How much does it pay? Pretty good I bet." He scoffed at this and she pulled back his coat. "I seen your gun, Cole. It's pure silver, ain't it?" He scoffed at this as well, and kept marching. "All I'm sayin' is don't go chintzy on me. Hey, what is this place?"

He was crossing another dark street and heading to a brick building that had once been squat and long, but now had a multiplex apartment heaped up on top of it, seven stories high. Corrina didn't like the look of it. The addition wasn't even treated polyfab, it was made of corrugated tin, warped wood, fencing, and the home-brewed concrete substitute called sand-crete, which was more or less pressed sand with a glue filler.

There were a lot of these sort of "buildings," and sooner or later they always came crashing down. Corrina felt safer underground.

Across the top of one door were words which she couldn't read, but she recognized the cross. "Hey, a Jova-freak is the last thing I need."

"It's an orphanage and you're an orphan. I need to dump you somewhere, so in you go."

"No way!" She tried to run, which was exactly what he was expecting. Cole was on her like a cat on a mouse, and in four seconds, she was pinned to the wall and had her hands cuffed behind her back.

Chapter 7

It took five minutes of hammering on the door before it was opened by a sleepy-eyed boy of nine. He tilted his buzzed head back to look up at Cole. "Yeah?"

He must have been new. "You don't say 'yeah.' You ask, may I help you?" Cole brushed him aside and stepped into the open room. It was long and wide, windowless and chill. It doubled as a church and a school—and apparently as a third dormitory. Twenty-three children were stretched out on the floor in pairs. Each pair shared a pillow and blanket.

"Where's Father Hernton?"

"Dead. He got the lung-junk fever two months ago."

Cole started to curse, biting it off at the last moment. "Alright, what about Jimmy Smith? He isn't dead, is he?"

"It's Father James now," the boy corrected. "He's in his room." Cole stared daggers at the kid until he mumbled, "I'll go get him."

The boy was small and skinny and his feet thumped softly up the stairs. Father James wasn't a very big man and yet his slippered feet could be heard descending from four stories down. The entire building creaked and groaned, and seemed to lean in the direction of the preformed poly-stairs.

"I'm not staying here," Corrina whispered under her breath. She was still cuffed and if Cole had his way, she'd remain that way until morning. By then the hunger for her next fix would be at least manageable. Cole was about to tell her that she was staying when Father James came down the last flight wearing a drab pair of wool pants and an equally drab shirt. Cole affixed the best smile he could in place, hoping that the guilt didn't show through. He had been rather merciless to James growing up in the orphanage together.

James was half a foot shorter than Cole and seven shades darker. Save for a scar that ran from the corner of one lip all the way to his right ear, he was a perfectly handsome man. When he smiled, his teeth seemed to radiate their own light. "Well, if it isn't my favorite part-time Christian," he said, flashing those white teeth briefly. "It's been too long, Cole."

"It's been a tough couple of years."

"That's when most people come to the All Father. But not you. You only come around when you're flush, splashing your money around. Why is that? Does success make you feel guilty? Or are you ashamed of failure?"

"Maybe it's because I don't like to come empty-handed. Speaking of which." He jerked a thumb at Corrina. "I have a present for you. This is Corrina Marie. She's doing her best to throw her life away and I figured you could straighten her out."

In the dim light cast off by a single wall sconce, James' handsome features became pained. "Sorry, but we're filled to overflowing as is. And besides, she's too old. You know that as well as anyone. We start integrating them outside the orphanage at thirteen and that's only if they can read and write."

"What about somewhere else? You know if the *Chain of Light* guys have any openings?"

"*Chain of Light?* That's a cult for goodness sakes! Either way, the answer's no. They've been sending their failures our way for months now. It's getting bad, Cole."

"It's always been bad." Cole was thirty years old, and as far as he knew there had never been a "good" time. No one reminisced about the good ol' days, except when it came to music. Every generation had their music, and every generation claimed the next generation listened to nothing but noise. "Come on, Jimmy someone has to take her. She's on the mule and if someone doesn't watch over her, she's going to slag-out pretty quickly."

James nodded somberly, but only for a moment, then his smile flashed anew. "I know who can do it. You." Cole glared at him in response, his hazel eyes a dark mottled grey. James wasn't impressed. "She may be exactly what you need, and you are clearly exactly what she needs. You know we don't keep kids in chains here."

"I'll let her go," Cole threatened. "I'll set her loose and she'll be right back to doing only God knows what."

"That'll be between you and God. If you wish, I will pray for both you and the child."

Cole only barely kept his composure. He didn't need prayers. He needed to offload the kid so he could get back to the hunt. There were at least two zombies running around New York and if he didn't bag one of them he would never have a chance of clearing his name.

"Alright," Cole said, pulling out his handcuff key and showing it to James. "I guess she goes free." Corrina turned around, happy to get the cuffs off. Cole started to work the key into the lock but stopped as James only stood there waiting. "Goddamn it, Jimmy! Some priest you are. You'd let a girl…" He raised a fist at James, but they both knew that was also a bluff. Cole wasn't going to punch a priest in the face with two-dozen young boys watching.

Instead, he grabbed James by the arm and pulled him into the hallway. "Fine, I'll take her, but I'm going to need some money." James burst out laughing at this, all of his pretty teeth showing. Again, Cole had to hold back. "I'm talking about a loan. And for just a few dollars. You know I'm good for it. Things are kind of…weird right now."

"I have eighty mouths to feed, Cole. Do you think I have a few dollars lying around to hand over to a gambler on the skids? No. Every penny is needed to keep a roof over their heads and clothes on their backs."

"Alright, fine!" This wasn't going the way Cole had envisioned at all. "What about some syn-ope? Or some calc? She's going to need something to come down on and if you want me to take her, I can't have her climbing the damned walls."

It felt good to wield the guilt sword for once. James' shoulders drooped and he left Cole in the hall. When he came back, he did so with a small bag of confiscated pills in one hand and Corrina in the other. He wished them good luck and then shut the door without another word.

"You gonna take these off, or what?" Corrina asked, holding out her wrists.

"First, take one of these." The pills were blue calc, which wasn't the best, but she was small and young. Chances were that she would be dead on her feet in minutes. Depressingly, she took the pill as if it were candy, not even asking what it was. He then led her outside where the rain had turned into a grey drizzle.

She was already yawning.

"We'll find a phone and then we'll get a room. And don't start in with me about that dollar business."

Finding a pay phone that worked could be a challenge. In this case, they got lucky on their third try. It was a waste of a nickel as the call went right to a machine. Cole left only the phone's number as a message and then dragged Corrina across the street to wait in an alley. The phone never rang, however a squad car did suddenly zip up after a few minutes.

More police cars arrived and fanned out, beaming lights into every nook and cranny. Cole waited in his hiding spot for half an hour with Corrina asleep next to him, her head resting on his leg.

Eventually, the cops went in ever wider circles until they gave up on the chase. When they were gone Cole picked her up and went in search of a room to let. Sixty-five cents got him a single bed and a glaring eye from a jowly woman with cheeks like slabs of pork. She shook a finger at Cole. "No funny business, ya hear?" she warned. "This ain't no honey-pot. This is a fine establishment."

The "fine" establishment had roaches and, by the sounds coming from the thin walls, rats.

Corrina was so out of it that she would have slept with her shoes on. Of course, they weren't her shoes at all. They were two sizes too big and the skin around her ankles was chaffed and blistered. Although her clothes were still wet, he decided against undressing her. On the other hand, he hung up his suit coat and pants. He laid the shirt as neatly as possible on the floor, before he climbed into the bed next to her, wearing nothing but his boxers.

It was weird, and if she had woken up and started mentioning dollars, he would have booted her onto the floor. Once she laid her head on the pillow, she was out and a minute later so was he.

They didn't wake until the jowly lady's husband banged on the door at exactly ten, demanding that they check out or be charged an extra day. He was very angry sounding right up until he got a look at Cole, then he tucked his tail and disappeared.

Cole paid an extra ten cents apiece for breakfast which consisted of a milk substitute, a bacon substitute, and oatmeal with a sugar substitute. They'd both eaten far worse and they left the apartment with full bellies.

Corrina started to get cranky and Cole dosed her with another pill. In minutes, her lids were heavy again and every time they stopped, she started to nod off. She didn't even notice that her blisters were popping around her ankles because of her shoes.

"I don't need this right now," he muttered when he saw the blood in her shoes. They had been pushing northeast across lower Manhattan, heading for Grand Central Station. If there was one place that a person could use a telephone and not be jumped on by the cops, it was there.

He had been hoping to avoid the cost of two train tickets, but now it looked as though he would have to spring for a pair of shoes. In a third-hand shop, they were a dime as was a new shirt and a proper jacket. She woke up enough to parade around in front of a mirror in her new clothes.

"It's red! It matches my pants."

Really it didn't. Her pants were burgundy and the jacket was cherry. The new shoes were midnight blue and ankle-high, and the socks were wool, thick and stolen. She suppressed a grin as she walked out of the store, wiggling her toes.

"This is where you say thank you." She opened her mouth to argue and he held up a hand. "Yeah, yeah, I owe you a dollar. Or two. Whatever."

"Sure, thanks. As long as we're on the same page about your debt. Gifts don't count. But, uh, say, while you're shelling out, can we get some make-up?" She tugged at her hair on the longer side trying to cover up the grey slag creeping up the left side of her neck.

With less than three dollars to his name, he wasn't about to drop two bits on powder. "If I get one of these bounties, I'll get you all the make-up you want. Until then, do what I say."

"No foolin?"

With ten large he could afford to push her onto James Smith. He would take her as long as she came with a "contribution."

"Yeah, no fooling. Just keep up." Even with the lure of make-up dangling in front of her, he half-expected her to take off while they were pushing through the faceless mob in Grand Central. Thousands of people were going in every direction, and all of them were in a great hurry. It would have been nothing for her to slip away and he wouldn't have done anything to stop her.

His charity only went so far.

But she stayed close, jogging to keep up with his long stride as he went deeper into the train station. They passed many banks of phones, and went up and down stairs before they came to the main lobby. It was an immense, monumental space that teemed with so many thousands of people that it made the earlier crowds seem small and tame.

With its cream-colored Botticino marble floors, towering Corinthian columns, imported Texas light bulbs, and the huge, gleaming brass clock, it was the fanciest place Corrina had ever been. Cole nearly lost her as she stared around, thinking how wonderful it would be to get high, lie down in the middle of the room, and let the world simply spin around her.

"What're you doing, Corrina? Come on. The phones are this way."

Cole took her by the arm and led her to one of the double banks of phones. They were constantly busy with people moving in and out, making calls, laughing, sometimes covering their mouths and whispering secrets.

She was fascinated by all the activity and again Cole had to shake her.

"There's one." He pulled her close. "I need you to watch those two police officers. See the ones over there by that bootblack? If they suddenly look this way let me know." The cops were lounging in a couple of raised chairs, taking up space meant for customers, much to the annoyance of the shoe-shine boys.

"You know this'll cost you, right? I already saved you once from the cops, remember? Last night when you grabbed my... "

A groan escaped him. He took her by the shoulders and turned her towards the police. "I said I'd get you the makeup. Now, watch them." He dropped a nickel in the slot and dialed the number to the Hall of Records. "Director Niederer, please," he said to the bored voice that answered. "This is Cole Younger. She's expecting my call."

"Hold the line."

A trace could take up to a minute. Then it would be another three before the right man at the right precinct was found who could contact the two officers. How long would he have then? One minute? Two?

Cole told himself he would hang up and walk away after five minutes no matter what. Of course, Jo came on the line with three seconds left and Corrina tugging nervously on his coat. The two cops had hopped up out of the chairs.

"The Grimmett family records have disappeared!" she hissed into the phone. "Normally, they give me a heads-up when they scrub a record, but this happened out of the blue, Cole. It was on my desk..."

He tuned her out as he lifted up slightly seeing the police officers coming down the rows of phones. More cops were hurrying into the atrium from other directions.

"Jo, shut up for a second. Go to the front desk. I'll call you right back at that number. This one's bugged." He hung up on her and grabbed Corrina who had been edging away, wanting to put some distance between herself and the man the cops were about to kill. He pulled her down onto his lap and handed her the phone. "Pretend you're talking to your Aunt Lucy."

"I don't have an…"

"Say hi to Aunt Lucy," Cole said, speaking louder as one of the cops came up. When Corrina only stared at him, he nudged her. "Don't forget to thank her for that dolly she sent you."

The cop was eyeing the man in the rumpled suit when Corrina said in a blaring voice, "Thanks for the dolly, Aunt Lucy. I really love it. It's the best. It's really, really great. Yeah, it's great."

Cole cursed under his breath. Then, in a whisper, he said, "Ask her how the kids are." Corrina asked, all the while staring at the cop. Cole took the phone from her. "Lucy," he said to the dial tone. "Our train got delayed. I think it might be a breakdown." The cop moved on, eyeing every man along the row who was alone. The moment he was gone, Cole slipped another nickel into the slot, dialing slowly, guessing that Jo at full speed wasn't much faster than Jo watching paint dry.

"Hello?" Jo answered, timidly.

"Are you alone?"

"Yes. I hope you know what you're doing. The Tinsleys are richer than God, and very well connected."

Cole hunched over the phone. "Who are the Tinsley's? I've never heard of them. I'm trying to find Santino's daughter."

"Her name is Christina Grimmett and she worked for the Tinsley's. It was on her tax record. *Was* being the operative word. Luckily that Tinsley name jumped out at me. Like I said, they're rich."

"Vamps, shit," Cole muttered. He hated dealing with vamps. They had even less scruples than the police and enough money to make any problem disappear, including a problem like Cole Younger. "Do you have an address on this Ashley Tinsley?" She gave him an upper east side address with a suffix of Sub-7. They'd be going deep.

"Good luck, Cole," Joanna whispered. "And be careful around the Tinleys." She didn't expand on her warning but only hung up the phone.

Cole was more worried about the police who were still combing the station. Luckily, they were still looking for a single man. Cole ducked into the crowd while holding Corrina's hand. He tried to get her to talk about "Aunt Lucy." She only wanted to talk about how much he owed her. By her estimation, it was eleven dollars.

"And that's me bein' nice," she told him as they walked up Park Avenue. "I bet I could get loads more if I turned you over to the cops."

She wasn't wrong. The police were throwing a lot into taking him down, which meant someone big or someone rich was after him. Was it the Tinsley family? Was he walking straight into the lion's den? He caught a glimpse of himself in a window and wondered if he would get even close to the lion's den. His short dark hair could've used some gel and a comb, he needed a shave, and his clothes were stained and wrinkled.

The little money left in his pocket would've helped to straighten him out, but what happened if the Tinsleys were a dead end? He would end up having to pawn the Crown simply to eat that night.

"A haircut isn't going to change what the vamps think of me," he said. Corrina frowned, thinking that he had ignored her. "I heard you. Eleven it is. As soon as I get paid, it's yours. That means you got to stick with me and do what I tell you. I'm going to have to leave you alone for a while. If you take off, that's on you. I won't go looking for you."

She found this strangely upsetting and didn't know why. "Where are you going?"

"I have to go talk to some vamps and I'll be lucky to get through the front door. I'd take you, but one look at that bit of slag of yours and they send us packin'."

Quickly, she covered her slag with her green hair. "I don't wanna see no vamps no how." She walked with her head down for a couple of blocks. The ache in her temples was coming on again and with it came a hunger to get high and forget about vamps and taxmen, and all the rest. None of it had anything to do with her, after all.

At the same time, eleven dollars was more money than she had ever seen in her life. If she had that much money, she could get a place and work like a proper honey. She was also curious about all this bounty hunting business. It was something different. It was also kind of scary.

"You worried they might suck you dry?" she asked.

He shot her a look. "Suck me dry? How so?"

"Well, they're vampires, ain't they? They drink blood. That's what I heard. And they never come out in the daytime. And they're evil. They look pretty on the outside, but on the inside they're black as hell."

Cole laughed at the description. "Sorry to burst your bubble, they're not real vampires like in the movies. They're just called that because they suck the city dry. They're rich and all they care about is getting richer." *Even if that means murdering a couple of nobodies like us,* he thought, but didn't add.

Chapter 8

As the two got closer to the address, the buildings became taller and went from ramshackle leaners, to brick and ramshackle, to brick and then to windowless steel monoliths. The vamps liked their privacy.

Corrina was hungry and Cole was forced to plunk down fifty cents for a sandwich and chips, afraid that if he didn't, she would've tried ginning-up some work for herself. Hooking wasn't illegal in the city, but in the nicer areas, people frowned on the idea of honeys on the corner showing off their wares.

"Fifty cents for a sandwich?" she asked, when he slid the quarters across to the smiling counterman.

"Yeah, everything uptown costs more so eat slow. I'll be back as soon as possible." He left her and hurried to the address and found himself in front of one of the monoliths. The shining steel doors were handleless. There was no way to get into the building unless one was invited from the inside.

"State your name and business here," a voice sounded from above. A camera and speaker had slid out of a hidden compartment eight feet off the ground.

The camera was the size and shape of a Colorado box gun and Cole couldn't help wondering if it could also fire bullets. *Probably*, he decided. He patted down his hair before answering: "Cole Younger. I'm a licensed bounty hunter with the city on official business. I would like to see Miss Ashley Tinsley in Sub-7."

"One second."

It was not one second. He waited seven minutes before the steel door hissed back and the voice said, "Enter."

He did not enter a lobby as he had expected. Instead, he found himself in a small empty room. The walls were the same silver steel as the outer structure, though not as seamless. In front of him was another door; again without a handle. Beside that was what looked like a cubby that slid out as he stepped in.

"Place your gun and ID in the bin."

It wasn't a question of whether he had a gun or not. They knew. He unloaded the Crown and put it in the bin next to his ID and license. The drawer hissed closed and there followed another even longer wait. Finally, the door in front opened and a very, very large man stood just beyond it. Cole was a big guy, but this man was something of a monster. The top of his head was higher than the doorway and his shoulders would scrape either side if he tried to step through. His blue silk suit barely held in his bulging muscles. They weren't natural.

Despite his fearsome size, he had a higher than expected voice and something of a lisp. "Mithter Younger. Follow me."

Cole stepped inside the lobby that he'd been expecting to see from the start. The floor was a slab of pure uncut marble of gleaming white. Above their heads were a hundred crystal dolphins hanging from golden filaments that ran down from a ceiling that was painted to look like the sky—just not the New York sky. It was blue and beautiful and gave off an ambient light that lit the room.

The brute of a man escorted Cole to the only feature in the lobby, a steel elevator door. There were no buttons of any sort. The door opened after only a pause and the guard placed a hand on Cole's back. He stepped inside and saw that once again there weren't any buttons. Before he could remark on it, the guard stepped inside with him. The man was so large that he took up almost all the space and Cole was forced to stand in his shadow, feeling small.

After another pause, the doors shut. Since they tended to break down every other week, Cole wasn't used to taking an elevator, and he certainly wasn't used to one that seemed to be slipping through silk. Most elevators snorted and shuddered, and tended to miss their mark by a few feet when they finally made it to their floor.

The ride down was not long, and yet it was terribly uncomfortable. The beast of a guard stared down at Cole, looking as though he were a sneeze away from leaping on him and tearing his head off. For all of a second, Cole was relieved when the elevator stopped and the doors slid soundlessly open.

He then saw that the security had doubled in intensity. In front of him were two hulking guards in form-fitting black suits. One was pale with watery blue eyes and hands that looked as though they could crush Cole's head simply by squeezing it. The other was a dark brown version of the first, except that his eyes were an unhealthy shade of yellow.

After a single nod from the pale guard, the blue-suited man stepped back and the doors closed in front of him without a sound. Silence enveloped Cole. Not a squeak, not a murmur, not even a breath could be heard. Neither of the two giants uttered a word. They communicated by gesture. The dark one pointed at the floor in front of him and held out his arms, obviously desiring that Cole step forward and do the same.

When he did, the pale man pulled his trench coat off him and then frisked him with near-indecent thoroughness. As the large hands roamed over him, Cole surveyed the room he found himself in.

The floors and walls were of simple polished white marble. The perfect white was offset by two long, narrow tables of ebony that were so black that they seemed wet and deep. On the tables were three-foot high alabaster and ivory statues of children playing. Everything about the room was exact and excruciatingly spotless…everything except for Cole, that is. He was disheveled and dirty.

The pale giant held Cole's trench coat over one massive arm and pointed to a white door at the far end of the room. He found himself sandwiched between the two guards as they entered a sprawling, open room that was as warm and inviting as the previous one had been sterile.

Two separate fires were burning in the room. One in the center of the room was bound by a low brass railing and surrounded by rich leather couches of deep brown. The other fire was at the far end of the room. It was smaller and cozier, and had three soft, plump chairs pointed at it. These sat on a tawny rug of lion fur.

The floor was gleaming lacquered mahogany and the cream-colored walls were covered in gold and silver picture frames depicting forests and rivers for the most part.

It was a stunning display of casual opulence, and it almost went unnoticed. Cole was enraptured by something greater than the material wealth. Across from the second fire was a grand piano that was as long as a car, and sleekly black.

Cole had seen pianos in pictures before, though none held a candle to this one, and he had heard a few records of piano music. They had sounded "clanky" and just plain wrong in a way he hadn't understood until just then. The pianist, a small dark-eyed slick with a hooked nose and a part in his hair an inch wide, didn't simply play the instrument. His fingers caressed the keys, touching each briefly, softly, sometimes dancing across them, sometimes coming down as lightly and chaotically as a swarm of butterflies.

With his hands he produced beauty.

Cole was instantly entranced and he followed after the pale guard with his mouth open. When the giant stopped, Cole was still staring at the piano and walked right into him as a result.

A woman asked, "Is it drunk?"

Sitting alone in one of the over-sized chairs by the second fire was a long, thin woman. She wore a smile that was equal parts contempt and malicious amusement.

He had seen a few vamps in his time and in certain ways they were all alike. Whatever their color, their skin was always impossibly, perfectly smooth. They bore no scars, no wrinkles and no laugh-lines. They had eyes that were unsettlingly large; almost to the point that they appeared alien. They had tall, straight noses that never flared, and cheek bones that were so sharp and prominent they looked as though they had been carved by a sculptor.

This vamp had skin that was freakishly white. It was almost as if it had been painted. Her lips and tongue were uncommonly red, which made her perfectly straight teeth seem even whiter than her flesh. Her eyes were gold as was her hair, which shimmered like silken metal. Dozens of sapphires were entwined in the silk.

The gems matched the color of the odd suit she wore. It mimicked a man's suit except that the pants narrowed down the legs and ended with darker blue cuffs just below the calves. The sleeves were equally stunted, which made the wide shoulders on the suit seem more so. She wore no shirt beneath the suit's coat and the sharp V of her lapels displayed an impressive cleavage.

Cole stole one look and quickly looked away, saying, "I'm not drunk, ma'am. It's the music." He wanted to say that it was good or great; however the music was indescribable and no compliment seemed proper.

"Bach's Variations," she drawled, turning her gold eyes to the pianist. "It sometimes strikes the perfect mood, which you have just managed to kill." She snapped her fingers and the slick stopped playing in mid note. "Leave."

Without a word, the slick stood, bowed and left through a door that seemed to magically open from a blank part of the wall.

"You are Miss Ashley Tinsley?"

She nodded, regarding Cole, staring him up and down, with a wintery look. "And you are some nobody." She put out a hand and the darker of the two giants handed her Cole's ID. "One of the governor's little monkey-men. Hmmm, Cole Younger. A made-up name."

"Every name is made-up. I want to talk to you about Christina Grimmett." He paused and when Ashley didn't react, he added, "She worked for you."

"Many people work for me," she said as she took a small black device from the pocket of her coat. She pointed it at each guard in turn before returning it to her pocket. "Now that they're muted, we can speak freely."

Cole frowned. "Muted? How do you mean?"

"I've cut the feed to their auditory implants. They can no longer hear us. Just pretend like they don't exist."

The idea of being switched off with the press of a button was horrible, but worse was how blasé she was about it. "You can just turn them on or off? Just like that?"

"I can *kill* them just like that." Her smile became predatory. "Does that bother you? Why, it does! What sort of bounty hunter are you? You're not like the last one, I hope."

"The last one?" His stomach began to sink.

She laughed softly, enjoying his discomfort. "Yes, the homosexual." She pronounced the word 'homo-setual.' Her laugh grew louder when she saw his dismay at being beaten to the punch yet again by Aaron. "Yes, your fancy friend was here ahead of you, asking all sorts of questions. He seemed to know a great deal about things he shouldn't know."

Cole stifled a groan.

How had Aaron gotten here first? Was it Jo? Was she double-dealing? And what sort of things did he know, exactly? More than Cole, that was for certain. He felt as if this case was unravelling around him and that all he was doing was just flailing about at random, hoping to get lucky. *Except, when am I ever lucky?* He sensed he was beginning to bottom out and he was on the verge of simply blurting: What did you tell him?

Ashley's smile suggested she was expecting exactly this. The smile mocked him. The smile told him that she wanted him to beg.

"Fuck that," he muttered, feeling the anger begin to burn. He had been getting the raw deal on this job from the very start and he was tired of it.

"I'm sorry, what did you just say to me?" One tawny eyebrow was raised and, much to Cole's delight, the smile had disappeared.

Cole decided not to answer, instead he stared at her as a man should, not like a frightened servant who could be muted or even deleted with one click. He looked past the fancy clothes, the expertly dyed hair and the strange golden eyes. Beneath all that, she was just a person.

He looked at her without fear and she didn't like it. Her ruby lips turned down, which made him smirk. "Vamps sure do hate to be judged."

"Do you think I care what a slag thinks about me?"

"I'm not a slag."

Her gold eyes bored in on him. "You're all slags up there. It's just a matter of when it'll show. If we tested you right now, what would your levels show?"

"Last time I was tested, I was ninety-nine percent pure." Of course, that had been eleven years before when he had applied at the police academy. He hadn't been tested since, and didn't plan on getting tested. It wouldn't change anything. Unlike the vamps, he couldn't afford to hide from the contamination that was slowly poisoning the world.

She scoffed at merely being ninety-nine percent pure. "And at what percentage does one officially become a slag? It's ninety-six percent isn't it?"

There was no "official" percentage that made a person a slag, but no one in the ninety-sixth percentile could legally have children. They couldn't hold a city job and there was no way in hell they would be allowed to emigrate, not even to a city like Boston or Washington, which were rumored to be even more slagged than New York.

"I'm still at least ninety-nine percent human," he said, "Which is more than you. Look at you. Fake tits, fake eyes, fake hair, fake teeth, fake nails. The only real thing about you are your ears."

Her gold eyes blazed in outrage and she drew in a deep breath, presumably to scream at him, but before she could, he calmly said, "So you do care what a slag thinks of you."

Surprise overcame anger. Her mouth opened wide and then shut with a click of her fine white teeth. "My, you are a cheeky one. That's what my mother would have said. You are correct about my ears. They're all natural." She turned her head to show off her small ears. They were quite delicate. "My lips are real, too. Not the color, of course."

"They are…" *Very kissable.* The thought just popped into his head and seemed to want to stay there. "Very nice." To get his mind off her lips he looked again at her ear. Ears, elbows and feet were not in any way sexy to Cole and he felt he was on safer ground. Her ears held diamond studs in the lobes. Although she could afford diamonds the size of his fist, the studds were actually quite small.

"So, you don't stretch out your lobes," he said as he reached into his pocket and pulled out the earring he had found in Santino's apartment. "Is this yours?" He had been standing across from her this entire time. Now, he took a step closer and handed her the small hoop.

She looked down at it and then shrugged. "Maybe. I own many earrings. I do like gold and I do like them small for the reason you stated. Too many women think that everything bigger is better. I prefer understatement to overstatement." Cole kept his face purposely bland so that she couldn't help but notice his utter "lack" of reaction. "I suppose to a slag…or whatever you call yourselves."

"People," Cole suggested.

"Really? You call yourselves people? Hmm. Either way, to you my apartments may seem ostentatious. I assure you they are not. Fourteen thousand square feet is little more than a hovel compared to most. My brother's place is thirty-thousand square feet. Of course, he has a child, so I guess the extra room is justified in his case."

These were numbers that Cole could not even comprehend. He tried to refocus back to the single earring. He pointed at it. "Christina had it in her possession."

As if it was covered in "people" germs, Ashley sneered at the earring sitting in her creaseless white palm. "Yes, I'm sure she did. Christina turned out to be something of a thief."

"What else did she steal from you?"

"My name, for starters. So, is she dead? Is that how you came by this?"

"It was at her home. She's missing, but her family is dead, so I'm not holding out much hope. What did you mean by taking your name? Is she trying to pass herself off as you?"

Ashley had her head tilted back as she regarded Cole. She gazed at him for some time before she asked, "How old are you, Mr. Younger? I'm just curious."

He had no reason to lie. "Thirty."

She sat back, the sapphires in her golden hair catching the light so that there seemed to be a tiny fire burning in each. "Thirty! You astound me. I would have thought you were at least forty. I asked your homo-setual friend how old he was, but he wouldn't tell me. So, I didn't answer any of his questions, either."

"But you'll tell me," Cole said.

"Yes, I suppose I will. Or I would if I knew anything at all about her. To me, she was nothing but a servant, a trained monkey who could fetch things on command. If she had a life outside of that, I didn't want to know."

Cole had a list of questions he'd been about to ask, but these all went right out the window. "You know nothing about her whatsoever? Who her friends were? What she did for fun? Where she lived? Her birthday?"

Ashley shook her head at each question. "Her birthday? Why on earth would I care about that? No, the only information about her that would be even remotely useful to you is that Christina was at a place called *The Leather Lounge* a few days back. If you can believe it, she was calling herself Allegro Albarossa." Ashley said this as if Cole should find it amusing. When he didn't laugh, she rolled her gold eyes. "Those are names of wines that I'm fond of. Either way, she kept throwing around my name, telling everyone who would listen that I was on my way. As if I would ever frequent a place called *The Leather Lounge*. Probably filled with slags from one end to the other. No offense to your kind."

"That's okay. I hear it's dull and overpriced. I think you should go. I get the feeling you would fit right in."

Her full red lips pursed, but again for only a moment. "Cheeky, cheeky, Mr. Younger. Very cheeky, yes." She grinned, leaning back and crossing her legs. "The Tinsley name is very powerful. You don't throw it around without repercussion." She tossed him the earring. "If you find Christina, kill her."

The earring was real gold, there was no question about that since it belonged to a vamp. It sat strangely heavy in his palm. But how heavy? A quarter of an ounce? A fifth? How much was it worth? Fifteen hundred dollars? Eighteen hundred? With that much money he could hold his head above water long enough to hunt down another Dead-eye, and this time he wouldn't burn through his money. He had learned his lesson about spending and the gambling...

Cole realized that he was already planning a future in which he was a murderer. Suddenly, he wanted out of the vamp's home. He held the gold hoop out to Ashley. She only looked at it disdainfully, so he tossed it into her lap. "I'm not a murderer."

Before she could say anything, he started walking back toward the front room with the guards closing in, keeping pace, eyeing him very closely. They would kill him without a qualm and probably for a lot less than the value of the earring. They eased away when Ashley came storming up. Even with her five-inch heels she was half a head shorter than he was.

"But you hunt people for cash! That is literally your job title." He said nothing to this. It would mean his life to explain what he really did. She shook her head in disbelief. "Tell me, how much do you make hunting people?"

"It depends."

She laughed. "No, it doesn't. Judging by your clothes and that hack-job of a hairstyle, I rather think you don't make much at all."

"What's your point?" He was crossing into the black and white room by then and wondering how he would call an elevator when there were no buttons.

"My point is..." Ashley stopped with an odd look on her white, white face. She was staring at him as if she had never seen a man before. "You really won't take money for killing her?" He shook his head and she let out a breath that was part rueful laugh. "How interesting. It's rare to run across an honest man, but to find an honest cop? I've never heard of such a thing."

Sadly, she wasn't wrong. "I'm not a cop, Miss Tinsley. May I have my ID back?"

"Yes, you're a bounty hunter. Do you ever wonder what happens to the people you capture? Do you care that they probably end up dead?" He couldn't answer that honestly. The Dead-eyes had to be eradicated, but the criminals that he brought in were a different story. He had no idea if they were innocent of the crimes they'd been convicted of—when the police were involved, justice was no longer a term that really meant anything.

"It's not my job to ask those questions. Now can I have my ID, please?" He glared down at her with his hand out.

Her question had been malicious and her grin had been alight with evil. Now, it turned impish. "First, ask me a question about me. You have been sneering at me since you walked in my home. I can see in your eyes that you think that all vamps are the same. I find it amazingly bigoted and wonderfully hypocritical of you."

She wasn't wrong about that either. A half-dozen snide questions sprang to mind, all designed to cut her down a peg. The way she had one gold eyebrow raised, it looked like she was expecting exactly those sorts of questions. He decided to ask a question that had been in the back of his mind since he had walked in.

"How old are you?" He stared into her beautiful face searching for the answer, but there were no clues to be found there. The age of a vamp was more of a mystery than that of a Mandarin. She could be eighty-five for all he knew.

"I'm thirty-two. Does that surprise you?"

"No. It only surprises me that you think I care."

Chapter 9

Cole groaned up into the rain. It was coming down in sheets and it seemed to wash the "vamp" off him. There was something unsavory about being so close to one, and despite the sterile conditions, he felt dirty as he strode from the steel tower.

The rain only helped so much. There was a metallic bite to the rain that was far from natural. Though it was true that after a lifetime in the city, he didn't really know what natural was. He was sure that there wasn't much natural about Ashley. Strangely, he thought the same about Corrina.

She was sitting in the corner of the restaurant, her hood cast over her head, jagging badly. Her nails hadn't been long to begin with; now they were bitten down to the quick. One knee was jangling up and down like it was attached to a live wire, and through the curtain of her green hair, he could see the paranoia in her eyes.

"You left me!" she hissed, the moment he came in through the door. An empty plate sat in front of her; every last crumb had been licked up. "You were gone forever and that counter guy keeps staring. I think he mighta called the taxmen down on us."

Cole glared the counterman back into the kitchens. "You're worried for nothing, and you shouldn't have worried about me, either. I'm here, aren't I? I told you I'd come back." He cast a disappointed eye at her plate, wishing she had left him at least a bite. His last meal had been the ten-cent breakfast eaten under the watchful suspicious eye of the jowly landlady, many hours before.

"Don't tell me not to worry," she said in a hissing whisper. "We're in vamp central. Everyone hates us here. We gotta get back down where they can't see or get us."

This was the mule talking. "Do you want another pill?" In answer, her hand flipped over and her fingers begged. "It'll be your last one until bedtime." *If you're even with me then.*

Her presence in his life was inexplicable. He didn't need her or want her, and there was really no reason he should feel responsible for her. "Are you sure there isn't someone you can stay with?" he asked, handing over the pill. It went down the hatch in a blink.

"Nope, but if you don't want me…"

"Stop it," he growled. He didn't want her but he also didn't want a pity party. "Come on. We got a lead on Santino's daughter."

She didn't know who that was, and really didn't show any interest, either. The pill acted quickly and she was glass-eyed as they stepped out into the rain and began marching back south. She moved robotically, splashing through puddles of muck without noticing. He wasn't much better. All he could think about was the damned earring and how much money he could've gotten for it. For damn sure, he could've off-loaded Corrina onto Father James.

"After that I would've gotten a steak," he said to himself. "A nice thick one, too." His stomach rumbled, reminding him that he was down to less than two dollars and fifty cents. A steak was out of the question. He sighed.

Corrina heard the longing in the sound and asked, "What was the vamp like? Did she have long teeth like they say? Was she all white like a ghost?"

He told her about the vamp and her fancy house and the giant guards. He tried to explain about the piano, however, he couldn't put the beauty of that into words. Corrina listened with a faraway look in her grey eyes.

"You gonna go back and tell her when we find this girl? If so, you think I could come along? I wanna see a vamp place before I die."

"Maybe," Cole lied. Ashley Tinsley would never let a slagged honey through her doors. They both lapsed into a dreamy sort of silence as the blocks passed beneath their feet. The afternoon was half gone before they came to *The Leather Lounge*.

Its neon sign was dim green and from across the street the long, low building seemed empty despite the Rango music thumping from every crevice. The machine gun drums perked Corrina up and she began to wobble her head and shoulders to the beat.

"No," Cole told her. "You're waiting here."

"Why? There ain't no vamp in there."

He took her shimmying shoulders and pressed her against the brick wall. "Because there might be trouble. This was the last place anyone saw Christina alive. You will stay here or I'm going to start subtracting dollars from what I owe you."

She didn't know what subtracting meant and he didn't have time to explain. Booze joints were slow during the day and if he was going to get any answers it was going to be right then.

"Stay put," he ordered, and then crossed the street, his hazel eyes shifting left and right, looking for danger in what was a typical day. The wet street was crowded with bikes, delivery trucks and the occasional taxi. The sidewalks were teeming with dull, grey-faced New Yorkers going about their dull, grey lives. Taxmen were nowhere in sight.

From the outside, there was nothing special about *The Leather Lounge*. Stepping inside, Cole paused to give his eyes a chance to get used to the dark. Not only was the place coated from one end to the other in a thick layer of heavy brown polyester "leather," it skimped on the lighting.

Gradually, he came to see that along the walls to the left and right were alcoves that were so deeply shadowed they could have been tunnels. In front of him was a wide area tiled in neon green linoleum. In the glow of the neon, he could see the outline of a few dive dancers sliding across the waxed floor as if it was ice. One slid backwards, her ass presented to Cole. She gave him a grin from over one shoulder.

"Want a dance?"

"Next time," he told her, going around the dance floor. Beyond it was a copper-trimmed bar. It was easily sixty feet long. Evenly spaced along it were three aging gin-johnnies nursing their drinks until the gin was more ice than alcohol.

Leaning against the line of kegs was a grizzled old slinger. He had his arms crossed over his beer-belly. His muddy eyes suggested he had been around the block more times than Cole could count. "You drinkin'?" The tone of his voice suggested he knew that Cole wouldn't be.

Cole pointed up at one of the cameras aimed towards the cash register. "I need to know what you got going on with them. They real?"

The slinger grunted, "Like I told your friend, they's just for show. If you want the song, you gotta pay the piper. Course, Red's busy. You'll have to wait your turn."

"Hold on," Cole said, familiar anger beginning to burn in him. "There's someone here? Is it about last Friday night?"

"Yup. There was a vamp slummin' it with Red Rod half the night. She was something else with her fancy bone corset all decked out with ivory and silver. And she had on these long, elbow-length gloves. I thought it was weird because one was white and the other was deep red. They were silk and that's about all I know, so too bad, taxman. If you want more'n that, you're gonna have to pay."

He started to turn away. Cole reached a long arm across the bar and turned him back. "I wasn't done with you. Where's Red?"

"I said wait your turn, taxman. Unless you got a little incentive for me. I never said no to an incentive."

The Crown was in Cole's hand before the bartender could blink. Cole shoved it into the man's ear. "This is all the incentive I need. Where the fuck is Red?" The barman pointed a shaking finger towards the back. In a fury, Cole stomped towards an unmarked door. The Crown was still in his hand and he was more than ready to shoot Aaron Reynolds the moment he saw him.

But it wasn't the Fox and his annoying smirk in the cramped little office. The door banged against a folding chair, which Cole thrust aside as he barged into the room. "Aaron, you got a lot of nerve…" The sight in front of him made Cole's throat instantly clamp shut. A man with slick red hair and dead white skin was staring up at the ceiling with blank eyes as a woman sucked dark blood from a neat little hole in his neck.

The hole had been made by a Dead-eye that knew how to cover her tracks. It was the blonde that had been with Santino before Cole had killed him. She wore a bright chameleon-green jacket and matching pants which made the slick and shiny bright blood on her chin look vibrantly red. In one hand she held the weapon she had murdered Red Rod with: a fountain pen. It was simple and perfect. No one besides a hunter would connect a small hole in the neck with a Dead-eye.

Before Cole could even process exactly what was happening, the blonde whistled the fountain pen at his face, missing his eye by an inch. He flinched and fired, hitting Red Rod in the chest as the Dead-eye was off of him in a blink, moving faster than Cole could follow. The next thing Cole knew, he was on his back, desperately trying to keep her teeth from his neck. She was hideously strong.

He fired the Crown but she had his wrist in a vice-like grip and the bullet missed the mark. It tore a chunk of muscle from her shoulder; she didn't even blink.

From the bar there was a hoarse shout, the sound of a bottle breaking and chairs being overturned. People were running. Cole could feel the floor shaking beneath him. They weren't running to help. The blonde didn't know this and leapt off of Cole, dashing for a back door. When it opened it let in a blinding grey light.

Cole pulled himself up and ran after her, hoping to be able to line up one clean shot. The chance of that went right out the window as he was lashed by a wall of stinging rain the moment he made it to the alley. She was already thirty yards away and sprinting as fast as he had ever seen anyone run.

You can't outrun a bullet, he thought as he brought up the Crown in one fluid motion. He fired just as she darted to the right past a mound of trash that was twice as tall as he was. He charged down the alley only by the time he got to the corner, she was gone, lost in the inner block maze.

There was still hope. A spray of black blood against the wall told him that he hadn't missed. He ran down the narrow alley until he came to a cross section of tenements. Ahead of him the alley narrowed to a foot or so; to the left and right were slightly wider lanes.

But which direction to take?

They were both lined with muck and trash, and each had a small river of rainwater washing down the center. Out of instinct, he chose the right and was rewarded by seeing a splash of black blood along one wall. He ran on, looking for blood drops. They came at uneven intervals, with these intervals growing shorter and shorter. She was tiring.

Or dying.

He hoped she was dying. A wounded Dead-eye was almost always more dangerous than one still thinking it could blend in.

The blood trail ran into a partly burned-out building. The warped ceiling dripped black tears onto a scorched polyfab floor. If there was more blood, it was all but invisible. Cole dug for his flashlight as he strode inside, every inch of his body tense, ready to fight for his life.

She would flee underground. Like roaches, Dead-eyes always felt safer hiding in the deep where the light couldn't reach them.

Movement on his left. Cole spun and pinned a tattooed slag to the wall with his light. The man cringed from the light. "There was a woman; where did she go?"

From his voice, the man knew Cole wasn't messing around. He pointed a stump of a finger down what had once been the center hall of the building. Now, it was only a melted tunnel of polyfab that looked like it had come from a nightmare. Running along the floor was a mass of sixty or seventy small black wires. Each represented stolen electricity. If he followed them, they would lead to a family of slags squatting in the ruin.

He wasn't after them.

"Where are the stairs down?" The slag crooked the same stump to his left. Cole didn't bother to thank the man. He simply ran down the hall and took the first left, ducking his head as he entered another twisted room. The stairs to the lower levels practically fell away, while the ones that went up, angled dangerously away from the wall.

Down was the direction he wanted; however the stairs led straight into rushing water. A main sewer line had ruptured and now thousands of gallons of water a minute were tunneling a new channel through the foundation of the building. Cole dropped down to one knee and shone the light back and forth. As much as Dead-eyes liked being underground, they hated being underwater.

He was just thinking that his prey might be desperate enough to take a chance on finding an air pocket, when he heard the stairs creak behind him. Instinctually, he twisted to his right, hoping to clear his gun so he could shoot, only once again, he was too slow.

The Dead-eye came leaping from the deep shadows, her face twisted in seething anger and eternal hunger. She crashed into him just as he turned and he was sent face first down into the water. As he put out his hands to stop himself, the tip of the gun got caught in a split in the warped polyfab and was torn from his grip. It disappeared in the racing water. Panicked and feeling helpless without a weapon, he tossed aside the flashlight and groped beneath the surface.

Before he could find it, the woman had him by the hair and shoved him deep. Even with a gaping hole in her abdomen and another in her shoulder, she was stronger than him and perfectly positioned to hold him under. There was nothing he could do. In vain, and in a growing terror, he fought as hard as he could, trying to push back against her, trying to buck her off or twist around.

I'm going to die.

Even though the thought somehow cut through the panic, it did not lend itself to a moment of clarity or of calm. It did not suddenly put him in a mental state in which he could placidly accept his fate and prepare for his on-rushing death.

No, the thought made him angry. Furious in fact. He was so enraged that his fear fell away and was replaced by an intense hunger for revenge.

You're going down with me, bitch! With that thought, he launched himself forward into the swirling blackness. Taken by surprise, the Dead-eye was slow to realize what Cole was doing, and she rode him down the stairs.

Just like that, their roles had been reversed. Now he trying to hold her back. It was like holding back a train. She was so strong that she tore the stairs apart trying to get to the surface. Flailing wildly, hunks of polyfab risers ripped away beneath her hooked fingernails. Then the banister bent and snapped off the wall completely, and still she clawed for the surface, pulling him along with her.

The instant they broke the surface, he began pounding his fist into the back of her head. She didn't care. Her only goal was to get to the landing. By then she was wobbling from the blows, while he was getting stronger with every breath. When his feet were underneath him, he took her bodily and rammed her face into the wall, breaking her nose and unhinging her jaw in a spray of water and black blood.

She lashed back with an elbow, striking him in the side of the head and staggering him. If she had been a thinking creature, she might have been able to eat him right there, but she was all animal at this point. Wounded as she was, she only cared about escape. She fled up the stairs, moving slower now, her wet trail easy to follow.

Cole dogged her, splashing along in her wake. They went up five stories until the building seemed to teeter around them. And still she fled, one hand holding in her guts. She ran down a long dark hall that was lit only by narrow shafts of grey light that somehow made it through the warped polyfab.

She ran until the building itself stopped her. The door at the far end of the hall had been melted in place and when she yanked at the doorknob, it came off in her hand.

She was trapped. Somewhere along the way, she had lost both of her contact lenses and when she turned, her black eyes gleamed. Like any animal, when cornered she would fight to the death.

He didn't rush in. Although she was weakened, she was still dangerous. "What did you want to see Red for?" he asked as he took off his trench coat; he felt thirty pounds lighter without it.

"Fock you," she said in a mumble, her broken jaw moving oddly.

"Yeah. That's what I thought." He had tried torturing a Dead-eye once. Fire, electricity, knives had all been a waste of time—if they felt pain it was probably the same way an insect did. To them a missing hand was only a distraction.

Cole held up his trench to the meager light. One of the sleeves was torn and a pocket was ripped. "Look what you did to my coat." When her eyes slipped to the coat, he threw it at her face and then sailed in swinging haymakers. One connected with her temple with a *Crack!* Another nearly knocked her jaw back into place.

She didn't seem to notice either blow. Her blood was up and she sent a punch into his chest that sent him flying into the wall. He bounced off of it and came right back, hammering her, knowing that his only hope was to cave in her skull. A Dead-eye could fight for some time with a bullet through its heart, but if you got to its brain, then it was lights out.

The two traded blows and went back and forth, smashing into the walls, making the building groan. She was fast, while he was trained. She was cunning while he was smart. She was small and amazingly strong; he was big with hands like sledgehammers. She relied too much on her teeth, but when she tried to bite him she could only smear black blood across his chest, because of her broken jaw.

In the end, her endurance was the deciding factor. A Dead-eye did not get tired. They went on and on without let up. Soon Cole was gasping for breath and his knuckles were bleeding. He began to slow and his punches became weaker. She grabbed him by the coat and slung him down, cracking his head against the floor with the sound of an explosion.

Stars shot across his vision. For seconds only, his eyes cleared, then she was on top of him with both hands around his neck, crushing down. Gradually, everything began to go hazy and dim. Even his fear became something distant. Without much care, he realized he would die this time, only just then there was a second explosion. The girl, a confused look on her bloody features, fell over him.

"Thanks for the assist." It was Aaron Reynolds wearing a plum suit with a gold vest and gold shoes. Gold beads dangled from his shoulder length hair. Leaving Cole lying there, he lit a cigarette and went to a window. Heaving back the lead-lined shutters, he let in a blinding light.

"What do you mean assist?" Cole said in a hiss, his throat felt like a can that had been crushed. Painfully, he heaved the body of the Dead-eye off of him, but for the moment, his head was too spinny to try standing. "There's no assist. That's my kill."

Aaron shook his head, making the beads rattle. "Not with my bullet in her head. No, the only kill you have under your belt today is Red Rod. The police are already looking for the murderer." He pointed his cigarette at Cole.

"How would they know I had anything to do with that? Unless you told them!" Cole started to scramble to his feet. He needed two tries to get up and when he was up, he stood, swaying with the building, his head swimming and a dull ache in his temple from…a fist? An elbow? Part of the wall? He didn't know and just then he didn't care. All he cared about was pounding Aaron into pieces.

Now Aaron pointed his Crown at him, the gold and silver glinting beautifully. "I couldn't tell them a Dead-eye was involved, now could I? Besides, your bullet is in him, your fingerprints are everywhere and there are four eyewitnesses. Lucky for you I told them you went north back to Vamp-town."

"Lucky? I should…"

Aaron cocked the hammer back, stopping Cole a second time. "Here's what you should do. One, you should thank me for saving your ass. And two, you should find a way out of town. Even if you could manage to bag a Dead-eye, you'll never live long enough to spend the cash. The police have a hard-on for you and sooner or later, they're going to nail your ass to the wall."

Chapter 10

Just then, Cole hated Aaron with a fiery passion. He hated his fancy plum suit and he hated his ridiculous gold shoes. He hated the damn smirk on his effeminate face and wanted to wipe it away with his fist.

"Gimme a cig," he muttered, going to the window and letting the rain wash over him. The Dead-eye blood had a rancid stink to it that made him want to vomit.

Aaron shook one loose and held it out. Of course, they were Confederates, each worth a dollar. When Cole lit it up, his head spun from the aroma. It had been a long time since he'd been able to afford a Confederate.

"Still no thank you?" Aaron scoffed, snapping his lighter closed. "First, I save your life, which admittedly isn't worth a nickel, but where's the gratitude for the cig?"

Cole grunted, "Go fuck yourself."

For some reason, Aaron grinned at this. "You were always the poet, Cole. Damn, look at you. Where's your Crown?"

"Lost it."

"What about your backup piece?"

Cole sucked in another lungful, feeling the burn in his throat where the Dead-eye had been crushing his windpipe. "Pawned it."

Aaron shook his head, rolling his eyes at the same time. "Rule one: never hunt without a backup piece. Rule two: never hunt without a semi-vax shot on hand. Let me guess, you pawned that as well?" Cole had used it a year ago and hadn't been able to afford a new one. He shrugged in answer and Aaron sighed. "Do you want to turn into one of them? Do you? If you aren't careful, I'll be hunting your ass down. It'll be easy money."

"They say the booster's good for a year. I should be fine." *I hope.* "And stop acting like you're doing me any favors. This was my kill. You did something to piss off Ashley Tinsley, which means the only reason you're here is because you were following me."

"Following you and saving you from your own stupidity. If you weren't so slow on the draw, you would be the one collecting. And so what if I followed you? It's hardly illegal. It's called overcoming obstacles. In this case, it was a vamp bitch. Pretty girls rarely trust a muncher, and do you want to know why? It's because they know that they can't shake their teats and expect us to go all gaga. You walked out of that building looking like you'd been slapped."

Cole finished the cigarette and tossed the butt out the window. He glanced down and then jerked back with a start. Below him the police were going through the maze of alleys with guns drawn. "Shit! I thought you said you sent them north."

Aaron took a look over the edge of the window and spat. "They're cops, what can I say? They aren't too bright. They are thorough, however. I bet they'll have this building locked down tight in under two minutes. Like I said, they got a thing for you."

Cops rarely came into the maze after a criminal—Aaron must have pointed them this way. Cole glared at the muncher, feeling helpless rage course through him. "I owe you a beat down, one that'll stay with you for a year or two," he growled.

The corners of his gold-tipped goatee turned up. "Sure Cole, whatever you say."

Cole had a lot to say and no time to say it. He left the room at a run, racing for the crooked stairs. His weight made them groan and bend. He couldn't help hoping that the whole building would collapse the moment he was out the door. A hundred slags would die but if it took out Aaron and a few taxmen, he felt it would be a fair trade.

He hurried past the ground floor and went down until the stairs were swallowed by the inky dark waters. His gun was down there somewhere. He went down five steps and fished around, searching along the risers. These stairs were even more unstable than the ones above and they slowly tore away from the wall, leaving him to fight the current using a flailing doggy-paddle; the only swimming style he knew.

By the time he climbed to safety, he could hear the heavy tread of metal strapped boots going up and down the hallway.

A quick glance from the stairwell revealed that the police were rousting out the slags in the building. They'd be rounded up, counted, beaten for information, "taxed" for stealing power and released to go back to their dreary lives.

As ragged as Cole looked, he couldn't pass for a slag. He started up the stairs only to stop when he heard a gunshot on the floor above him. "Fuuuuck," he whispered, drawing out the word as he turned around—there was only one way out of the building and that was through the rushing water. It was one thing to doggy-paddle five feet to safety, it was another thing altogether to trust the stroke under water that was black as night.

But he didn't have a choice. He sucked in a huge breath and slipped under, thinking that the racing current would carry him along. Instead it sucked him deep and spun him like a top. The three subbasements beneath the building had been made of sand-crete and were eroding at an alarming rate. Already a veritable canyon had been dug away by the swirling water.

It was not empty, however. Limp corpses danced in the current and thousands of bits of trash spun in an amazing vortex. The watery cyclone had an irresistible pull, and sucked him ever downward. In vain, he paddled like mad against it and it was only luck that he hit a wall jutting out into the gorge.

He couldn't swim, but he could climb and he could kick off with his powerful legs.

The darkness was not absolute. Here and there were shafts of dim light. Holding his breath, he went from wall to wall, aiming for one that gave off a greenish glow. It was an opening of sorts: a sewer grate from which long tendrils of green slime rippled gently as if waving goodbye to the passing corpses.

A section of the grate was bent inward and he managed to hook his fingers around one end, which kept him from being swept on to his death. He had been under water for over a minute and the need to breathe, even to breathe in the foul water was overpowering. If the grate hadn't been weakened by radiation and rust, he would've died right there. With a burst of bubbles, he heaved it back and the rusting hinges snapped off.

For once he was too tired to even curse as he crawled up through the green slime and into the gutter. He lay there in the filth, gasping, looking now so much like a slag that a police officer walked by and barely gave him a glance. The waters had carried him one street over, and here the slags were fleeing the maze before the police snatched them up. Many of them were loaded down with bags and packs and odd bits of furniture.

Cole staggered up and wandered along in the crowd, letting the driving rain wash away as much of the slime as it would. What was left behind was a black-green stain that made it seem as though Cole had been sleeping under a dumpster for the last month. He felt that way as well. He felt like one giant bruise.

Ducking away from the crowd, he walked in a loop and came up across the street from *The Leather Lounge* and stood in the shadows, watching as the Contamination Team began to cordon off the block. Already a hundred white-clad scrubbers were there, with more showing up every second. Within the sea of white, Aaron in his plum suit stood out like a sore thumb. Cole knew he was giving his prelim report.

Then he would do a walk through with the team leader. After that he would go downtown to fill out his official report and meet with Lloyd.

It would be hours before he could get back out on the streets, sniffing out clues. Cole still had a chance to hunt down that second Dead-eye. He could picture her perfectly: long dark brown hair, a pert deadly smile, a bump of a nose, a hole in her chest where he had shot her.

A bullet wouldn't stop a Dead-eye. She was still out there searching for Santino's daughter. "But why?" Why did anyone care about Christina? She was a nobody. She was only a maid. "Maybe not. She was a maid to a millionaire, and that had to mean something."

"Who's a maid to a millionaire?"

Cole jumped, his hand going for the empty holster beneath his suit coat. It was just Corrina, her green hair hanging limp and wet in front of her face. She had pulled back when the police arrived, but when she saw Cole skulking around, she had slipped up on cat's paws.

The fright not only made Cole feel stupid, it took the last bit of energy out of him. He sat down on the curb and watched the scrubbers haul hoses from their trucks. "A girl named Christina. Everyone is after her. I just don't know why."

It was more of a mystery than Corrina could bother with. "Oh, well that sucks. You know you look like shit, Cole. And you're bleeding. What happened in there? I heard shooting. You kill anyone?"

"Yeah, sorta."

"Did you get my money?"

Cole groaned. "All you care about is your damned..." He stopped as another cruiser pulled up, lights flashing. Sergeant Bruce Hamilton climbed out of it. "Son of a bitch. We have to scoot." He wound his way through the next maze without looking back as Corrina hurried along in his wake, muttering about how much money was owed to her. He didn't want to hear it just then.

He had lost another bounty, and his gun, and his trench coat. His best suit was in tatters and his shoes were scuffed into ruin. "At this rate, I'll be naked by the time we catch up to Christina." Naked and broke. In his pocket was two dollars and forty-five cents. "Fuuuck," he whispered, regretting the earring he had refused. Fifteen hundred dollars was enough to get out of the city.

Was it also enough to get him an entry visa into the Carolinas? Probably not. It might be enough to make it to

Boston, but from what everyone said, Boston was as bad off as New York.

The lure of the money ate away at his insides as he marched north in the stinging rain. To get it, he would have to murder what could be an innocent woman. Christina might have been only borrowing the earrings, and there was certainly no law against dropping a vamp's name, no matter what Ashley Tinsley had said. *The Tinsley name is very powerful. You don't throw it around without repercussions.*

It had been an oddly hateful thing to say and Cole regretted even considering taking the money. He stopped in his tracks, realizing his feet had been taking him uptown. Corrina bumped into him. She'd been walking with her hood thrown over her head.

What the hell am I going to do with her? he wondered. He couldn't have her tagging along with him, especially now that he had lost his gun. Hunting Dead-eyes was dangerous enough when armed, trying to do it without a gun might very well be a form of suicide.

Then again, so was working the honey tree. Even with a daddy, honeys turned up dead every day.

She looked up at him, the rain dripping from her green hair. There was suspicion in her grey eyes. "What?"

"Hmm? Nothing. We're just going the wrong way. The slinger let drop that a Krupp van was there the night Christina disappeared. As far as clues go, it's pretty thin. Still, it's all we got."

"What's a slinger?" she asked once they were turned around and heading south again. Krupp was the largest metal recovery operation in the city and took up a half-mile of the island at the southern tip.

"A slinger's just a bartender."

She grunted and was silent for a few blocks before picking up the conversation as if only a second had passed. "I thought it might be that guy in purple that was there. Now, he looked loaded."

"He's also a lying, two-faced son of a bitch."

Again, there was a long pause. "You know what? I'd rather be a lying, two-faced son of a bitch with a full belly than whatever we are without one. I bet *he* pays his debts."

Cole glared down at her and she glared right back. "Look, Corrina. Maybe you should take off. I got forty-five cents. Consider it a down payment. If I can get a bounty, I'll drop off the rest with Father James. If you'll go by there every few days…"

"Forty-five cents!" she shouted in outrage. "You owe me eleven dollars! And what do you mean by down payment? Is that your way of being a lying, two-faced son of a bitch, because that sure sounds like it!"

"It means I give you some now and the rest when I get my damned bounty." They glared once more at each other and then lapsed into a long silence that ate more than a mile. As she walked her lips moved and she would hold up her fingers and look at them in dissatisfaction. "What are you mumbling about?"

Quickly she stuck her hands back down into her pockets. "Nothing. It's just that I think you should give me half my money now and half later. How much is that? Four dollars?" As she asked this, she eyed him very closely, looking for any sign that she was being cheated.

A street honey like Corrina could rarely count past ten and even simple division was completely beyond them. They liked to work with exact change and even numbers. "It's five-fifty." She perked up at this. "And I don't have it."

Her frown came crashing back down. "Maybe that purple guy would pay. Maybe I should go tell him about that Santino guy." She stopped and the crowd flowed around them without pause. "He'd give me more'n eleven for a good word, I bet. He had gold in his hair!" She looked around to see if he was nearby.

Cole did as well out of a touch of paranoia. There was no way Aaron would be on his trail so quickly. Aaron would've stood out in the bland crowd. People generally wore grey, black, or dull brown, though women tried to add splashes of color: beads in their hair, a bright scarf, a tattered ribbon depending on what they could afford. When they did wear color like Corrina, it was always washed out.

Someone as well off as Aaron would keep off the streets entirely. "Good luck finding him," Cole said to her.

"Good luck yourself," she replied stiffly. "You were gonna pull a ditch on me from the start, I know it. And you 'spect me to believe that you're good for eleven dollars? You know what you can do? You can go…"

She was interrupted by the heavy rumbling note of a Cat-3 bell. There were ten-thousand people on the street around them and at the sound of the huge iron bell, everyone froze. A Cat-3 only happened a few times a year and it was always like this. People stopped at the first bell and then ran at the second.

The radiation given off by a Cat-3 storm could turn a "pure" like Cole into a trog in a matter of minutes.

As Cole knew it would, at the second tolling bell, the crowd panicked and suddenly started running in all directions, the bigger, faster people trampled the small and the weak. Corrina's eyes went wide as a wall of men turned and rushed down on her, sprinting for the entrance to a subway they had passed the minute before.

The effects of the radiation were so abrupt and so ghastly that Cole felt the desire to run as well and had he been alone, he might have trampled a few people to get to the subway. Instead he barreled right past Corrina and smashed into a man who had been about to run her down. The collision sent them both tumbling to the ground.

"Go!" Cole yelled, however, his voice was drowned out by a thousand screams and Corrina only stood there, one foot in the street, one on the sidewalk.

Someone fell over Cole, starting a chain reaction and in seconds, he was buried. Feet and knees pummeled him as he fought upright in the middle of the scrum. Now, he really did have to trample people. It was the only way to get to safety.

He caught sight of Corrina's red jacket. She was in the back of a crowd battling to get down into the subway.

Racing over, he grabbed her by the arm. "Forget it!" he screamed into her ear. "There's no time!" The bells did not tell you how close the radiation surge was. For all Cole knew, it was already coming down.

With a thousand people trying to force themselves through one opening, Cole ran for the nearest building, dragging Corrina behind him. There were thirty people trying to force open a door, while a like number was doing everything they could to close it. Cole added his strength and still more people crowded in from behind, pressing forward until the door banged open and the crowd surged.

A woman fell in front of Cole and before he knew it, his heel came down on her hand. It felt like stepping on a bag of peanuts. Her scream was added to the rest. In vain, he tried to grab her with his free hand. There was too much momentum to the crowd and it was all he could do to keep his feet and hold onto Corrina.

People fought to get into the building, then, once inside, they fought to keep everyone else out. The doors had to be shut and sealed. Cole was one of those who turned from invader to defender the moment he passed over the threshold. Along with three other big men, he braced his back against the door and heaved backward, straining with every muscle in his body—without any result. The crowd was too great, too strong.

This was one of the few buildings that hadn't barred their door quick enough and the mob outside had turned into an unstoppable mass. A groan escaped the door and someone cried, "Stop! You're bending it!" The people outside didn't care. All that mattered to them was escaping the fallout.

Only the threat of immediate death could penetrate their panicked minds. An East River Rasta, with thick, yarny dreads provided the threat and then some. The moment he had pushed his way through, he turned and pulled a .45 caliber Bulldog revolver from his coat. He gave no warning and he made no allowances for age, race or sex as he fired through the doorway with calm deliberation.

The screams of the crowd doubled in volume for a few seconds then gave way to a rush of feet away from the building. No one said a word. Cole hated the rasta for what he had done. It didn't matter that if he'd still had his Crown he would have done the same thing, and nor did it matter that he was limp with relief. Prejudice didn't need to make sense.

Once the dead and dying were pushed outside and the door slammed shut and barred, Cole looked around for Corrina. A hundred people, all stinking like wet dogs, were crammed into a lobby that held little but defunct elevators and a security desk. He pushed through the crowd, searching for her without luck. He didn't search all that hard, however.

He was in no position to care for her or to protect her. "Chances are she'll outlive me," he told himself, rationalizing his desire to be rid of the girl.

Chapter 11

It seemed that the bells would never stop ringing. For hours, they rang without let up. They rang in Cole's dreams. He had thought about testing out the tunnels, only the building watch party had sealed off their sole tunnel entrance and wouldn't let anyone up or down. So, he found a corner and slept.

At some point, the bells switched to klaxons and then, after three hours, these abruptly switched off.

It was so late at night by then that the dawn wasn't far off—and the rain was still coming down. That was a good thing. It was common knowledge that in the Great Nebraskan Desert, where it only rained four times a year, fallout could linger for months on end. Now, it was being washed away down into the sewers where it would eventually find its way out into the Hudson.

Despite the sudden silence, no one rushed out from the safety of the building. They waited for someone else to make the first move. Even Cole, who had all the reason in the world to get out of there, waited until he saw people begin to emerge from the subway. As always, it was the slags who went out first. They had less to lose.

They huddled in their coats and hurried up the sidewalk, avoiding the dead bodies. Cole didn't chance the street until he saw the first suit go by, then he lifted the bar from the door.

"Hey mon, are you goin' east?" It was the rasta, his Bulldog back in its holster. Closer now, Cole saw that his nose was wide and dented across the bridge, and that he had slag reducing his right ear to a nub. "We can get a cab runnin' if so."

Cabs were lead-lined and used expensive filters to keep the air inside breathable. Beside the subways, they were the safest way to travel after a Cat-3.

"No. I'm heading south." *And I can't afford a cab ride, especially now.* Everyone knew that cabbies always jacked up their rates after a Cat-3. He gave the rasta a brief nod and stepped out into the rainy night. Just like that, it seemed as though Cole had opened the floodgates. Hundreds of thousands of people who had been trapped by the fallout storm suddenly poured out into the streets, each hurrying home or to work. Each muttering curses at their ill luck.

Thankfully, most were not heading south and Cole didn't have to swim against a river of humanity. It was the only good thing going for him at that moment. If Aaron had caught a cab as soon as he heard the bells, he would be done with his report by then and, more than likely, be walking around with a fat check in his pocket.

"Riding in a cab, more'n like," Cole muttered, enviously picturing Aaron riding in style to his bank.

Cole himself had a three-mile hike and every step was accompanied by a growl from his empty stomach. His last meal had been breakfast the day before and he felt somewhat thin and wobbly as he came to the brick monstrosity that was the Krupp Metal Works facility. It was a great brick rectangle from which dozens of smokestacks belched out clouds of black smoke and green poison. Rumor had it that chimney sweeps who were caught in one of those clouds died like flies after only a single breath.

A line of slags wrapped around the building, each vying for the chance to be one of those chimney sweeps or perhaps a furnace feeder where the temperatures had to be kept at a minimum temperature of a thousand degrees. Or they would be skimmers who wore puffed-up wool suits three inches thick, but who still went home covered in blisters.

And they always came back. Unlike so many other places, Krupp paid daily. They even fed the workers a full meal during a twelve-hour shift. It was true that a worker had to actually finish the shift or the bland food was docked from their hourly. Of course, there were no benefits and no one had a permanent position. They had to come every day and hope that they were early enough to pick up a spot.

Cole walked down the line to the great gleaming gates, passing tattooed and bearded men, their eyes shorn of whatever promises life had once offered. The women slags wore their hair long and stood stooped, letting it fall in front of their faces. Everyone in line who looked at Cole as he passed saw one of their own. His color wasn't human and there was blood mixed in with grime on the collar of his shirt.

At the gate, he lurked in the early morning shadows. Something told him that flashing his license would not get him the information he needed. There was no way he could waltz in there as a bounty hunter without being surrounded by a million lawyers who'd be phoning every police contact they knew. Cole would be arrested, or worse, before he could ask one question.

Besides, how likely was it that Krupp knowingly had zombies driving their trucks around?

"But there had been a Krupp truck at *The Leather Lounge*. A recycle pickup? Had the driver seen something out of the ordinary?" What Cole needed was to get inside, find the motorpool and inspect the dates and times each vehicle had been used last. He glanced up at the brick wall. Sixty feet high, perfectly vertical and utterly windowless. Getting in would be easy, getting out again was what made him nervous.

"One thing at a time," he muttered and strode back down the line. The slags stared as he passed. *They* never strode with that purposeful air. Sometimes they hurried with quick nervous steps, but usually they moved at a stagnant walk as if they dreaded their destination. Seeing the looks he was getting, Cole slowed and kept his face down as he neared the back of the line.

In the last few minutes it had grown by a full city block. Cole took up a position behind the last man. He was a gaunt character, his cheekbones jutted from his stretched skin like axe heads. The slag had a good hold of him and had nearly rotted away his lips and nose.

"Lucky today," he said, giving Cole a riddled smile.
"Yeah?"

"The alarm. The line's short. See?" He pointed at the line in front of them as if Cole didn't know what a line was. "I never get this close. I hope I can get the copper pit today. You ever work the copper pit?"

A woman in a shabby house coat with patches over patches on the elbows took up a spot behind Cole. She wore a green scarf over a face that was slowly withering away to nothing. She wouldn't look up from the sidewalk.

"No. This is my first day. Do you happen to know where…"

"Gawd! Your first day? How is that even possible? Krupp's been around ages. They been here even before the bombs is what they say."

Cole put a hand on the man's bony shoulder and squeezed. "Maybe you should quiet down friend. This is my first day because I had other jobs. Do you understand?" He didn't, it showed in his eyes. "That's okay, friend. Do you happen to know where the motorpool is?"

"You mean for cars? No. I ain't never drived once in my whole life."

That hadn't been the question, but Cole didn't think he would get a straight answer one way or the other. The slag had worked its way deep into the man's brain. "What about you, ma'am? Do you know where the motorpool is?"

"I know where the kitchens be at."

Right then, Cole decided he would kill himself before he ever took a job at Krupp's.

The line shuffled forward quicker than Cole had expected and within a few minutes, he was through the gates and into the building. The gates, which were guarded by thirty men armed with blunt-nosed submachine guns everyone called "Hosers," opened into the Charging Room. This was a long hall that was brilliantly lit and painfully white. It smelled strongly of bleach.

Women had a single line of their own, while the men's branched into seven, each ending at a desk. Behind each desk was an officious man wearing one-piece green overalls, the words *Tier 3* printed across their breast. On the desks in front of them were clip boards. Behind them was a lone desk where a man in white overalls sat reading a newspaper. Cole guessed that he was Tier 4.

The slags in the line were dead silent. It was only when they reached the front that they could be heard mumbling to the Tier 3 men. The slags kept their heads down and stood as tall as they could, while the desk men sat in a slouched hump, slowly becoming one with their chairs. They didn't look up either.

Cole went to the far line on the right and when it was his turn, the man behind the desk slid a white pin across to Cole and sighed, "You're gonna be 4159. Where you been working?"

A slight hesitation and then Cole spat out, "Driving. I can drive."

The Tier 3 looked up at this, craning his head back as far as it would go, which was not far because of his hunched back. He had a big head that was sparsely decorated by thin, weedy hair. His dark eyes sat over a cracked bloodshot mesh of a nose. "Ain't no nobody slag from off the street gonna drive nothin' round here. Ain't hardly no slag can drive at all. Tellin' me you can drive, humph! I oughtta stick you on a skimmer for that."

"I can also read if you have positions that call for that." The man's dark eyes narrowed making his nose seem even larger. Before he could raise his voice again, Cole pointed at the top clipboard. "That says: Tungsten high run pit—Fill first. I was a driver on the docks before this. You had to know how to read."

The desk man seemed confused. "Then why you here?"

"Trouble," Cole answered. Trouble was painted in purple bruises along one side of his face and across the ridges of his scabbed-over knuckles.

"Your loss my gain. I need a flow manager on the Manganese line. Sign here." The ink in the pen was in the process of running out and every third letter belonged to some sort of ghost alphabet. It was just as well since Cole signed in as Aaron Reynolds. The Tier 3 man kept talking, now in a dulled-out repetitive manner. "The pay is five cents 'n hour. You get two fifteen-minute bathroom breaks every shift and a thirty-minute lunch. Once you change into your uni, take this form to level 5, section G. Next!"

Cole took his form and his pin through a doorway and into a room larger than the first. It was filled with lockers and the stench of unwashed bodies. A man in a grey jumper looked at Cole's number and said, "Fours are that way." Cole came to another man in grey who pointed down a second lane. "This is ones."

Now Cole understood. They were directing the slags to their lockers, which corresponded to their pin number. At least half of the slags would have gotten lost without the help. In the locker was a key and a set of brown overalls with the words Tier 1 stitched across the breast. They were one size fits all and could be buttoned up at the ankle and wrist if the wearer was too short. Cole had to squeeze his big frame into his.

Another person at the end of the locker room told Cole to go up the stairs until he saw a "Big 5." He showed Cole what a five was on the paperwork. Up he went along with hundreds of other people garbed in brown. The air smelled now of metal and poison. In the span of a single flight of stairs, Cole's head began to thump.

The fifth level housed a series of immense blast furnaces seventy feet in height. Cole only saw them as fantastically hot collections of stairs and pipes. It was impossible to tell how they were operated. Sitting at the top of the stairs in a glaze of sweat was another of the stationary guides. This one had drooping cheeks and dull eyes that held all the miserable secrets found at the bottom of a bottle of gin. The poisonous air seemed to be killing him faster than anyone. He pointed at the form. "You see that? That's a G. Head that way until you see one just like it on the wall. When you get there, find Jack. You're his replacement."

"And what do I do?"

"He'll tell you."

As Cole walked through the sections, he kept as far from the furnaces as he could and still it felt as though the skin of his face was stretching and turning dry and brittle as an old leaf. He presumed Jack could read, and when he got to G he looked for anyone with a clipboard. "Well, it's about damn time," Jack said when Cole finally found him. He spoke in an annoying chaffing tone as if he yelled habitually and had to hold himself back. "I clock out at six sharp and it ain't gonna be on me if you don't know what you're doing."

Cole had a near irresistible desire to slap Jack across his grey face. "Here's what you're going to do," Cole told him. "You're going to fill me in on this operation and do it at my pace or I'll take my fist and shove it down your throat until you choke on it. How does that sound?"

Jack gave Cole a closer look and didn't like what he saw. "Not so good, I guess. You can read?" He handed Cole the clipboard.

"Yeah." Cole wasn't about to demonstrate for Jack. Instead he glanced down at a six columned piece of paper and read across the top: Beginning Fuel Level—Hourly Fuel Level—Gross Incoming—Gross Impurities—Aluminum Alloy Weight —Raw Manganese Weight. As Cole tried to make sense of the columns Jack breathed annoyingly loud. His breath went out in a downward rumble and in with an upward wheeze.

"It's simple." Jack told him. "You measure the fuel at the start of your shift and then every hour after that. Normally you will have to do a refill in about nine hours. Make sure you mark that. Then you weigh every batch before it goes in the cooker. Then when the skimmers scrape off the impurities, you let it cool and then weigh that. Then you weigh the aluminum, then the manganese when the cook is done. Easy, right?"

"What about once you've weighed the manganese? Where does it go from here?"

Jack shook his head, looking at Cole as if he were an exceptionally stupid slag. "That's not your job, dip shit so don't worry about it. All you…" Cole snatched his overalls in one fist and raised the other. Jack shied back with his hands up. "I don't know. Maybe the purifier, I guess. Everything goes to the purifier."

"And after that? Is there a transportation section here?"

"I guess. The garage is down on subfloor three. They have a tunnel out of here. I worked there once. It was a bunch of loading and unloading. Killed my back." He clapped his hands together. "So, are we good?"

Cole wanted to ask about security, but felt he had pressed his luck too far already and didn't want to draw any more attention to himself. So far, the security inside the building had consisted of only a few wandering guards and a smattering of Tier 3 and 4 managers. No one expected much trouble from the slags. He guessed that the security at the garage would be much tighter.

Jack left the moment Cole's attention wandered from him and now Cole was somewhat stuck having to weigh and measure and record with a Tier 3 stopping by every half hour. The heat from the blast furnace was overwhelming at times and Cole made a trip to the water fountain every fifteen minutes and still felt as though he was on the verge of turning to dust.

Taking in so much water made him have to piss so badly he thought he might actually wet himself. He held it in, not wanting to waste one of his breaks. His plan was to take a break right before lunch and then a second one right after. It would give him an hour to try to slip into the garage.

The slags and their managers worked in a daze from the heat. They hauled metal in by the cartload, weighed it and then hauled it to the top of the blast furnace. When the metal was skimmed, it was hauled, weighed, and carted out again. Men were burned. They would hiss curses and blow on their hands and some would dance from foot to foot, but none ever left the line.

During the long hours, Cole asked everyone in his section about the garage and discovered that he wouldn't be able to simply walk down there and start poking about.

Since bars of unsullied metal were so valuable, workers had their pin numbers checked upon entering, and yes, there were dozens of guards with guns.

Still, the picture wasn't entirely bleak. Cole had two dollars and forty-five cents in his pocket, just enough to throw around a bribe or two. As far as he could tell, slags were interchangeable. No one paid any attention to faces. The only thing that mattered were pin numbers.

At exactly fifteen minutes before the lunch bell, Cole told his Tier 3 that his back teeth were floating and promptly jogged to the bathroom. Six minutes later his aching bladder was empty and he hurried down the stairs fighting a wave of slags who were returning from one of the staggered lunch breaks. He was big and they were weak; his elbows gave him all the room he needed. With each flight down the heat dissipated and by the third level he could breathe the poison atmosphere without swooning.

"Now to find the right guy," he muttered as he made his way to the garage level. Every slag in a brown overall that he passed was asked the same question: "Do you work in the garage?"

The first ten said they worked in the "shaft." He definitely didn't want to know what that was. The stench coming off of them was unbelievable and they seemed even more confused than most slags. Their words came out soft and phlegmy, without conviction. Behind them came a Tier 2 manager who looked as though his only job was to get them to the cafeteria and back again.

The eleventh man Cole ran into came limping up the stairs, blood seeping through the leg of his pants. "You alright?" Cole asked, pretending to care.

"Does it look like I'm fuckin' alright?"

"I suppose not. Do you work in the garage?"

A moan escaped the man and he paused on the stair, his face suddenly losing its angry edge. "I did. I don't work anywhere now." A handcart had overturned and a pallet of iron ingots had fallen on him. Although it hadn't been his fault, he'd been fired on the spot. Krupp didn't pay men to limp around bleeding on their floors. "What am I going to do?"

"You can change pin numbers with me," Cole suggested. "I'm up on five. You don't have to lift anything. You just have to write down numbers. Do you know your numbers?"

Even hurt and looking at an impossible walk home, the man was suspicious. "Yeah, most of them. You not trying to get me in trouble, are you? Oh wait, I get it now. You did something and you're trying to put it on me. The answer's no, buster." He tried to limp past Cole.

"Not so fast, friend," Cole said, stepping in front of him. "That's not it at all. I'm actually a Christian. You know what that is?"

"Yeah, a sucker."

It usually felt like that. "No, it means that sometimes I have to do nice things for people."

The man appraised Cole with half-lidded reptilian eyes, his hurt leg almost forgotten. "Don't you have to give to the poor, too?"

I am poor! Cole wanted to scream. Instead, he forced a smile onto his battered face and dug out a dime. He held it up but didn't hand it over. "The badge first." They exchanged pin badges and Cole told him to get up to 5G before lunch ran out.

"So, I'm gonna miss lunch twice over," the man griped, giving Cole a look that suggests he's going to be even more poor without that lunch.

As Cole had gone a day and a half without eating, he wasn't affected by the guilt. "Shit happens, friend," he said, leaving the man and forgetting him after only a few steps. His mind was focused on what lay ahead. Would someone realize that Pin # 3381 had just returned, miraculously healed? Or would they not even notice as he blended in with the other slags?

There was a steady flow of people into the garage and Cole inserted himself in among them, trying to look as small and meek as possible. The man in front of him told the guard that he was returning from his piss break and so

Cole said the same thing and after his number was checked, he strode right into an immense underground chamber that was larger than most tenements.

It was more of a warehouse than a standard garage. At one end of the room flatbed trucks and vans sat in a long line waiting to receive their loads, at the other end, looking small with the distance were other vehicles waiting to drop off theirs. Closer to Cole were rows and rows of industrial shelving three stories high and a hundred yards long.

"Loader or picker?" a Tier 2 asked Cole when he stood in the doorway too long. Cole gave him a typical slaggy look of non-understanding, and the man said. "The loading teams are across the way." Cole followed his outstretched hand and saw a line of forty or so men. They were being called by two or three to haul down pallets and drag them to the trucks.

"No, that's not me," Cole said. He didn't want to be stuck hauling metal for the rest of the day.

"Then the pickers are through that door on the right."

Cole started in that direction, but then noticed that some men were dashing back and forth between the loading teams and a set of doors along the wall. Most of the doors were marked with a big red hand that suggested that the slags were not allowed inside. Written above the doors were things like: Order Management, Fuel Management, Inventory Management, and Fleet Management.

It was the last one that he wanted.

As he watched the men, he saw that they were carrying pieces of paper. They would dash to a Tier 3, present the paper, wait for it to be signed and then run back with the copy. These had to be written orders. If Cole could get a blank form and the name of someone high-up, he could have the delivery records pulled in minutes. There was only one way to get a form and that was to jump in and start running back and forth with the rest.

No one questioned him. That would take initiative and that human characteristic was a nonexistent phenomenon at Krupp. Orders were given, orders were carried out.

Orders were not questioned. The only time they were was when something deviated significantly from the norm.

Cole decided to start with running messages from Order Management since it seemed the most likely place to find a bigwig name he could steal. This was not difficult. Unlike the other runners who waited their turn with vague expressions and open, slack jaws. Cole listened to the dozen or so secretaries who were answering calls and jotting down the requests on their proper forms. Every last one of them would repeat the orders that were given to them.

In the short time between three runs, Cole got the names of the Marshaling Supervisor, the Vice President of the Finance Division and the Vice President of Human Resources.

"Can I borrow one of those forms?" Cole asked one of the secretaries, leaning his long frame over the counter and violating two rules at once: he wasn't supposed to talk to the secretaries and he certainly wasn't supposed to get out of line. The other runners suddenly perked up, waiting for the hammer to fall on the new guy. In the back of the room was a Tier 4 in white standing over one of the secretaries, his hands on his hips in a position of furious indignation over some minor clerical error.

Cole could feel the tension rising in the normally stale air. "It's just that I remembered something I had to do and I don't want to forget it. You understand, right?"

The secretaries were all women in black skirts and white shirts, each of them trying valiantly to hide the slag breaking through their flesh. They spent whatever free money they had on cosmetics to cover it. This particular woman wore her thick brown hair like a scarf. "I like your hair, by the way. It's very stylish." He knew that when he remembered to smile, women thought he was handsome. He gave the secretary his best smile.

She looked around in something of alarm, sneaking a look at the Tier 4 man. Thankfully, he was still engrossed in browbeating the other secretary. "I would if I could, but

I'm not allowed to. The slips are numbered and we get docked a penny if we ruin one."

"That's okay because I have a nickel to cover it." He held out a shiny coin. Her eyes went wide and once more she gave a look around. Half the office was staring now. Still, four cents was four cents. She made a tiny tear at the top corner and said, loudly, "Oops, this one's messed up."

She made the trade as if she was selling blood on the black market. "Can I borrow a pen as well?" When she hesitated he asked, "What's your name, by the way?"

"Leah Middleton. What's yours?"

"Aaron Reynolds," he told her and then pointed to the paper. "Will you give me just a second?" The form was straight forward and in moments the Marshaling Supervisor had "requested" the fleet log for June 3rd, 2161. He left Leah with another smile and jogged from the room like any other runner.

Although he went only twenty feet or so, he burst into the Fleet Management offices as if he had run a mile. He gasped and handed the form to the first secretary. She frowned as she read it.

"I thought the police were coming to get them," she said.

"The records?" Cole blurted, feeling a sudden tightness in his chest.

She nodded and pointed to a slim file that was set with perfect symmetry on the edge of her desk. "We just got a call from Mr. Hemmings not five minutes ago. He said the officer was coming down himself."

Cole had to hold back the fantastic desire to look over his shoulder, afraid that he would see Bruce Hamilton strolling in. "I-I think there might have been a change of plans. I just got this message. I'm supposed to run them up right away." Slowly, he reached out his hand for the file. When she didn't stop him, he picked it up and clutched it to his chest.

"Wait," she said, as he turned to go. Again, he felt that electric flash of fear. "Don't you need a copy of the request form?" He nodded and watched as she signed the form, tore off the top page and gave him the copy.

He was gone a second later, jogging for the stairs. Two flights up, he saw Aaron Reynolds heading down. The Fox, wearing a suit of deepest red with silver shoes and cuffs, was surrounded by two guards and two tight-faced men in suits. Their pinched expressions told Cole they were lawyers. None of them noticed the slag in the brown overalls. The moment he passed them, Cole ran for his life.

Chapter 12

Cole was half out of the brown uniform before he even entered the changing room and by the time he found his locker, he had it stripped off altogether. He threw on his pants and jacket, leaving his shirt bundled in his hand. The cover of the file was too bulky to hide and so he tore out the pages, folded them up, and stuck them in the inner pocket of the coat.

Then he limped out of the room as if he was the real # 3381. "A pallet fell on me," he grumbled to one of the Tier 3 men who had desks barring the way to the exit.

"That's really too bad," he said, and then added in perfect Krupp fashion, "Don't bother coming back tomorrow." The Tier 3 had him sign a paystub and then handed over thirty-five cents.

Not a bad day, Cole thought, pocketing the change. He had made thirty-five cents, picked up a possible piece to the puzzle he was trying to unravel, and had finally managed to get ahead of the Fox. He was grinning as he hurried to lose himself in the crowd. It was a strangely bright afternoon. The sky was lead grey with a glare to it that wasn't normal. Looking up, he saw a little disc high up in the haze. It was the sun. That wasn't so good.

He liked the anonymity of the rain, it made a humped sameness out of people. As he walked, he kept glancing back at the Krupp building, worried that at any second a hundred security guards would come pouring out of the place. But the trouble didn't come from behind. A police siren suddenly started wailing ahead of him. It was blocks away, but Cole didn't wait to see if the cruiser was coming for him. He took off across the street and ran for the end of the block at a sprint, thinking he would take a quick turn and run for one of the little alleys that cut the block into a maze.

Just as he came to the corner he saw the lights of the police car; they were slashing through the glare only two blocks away. The sound of its engine was a scream. He was so engrossed by the lights that he smashed into a woman carrying a sack of groceries. She went right down with a squawk.

"Sorry!" Cole lifted her to her feet and was about to take off running again when he saw a skinny green-haired girl in red. It was Corrina. She had been on the opposite corner talking up a slag, trying to get him to part with his day's wages for a quick romp.

"Cole, this way." She waved him over, her head swinging back and forth, looking up and down the street. She was afraid. That fear was the only reason he ran through the traffic to get to her. Nothing else had changed between them.

By the time he crossed, she was up the steps of the corner building and standing in the shadows inside, going from foot to foot. "You were followed," she said, shutting the door as soon as he made it inside.

"Followed? By who?"

She was already gone, dashing into the building towards the central stair. As expected she went down. "That rasta, the one we were trapped with. I saw him watching you when you were sleeping and then when the sirens cut out, he followed you all the way down here. Hey, you got that flashlight still?"

There were two sub-basements and each was darker than the next. The tunnel that ran at a forty-five degree angle from the second was dark as pitch. "No, I lost it. So how did you get here? Did you follow me, too?"

"Sorta, except not really. I actually followed the rasta and only because I was curious, and because you owe me eleven dollars...twelve now since I saved you from the cops again. Maybe it's even thirteen because of the rasta. He's good, Cole. He had your scent. Oh, hold on, was that the third right?"

They were moving with their hands out, trailing their fingertips along the walls. When they came to openings they could only tell if they were alcoves by the close, heavy stink and the fact that the walls widened out. "It was the second. Where are we?"

"I'm not sure. This guy said that the third tunnel on the right ran uptown for a mile."

The guy? "What guy?" he asked, only just then he heard the change jingling in her pocket. She'd been "working" while he'd been inside the Krupp facility. Thinking about that made his stomach edgy.

"Just some guy," she answered, trying to sound innocent. "Ha! I see something." Seconds later they found the third tunnel. There was a gold glow far down it that drew them on. As they walked, they each glanced secretly at the other and maintained a stiff silence.

It lasted until the light began to flicker. They were coming on a fire. Cole slid Corrina to his right and slowed as he came up on a little carved out room. There were six men inside, sitting around a fire made from shards of pressed sawdust. It was a small fire, barely a foot across and yet it was blinding, and the men did not see the two until they were past the opening.

"Hey fella!" one barked. "Where you goin? This here is our tunnel." The six jumped to their feet with the leader brandishing a serrated steak knife of ancient origin. He was riddled with slag, his hair coming out in strange tufts giving him a mangy look. Next to him was a creature with an empty socket where his right eye had been; inside the hole was black goo. The men behind these two were mere shadows. They were smaller, stooped and gnarled. They had the acid stench of men who hadn't seen the inside of a shower in years.

"We're just passing through," Cole replied, stopping and turning, standing with his right foot back.

"Not without payin' yer tax," the one-eyed man said. He smiled and showed off three black teeth. The one on top had a string of thick drool hanging from it. He too had a knife; its point was snapped off.

"If you insist," Cole said and then launched himself at the man with the steak knife, landing a front kick with his entire two-hundred and ten pounds behind it. It was the simplest, most effective attack in the cramped, dark conditions. Air shot from the man's dirty lips as he went flying back into the others.

One-eye froze for a second before jabbing at Cole with his blunt knife. The move was both feeble and tactically foolish. He held the knife in his right hand, presumably his dominant hand and when it scraped across Cole's coat, he knew there wouldn't be a follow up attack. As if they were dancing, Cole stepped past the man, taking his right wrist in an iron grip. He then twisted, bent and spun, throwing One-eye over his hip.

The man landed in the fire, blotting out the light. There was a sizzling hiss and then a scream, followed by shouts. Cole was already moving along the tunnel, taking Corrina by the arm. She kept looking back over her shoulder. At first all she saw was darkness then there came a red glow—and still the yelling went on.

"Holy shit," she said, breathlessly. "You kungfu'd the crap out of them."

"They were slags. There's no honor in beating up a slag. It's like beating up a girl."

She raised an eyebrow that he didn't see. He felt her indignation, however. "I knowd some girls who were the best fighters ever," she declared. "Way better'n you, that's for certain. They wouldn't of lost their guns to a little man in purple. I know that for a fact."

"Then maybe they can keep you alive. If you had come down here by yourself, those men would've eaten you. You know that's a thing, right? It's not just a scary story." She shrugged with pursed lips, the ultimate apathetic response. "If you don't care what happens to you then I don't care either."

She grabbed his arm. "You're still going to get me my money, right? You have to since you're one of them Jova guys. That's what them guys always say. Be good or you go to the fire."

"I told you that when I get paid, then you get paid."

"Thirteen dollars?"

Just then thirteen dollars seemed to Cole like an unattainable amount. But if he could get one bounty, it would be nothing. *How am I going to do that without a gun? The Dead-eyes were so terribly strong that without a gun...* His mind suddenly strayed to the rasta and his massive .45 caliber Bulldog. Chances were he was working for Reynolds. The muncher stood out no matter where he went, especially in that stupid plum suit he'd been wearing. Cole would have spotted him from a mile away, but he hadn't seen the rasta until he had pulled out his gun. Even with his long dreads, the rasta had fit in among the crowds. He was a nobody in a sea of nobodies.

If he worked for the Fox that meant he was fair game. Christian or not, Cole was going to put a beating on them both. But how to "allow" the rasta to find him without also being scooped up by the police?

"Well?" Corrina demanded. "What about my thirteen dollars?"

"How about we make it fourteen? I need another favor from you."

With her thighs rubbed raw and her "down under" still burning, she wasn't about to turn down an easy dollar. "Sure, you know me. I'll do anything for a dollar." Even in the dark she could see his scowl and it made her laugh. She was giddy with the idea of fourteen dollars.

What he wanted from her was pretty much the same thing she'd been doing for him ever since she had met him. He wanted her to watch his back—a dollar for doing what the back alley crews paid a nickel for. Yeah, he was a sucker, but not as big a one as he let on.

He didn't hand over the money right away. "Before we go up top, give me your money." She protested and he grabbed her by the back of her red coat. "I'm not going to have you try to slip off and buy some mule leaving my ass in the wind. And I know that's what you've been thinking because that's what junkies do. Now, give me the money or leave. It's your choice."

The mule had been galloping through her mind ever since the john had plunked down the two quarters. It had been almost all she could think about. Then she remembered the rasta and the eleven dollars that Cole owed her. Only now it was thirteen dollars he owed her, fourteen if she stuck around. It was an amount that was becoming monumental in her mind. It was such a huge number that it drove back the cravings and she gave over the coins, making sure to note which pocket he'd stuffed them in. Only then did they trudge up out of the darkness.

Their first order of business was to fill their empty bellies. Fish paste soup never tasted so good and they both licked up every drop. Then they were off trudging along the streets, both tired and dull-eyed. It was mid-afternoon and the sun was desperately trying to break through the clouds. It was beginning to get muggy and there was absolutely nothing worse than a muggy New York afternoon. The stink of the city rose up out of the gutters and clung to a person, clogging their pores with rot.

Cole pulled off his coat before he sweated through it and turned the file he had stolen to mush. It was already wilting and didn't make that crinkling sound as it had.

Although there was no way they could have been followed, they both glanced back every few seconds, noting the nobodies, counting the cheap suits with the worn shoes, worrying over the few slags who managed to keep pace as they walked block after block.

To throw off any pursuers, Cole made a series of sudden changes in direction, crossing and then re-crossing streets, hurrying down alleys, doing everything to make their destination less obvious. All of this added an extra mile to their trek and Corrina was beginning to get buggy again. He handed her another Blue Calc, considered taking one himself, but decided he needed to be as clearheaded as possible.

"What are you doing?" she asked. They had finally stopped and he was now staring at her, thinking. She didn't like it. And she didn't like the heat and the glare. She began thinking about riding the mule again, only he had taken her fifty cents.

"Take off your coat. The rasta might have seen you in it. Good. Now, watch these two cross streets. If you see any cops, scream 'daddy.' If you see the rasta, scream 'mommy,' got it? For now, I'm going to be right there." He pointed to a long bank of phones down the block.

She said she understood and watched as Cole hurried to the phones, chose the center one and fed a nickel into the slot.

Lieutenant Lloyd's secretary was a nasal sounding bitch who must have had the goods on Lloyd because her attitude was crap. She had never liked Cole, then again, she never liked anyone. He affected a bored attitude and gave her the name of another hunter instead of his own. "Hold," was all she said in reply.

"Whatchu want, Demott?" Lloyd rumbled into the phone, sounding just as tired as ever. Cole could picture him slouched over the phone, his baggy eyes barely open.

"It ain't Demott, it's Cole. There's too much weird shit going on around here to give just anyone my real name. But I can trust you, can't I?"

Cole could hear Lloyd's chair groan as he leaned back in it. "Oh yeah, sure, buddy. You an' I go way back. Where are you? We need to talk about that human you killed. You stabbed him in the neck and then shot him? What's up with that? You goin' psycho on us, Cole?"

"Don't be an idiot. The Dead-eye beat me there and had already killed Red by the time I showed up. His body got hit when I was trying to hit the chick."

"That's not what the autopsy report reads. You know I believe you but my…"

Cole banged the phone against the side of the booth. "I don't care what you believe! What I care about is that damned report. She was sucking blood from that hole in his neck." For a moment, this silenced Lloyd, who had been stammering through a series of curses at being cut off.

"No shit?"

"No shit. The chick was good. She got him clean through the carotid. If you check the report, you'll see that Red was suspiciously low on blood. If you can get that cleared up, I'll bring in another Dead-eye that I'm trailing. If not, I'll take her out and burn the remains."

The chair squeaked as Lloyd slammed his bulk forward. "Hold on, Cole. Don't be like that," he said, his voice was higher and there was a slight begging quality to it. Lloyd picked up a grand for every Dead-eye one of his men bagged. He got nothing for a charred body. "You know I'll do everything I can for you. Where the hell are you?"

"Remember that Mandarin place from my last kill? I caught sight of the Dead-eye leaving it about an hour ago. I lost her when she jumped a cab. I have some other leads but I know that Wu knows something that he's not letting on. I'm gonna give him a little visit."

Lloyd sounded like a bull with a cold as he dragged air into his lungs. "Wu's? All I ask is that you don't shoot anyone, Cole. That little chink fucker sent us a damned bill for that aquarium you took out. And what was that about, Cole? Can you even shoot straight anymore? Do I need to make you qualify again?"

"I can shoot just fine," Cole said. "Don't worry about that. You just worry about getting my name cleared, because if I put out feelers and the cops are still on my ass, that Dead-eye disappears and so will anyone that she might have turned. Got it?"

"I got it, fuck-wad. You just remember that reports can be changed back again if you don't come through."

Cole knew all too well the power his boss could wield. "I can only come through if I don't have the taxmen hounding me, so you do your thing and I'll do mine." Cole hung up and stared across the street at the Mandarin joint. He was pretty much fucked. In four years, Lloyd had never asked him where he was. Never. He hadn't ever given a rat's ass where Cole was just as long as he brought in the stiffs. It was telling that he'd asked twice in one short conversation.

If the police showed up Cole might as well pack it in. It would mean that someone much higher up the food chain was after him. If Reynolds or the rasta showed up, it would mean that Lloyd was getting kickbacks.

Either way, Cole had a few minutes and he used that time to reposition Corrina. He stashed her in the alley behind the restaurant, while he went to the building across the street and knocked on every door that faced the joint. It took three tries and the loss of a dime to a pale teen with a wispy blonde beard before he had a spot where he could overlook Wu's.

It was the rasta who showed up. He crossed the street up the block and casually strolled by the joint, taking a not so casual peek through the door as a customer left. He kept walking, now with his chin down but his eyes up. Could he smell the trap? Did he feel its jaws closing in on him?

At the corner, he took a long pause to tie his boot. As he knotted and re-knotted, he looked around, scanning the faces in the crowd. He would go into the joint next and after he found the place undisturbed and Cole not in attendance, he would slip around back.

Or so Cole hoped.

"Thanks," he said to the frail teen as he slipped out of the apartment and dashed down the hall to the stairs. He was out into the sticky air in seconds, and fast-walking across the street before the rasta was even inside the restaurant. Cole slowed to hide among the crowd, watching as the rasta ducked inside. The second he did, Cole jogged to the corner and slipped down the dim alley. Whatever brightness there was to the day it didn't extend to the alley, which existed in a perpetual old-fish smelling twilight.

Cole slowed, casting about for a good-sized chunk of a brick. Corrina was peeking out from the mound of trash he had stuck her behind and she saw him. She hissed, "Is he here?"

She had come crouching out of her hiding place and he went to push her back. "Yeah. Stay out of sight. He should be coming down here in the next minute." The words had just left his mouth when the back door of the Mandarin joint opened and there was the rasta, his Bulldog in hand. Its hammer was back.

Chapter 13

Cole went stiff, his coat in one hand and clutching the inadequate chunk of brick to his chest with the other. The rasta had him dead to rights. His only chance was if the man simply walked away and how likely was that?

Do I spin and throw the rock? Do I give up and let him take the Krupp file, and then go somewhere and die a slag's death? Do I just stand here like an idiot as the seconds tick away?

He didn't normally come unglued so quickly and yet, he was going with option three.

Corrina saved him. She was already in a crouch and now she leaned forward, going to her knees in front of him. "It'll be the best fitty-cent you ever spent, baby," she said, as she reached for his belt. If he was frozen into inaction before, he was now a statue. The only thing moving were his eyes which popped open in shock.

He didn't move as her hands completely undid his belt and went to work on his fly. "Oh yeah, baby. I can tell it gonna be big. I like it big." Finally, he blinked and jerked as the rasta stepped closer.

The tiny, eighty-pound girl leaned around Cole's hip and barked, "Wait your turn! And if you watch it'll be extra. I don't do no free shows."

"Go fuck yourself," the rasta said, but without rancor. It was more of a habitual response. Turning away was an instinctive one. No one wanted to see a slag get blown by an alley whore with her knees in the mud. The moment he turned, Cole saw it out of the corner of his eye, and he moved as if all his previous hesitation had been pumping energy into his feet. In a flash, he was on the rasta, the chunk of concrete poised.

With a full swing, three pounds of rock could kill the man. Cole checked the speed of his strike but still managed to crack the brick in half. The rasta's legs buckled and he went spaghetti limp, falling face first into the mud. He was one tough son of a bitch and was still not out, despite having his brains scrambled.

"Wha the fuck, mon?" he said, through thick slurry lips.

Cole dropped the brick and cracked him with a fist. This time his eyes went gauzy and his lids were heavy. It was good enough. Cole snatched the fallen Bulldog then went through the man's pockets, finding nine extra shells, a wallet with eighteen dollars and change, a bag of dried plantains, and another holding a couple of ounces of uptown ice. Cole took it all.

"How much he got?" Corrina asked, her eyes ablaze. She had seen the ice and although it wasn't her favorite, she was hungry for anything. But first, she wanted her money.

"Not enough," he said, pulling the rasta out of the center of the alley. If a trog saw the rasta he would strip him bare.

The hunger in Corrina flared into anger. "What do you mean, not enough?" Unexpectedly, she launched herself at Cole, digging her small grubby hands into his jacket pocket. Even caught off guard, Cole was quick. He caught her wrists in one of his big paws before she could work the cork button from the eyelet.

"You got enough. I seen it. And besides, you owe me extra for my, you know, my smart thinking. You woulda been in big trouble if I hadn't saved you. Now you owe me fourteen dollars!"

"That's how much I owed you before," Cole told her and then turned on his heel and began marching from the alley. It did not pay to linger over the scene of a crime. Though it hardly seemed like a crime to defend yourself against a man with a gun. Of course, Cole had no idea if the rasta was going to kill him or not. Chances were he was just going after the file. Still, there was a chance that he was coming for both the file and his life.

Corrina trailed after him trying to work out the math. Once she found herself in the teens, she was getting into some dizzying numbers and sometimes couldn't keep them straight. "So how much do you owe me now?"

"Fifteen," he answered. It was a fair amount considering her life might have been in danger as well.

"That's what I thought," she said, trying to appear wise despite her muddy knees. "So, if you could hand it over, we can call it quits. It's been fun, an' all but my mom's probably getting worried."

Cole glanced down at her. "Your mom's dead, so don't try to feed me that bull." He marched on, once more wondering what to do with her. If he gave her the money, she'd more than likely overdose within a day. Once someone got a baggy of mule, it was hard to stop until it was all gone and fifteen dollars' worth would kill the little girl. And even if she somehow managed to escape that fate, she'd be back to working the honey tree in no time, with all of its attendant horrors and dangers.

"I think I need a drink," he muttered. His feet took him south into Red Dog territory and Cole told her to put on her jacket. When she complained about the heat, he said, "When in Rome, do as the Romans do."

This stopped her and she gazed hard at him, wondering if he had dipped into the ice. "This ain't no Rome, Cole. This is Manhattan."

"Yeah, I know. It's an expression that means you should blend in with the locals. This is Red Dog territory, so if you have red, it makes sense to wear it." He pointed at the sudden influx of red among the people on the bustling street.

She put on the coat and walked next to him for a while before she finally spat out: "So what kind of gang are the Romans? What do they push?" Although most gangs dabbled in everything, they tried to corner the market on some illegal activity.

"Western civilization," he answered and then laughed bitterly at his own unfunny joke. "I'm sorry. The Romans are long gone. It's probably been fifteen hundred years at least. Never mind. It's just useless knowledge the priests foisted on us. The word foisted is another useless thing we had to learn."

"I know moisted but I don't know foisted," Corrina said. "So these Roman guys, was it the bombs what got 'em or the Dead-eyes?"

Most of the priests blamed Germanic tribes, or the goths, who were Celtic in origin, but Father Hernton always said it was the Romans who lost Rome, just as he said it was Americans who had lost America. This concept was beyond Corrina. In her mind, the world and everything in it had sprung into existence around the time she was born. The small kids sometime after.

He sighed. Rome was gone for good, now. "Both. The Dead-eyes infiltrated Italy from the south and the Union took them out with nukes." That had been seventy years ago and currently all of Italy right up to the Alps was a radioactive wasteland. A good chunk of the world was like that.

Half a mile into Red Dog territory, Cole found a gin joint. He didn't care for gin but it was the cheapest booze in the city and he still had to make a dollar last.

He'd almost died in the last bar he'd been in and Cole paused just in the doorway to get a look around. Everything about the place suggested it was low rent. Its ceilings loomed a half-foot over his head, its linoleum floors were re-stretched and reworked, the chairs around the worn and dented bar were hard poly-fab; durable, easy to clean but uncomfortable after only a few minutes.

Other than a few gin-johnnies, a bar girl in a tight skirt, and the usual gaunt slinger, the place was empty.

"You think they got any wine?" Corrina asked in a whisper.

"Probably, but I'm not buying it for you. If you want a fizz, I'll take care of that."

Corrina rolled her eyes. "A fizz? I'm not a baby, you know. And at least half that money is mine. When you gonna hand it over?"

Cole ignored her. Addressing the slinger, he said, "One fizz and a gin sour. Whatever's in the well."

"Grape or lemon on that fizz? The lemon actually tastes like lemons. The grapes…" He made a face.

"I'll get the lemon then," Corrina answered without enthusiasm. The slinger gave her a wink, making Cole scowl. She laughed at him, higher than necessary, and she practically pranced to the back table Cole had picked out. When the slinger came back with their drinks, Cole was still scowling. "You got any wine?" she asked, smiling up at him.

He smiled back the way a hungry wolf might. "Oh yeah, little honey, but it's a buck a glass. Maybe we can work out a proper…"

"Maybe you get your ass back behind that bar," Cole snapped, "before I rearrange that smile of yours."

Cole's look suggested that not only would he rearrange the man's smile, he would enjoy doing it, too. The slinger backed away from the table, no longer smiling. Now it was Corrina's turn to scowl. "He was nice! And maybe he coulda been a customer. If you ain't gonna pay me, I gotta make my money somehow."

"He isn't a customer, he's a degenerate trying to latch onto a…how old are you?" She shrugged, neither knowing nor caring about her age. "Well, you can't be more'n thirteen and that's messed up."

And yet it happened every single day and no one batted an eye. For Corrina it was simply a fact of life. Turning tricks was better than working in one of the sweatshops in Brooklyn. At the hazy edge of her memory, she could remember working in one making pens. Her "line" had been her family. Nine little girls chained at the ankle in a row; they worked together at a long ink-stained bench; they slept together, cuddled like puppies, each trying to get as much of the blanket as they could; they ate together from dirty bowls that were never once full. They even went potty together, squatting in turn above a hellish black hole in the floor.

The other kids said that hole went all the way down to hell and that if you fell in, the shit-demons that lived down there would eat you.

As an orphan, the city held her indentured license and collected her "wages." Supposedly, she had earned money from her work, but when her two-year contract was up, the company subtracted child support and assistance fees which left very little. Most of the rest was taxed away by the city. Corrina walked out into the harsh light of a stinging cold day with one dollar and forty cents to show for two years of work.

A kindly old lady whom she had never met before took her to a restaurant and gave her a full bowl of meat stew, a middle piece of black bread and a cherry fizz. And as Corrina ate, the woman told her all about a wonderful opportunity in a sneaker factory. She made it sound like heaven compared to the pen factory: warm beds, full bowls with cookies on Sundays, and Thursday evenings off. "And much better pay. What you just got is a crying shame. Tarblesons would never steal from you. You trust me, right?"

Although she had a sweet grandmotherly smile and spoke with such fervor, Corrina did not trust her. The older kids had warned her that this was going to happen. "They lie. They all lie," a toothless ten-year-old had said.

"But what else is there to do?" another kid in her line had asked. "I nearly starved the last time my contract was up."

"I asked for seconds before I signed," said another, arching a slagged eyebrow. Half her face looked like grey, melted cheese and yet she was inordinately proud of that second bowl of stew.

Corrina decided she would ask for that second bowl.

"After you sign," the grandmother insisted. "You'll get too sleepy otherwise and then you'll get snapped up by one of the battery makers, and let me tell you those places are hell." She nodded towards another of the grandmothers who was chatting with the other newly scrubbed little girls from Corrina's line. "She would lie right to your face to get your contract. Can you believe that?"

"Yeah." Corrina believed it. She didn't get that second bowl of soup, although in retrospect, she could have if she had pushed just a little harder. But she had learned two valuable lessons. The first was that everyone lies and they lie all the time. The second was that people will *always* try to screw you over.

Cole was a prime example. He was doing everything he could not to give her the money he had promised. And worse, he had taken the cash she had earned hooking up with that drooly slag. He had been like a Saint Bernard and what did she have to show for it?

She stared at Cole, deciding that the next time he slept she would snatch his wallet and run. Just then he was squinting over the tiny numbers and letters that ran in wavering lines up and down the paper he had stolen from the Krupp factory. She couldn't understand anything on the form. It might as well have been written in Mandarin for all she could read of it.

"What is all that, daddy?"

His hazel eyes went dark green and he turned that ferocious glare on her. "Don't ever call me that."

"Why not? You tell me who I can turn a trick with, you take my fuck-money and you're a big jerk. That's what a daddy is…daddy."

He balled a huge fist while she took an innocent sip of fizz. "I'm trying to keep you alive," he said through a clenched jaw. "You'll get your money when I figure out how to do that. Now, if you don't mind shutting up altogether, I might be able to figure this out."

"Whatever you say, daddy." She sipped her fizz and tried her best to keep quiet, but whenever she was bored, the mule began to gallop and the mule didn't gallop like a thoroughbred, smooth as silk and beautiful to behold. No, the mule kicked, and bucked and stuttered, and made a jangly mess of her nerves until she was dying for another hit, or a smoke from a pipe or even a splash of Cole's nasty gin.

She slid the glass over and took a healthy swig and nearly coughed the entire thing over his papers. "Gross!" He smirked and slid the glass back, taking a sip. "Why is wine so expensive?" she moaned. "Do you think dock wine is a dollar too?"

Every boat on the sea made their own wine from a fermented mash of whatever vegetable or fruit that had gone bad during their voyages. Cole only shrugged and went back to the paper.

"Something's wrong with this world," Corrina stated after only a minute. "Gin should cost a dollar, not wine. They probably just make you pay a dollar because they can. You know, because it's so good."

Cole rubbed his face with both hands. His eyes were tired and his cheeks were sandpaper rough. "If I tell you why gin is cheap, will you shut up for once?" She said she would. "Good. Gin is cheap because it comes from Juniper berries and apparently nothing kills a Juniper bush, not even nuclear bombs. Wine comes from grapes and people eat grapes, making them harder to come by. When something is scarce, it makes it more expensive. Do you understand?"

"I guess." She tried harder this time to be quiet like she had promised, but the *need* was making her jittery. Her nerves were like out of tune guitar strings being scraped by a toilet brush. "Say, what is all that?" she asked when she couldn't stand the silence any longer.

"It's a bunch of lies." Cole had never been in the corporate world, however he had seen enough fudged paperwork to recognize that someone had gone in and made quite a few changes. "Most of this is straight forward. Like here. Van number 635 left at seven in the morning to pick up scrap at Pier 39 in Brooklyn. It returned at two-thirteen with a load of eight-hundred and twenty-six pounds. What we need is a van that was on the move late that night picking up or dropping off somewhere near *The Leather Lounge*."

Corrina roved her eyes over the letters and numbers, picking out the ones she recognized. "Does it say *Leather Lounge* on any of that?"

"No. And the only ones that drove close look very straight forward. No smudges, no whiteout, no corrections and no blanks. Even the ink matches." Ink color, stroke thickness, and overall penmanship were usually dead giveaways when it came to fixes. To an untrained eye, it looked as though every van that had gone out that night had come back without incident.

It was impossible. Twenty-six vans and not one of them delayed. Not one had broken down or had a flat. Only in the corporate world was such rampant falsification so blatant. The bigwigs upstairs demanded impossibilities and the only way to meet those demands was to fake the outcome.

"So, what do we do?" Corrina asked. She only partly cared. She had been distracted enough to forget her hunger for her drug, but not so distracted that she could ignore her growling stomach. That was something they never told you. When you came down off the mule, you were perpetually hungry.

"We go line by line, column by column." There was nothing else he could do. If he'd had the full weight of the police behind him, he could bring in the dispatchers and grill them, backroom style. Without that, he could only hope.

Five minutes later, "Can I get something to eat?"

He groaned, "You're hungry again?"

"I wouldn't have asked you if I had some of my own money...daddy." He fished out a dime and slid it across, his scowl pegging the anger meter. When she was gone, he looked blearily down at the papers. "Crap. Where was I?" He'd started at the top and after running his finger down the list, he realized that he should have started at the bottom of the last page. If a van had been out at *The Leather Lounge* at eleven, it would've checked in very late. Sure enough, there were three that had come in at exactly 11:59.

"Yeah right."

One had gone to south Brooklyn at ten that night and it was no wonder it didn't get back in time. Another had gone out to the Hempstead Wall at around six. The wall marked the last edge of the "Clean Zone" on Long Island.

Everything west of it was inundated daily by Cat-1 storms. Sometimes trogs went there to die. From the Krupp factory it was twenty-five miles as the crow flies.

That would've been a "maybe," if the third one hadn't gone on a pick up at a Harlem reclamation joint at 7:30. It was a two-hour trip there and back, and yet the driver supposedly checked in at 11:59 and with a load of exactly eight-hundred pounds? Cole didn't think so. Out of three-hundred odd deliveries, there had been only two exact-to-the-pound weights that day.

"Now we know who drove the van," Cole said, grinning at Corrina, not caring that she had spent the dime on a slice of a molasses pie instead of getting a nickel's worth of soup.

"Oh yeah?" She wasn't quite sure what was going on, but as long as she was eating molasses pie and drinking fizzes she was okay. "Who was it?"

"Pin number 0329. We'll get his real name when we get to Harlem. Everything has to be signed for, after all."

Chapter 14

The rain again. The afternoon had worn away to a dreary wet evening when Cole stepped out of the gin joint. He felt dog-tired after the long day and all he wanted was to go home, take a hot shower, lie down in his own bed and sleep until dawn.

But he couldn't. The Fox was too good. Even with the Krupp lawyers hounding him and Cole stealing the file, he had a way of discovering things, of getting at secrets. Cole had a gnawing worry in his gut that even then Reynolds was far ahead of him. Maybe he was already uptown, snooping around the reclamation joint, or maybe he was already off on a better lead.

It seemed smart to go as soon as possible. "After a shower and a change of clothes." He was tired of looking and feeling like a slag. But he couldn't simply make a blind stab at his apartment. He had to make sure the cops weren't still on his ass.

"Come on," he said to Corrina and zipped across the street as fat, heavy raindrops fell like pennies from the slate-black sky. They were soaked by the time they got to a bank of pay phones.

As Corrina hugged herself inches from a curtain of rain falling from an overhang, he fed a nickel into the phone. "This is Cole Younger, I need to talk to Lloyd," he said to the secretary.

Steffi Foller sucked in a breath. "Cole? Well okay, Cole. The thing is…well, the thing is he already left for the day. Sorry. I'd try again in the morning." She hung up before Cole could call her a liar. She never stayed a second later than Lloyd. If he had left, she wouldn't have picked up the phone. In fact, he had probably been standing right there shaking his head.

"Fuuuck," growled Cole, "Looks like we aren't gonna make a pitstop."

"Well, I ain't walkin' all the way to Harlem."

A cab ride would be at least seven dollars—was the Fox already at the reclamation joint? Or was he onto a new lead? Or was he trying to find the rasta? Either way a cab ride just seemed too expensive. He took her by the arm and led her from the shelter of the booth, where they were again pelted. "We'll take the train," he yelled, pulling her close so she could huddle beneath his coat. The raindrops had gotten larger and now burst on impact with a *thwap!*

Corrina didn't like the trains. They were too confining. There was nowhere to run. And many times it felt like she was sitting in a long cage with a dozen hungry lions and two dozen sheep. She was one of the sheep and not a very big one at that. At least she had Cole. He was one of the lions and there was no doubt about that. He shouldered his way through the crowds, his eyes sweeping back and forth looking for danger, his right hand touching his lapel, an inch from the holstered Bulldog.

The gun was bigger than the Crown had been and constantly wanted to slip out of the holster. He couldn't have that. There were cops in the station. Cole, and men like him, kept their distance, watching them from the corner of their eyes.

Around the two of them the crowd shrunk and swelled, as trains came and went. An hour went by before the Uptown 3 chugged slowly into the station, its cars rattling and its brakes screeching as if it were in pain. When it stopped, it let out a sad gasp from beneath the engine.

There were seats, however Cole preferred to stand in the corner near the back. He too disliked taking the train. They were a gamble. You never knew if they were going to break down and leave you stranded beneath the East River. And you never knew if thirty gangsters would board at the next stop and rob everyone blind. And like Corrina, he didn't care for the fact that there was nowhere to run and no room to fight.

The ride was uneventful and so dreadfully slow that Corrina was fast asleep before they reached 42nd Street. In sleep she looked even younger than usual. She looked like a child. A thin, malnourished child who needed to be protected. "By a mom," he muttered, glancing around the car, with the vague hope of seeing a motherly woman gazing fondly on the girl in mismatched red.

The only women of the right age sat stiffly, clutching their purses, casting nervous glances about as if they were on the verge of being attacked. Corrina needed a strong hand, not a frightened one.

Father James could be that hand if Cole could collect a bounty. Cole mulled over how low he could waggle James down to, and before he knew it they were crossing into Spanish Harlem. The Number 3 train ran down the border between the Rican Reds and the Kings. Gang fights onboard the cars were common and deadly.

Cole figured the heavy rain was keeping them inside because all three stops were uneventful. The few bangers that came into the car only sneered at each other, then sneered at everyone else. This was normal enough. New Yorkers had always been equal opportunity haters; they hated everyone equally. Cole got his share of sneers, but no one was stupid enough to press it any further than that.

They got off at 135th Street and were forced to walk two blocks through the rain until they came to *River Reclamation*. It was a fancy word for a chop shop which made it strange that the rambling building was dark and silent. Usually night was when a place that specialized in parting-out stolen cars was most active. Cole stopped up the block, noting how quiet and desolate the street was.

"Something's not right," he said to Corrina. "Wait here and keep out of sight." For once, she didn't argue. She felt the tension in the air as well.

She ducked down into a short stairwell leading to the garden level entrance of a seven-floor tenement, while he started toward the chop shop with the Bulldog in hand. The only entrances were twenty-foot tall bay doors that had sixty years' worth of graffiti scrawled over them in a layer half an inch thick. One of the doors was open. Just in front of it was a waterfall of rain. What lay beyond the curtain of water couldn't be seen or heard. The rain thrummed on the tin roof like a tone-deaf army of drummers banging endlessly on snares.

The revolver parted the falling rain water first, then Cole came through in a crouch, ready to shoot the first thing that moved. Nothing did. The dark, oily air hung as if suspended in a jelly jar. In front of him were the skeletal remains of a dock truck; its tires were gone, its panels, roof and hood had been cut away. There were hunks of rust and ruin sitting off to the side, waiting to be sent to Krupp.

The real treasure was the engine. After the kickbacks, the bribes and the taxes paid to the local police, a stolen engine in good condition could be sold for five hundred dollars—well worth the danger involved in stealing from the infamous Truckers Guild. People who got caught stealing from the Guild never went to prison; they never lived that long.

Lying face down next to the truck was a body. He was a black man in grease-stained overalls. His blood was as dark as the oil it mixed with. Cole could tell he hadn't been dead for more than a few minutes; the rats hadn't yet come out to feast.

There wasn't enough light to see how the man had died. It didn't matter. This was no Guild hit. Cole just wasn't that lucky. He stepped past the body and the van, and looked down the row to the next bay where a huge shadow of metal and rubber hung over the room. It was a truck of some sort. In the dark it was impossible to tell what kind. Cole didn't care one way or the other. It was the second body that drew his attention.

Another black man. This one had died with a cutting torch in hand and a face shield still in place. He had died while the power was still going. Cole eased closer, stepping over the hunks of metal that had been cut away from the truck. Up close he saw a hole in the back of the man's head—he'd been killed execution style. There would be more bodies.

He found two more in the next bay and two in a hall leading away. Here Cole paused, trying to piece together what had happened. The two bodies in the hall were heaped together one on top of the other in something of an X. The strange position drew Cole's attention and he knelt over them trying to make sense of the shadowy convulsion of arms and legs and…a glint of silver caught his eye.

"Son of a bitch," he whispered, realizing that one of the men was Aaron Reynolds. The Fox was dead, but in a manner unlike the others. He'd died with a gun in hand. The Crown was still warm, the acrid smell of burnt propellant hung about the bore. The Fox had got off a few shots. But at who…or what?

The rain was still drumming too loud to hear much of anything, however just as he slid the new, flashy Crown into his old battered holster, something metallic dropped, hitting a high singing note that cut through the background noise.

Cole froze, his breath caught in his throat, fear slithering into his belly, like a coiled snake. He lived in a hard world where fear was worse than useless. Normally, he could shrug aside that tingle and move on, but just then the idea of running away was almost a compulsion and he actually took a step back. Had he been flush and his wallet fat, he might have left, he might have crept out into the rain and taken up a position down the block, hoping to pickoff the killer as he came out.

But what if there was another exit? What if this was his only chance to take down the Dead-eye? There was nothing for him out in the rain but a little whore, who even then might be on her knees working to get her next fix.

Need drove him on. It was survival that made him heft the Bulldog and head down the hall, passing a storage room with its door flung open, a reeking bathroom, and two bedrooms with half a dozen mattresses strewn on the filthy floors.

The hall t-boned another. To the left the hall went on in growing darkness until it seemed to end in nothing. To the right the hall dead-ended at a simple doorway, the edge of which was lit momentarily by a beam of light before it swept away. Oddly, the very fact of the light cooled the fear inside him. Weak things needed lights. The truly terrible things in the world operated in the dark.

Cole prowled to the door and glanced inside. It was the shop's office. Thirty feet long, low-ceilinged, and filled with desks, cabinets, files and tons of paper. There was enough paper stacked about that Cole figured half a forest had been felled to make it all. The paper wasn't just sitting neatly in stacks and files and in cabinets, it was everywhere. Had a hurricane blown through the office it couldn't have added to the mess.

In the room were two people in black, wielding separate lights. One was squatted down studying something in an open drawer, while the other was picking through a stack on one of the desks. Cole should have just started shooting right there and then. At best they were killers, but more than likely they were Dead-eyes.

Foolishly, he yelled, "Freeze! Police!"

It was something of a surprise that they both actually froze in place, moving only enough to glance at each other. With their flashlights pointed down, the shadows pooled in the shallows of their eyes, making them appear deep as caves and wider than normal. It made it look as though they were wearing nightmare masks.

The one standing nodded to the other and put a hand to his hip where a pistol was shoved down into the waist of his pants.

Cole had a perfect bead on him. He couldn't miss. "Don't do it." It was all the warning he was prepared to give. The man yanked the gun from his pants and Cole shot him. He'd been aiming for the head, but had been surprised by the Bulldog's heavier than expected trigger pull, which caused the bullet to yank low and to the right. It struck the man below the eye and tore off half his face. A spray of red splattered the wall, while the splintered fragments of a dozen teeth rattled off a filing cabinet.

The haunted expression on the man's ruined face changed, not to horrified pain, but instead to one of surprise.

This was all the proof Cole needed; it was clearly a Dead-eye. The bullet didn't even make the thing blink, and it certainly didn't slow it down. However, it did screw with its aim. It fired its gun as fast it could pull the trigger. It shot the floor, then a desk, then a second desk, and finally the wall a few feet from Cole, who had no idea where any of the bullets were going.

In the dark all he saw were stabs of light, and all he heard beneath the rain was what sounded like thunderbolts. Cole ignored all of this and concentrated on aiming the Bulldog. Compared to his Crown, it was a big ugly blocky weapon. Its balance was off and its grip was sticky with a substance some mercs called "Yak-tar." Supposedly it made a weapon sure-handed in any situation.

Cole's hands were already as sure as they would ever get as he lined up a second shot and squeezed the trigger. He missed completely this time! Since he was using an unfamiliar weapon, firing in the dark from twenty feet away and trying to hit a target that was roughly three inches by three inches, it shouldn't have been a surprise.

Rationalizing the moment wasn't going to keep him alive. "Fuck!" he cried, thumbing back the hammer and firing again, missing a second time, but not so badly. Instead of popping a black hole through the thing's forehead, the bullet plowed through the beast's eye, tunneled through its head and blasted out the back taking a palm-sized hunk of skull with it.

Every muscle in its body went instantly slack and the creature collapsed in place.

Even as its legs were buckling, Cole was turning, bringing his smoking weapon to bear on the other Dead-eye and got a face-full of light. The other Dead-eye was digging in a pocket for its gun with one hand and blinding Cole with a flashlight with the other.

Cole fired into the light. Under the explosion of the revolver, there was a metallic whine. He had missed again! Furiously, he fired twice more. There was no whine this time and yet the light hadn't budged. The Dead-eye was still standing. At that moment, Cole hated the Bulldog more than he'd hated anything in his life. He put the blame squarely on the gun, cursing it for a piece of shit as he thumbed the hammer back so there'd be no excuse about the trigger this time. Then he squeezed the trigger, and the hammer came down on an empty chamber with an amazingly loud *Click!*

He couldn't blame the Bulldog for not having been smart enough to count to six or for wasting shots when the gun held so few.

"What a moron," the Dead-eye said as she finally got her pistol out of her pocket. It was a woman and Cole guessed it was the brunette with the pert little nose.

Cole caught only a flash of silver before he tossed aside the Bulldog and threw himself back into the hallway. Bullets buzzed by so close that one seemed to whisper a breath into his ear. He fled, flailing left and right, caroming from wall to wall. He was halfway down the hall by the time she leapt over the desks and piles of paper. He could feel her presence behind him looming—she would shoot him in the spine as he ran. He *knew* it. He was almost sick with fear and when she fired, he came very close to screaming.

To his left was an open door that led to one of the little storage rooms. Without hesitation, he threw himself inside just as she fired again. Her previous shot had singed a hole into the flap of his coat. This last one hit him high up on the side with a strange muffled *Tank* noise.

The noise was perplexing, but not something he could dwell on as he smashed into a pile of foul blocky shapes that smelled so strongly of acid that Cole's vision doubled. Not that he could see anything in the pitch-black room. All he could see was that the door was open; it had to be shut.

He lunged at it and slammed it shut, throwing his weight behind it. "Come on, bitch!" Cole yelled, dragging out Aaron's Crown. Normally, drawing a Crown was such a smooth motion that it was like pulling a silk handkerchief from a pocket. This was different. The damned thing snagged on his holster and he had to yank it out.

At first he thought that the problem was with his holster. The Crown was the latest model and he thought that his holster wasn't sized properly for it. Then as he stepped back from the door, aiming the gun, he saw, to his utter horror that the beautiful gun was mangled. The bullet from the Dead-eye's gun had smashed into it just above the trigger assembly. He ran his hands over it and little pieces began to fall to the floor.

"Fuuuck," Cole whined in a high whisper. It was ruined. The Crown had been a piece of art. It had been nearly priceless, and now…Cole almost wished the bullet had hit him instead.

Thinking that maybe he could fix it, he set it aside on a stack of whatever the blocky things were and turned back to the door. There was a heavy deadbolt on it, which he turned. It wasn't so heavy that it would stop a bullet. One or two shots and the Dead-eye would be able to kick her way in. Quickly, he began running his hands over the wall looking for a light switch. When he found it and flicked it up, a single dusty lightbulb lit the room, which was small and cramped, and made more so by the hundred-odd car batteries that were piled one on top of the other all the way to the low ceiling. It explained the acid stink that seared his nostrils with each breath.

He grabbed one and heaved it in front of the door. "What're you waiting for?" he yelled, and picked up a second battery. "Or are you just realizing that you left me Aaron's gun? Stupid move, you dead bitch." He kept shifting the batteries until he had a little pyramid of them before the door. Even a Dead-eye wasn't going to be able to open the door very easily.

She hadn't even tried, which he found odd. Putting his ear to the door, he listened but could hear nothing but the rain. Seconds ticked by. Cole could imagine her sitting crouched down the hall in the dark, her gun trained on the doorway, waiting for him to open it like some sort of stupid schmuck.

"Well, sorry bitch," he muttered. "That ain't gonna hap…" The sound of a police siren stopped him. Now he understood her game. She had trapped him and now was going to leave him holding the bag, on the hook for half a dozen murders. But that wasn't going to work because he had the body of her friend. All it took was one Dead-eye on scene and a hundred murder charges would disappear.

Cole threw down the stack of batteries as fast as he could and shoved the door back far enough to squirm through the opening. There was a shimmering gold light coming from the direction of the office. "No!" He pounded down the hall, thinking that she was burning the one piece of evidence that could clear him of the murders.

But it was worse than that.

She had set the room on fire and had taken the body with her. Now, the police would have him for arson *and* murder.

Chapter 15

With the blare of sirens cutting through the rain like knives, Cole knew that if he had a minute to get away before the police showed up, he'd be lucky—and when was he ever lucky? The smart thing to do was to get out of there as fast as he could. "But when am I ever smart?"

He was no one's genius, still he knew that the fire hadn't been set as a distraction or to pin an arson charge on him. No, the Dead-eye had wanted to destroy evidence. They had been searching for something when he had interrupted them, and whatever they wanted was still there.

"Were they after the same Krupp invoice as me?" More than likely, but *why* they would be was beyond him. He hurried over to the file cabinet the woman had been digging through, but could only get so close because of the flames, which were growing by the second. He could only read the label on the bottom drawer: *Outbound A-1 Inventory April 2161*. It was something of a fancy title for a place that fleeced stolen auto parts.

It struck Cole that the Dead-eyes were looking in the wrong place for an invoice created just four days before. The entire office was an immense pigsty. Papers were everywhere, which suggested that filing took place on a haphazard basis, if at all. If there was an invoice, it would still be on one of the desks.

Cole spun around. With the light of the fire filling the room, he picked out a handwritten sign over a cardboard box: *Nu Papor werk* it read. He ran to it. Inside was a jumble of receipts, invoices, and forms crammed one on top of the other. With the sirens screaming down the block, there was not enough time to pick through it all, so he grabbed the entire box. He took it and ran, stopping only long enough to grab the empty Bulldog he had chucked aside earlier. His one chance to escape the police was to find a back exit. It wasn't difficult. All he had to do was follow the trail of black blood that ran from the office. The Dead-eyes had come in through the rear, using the pounding rain to cover the sound of their approach.

A back door had been shouldered in and part of the chainlink fence had been torn free from a metal post. Cole was out in the rain and slipping through the fence just as the first squad car came roaring up in front.

He hurried down an alley, hunched over the cardboard box, once more regretting Corrina's presence in his life. Because of her, he couldn't just run away. He had to go all the way around the block to get her and with the police flooding the area, he was afraid one of them would notice a man walking around holding a box filled with paper in the middle of a rainstorm. His fear turned out to be ungrounded.

As much as people hated the police, they were fascinated by fire and a hundred people had appeared like magic to watch as the building went up in flames. In the time it took Cole to scurry around the block, half the chop shop was ablaze. The office with its overflowing files had been a bonfire waiting to happen and once the flames got going, they quickly spread to the room next door which held a mishmash of metal and plastic containers, each filled with old motor oil. They were burning like mad, warping the corrugated tin roof, which was hissing like a frying pan as the rain evaporated on contact.

Unfortunately, the fire hadn't yet reached the cutting bays and the police were able to recover a few of the bodies. The crowd oohed as each was pulled out and left in the street. The last body was that of Aaron Reynolds.

"Perfect," Cole muttered. If Aaron had never been found, then there would be nothing at all linking Cole to the crime scene. Now, it wouldn't take much to connect the dots.

"What's perfect?" Corrina asked, looking in the box. She turned her nose up at the papers. "What did you do to your coat?"

A glance down showed that the sulfuric acid from the batteries had already eaten holes in his black coat. Where the acid hadn't burned all the way through, it had stained the material a light grey color. "Son of a bitch," he moaned.

Corrina gave a little sigh. "Sorry about your coat an' all. So, you get my money yet?" He glared down at her ferociously, but she was no longer even mildly afraid of him. "Don't play with me, Cole. You killed all those people, which means you musta got something. Stop holding out on me or so help me, I'll scream right here. I'll let everyone know that Cole…what's your last name?"

"Shut up. I didn't kill any of those guys. I was trying to kill the thing that did, but it didn't work out."

"It never works out. Look Cole, I ain't trying to be mean or nothing, it's just, you keep running here and there, and every time, you come out a little worser off than when you went in."

"Yeah and I get closer every time, too." An apartment building across the street had a lit lobby and an open door. Half the building's renters were out watching the fire, chatting and laughing. Cole dashed across the street and pushed through the residents.

One of them muttered, "Fucking slags don't belong," but none dared to look Cole in the eye and they gave him a wide birth as he went to stand beneath the ceiling light in the center of the lobby. He began peeling away the recently added top layers of paper in the box to get to the drier ones below.

"Ah, here we go, June 3rd. Here, hold this stuff." He handed Corrina the top three inches of wet paper which she let fall.

"So, I was thinking," she said to him. "Maybe if you just give me that gun and a few bullets, we can call it even. A gun'll come in handy. You do want me safe, right? I mean, here I am a honey without a daddy. That's not safe. And I did save you all those times. Without me, you woulda been a goner a long time ago. So, what do you think?"

He hadn't been listening. Beneath a request order for a new nuclear filter, he had found a Krupp receiving receipt dated on the 3rd. This had to be it. The form had been filled out by someone who wrote in childish block letters and, other than the signature, which was only a wavering

X, it was surprisingly legible. Below the signature line was one marked: Print Name. "Is that a K?" Cole asked.

Corrina screwed up her grey eyes and stared at the squiggles. She didn't know a K from a platypus. "I can't tell. So, what do you think?"

"I don't think it matters. It's either Mike or Mire McDonald. I don't think Mire is a name. Still, there can't be too many of either at Krupp."

"Krupp?" She rolled her eyes in dramatic form. "Not again. Come on, Cole. It's been fun an' all, but you been dragging me all over New York. I think you need to face facts, I'm not gonna tag along with you forever...hey, wait up." He had tossed aside the box and was once more pushing through the crowd, pausing only for a second to crumple up the Krupp invoice and toss it in a puddle. The crowd was too mesmerized by the fire to notice the man in the ratty clothes striding away, or the little girl jogging to keep up with him.

"So, what do you think?" she asked, breathlessly.

He had been wondering how he was going to get into the records section at Krupp and hadn't heard a word she'd been saying. "What do I think about what?"

"About handing over that big gun, you know, the one you took from the rasta. Even though it is stolen property, I'll be willing to trade it for what you owe me. It's only fair after everything I've done for you. I musta saved your life ten times by now. What do you think?"

She came up to his elbow and she wanted to carry this monster of a gun? "I think you might be crazy. The gun weighs almost as much as you do. And you know what? Even if it was a .22, I wouldn't let you have it. If you don't like being a honey, then do something else."

"Like what? You want me to sell my work license to one of the factories? Fuck that noise, mister. I done that already and I ain't going back to slag out, no way. Are you listening to me?"

He hadn't been. They had turned south onto Fifth and Cole noticed a sleek black car that screamed elegance suddenly pull away from the curb behind them. Instead of heading down the street, it came purring up next to them. Cole was suddenly very aware that he hadn't reloaded the Bulldog yet.

It was a long stretch of shining black with mirrored windows. The very back one slid noiselessly down and from the dark interior of the car a voice asked, "Cole Younger?"

"Who wants to know?"

The owner of the voice was a man, thin-faced and so thin-lipped, he didn't appear to have lips at all, and yet these non-existent lips were twisted into a look of disgust. "My name is Gavin Baker. Miss Tinsley would like a word."

As much as Cole hated the idea of dealing with the vamp, he also wanted to get away from the crime scene as fast as possible. He tried to look past the mirrored window and only managed to squint at himself. "Is she in the car?" he asked, reaching for the door handle. It was locked.

"She is not," Gavin said. "You are to meet Miss Tinsley for dinner. Just you. The girl is not invited."

"We're sort of a package deal," Cole said, stepping back.

The man seemed to have only two expressions: contempt and disgust. He had switched to contempt. "That's not how this works. When Miss Tinsley asks for something, her orders are carried out precisely. We will do this the easy way or the hard way. Mr. Orand will gladly undertake the hard way. Althalis, if you please."

Cole expected a monster to emerge from the passenger side and it was exactly what he got: Althalis Orand seven feet of muscle topped by a pinkish head that seemed comparably small. The giant's black suit seemed to be throttling him and thus the pink coloration.

"There's one other way," Cole said as the beast of a man came around the long hood of the car. Cole pulled the empty Bulldog and pointed it at the giant. "There's also my way."

A sigh escaped out the rear window. "Is that necessary? You're simply being invited to dinner."

"It looks as though I'm being forced against my will. Some might call it kidnapping. Others might call it interfering with a bounty hunter during an investigation, which is a class one felony for all involved."

Although the gun stopped Althalis, it only elicited a new put-upon sigh from the car. "How about this, Mr. Younger. I'll keep the girl safe and sound in the car while you and Miss Tinsley have your dinner. Does that sound like a proper compromise?"

"Not to me it don't," Corrina said, balling her fists and planting them on her pointy little hips. "How come I don't get no dinner? I'm just as much a part of this investigation as him."

Gavin didn't seem able to exhale in a normal manner and he sighed for a third time in the last minute. "I will make sure you are fed, though you may not eat in the car."

"Okay," Corrina said, grinning. Trying the door, she found it to be now unlocked and she popped inside bringing with her five gallons of rainwater. Cole was about to slide the Bulldog away when Althalis wagged a finger at him and then held out a hand the size of a serving platter.

"It was empty anyway," he said and slid in after Corrina. The inside was as fancy as he had expected and yet he still had to refrain from gaping around like a Barrio slag—the way Corrina was. She had been in very few cars and none had ever been this big or this nice. The gleaming wood was real, as was the silver trim and the leather seats.

She wanted to touch everything, especially the crystal glasses and the long-stemmed champagne flutes. They were wonderful and perfect, the most perfect things she had ever seen. "How do they get them so round? And so exact? Look how they're all the same size. And what does this button do?" Cole grabbed her hand before she had a chance to break anything.

Gavin looked like he had regretted inviting the girl in. He was a spare man in every way. Thin, yes, but also small to the point of being dainty. Over his mini frame he wore a black suit that was so tight it scarcely gave him room to breathe. He had to sit perfectly upright and perfectly stiff to keep from popping a button. His shirt was brilliantly white and his bow tie was as well, and Cole didn't notice it at first.

"So, what are you?" Cole asked. "A butler?"

"Hardly. I am the lady's majordomo."

Cole didn't know what that was, but Gavin looked like a fancy butler to him. "So, what's the lady want with me? If it's to kill Christina, I hate to say it but she's wasting her time."

Corrina elbowed him and then sat up as straight as she could and clasped her hands together. "We should hear what the lady has to say 'fore we go saying no."

"There ain't no we in this. And why are you sitting like that?"

"When in Rome," she answered. She had never seen a vamp before and at first, all she could think about was how desperately she wanted to see one. Now, it was slowly dawning on her what a golden opportunity this was. From what she knew of vamps, they always had stacks of cash lying around and if she could get lucky, she hoped to snag one and make a break for it.

But first she had to fit in. She couldn't be a kid at a time like this. She had to appear as if she was picked up by vamps all the time.

"This is a nice car, though kinda small," she said, gazing around as if she hadn't been gushing over it only a minute before. "I was in one twice this size before."

Gavin turned his lizard-like gaze at Cole and asked, "Please tell me she has a mute button?"

"No. She only stops talking when you feed her, so I'd stuff her silly." Corrina opened her mouth to protest the shabby treatment she was receiving, only just then Cole put his hand on her knee and gave her a warning squeeze. Something wasn't right. "Where are we going? Your man turned too soon."

"We're going to get you cleaned up a bit first," Gavin answered. "You can't possibly be seen in public with Miss Tinsley looking like that." He sniffed and raised his eyebrows, which Cole just noticed were actually penciled in. "Or smelling like that."

Cole was both embarrassed and relieved. He knew he looked like a slag and he was sure he smelled worse. The car turned two corners and then came to a descending ramp blocked by a steel wall. At their approach, the wall slid upward and they entered an underground city that only vamps could access.

Above them Manhattan was dark, dirty, and dangerous. This city was brilliantly lit and beautiful. The streets were so smoothly paved it was as if the car was rolling along velvet. On either side of the street were swanky shops that boasted of real turtle shell shoes, cashmere leggings, buffalo hide belts, and armadillo-skin gloves.

They passed a jewelry store that had Corrina drooling. There was enough gold in the window to cover both her and Cole head to toe. "Fuuuck," she whispered, as they swept slowly by. He jabbed her with his elbow but she only continued to stare, craning her neck further and further around until the store was too far back.

Then there was a new sight for her to behold. A woman wearing a deep blue outfit that seemed to flow like water. She had metallic silver hair and nails. Around one wrist was a fine silver chain that ran down to the ground and wrapped around the neck of a tiny creature.

"Is that a..." Corrina began to ask. She thought the animal was a fancy rat, but that didn't seem right. "What is that?"

Gavin turned his languid gaze out the window. "It's a mod. Probably was a dog at one time." He saw the question rise on her lips. "A mod is a modified animal."

"A dog? Wow." She had never seen a real dog before. Only when they were past it did she remember she was trying to fit in "Of course it was a mod. I knew that. I was just wondering, you know, what it had been. I thought it was..." They were passing a wig shop. In the front window were two scantily clad women with long flowing hair. One had hair as black as midnight and the other's was like new snow. They alternated between posing, one second letting their hair hang like gorgeous waterfalls, and the next, whipping it about to a grinding, oddly compelling musical beat.

In the next window was a fat man in a white dusted uniform creating art out of muffins and cupcakes. Each looked like you could either hang it on your wall or scarf it down. After that was a shoe shop that had Corrina drooling as much as she had for the cupcakes.

Finally, the car took another turn and slid into an open garage that expanded outward. It could fit a dozen vehicles as large as the one they were driving in, but theirs was only one of three. When the car stopped, Gavin sat, waiting patiently until the giant in the front seat got out and opened the door. He didn't move except to gesture at the door.

"Time for you to get out, Mr. Younger. This is where you get modified."

Chapter 16

The giant put a huge hand on Cole's shoulder, nearly buckling his knees. He didn't speak, he simply pushed Cole toward a door. When he hammered on it, the metal door thundered and shook.

"Oh stop it, you big gorilla," a woman said from the other side of the door. "I saw you coming, just let me get my keys. Ah, here we go."

When the door opened, Cole was surprised to see that it wasn't a woman after all. It was a man, average height, dark complected, and skinny. He wore a purple miniskirt that matched the color of his inch-high afro, green sneakers and a gold wife-beater t-shirt that showed off his lack of musculature. Despite the shirt, it was clear he did not have a wife to beat. He was a muncher all the way.

Normally, his flamboyant presence would have rankled Cole on a genetic level, but Aaron's death was too fresh.

The muncher looked Cole up and down, shaking his head. "Oh my. Oh my, oh my, oh my. I don't know. I. Just. Don't. Know. A slag? Miss Ashley sends me a slag? This may be beyond even me."

The giant grunted and shook his head. Before Cole knew it, the beast had grabbed him from behind with one hand holding a fierce grip in his hair. As if he were nothing but a ragdoll, he jerked Cole's head left and right, then up and down.

"Huh?" the muncher said. "What are you trying to say?"

Cole pulled out of the man's grip. "He's trying to say that I'm not a slag. I've just had a run of bad luck."

"To me it looks like you're lucky to be alive. Well, it's good that you're not a slag, but all the same, I don't need a headache. Are you going to be a headache? Because I told Miss Ashley that I *might* be able to help as a personal favor to her. And here you show up with a gorilla. Is he really necessary? She said you'd be challenging, but this is too much."

"I'm not even sure what I'm doing here," Cole told him. "I don't plan on making trouble, but I won't shy from it either." This last he said while glaring up at the giant.

A grin spread across the muncher's face. "Okay now I'm seeing it. Okay, yeah. Alright, follow Miss Bobby inside and we'll get you fixed up right."

"Miss Bobby?" There was only the three of them.

The muncher started to put out a hand and then thought better of it. "I'm Miss Bobby and that is how you'll refer to me. Call me Bob or Bobby even once and I'll have the gorilla break your arm."

Cole rubbed his forehead, feeling the weight of the last few days descend on him. "Sure, whatever you say, Miss Bobby."

Miss Bobby smiled. "Now that's the proper attitude, and if you do whatever I say, I will make you look fabulous. But not too fabulous. I know Ashley. If she wanted fabulous, she wouldn't have chosen you, honey."

"Thanks, I think." Before walking into his salon, Cole had expected to be given a washtub to use and a jacket to borrow. Right away, he knew this was going to be far more in-depth than he really wanted. Perhaps that was why the giant came in after him, a smirk on his over-sized face.

The salon was a color explosion. Even the back hall was bedecked in rainbow streamers and shining gold floors. The place smelled mostly of perfume, but beneath that was a hint of chemicals, which was to be expected since the people who exited the salon came out unnaturally beautiful.

"The showers are in here, darling," Miss Bobby said. "If you need any help, I'll be right outside." He winked at Cole.

"I'm good, thanks." He scrubbed away the day's worth of grime and pollutants using soap that smelled of lavender. When he was done he dried and wrapped himself in a towel that barely fit across his lean hips. Right away he noticed that his clothes were missing.

"Hello? My clothes?"

"First things first," Miss Bobby said, coming in, his dark eyes drinking up Cole's body. "A shave and a quick trim. Trust me, I won't take off much. Come on." He reached out a hand and looked as though he expected Cole to take it. Cole declined.

Miss Bobby didn't take offense, he only laughed high and sweet as he walked Cole through to another room, this one with a single plush barber's chair made of white leather. There were two women in the room, both tiny delicate little Mandarins in form-fitting white body suits.

"Have a seat," Miss Bobby said, indicating the chair. Cole sat, distinctly aware that his towel barely made it to the top of his thighs. When he sat, the two women tittered, speaking in Mandarin. Miss Bobby laughed with them, but for only a second, then he was all business. As the two women went to work on his feet, Bobby lathered his face and then broke out a wickedly sharp razor. When he held it up for Cole to see, Cole felt his testicles pull up almost into his body to the delight of the two women, who giggled again.

"Enough," Miss Bobby growled and then applied the blade. Cole had been shaved by a barber before, but never had he been shaved with such a delicate touch. The blade slicked across his face without the slightest hitch and when he was done, Cole knew he hadn't been nicked once.

Miss Bobby held up a mirror and waited for the expected compliment. Cole, who was sparing with his compliments, said, "Excellent."

"For a man as verbally challenged as you are, I'll take that as your highest compliment. Now let's do something about this bit of hair on your head. Don't you know the style is shoulder length?" Cole didn't know what the vamp style was, and he really didn't care. Miss Bobby swung a leg over his and squatted across his knees, staring at his head. "I can add a few inches. No one will know but you, me and the giant makes three. What do you say?"

"I say you should probably get off me."

Bobby kicked his leg back over, narrowly missing one of the women. "So tough with the girls are you? How about a touch of color? I can do the tips midnight blue or better yet, forest green to match your eyes. You have nice eyes." Cole grunted a no and Miss Bobby said, "Your loss," before wading in with scissors, gel, combs and a great deal of teasing, and even more chattering to which Cole only grunted.

It took five grunts before Miss Bobby took the hint and finished in silence. Once more he had done an excellent job and Cole told him so.

"Now let's see if clothes make the man because sadly you can't wear that towel to dinner." He led Cole to another room where a black suit was hanging off a rack. "It's a Valorie Gemme. Herringbone wool, basted sleeves, double-vented, slash pockets. Beautiful, isn't it?"

"I uh, can't afford it."

This elicited a high squealing laugh from Miss Bobby. "You can't even afford the tie! I saw your wallet. Nineteen dollars and change." He laughed again until he was weak in the knee and "had to" lean against Cole for support. "Oh honey, this is just a loaner for your dinner. Come, let's get you into it. I hope you don't mind, but I peeked when you were showering. Just to measure you up, of course."

One thing was certain, Miss Bobby had an eye for measurement. The suit fit Cole like a glove right down to the shoes. "One last piece: the hat. I suggest you go with one of the Homburgs. It's the height of class." On a rack were eight different hats, all in black. There were three Homburgs, two sharp-peaked Belfasts, two baby Stetsons and lastly a Fedora.

He chose the Fedora because he liked the look and because it was not the height of fashion. The height of fashion meant that he was going to be just like everyone else.

"How forties of you," Miss Bobby said, with a look of disappointment. "Just do me one teeny tiny favor." He took the black band from it and added a green one. "There and now we change out your pocket square for a green one and we exchange the tie…"

Cole took hold of his tie. "It stays, but thank you. I feel a thousand times better."

"Just a thousand?" Miss Bobby asked, sounding miffed. "I guess you didn't see yourself when you came in. I suppose you won't let me put a little make-up on those bruises. No? Well, enjoy your dinner. Go on." He shooed Cole from his salon and out into the garage where the long black car had been turned around and was running with a soft purr. Corrina was sitting on the cement next to it, licking pink icing from her fingers.

She didn't recognize Cole at first and when she did she jumped up, mouth hanging open. "Holy crap, Cole, they made you into a vamp. Well almost. You still got that bruise on the side of your face and those scabs on your eyebrow, but wow. You look rich. Did you check the pockets for money? I bet they got fifties sewn up in 'em."

"It wouldn't be my money even if they had."

Corrina looked perplexed at this. Found money was always up for grabs, even if it happened to be found in a pocket of a borrowed coat, on a dresser or even in a wallet. Generally, if money was in reach, she would claim it. She thought about slipping her hand in Cole's pocket, but the giant was eyeing her too closely as he opened the door for her.

"A remarkable transformation," was all Gavin said as Cole slid in. The approval did not touch his reptilian eyes. He looked at Cole without expression. Corrina got a frown, which for her was par for the course. While Cole had been getting his make-over, she had tried to casually search for hidden compartments in the car. She was sure it had any number of them, just as she was sure they were stuffed with cash or jewels. Gavin had finally kicked her out of the car.

"Do not touch anything with those sticky hands," Gavin warned Corrina. "Not that it matters," he muttered, staring out the window as the car slid from the garage. "We'll probably have to burn this car."

It struck Cole that torching a car that had been "contaminated" by the presence of a slag was something a vamp might very well do. *Would they burn the suit as well?* he wondered. The thought sickened him. He had already grown fond of it. Even in his heyday, when he was taking down Dead-eyes every few months, he had never owned a suit like this one.

He was sorely tempted to ask how much it had cost, but he knew that Gavin would only sniff and say something like: *More than your life and the lives of your unborn children.* And he wouldn't be wrong.

The car arrived at the restaurant minutes later, just about the time Corrina got her hand stuck between the seats as she was rummaging for gold coins. She was turned sideways so Gavin wouldn't see. "You got any more of them pills?" Sitting alone in a car with Gavin was going to be a trial that she didn't want to face completely straight.

"You don't need pills. I probably won't be that long." Cole yanked her hand out of the seats before sliding from the car. He paused to glance around. Although they were deep underground, it didn't feel that way. There was a soft breeze coming from up the street and there were interesting night sounds: crickets, an occasional bird, and very faintly, waves rumbling up on a shore. Above him, the ceiling of the cavern was very high overhead and painted deep black. Within that darkness were tiny lights that resembled stars.

On the clearest New York night, Cole might be able to see an even dozen stars. Above him were hundreds. It was breathtaking.

He was nearly mesmerized and had to force his eyes away.

They had pulled up in front of a building made entirely of obsidian. It was polished to such a sheen that it looked like black glass. A dapper man with slicked back hair in a light grey suit greeted Cole. Although his smile appeared genuine, there was the tiniest bit of hesitation in his pale eyes as if he saw past the suit and recognized Cole as one who didn't belong. Maybe even a kindred spirit. There was even a look in those eyes that was something of a warning. *Be careful*, it said, *you're swimming with sharks*.

"The name on the reservation?"

"Ashley Tinsley."

The man's eyebrow went up a millimeter. It was all the surprise that he was permitted to show. "She has not yet arrived. I can show you to her table if you wish, or you can have a drink at the bar. Our barman makes a mean Roscoe." He nodded in a companionable way, telling Cole that the Roscoe was the way to go.

"The table, I think," Cole told him. Cole didn't think he would actually make it through the meal. He was sure that she was going to offer him more money to kill Christina Grimmett and his answer was going to be a firm no.

He followed a lithe attractive young thing in a shimmering, form-fitting dress of peach through the restaurant. Once more Cole forced himself not to stare around like a hick fresh off the train. There was plenty to stare at. The walls were high sheets of flowing silk that gradually changed colors, silver becoming gold, gold into mother of pearl and so on. Between the silk were columns of glass, inside which were insects and birds and animals, many of which had not been seen in New York since the bombs dropped.

The birds seemed to chirp in tune with a twelve-piece orchestra that took up a corner of the restaurant. It was made up of a three thrumming cellos, a harp and and seven violins. Cole nearly ran into a table as the beat picked up and the violins began stabbing the air in perfect unison. The sound was beguiling for someone not prepared for it.

As Cole passed through the restaurant, the din of conversation dimmed, and he could feel every eye in the place on him. For a man accustomed to moving about without being noticed, the attention was unnerving. Perhaps sensing the effect Cole was having on the other patrons, the woman offered Cole a seat facing away from the room. As was his habit, Cole chose the seat that put his back to the wall. "That's Miss Tinsley's chair," the woman said. "I'm sure you'll find this one to your liking."

Cole didn't budge. The woman looked like she was on the verge of insisting; however, Cole's stare was ice and she went away afraid for her job. The waiter in a uniform of brilliant white had the same expression when he came up. "I'd like a Roscoe, please," Cole said after a single glance at the man. He was more interested in the vamps.

The men wore haughty, bored expressions as if they had been there, dining on the same food with the same people for the last hundred years. They were all tall and muscular, but Cole guessed that there wasn't much strength behind the muscles. Their hands were too soft to know the weight of a barbell. Like the women, their features were perfectly seamless. They had no lines, no wrinkles, no scars, and certainly no scabs.

Without exception, they wore sharp suits of either blue or black, and on the seats next to them were matching Homburgs.

Superficially, there was far less uniformity among the women. They wore wigs of every color and style and height. One woman had braids of alternating colors that were spun two feet above the crown of her head. Another had a flow of canary yellow that spilled in a river onto the floor. The waiters made wide detours around it. Their dresses were equally outrageous. There was every color in the book, including clear. One woman wore a see-through dress.

Cole quickly looked away.

His Roscoe showed up a minute later. It was whiskey mixed with spices Cole couldn't name, and it was easily the best tasting drink he'd ever had. He had just ordered a second when Ashley Tinsley arrived, though it took Cole two looks before he realized it was her. She wore a gown of deepest green that extended from mid-breast down to the floor in front and trailed slightly in the back. Around her neck she wore a string of black pearls that came together in the middle clasping an enormous onyx the shape of a teardrop.

Cole stood and offered her a chair, which she ignored. Instead she sat in Cole's vacated spot.

"Even if it's just a chair, I get what I want, Mr. Younger. You will soon learn that." Her eyes were black now. Without being able to tell where the iris merged with the pupil, they looked alien. They were also enthralling and Cole found himself staring into them.

He shook his head to break the spell. "Perhaps I will, and perhaps you'll learn that not everything is for sale."

Her soft smile turned into a full-bellied laugh, which went on and on, louder and louder. Cole was glad now that his back was to the rest of the room. She laughed even harder when she saw how his jaw was clenched tight as a fist. When the laughter finally subsided, she reached across the table and put her hand on his arm, rubbing the soft wool.

"You are such a treat, Cole. Can I call you Cole? Of course I can, and you can call me Ashley if you wish. Either way, my dear boy, everything and everyone has its price. You must get it out of your head that the price may not be in cold hard cash per se. Take that little slag you keep tagging along after you. What would you do to keep her safe? And what price do you put on that orphanage you grew up in? An accidental fire would be easy to arrange."

A knife of cold sweat went down his spine. This wasn't an idle threat on her part. She had the resources to torch half of Manhattan if she wished.

"If anything happens to the girl or any of those kids, it'll cost the world one useless vamp. I'd say that was pricey."

Instead of looking frightened or appalled, her smile grew, as if the idea of a challenge appealed to her. She abruptly pulled her hand back and leaned away as two waiters arrived with bowls of soup. "I hope you don't mind that I ordered for us," she said, allowing a third waiter to drape a napkin across her lap. "I heard that you were out in the rain this evening. Nothing cures the chills like a hearty bisque."

He was oddly disappointed that soup was being served. He'd eaten soup in one form or another almost every day. Of course, this was different. It was indescribably rich and wonderful. Ashley watched as he tried not to scarf it down too quickly.

"Maybe I should consider paying you in bisque. It's lobster and Chilean sea bass. Two bowls and I'll have you eating out of my hand." She laughed again as he put down his spoon. "Don't be like that. I know you. I know now you can't be bought. You're the White Knight of the 7th Precinct. You couldn't be bought off like all the other taxmen and so your brothers tried to kill you, not once but twice." A new laugh escaped her, this one stilted by anger. "And I thought my family was broken."

"They weren't trying to kill me," Cole said, feeling the strange desire to stand up for his one-time comrades in arms. "They were just sending me a message."

She ran a hand through her black hair before shaking it out in a beautiful display designed to get the attention of everyone in the room. "They could have sent a letter. Is the postal service still a thing up top?"

Now it was Cole's turn to laugh. "It was gone before either of us were born. There are runners you can hire, but they aren't too reliable. When was the last time you were up top? Outside a car, that is." She thought for a moment and as she did, he attacked his soup again.

"I go up a few times a year to check my family's holdings, or I used to. Which brings me to why I asked you here tonight."

He set aside his spoon again. "Don't mention Christina."

"Hold on. Hear me out." She had just set aside her spoon and the moment she leaned back, a waiter appeared and whisked away both bowls. Angry as he was, Cole still watched his go with a pang of regret. "I need you to find her…" She stopped as he slid his chair back.

Her eyes flashed in sudden fury and in a controlled voice she said, "Sit down. You forget I still have the girl slag. So you will do me the courtesy of listening politely until I finish speaking. If you embarrass me, I'll see that she's the one who pays."

Cole could feel his pulse hammering in his temples. He could be across the table in a blink, a knife to her throat. He could force her to give up Corrina—but then what? How long could he protect her? And what about Jimmy Smith and the orphanage?

The conversation in the restaurant had become muted. The vamps could feel when reality entered their world. First it was in the form of Cole and now there was real anger in the air. Eyes shifted their way. He could feel them rove over his tense shoulders, his scarred knuckles, the way he sat as if spring-loaded. If he had to guess, he figured that everyone in the restaurant was hoping for some explosion on his part.

He wasn't about to give them the satisfaction as he slowly eased his chair forward again.

Immediately the conversations around them picked up again. Cole's and Ashley's did not. The two sat staring at each other until a rack of lamb was set between them. The smell had Cole salivating. A cut was put on his plate along with spears of beautifully green asparagus and something purple that had been whipped and sculpted so that it appeared to take on the form of a bird's nest. In the center was a pool of clear gravy that was intriguing in every way. Cole refused to pick up his fork.

Ashley's anger disappeared with dinner. She cut a bite of the lamb and after taking a bite, moaned in a way that was practically sexual. "A lamb died for you. There's no sense letting his sacrifice go to waste."

That was logic and the smell was driving Cole mad. At the same time, he felt as though she was treating him the way a drug dealer treats a new user. He was getting a taste for free. She was trying to get him hooked. When she saw that he wasn't going to eat, she steepled her long fingers in front of her and said, "Okay, I sort of lied before when I said that it wasn't good for people to throw around my family name. That's bad, it's true, but I was more concerned that *my* name was being brought up in connection to disappearances and murderers and who knows what else. Look at these people around us, Cole. They're jackals waiting for me to slip up."

"And contracting murder will help that?" He had meant for that to be a dig, but she nodded.

"Actually, yes. In this world, might makes right. They understand ruthlessness. They understand consequence. What they do not understand is someone like you."

He was taking another drink of his second Roscoe before he even realized what he was doing. Quickly, he set it down. "And you do?"

She shrugged. "The other day I thought you were playing hard to get. You know, trying to make me want what I couldn't have. I know now that you are truly… this." She was still having trouble putting into words exactly what Cole was. In their world, he was unique. "I understand now that you won't bend. It's interesting."

"I'm interesting? Is that why I'm here? Because you're just bored like all the rest and want to see me dance?"

"No. I have a job offer for you. I want you to find Christina and make her disappear…" Cole started to push his chair back again, but she glared him back down. "Let me finish. I want you to make her disappear your way. Put her on a boat to the Carolinas or set her up with a false name. I don't care, just as long as she ceases to exist. And of course you will warn her what the penalty will be if she ever utters my name again."

Now it was Cole's turn to be interested in Ashley, and for once he looked at her like a person instead of as a vamp. Beneath the layers of makeup, Ashley had something of a pinched look. She needed this. It was important to her. *But why? Because of her reputation?* he wondered.

"If you're worried about your reputation, why have dinner with me in public? Won't people say that you're slumming it?"

Her serene smile returned, covering over the pinched look. "Like I said, you're interesting. They all think so, too. You are real. The scars, the scabs, the…everything." Her smile became briefly mischievous before her eyes turned cold. "So? How does a thousand dollars, not including expenses sound?"

It sounded almost too good to be true. It sounded like she was buying him on the installment plan. A suit, a fancy dinner, a thousand dollars, what's next? Maybe a new Crown to replace his lost one? Or perhaps a car? Would she keep going until one day he was hooked by it all? Still, he needed the money. "If I do this, you'll have to trust me. When she disappears, I'm not going to tell you where she's gone or under what name."

Ashley was not used to trusting people and her black eyes narrowed as she gazed for a long time at Cole. She was silent for so long that after a minute he shrugged and began to gorge himself on his lamb and whatever the purple stuff was.

"A deal based on trust," she finally said, with a little chin waggle of disbelief. "The closest thing to that in my world is a deal based on mutual destruction, which is a trust in its way I suppose. My problem with this is you, Cole. You almost seem to be too good to be true."

"Funny, I was just thinking the same thing about you."

Her white smile was back. "So, we don't trust each other? I can live with that. For me, that's the most natural feeling in the world."

Chapter 17

Gavin slipped Cole an envelope just as they stepped out of the car in front of the 10th Avenue orphanage/church/school. "This is for expenses only." He cast a disparaging look at the ramshackle building leaning over them. "Make donations on your own dime. Take my card. Call me once you find Miss Christina."

"Sure," Cole grunted. "Whatever you say. Hey, Corrina. Time to wake up." Exhaustion combined with Blue Calc and a full belly had the girl snoring. She was a rag doll as he pulled her out and set her on unsteady feet.

She was still half asleep and didn't recognize the building. "Where are we?" The storm had blown itself out and the night was one of those rare cloudless ones. She tilted her head way back and gazed up at three stars set in a black sky. Compared to the fake sky in the underground vamp world, it was depressing.

"We're getting a place to stay," Cole said and pulled her back from the shiny black car, which was slowly easing away from the curb.

It slowed and the back window rolled down. Gavin stuck his thin head from it. "I'll be keeping an eye on you, Mr. Younger."

When it was gone, Cole muttered, "That wasn't creepy at all. Come on Corrina." She leaned into him as he mounted the stairs and knocked on the door. It was well after eleven by then and the orphanage was dead quiet. It took four of his hammer-like blows before a sleepy-eyed boy answered.

"Get me Father James," Cole demanded and then caught hold of the back of Corrina's red coat just as she tried to run. "It's just until I figure out what to do with you." This was a lie. He fully intended to drop her off with a large cash donation and never come back. It was all the charity he could manage under the circumstances.

Father James took five long minutes to come down and when he did, he was dressed in his working garments: plain black shirt and pants, a white collar tight around his throat. He was shaking his head as he approached, "I can't, Cole."

"You can. I can pay for her living expenses, plus a little bit on top."

"Yes, I can see by your suit, and I would if I could, but the police have been here asking about you. A Sergeant Hamilton seemed very intent on finding you and the girl. He said he'd be back."

Cole was struck dumb by this. He could understand Hamilton coming after him, but why on earth would he want Corrina? How would he even know about her? "That doesn't make any sense. Hamilton's never even seen her. How would he..." James' eyes darted away and Cole knew. "You told him!"

"Yes. He threatened us. You know this place isn't exactly legal." Not only was the school portion of the church illegal, none of the children were technically registered. They didn't have work licenses and didn't pay the yearly head-tax. It was a situation that the city usually overlooked since it kept the children off the street, where they would otherwise be a nuisance at best. Still, if Hamilton wanted to shut the place down and arrest Father James, no one would say a word.

"Damn it, Jimmy! This is how you treat an old friend? The least you could have done is..." Corrina grabbed his arm a half second before he heard the screech of a tire. A car had taken the turn onto 10th Avenue fast enough to lose a hubcap. James was looking down again in shame. "You called them!"

"I had to." He was about to go on with his lame excuses, but Cole was already pushing past him, racing for the stairs.

"Is the tunnel still open?" he yelled over his shoulder.

Father James wouldn't answer, however a boy of twelve cried out, "Yes! The third left leads to Penn Station."

Cole knew the tunnels below the orphanage better than anyone. He had spent half his nights slipping through them, desperate to end up somewhere better. At the time, anywhere seemed better than having to eat cold porridge every day and sleeping on hard boards, freezing in the winters and sweltering in the summers.

He dashed into the cramped cellar, pulled off the heavy bar that kept tunnel people from coming up into the building and threw open the door that led down. But he didn't race down into the darkness, instead he grabbed Corrina and ran lightly to the old furnace that sat like a squatting demon in the corner. It was a go-to spot for hide and seek because behind it was an alcove where wood had once been stored long before Cole was born.

It had burned coal for the last forty years and as there was never enough, the coal sat in a bucket next to the wall.

From where Cole and Corrina crouched, they could hear Father James rat them out plain as day: "They're in the tunnels, heading for Penn Station. It's the third left."

"You two!" they heard Sergeant Hamilton yell. "Get to Penn Station and ready the platoon there. I want all the tunnels watched. Have them on the lookout for a man and a ten-year-old girl."

"I ain't ten," Corrina groused.

Cole shushed her. Seconds later, the heavy tread of boots came stomping down the stairs. Father James' rubber-soled shoes were lost in the rumble. "Right down there," he told them, pointing at the opening.

Sergeant Hamilton didn't bother to thank the priest. He and his partner went racing into the darkness, flicking on their chest lights. James watched them for a few seconds before letting out a long weary sigh. He then walked slowly upstairs and began ordering the orphanage back into its previous sleepy state.

After a minute, Cole crept from his hiding place and went to the tunnel door. He gently shut it and re-barred it. Then he and Corrina stole upstairs like mice and found Father James at the door to the street staring down at Sergeant Hamilton's squad car. Cole tapped him once on the shoulder and then, when he turned around, Cole punched him once in his brilliant white grill, knocking him down the stairs.

"I pulled that punch, Jimmy," Cole said as he walked past him, groaning in the gutter. "I shouldn't have, and I won't next time."

"What would you have me do? Lie? I'm a priest, Cole."

Cole grunted a short laugh. "It's what I would've done. If they had been here thirty seconds earlier, you would've had fucking blood on your hands instead of a smudge on your soul. Now you're going to be an accessory to grand theft."

"We're takin' the cop car?" Corrina asked, excitement lighting up her grey eyes. She ran to it and tried the door. It was locked. She scrambled in the gutter for a brick and held it up to Cole.

"We're not going to need that. Hamilton always had the same key code back when we were partners. 107, it's his birthday." He pressed the metal studs on the door and the lock clicked open. Once inside, he hit the start engine button and had to feed the cruiser a little gas to keep it going. Once it did, it rumbled nicely. The cruiser didn't have a fancy electric motor driving the windows up and down. They had to be cranked down by hand, something that wasn't easy because the windows were an inch thick.

James was sitting on the curb checking his bloody teeth to see if any of them were loose. "Good luck with Hamilton. You're going to need it." Corrina waved as they pulled away. Cole had no idea where he was going to go. The police were still after him, which meant he couldn't just waltz into Krupp and start making demands to see their personnel files. It wouldn't be just their lawyers he would have to worry about. In no time Cole would be worked over by Krupp goons and when he was beaten to a pulp, they would call their police contacts.

If he survived, he'd have to face Sergeant Hamilton and his wrath. Just picturing it made him rethink stealing the police car. But only for a moment, then he gunned the engine and shot out of there with Corrina whooping it up next to him. As much as he wanted to blow past the 100-mph mark, there were still too many people on the streets.

He slowed, much to Corrina's disappointment. "What do you wanna do with it?" she asked. "I say we drive it off a bridge! That would be so cool."

It would be. He laughed, picturing Hamilton's face when they fished his ride from the East River. It would be fun, but wasteful. The squad car was too valuable to toss away just yet. The first thing he had to do was get it off the streets. There were too few cars running about and it stood out.

At the first sub-street entrance, he took a tunnel and headed south—towards Krupp. At first, he thought Krupp was the only way he would be able to find out who Mike McDonald was. Then he remembered Joanna Niederer. *Everyone has a record*, she had said.

"We're getting a motel room," he told Corrina. It was too late to try calling the Hall of Records. He would try in the morning. Until then, he knew a mid-priced subterranean motel nearby. For an extra dollar, they wouldn't ask about the squad car parked in their six-slot garage.

Next to him, Corrina looked torn. "It's been fun an' all, but maybe it's time I bugged out." He let out a sigh but before he could say anything, she said, "I know you don't really want me around. And that's fine because you know what? You're all up in my works, too. I know you gots money now. So…how 'bout you pay me and we'll call it quits."

"There are other orphanages."

She crossed her arms over the nubs of her breasts. "And I don't want to go to them. They ain't right for me and you know it."

"Fuuuck," he grumbled, turning into the low, cramped tunnel that led to the motel. The squad car barely fit. "You're a pain, you know that? I'm trying to do the right thing by you."

"You know what I learned from all this? Sometimes there isn't a right thing. When a priest screws you over, that tells you something. Maybe it's telling you to give up."

The garage held only one ugly little Brooklyn Grump. The Grump had a two-piston engine that sounded like a plunger going up and down, fop, fop, fop. He tore his eyes from it and regarded the girl in red, realizing that he didn't want her to go, as much for his sake as for hers. She was a twelve-year-old mule-kicked whore and was pretty much the only person Cole trusted.

"I can't give up," he told her. It wasn't just the money. Dead-eyes were dangerous. One could become twenty in a blink, and twenty could be a thousand in a week. It was the law that every baby born was inoculated with the semi-vax at birth, but there were hundreds of illegal babies born every year. And the semi-vax was named that for a reason. It gave a person only partial protection. Cole had a duty that he couldn't set aside when things got tough.

"I can," Corrina said. "Sometimes you gotta know when it's time to run. We're gonna get hooked for sure if you keep this car."

"Maybe, maybe not. There are thousands of little crannies like this beneath the streets and they can't look in them all. We'll be safe tonight. And I might need you tomorrow. It'll be another buck."

Her lips pursed. "What good's a buck I can't spend? If you get hooked, they'll take your money and then where will I be?"

"You'll be no worse off than when I met you. Now, stop your whining. How many money-honeys your age ever made sixteen dollars in three days? None." He really didn't know if this was true, but he certainly hoped it was.

The counter man didn't know what to make of the two of them. The big mean-looking Bulldog jutting from Cole's leather belt didn't go with the expensive suit any more than the little slag whore did. He could tell by the look in Cole's eyes that it was best not to ask questions. Cole plunked down seventy-five cents for the room and a dollar for the counterman not to notice the police cruiser.

Thankfully, there was a room with two beds and Cole was able to stretch out without worry, wearing only his new satin boxers. His suit was hung up, his Bulldog was under his pillow and his cash was stuffed far under his mattress, out of reach of Corrina's short arms. He trusted her with his life, not with his money.

In the morning he woke and was happily surprised to see Corrina was still there. She was a green-headed lump asleep in a mound of blankets. "Hey, Corrina, let's move. We have to make a phone call and then we'll get some breakfast. You like eggs?"

She pushed herself up. "Real eggs? Or the powdered ones?"

"Real ones. First, the phone call." He had a new plan when it came to calling the Hall of Records. He would cut through some of the union slowness by impersonating the Deputy Governor of Interior Services. His was a catch-all position that oversaw those city functions that fell outside the purview of the larger positions such as Judicial Services, Infrastructure, and Revenue.

Normally, it would be the death of his career for Cole to try something so crazy, but he was beginning to think he wasn't going to have much of a career left if he didn't bring in a Dead-eye soon…and maybe not even then.

Leaving the squad car, he and Corrina went topside and found a phone. While she kept watch, he dialed the number to the Hall of Records. "Director Niederer please, this is Wendle Holmes, assistant to the Deputy Governor of Interior Services."

The sleepy voice on the other end of the line perked up. "Just a moment."

There was a click and a buzz, followed by half a minute of dead air, then Jo came on. She was too old to get worked up when a deputy governor was on the line. "What do you want, Phil?"

"Sorry, Jo. This is Cole Younger. I need your help. Can you call…"

"You have a lot of nerve, Cole. And no, I won't call you back. All the lines on this floor are being monitored twenty-four seven. Thanks to you."

As angry as she was, she left a lot of dead air after her sentence. It was practically an invitation for him to speak.

And why had she told him about all the phone lines on the floor being monitored? Although her voice was filled with emotion, she wasn't as mad as she was letting on. She was afraid.

"Listen Jo, I'm on the job, so it's okay. We're talking about *special*, specials, do you understand? I need to find out everything I can about a fellow named Mire or Mike McDonald. He works at the Kr…"

"I'm sorry, Cole I can't. Don't call me anymore."

She hung up, leaving Cole standing in the bright light of day, staring at the phone in his hand. "Fuuuck," he muttered, thinking he had completely misjudged Jo. He hung up and gazed around him at the city. It looked strangely bright. A glance up showed him that the cloudless black sky from the night before had become a brilliant cloudless morning.

Between the black fumes spewing from a thousand smokestacks in Brooklyn and the brown haze that permanently shimmered over New Jersey, the sky was a beautiful robin's egg blue. Cole sneered at it before hanging up the phone.

"Now what?" McDonald was his only lead. Without him, Cole was lost. There was a chance that there was some information on him at Krupp. He had been a driver and from Cole's brief talk with the in-processing Tier 3 man, drivers were not chosen quite so randomly as the rest of the rabble.

"Can I get access to his files the same way as I did before?" Unlikely. It had been only a day and because of his size, he had a tendency to stand out. He needed a new plan. One that would let him get in deep…and then out again, if he could.

An idea was swishing around in his mind when the phone rang, making him jump. "Hello?" he asked cautiously.

"Cole? This is Jo. Something's not right in any of this."

"How so?"

"There are four-hundred and twenty live files with the name of either Mire or Mike McDonald. There's one missing. It was pulled sometime last night. I think I know the culprit on my end, but even if I catch her, it's not going to help you much. Sorry."

He almost muttered his trademark curse, but he didn't think it was proper to curse in front of someone's grandmother. "Thanks for trying."

"You're welcome. You probably shouldn't call here anymore. It's too dangerous for both of us."

"Yeah." They both said quiet goodbyes and hung up.

Cole walked slowly back to where he had left Corrina. "More bad news?" she asked and then quickly answered her own question. "Of course it's more bad news. With you there's only one sort of news; bad. The only question is how bad? Do I still get breakfast?"

He grunted a yes, and she smiled, showing off her gapped teeth. "Then it can't be that bad." She wanted to go back uptown and eat at a vamp place, and he didn't blame her. Common sense prevailed over their rumbling bellies. Hamilton's squad car was too conspicuous and couldn't be used to zip about for fun. That didn't mean it couldn't be driven at all. In fact, as Cole worked his way through three eggs, two patties of donkey sausage and Georgian bread, he mulled over the uses of the car.

His hazel eyes were almost blue in the light of the day. They were far off and picturing the garage beneath the Krupp factory. Security was tight with outbound vehicles, but inbound vans had been waved inside without an issue. "The car just might get me inside Krupp and maybe out again, too."

"You gonna ram your way in?" Corrina asked. She had jelly at the corners of her mouth that she couldn't reach with her tongue, despite her best efforts.

"Use your napkin. And no, I'm not going to ram my way in. I'm going to pull a Trojan Horse on them."

Her eyes got big. "Is that like Rican mule?"

"No, it's better."

Chapter 18

"This is gonna cost you two dollars, Cole," Corrina said from the passenger seat of the squad car as it careened through traffic with its lights going. A block ahead of them was a Krupp van, tooling along, oblivious to the silent cruiser. "How much will that be?"

"Seventeen dollars. Hold on!" The car's tires screeched as a bicyclist darted out in front of them. "Moron!" Cole yelled at him. "What is it with everyone today? They're all staring up as if this is the first time they've seen a blue sky."

Corrina had her feet braced on the dash. She canted her head to look up. "I think it's awful pretty." The one glance was all she gave it, then she was back to business. "Seventeen dollars? Are you sure? I thought it would be more."

"How would you know? You can't even count that high. And listen up, you only get the money if you stay put. Yes, thank God. He's pulling over. I need you to get down low. If he sees you, the jig will be up." The driver of the van was Puerto Rican and like most Puerto Ricans these days, he had lost his natural tan. He was sallow and sweating. Cole got on the speaker. "Turn into the alley."

The Rican's face was visible in his side mirror and Cole saw him mouth the words, *Mother Fucker*. He figured he was about to be shaken down by the taxmen, but when he saw Cole he went from frightened to angry. When he saw the honking big Bulldog that Cole carried, he went back to being afraid. Cole marched him back to the squad car and had him strip out of his brown coveralls at gunpoint.

Cole not only took the man's clothes and his ride, he also left him handcuffed in the backseat of the cruiser with Corrina watching over him, the Bulldog held in both hands.

The one-size fits all overalls were even tighter than usual as Cole put them on over a set of white overalls that he had picked up an hour before at a nearby pawnshop.

"Don't talk to her," he warned the driver. "She gets a nickel for every word you utter and you get a punch in the face."

Cole left in the van, glancing down at his number a couple of times to make sure he had it memorized. The van was a rattletrap and had a bad shimmy in the right front wheel. Being a part time Christian, Cole prayed that the "piece of crap" would hold together long enough to get him to the Krupp factory.

It stayed in one piece and Cole followed another van down into the garage, where he passed through security with barely a glance. Once inside, he watched the van in front of him closely. A runner took something from the driver, who then turned his van, following arrows that led toward another tunnel.

Once he moved, Cole slid the van up to take his place. When another runner came up, Cole handed over the entire clipboard that sat on the console.

"Huh?" the runner asked, holding the clipboard sideways. "Is this the receiving form? It's all I'm supposed to get."

"Right, sorry." Cole glanced through the papers and found one marked "Receiving." He gave it over and the man brightened. Cole quickly followed after the first van and was in time to see it being unloaded by a platoon of slags. The van left through the only exit. As it did, Cole pulled up to a yellow line and watched as the same platoon hauled away a ton of metal, tossing it down into an immense pit. It was hundreds of feet deep and about half that wide. It was half filled with metal and trash; a strange heat was shimmering up from it.

"The infinity pit," a Tier 2 in blue overalls said. "You new?"

"Yeah. Just got the job. Is that heat…what is that coming from the pit? Is it on fire?"

The Tier 2 laughed. "Yeah. Has been for years. It's deep down. They say it's the pressure and the constant grinding. I think it's the oil. They throw the engines in whole and all that oil drains down of course. The heat and the fumes really mess up the slags, the poor fucks. You know where you're going? Right down the passage. Take the first right and follow it to where you turn in your ride. It's right where you picked it up."

Cole thanked him and puttered away, going slowly. This is where things would get dicey. He didn't look Puerto Rican. He didn't look like someone named Alvarez. It wasn't good that the Tier 2 guy had noticed right away that he was new. Certainly the dispatchers would notice the same thing, and if any of them questioned Cole for over a minute, they would realize that he was a fake.

His solution was a poor one. He stopped the van in the middle of the tunnel, popped the hood. If asked, he would say that the van conked out and to that end, he took a look under the hood and gazed in at an engine that was constructed of an aluminum alloy and duct-tape. The Krupp mechanics were clearly some of the best. By improvising parts and jury-rigging every which way, they had managed to keep the van going a decade or two longer than possible.

"Sorry," Cole muttered and pulled at a hose and some worn wire that had once been attached to a lamp.

He then turned and stuffed his hands down into his mostly filled pockets to hide the fact they bulged. On his first trip to Krupp, he had noticed that no one had pockets that bulged. Certainly no one else was smuggling in neuro-tech grenades.

Sixty yards on, the tunnel opened into an immense gallery. The incoming trucks and vans were parked in front of him and were being inspected by Tier 3 men with a few slags in brown overalls nearby to run errands and lift anything that might need to be lifted. Once the vans were inspected they went to be filled up and then were sent through a heavily guarded bay. Krupp didn't want even an ounce of metal smuggled from their factory.

Cole was noticed right away by a frowning Tier 3. "Uhh, where the bathrooms at?" Cole asked, doing his best slag imitation.

"You damn right better use the damned bathroom," the Tier 3 snapped. "I'll dock the pay of the next one of you fucks who pees on the damn wall. Just because it's rock don't mean it's free game." He jerked a thumb over his shoulder at a building that was set into the carved-out bay. "The bathrooms are that way."

The building was bustling with dozens of secretaries trying to type with telephones nestled up to their necks, drivers sitting in a corner picking their teeth, runners dashing here and there, and upper management frowning at everything. The bathroom was only steps away from a door marked "Exit." There was a sign out sheet for the bathroom. Cole bent over it long enough to take the sheet and fold in half.

Pretending he was a runner, he held the paper in front of him and hurried importantly through the exit and didn't look back.

As before, there were Tier 2 men scattered about the giant factory whose job it was to point the slags in the right direction. "Human Resources?" Cole asked the first one he found.

"Third floor section QQ. That's two Qs not one." Helpfully, he held up two fingers. "Do you know what a Q is? It's sort of a circle with a daffle hanging off the bottom."

"A daffle?"

"Yes, a daffle," he said with perfect sincerity. "You would think it would be called a tail, but it's in front and since you can't call it a dick, it's a daffle."

Cole wondered if the slag was getting to the man. Regardless, he thanked him and then jogged off, looking for a bathroom, hoping they would be different than the ones on the upper floors. The one he had used the day before had been a one-room affair with two lines of toilets facing each other with so little room between them that men knocked knees when they sat down. Unfortunately the bathroom here was the same. Cole couldn't go from being a slag to a Tier 4 in front of witnesses.

Out of desperation, Cole tried various unmarked doors until he found a little closet that held only a sink, a mop bucket, a few rags on a shelf and three push-brooms. Cole ducked into it and stripped off the outer overalls to expose the white ones beneath. When he came out of the closet, he marched importantly, glaring at anyone who glanced his way. This was how all the Tier 4s acted. They even glared at each other.

The further down the hall Cole walked, the more Tier 4s he saw. It seemed there were one per office and they clearly disliked any other Tier 4 getting close to their territory.

The human resources department was broken into about twenty subsections and these were scattered up and down a wide hall that was, unlike so much of the factory, more than just functional. The floors were real granite tile and on the white walls were paintings in pastels, and actual color pictures. Cole barely noticed any of it. He was too preoccupied trying to figure out how he was going to get the records he needed. He doubted that he'd be able to bluff the Tier 4 in charge.

"What I need is a runner to fetch it for me." This represented an entirely new problem. A bribe wasn't going to work this time. Tier 4s didn't need to bribe anyone and even the suggestion would raise eyebrows. Charming some secretary was also out of the question. So far, Cole hadn't seen a single one of the Tier 4s exude even a whiff of charm. Their factory settings consisted solely of angry impatience.

"When in Rome, I guess," he muttered, watching the people moving about the hall. There weren't many and they didn't dawdle. Everyone hurried as if they were being timed going from one office to another. Cole was just about the only one who didn't. He stopped frequently to tie and re-tie his shoes, waiting for a Tier 4 to leave his office.

The first to do so was a baggy-eyed Mandarin with a ball of a belly that plumped out the front of his white overalls. Cole waited until he had turned a corner before he hurried into the man's office. It was an open area filled with an even dozen desks. Half belonged to Tier 3 men, who were on phones talking quietly, the other half were for their secretaries who typed with a steady clacking so that it sounded as if it were raining small marbles in the room.

In front of all of this was a receptionist's desk where a tiny, timid Mandarin lady with frightened eyes sat.

"Whose office is this?" Cole demanded, sharply.

"Mr. Matu, sir. This is Foreign Sales; Texas Department."

"Good. Let me talk to him. We have a meeting."

The frightened look grew into a panicked one. If Mr. Matu missed a meeting it would be on her head. "I'm sorry, sir but he just stepped out. I can run and get him for you." She was half out of her seat before Cole stopped her.

"No. That won't be necessary. I'll wait." Cole acted put out, drumming his fingers on the woman's desk as he stared hard at the top of her head. She wouldn't look up. He counted to thirty before speaking again. "You know what you could do for me. You could call up a runner and get me a request form. I need a file from records."

Although what he was asking was unheard of, she didn't hesitate to pick up the phone. The runner arrived seconds after he had filled out the form, signing it with a scribble in imitation of another form on the receptionist's desk. Once the runner had sped the form away it became a waiting game. Who would return first? Mr. Matu or the runner?

Cole's string of bad luck continued.

Mr. Matu walked in, stopped a foot from Cole and stared up at him with deep suspicion in his dark eyes. "What is this? Is Mr. Wren timing my bathroom breaks again? Huh? Is that it? Well, I signed out at exactly a quarter of two. Tell him that. And tell him it's not even two, now."

The level of micro-managing was shocking to Cole. Still, it was as good a cover as anything he could think of. "Mr. Wren follows the rules and expects the same of his subordinates. He's happy that you were able to confine yourself to the appropriate time. He's happy…for now."

Seeing Mr. Matu as nervous as his secretary was the only thing about the exchange that smacked of victory for Cole. Now his only chance to get the file was to waylay the runner and either bribe, threaten or charm him into doing something that would get the man fired. To do this, Cole had to loiter in a sparsely populated hallway where the chances of getting caught grew with every second.

This was especially true as a pair of black-garbed guards came sauntering down the hall. Although they acted like they were just making their rounds, Cole noticed how their eyes flicked about, scanning the faces of everyone they passed. Without a thought, Cole spun on his heel and headed back the other way only to see two more guards moving in.

Cole figured they'd be looking for a Tier 4 and so he walked straight away to the closet he had changed in earlier. He acted like it was the executive lounge as he walked in. A second later as he was tearing off the white overalls he accidentally dropped one of the neuro-tech gas grenades he had smuggled into the building. It landed with a clank. Cole froze, staring at it, knowing that if it exploded right there in the closet he'd be a dead man in seconds.

After a count of ten, he realized that the grenade wasn't going to explode and he quickly finished changing back into a Tier 1 nobody. The two grenades went back into his pocket before he cracked the door and stared out. His timing was spot on because he saw a runner with a file clutched in both hands approaching Mr. Matu's office. He was oblivious to the guards—there were six of them now. There were so many that Cole almost missed a slim young woman in an off-white pantsuit following after them.

It was the brunette Dead-eye who had ambushed him at Santino's apartment. "Jesus," he whispered, suddenly feeling very small and very alone. "She works here? With McDonald?" His mind was so spun that he watched what happened next as if detached from the situation.

She and the guards closed in on the runner but did not stop him from entering Mr. Matu's office. The guards surrounded him so closely that he couldn't move except to open the door and go through. The slag was so frightened that his hand shook as he reached for the doorknob and he opened the door with his shoulders hunched as if expecting something terrible to happen—and something did. The second the door came open, the guards charged over him, sending him sprawling on the tile.

Two of them grabbed Mr. Matu and threw him on the ground, while the other four fanned out with guns drawn. The last to enter was the brunette, who paused long enough to take the file from the runner's hand. He scurried away as she stepped into the room.

"Mr. Matu, we have a lot to talk about." She was about ten seconds away from finding out that Mr. Matu had nothing to do with the file. Then Cole would be on the run for his life empty-handed

"If I'm gonna run, it's not going to be empty handed." Cole grabbed one of the rags from the shelf, splashed water on it and then hurried from the closet, pulling out one of the Neuro grenades. "Look out," he said to the runner, yanking him from the doorway. Then, even as the Dead-eye turned at the sound of his voice, Cole twisted the top the grenade, tossed it inside and slammed the door shut.

There was a *Foomp!* sound from within. The grenade had gone off. In a small office, the effects would be close to instantaneous. Still, Cole counted to eight as he wrapped his face with the wet cloth. Taking a deep breath, he opened the door and saw that the gas had done its job on nineteen of the twenty individuals in the room. Only the Dead-eye was still standing and then, only barely.

Cole launched his bulk in a flying front kick that struck her square in the chest with bone-crushing force that sent her flying back into the denser clouds. The file had dropped from her numb fingers. He snatched it up and darted outside, throwing aside the damp rag and hurrying away from the office. There was a small crowd that gave way before both him and the gentle smoke coming from the doorway.

No one seemed to know what had happened and for a few seconds Cole thought that he might be able to get away. Then the Dead-eye lurched from the office. She shouldn't have been able to move. She should've been lying in a twitching heap like Mr. Matu and his secretary and all the others.

Instead she was charging down the hall smashing into men twice her size and knocking them to the ground without slowing. Nothing would slow her except for a bullet to the head—and Cole had left his gun with a twelve-year-old whore. He could do nothing but turn and run for his life.

Chapter 19

Cole ran for the stairs, the hall magically filling up in front of him. For the last half hour or so, the hall had been practically empty. Now, just when he needed room to run, there was a surge of people.

It was the last shift to take a lunch break and as the workers were docked pay if they came back even a minute late, no one straggled from their offices. But they weren't running either. Cole had to dart among them. The Dead-eye was far less delicate. She was a "human" wrecking ball. By sheer strength, she cleared a path to the stairs.

From there things slowed for her. Knocking people down stairs created a chain reaction and soon three flights of stairs were filled with screaming undulating bodies. The Dead-eye had no qualms about using the bodies as a carpet to walk across and had her limbs been functioning, she would have tap danced across thirty faces to get at Cole. Instead she fell over the first person, wriggled free and fell again.

Cole was pushy enough to get to the front of the little parade and went flying down the stairs, taking them five at a time. He had no idea where he was going. He knew of only two exits and he wouldn't be able to stroll out of either of them, not while he was wearing company overalls. The guards would stop him and make him go back and change, which would've been fine if he had five extra minutes and something to change into. The Puerto Rican he had stolen the overalls from had worn them with the ankles and wrists rolled well up.

What he needed was a distraction. If the building had a fire alarm system he would have pulled it, but the only alarms in the Krupp facility were on the floors with the blast furnaces. Upper management didn't want the other workers in the building interrupted by alarms about fires that *probably* wouldn't affect them.

This left Cole needing to create a distraction and he had just the thing in the form of his second neuro-toxin grenade.

Passing the door leading to the first floor, he kept going down until he came to the garage level. "Loader or picker?" the same Tier 2 from the day before asked him.

Cole held up the file. "Runner," he told the man and then jogged toward the vehicle receiving building he had been in earlier. "Runner," he announced to the Tier 3 man. "I got lost."

"I don't want to hear about it, you dumb fuck," the man answered.

"You're the dumb fuck," Cole snarled as he reached the top of the stairs. Behind him, the Tier 3 man began to blabber incoherent insults as he charged after Cole. When he entered the room, his foot kicked the grenade just as it went off. The room was filled in two seconds, about the time it took for Cole to make it into the stairwell. He could feel the burning toxin on his scalp and the tips of his ears. Behind him there was mayhem. The Tier 3 man had fallen unconscious in the doorway and everyone in the bay area thought a real bomb had gone off.

Security flooded the level but by then, Cole was on the first floor, the file stuffed down the front of his overalls. As he hurried for the main exit, he dug out three dollars and looked for anyone that was close to his height. There were a few.

"I'll give you two dollars for the clothes in your locker," he asked the first of them. "It's an emergency," he added when the man hesitated.

There was slag rot across his neck, but he was still bright enough to haggle. "Two-fitty."

"Give me your locker key right this second and I'll make it three."

"Done!"

The exchange was made and then Cole was racing for the exit. A Tier 2 at the locker room door started to ask a question, but Cole beat him to it. "It's an emergency! My wife's dying." This got him into the locker room, where he tore off the overalls in seconds and opened the locker. The smell hit him like a punch. He had paid three dollars for clothes the slag had taken from a gutter corpse a few days back.

As Cole fake-limped towards the exit he struggled to keep from vomiting.

"I was told to go home," he said to the Tier 3. For the moment the exit hall was quiet, no hint of an emergency in the air. During busy times there were twelve or more lines to process the slags, but just then there were only three and not even a dozen guards.

"I don't have all the latest break reports," the Tier 3 told Cole. The man's upper lip was curled from the waves of stink coming off Cole. "Where were you working?"

Cole looked back over his shoulder, saying, "Ummm, uh, I. There was moving stuff."

"You don't know? Let's have your pin number then."

This was taking too long. "I lost it."

"Then I can't out-process you. So, go back and figure out what it was and then come back with…"

"Can't I just go home?"

The Tier 3 had no problem with that and leaned back from his desk and made a sweeping gesture toward the large doors that led out to the street. "We ain't a sweat shop here. You can go anytime. You can also wash your clothes anytime. Maybe do that when you get home."

Cole had to bite his tongue to keep from telling the man to fuck off. It was, more or less an ingrained response, but he needed to get out of there as fast as he could. He only offered a grunt and started limping toward the exit, stopping only to get wanded by a bored security guard.

He was all of ten steps from the doors when he heard a shout from behind. "Seal the doors!" It was a woman's screech and he didn't have to look back to know that his distraction down in the garage hadn't been as successful as he had hoped. He took off running, sprinting through the doors before the guards really understood what was going on. One yelled at him to stop, which Cole had no intention of doing. They would have to shoot him to get him to stop. It was an unpleasant possibility that he reduced by darting out into traffic, crossing the street in front of a cabby, who wasn't about to brake for a slag. He jerked his car to the right, while cursing Cole.

A bike swerved to avoid the cab and hit Cole, sending them both crashing to the street. Cole had no idea if he was hurt. His leg could have been broken in two places for all he knew or cared. When guns were pointed your way and a Dead-eye was hot after you, a bike crash was no more significant than a sneeze.

From the ground he saw the woman smashing through the guards, almost all of whom had no idea what they were supposed to be doing. Those who had tried to grab the Dead-eye were quick to regret it. She was stronger than any two of them put together and in a blink of an eye, men were on the ground screaming in pain.

The guards closest to the doors tried to slam it shut in her face. The doors were tall with ornate metal scrolling, but they were also functional. Each was four inches thick and weighed half a ton. They were almost shut when she slammed her shoulder into one with the force of a truck, sending three guards flying back.

By then Cole was up and sprinting for the squad car he had left in an alley a few blocks away. Even with a fifty-yard head start, he didn't think he'd make it. She was just too fast!

She was so focused on her prey that she didn't see the second cab until it was almost too late. Once more, the cabby didn't slow. Like the other one, it tried to dart around the crazy woman, but her speed was too great and he hit her. At the last second she realized her danger and leaped so that her right hip and thigh struck the windshield. The impact spun and twisted her in the air, sending a shoe whipping away.

She landed on the pavement with a slap that went unheard beneath the sound of screeching tires. Unbelievably she was up again in two seconds. Her partially shoeless state slowed her down some and Cole increased his lead…at first. A two-hundred yard race was hard on a human; it was nothing for a Dead-eye. They did not tire and they did not feel pain. All they knew was rage and endless hunger.

When Cole looked back, he saw the woman eating into his lead. "Corrina!" he screamed. "Start the engine!" He could see the squad car right where he had left it. Corrina was in the driver's seat turned partially around, talking to the hostage. When she heard Cole's scream, she looked back and couldn't understand the fear in his voice. He was running from a girl.

"Start the engine!" he yelled again.

"Maybe she has a gun," the Puerto Rican suggested. He had been slowly working on the girl, who had talked nearly nonstop from the moment Cole had left. He had been trying to get her on his side of things but hadn't made much headway, and with Cole returning he had to change tactics. "You better do what he says. Just turn the key to the right. No, the other way. Now give it gas."

Corrina looked down at the pedals. "Which one's the gas?"

"On the right," the Rican said, his voice going higher. It wasn't the man that was making him nervous. It was the woman. One of her eyes was normal: it had a white outer part and a blue inner. The other eye was all black. And the blood coming from a cut on her arm was black, too. And the way she ran—there was something animalistic about it; it was as if she was part hyena.

The engine gave a howl of rage as Corrina held her foot down. "What's wrong with her?" she asked the Puerto Rican. She could just see over the wheel.

He didn't want to know. There were more diseases going around than he could count. All he knew was that his gut told him they had to get away. "Open the door and slide over!" he yelled.

Corrina pushed the door open just as Cole ran up, sweat in his hair, his breath ragged in his throat. She tried to get back over to the passenger side, but he was suddenly on top of her, trying to shut the door while entwined in a tangle of arms and legs.

"Where's the gun?" Cole yelled just before the woman leapt full on the hood of the squad car.

Corrina saw her plain as day, that one black eye wet and glistening like some sort of insect eye. The girl was paralyzed with fright by the eye. It held her spellbound and she could only watch as the woman pulled a fist back and then punched the heavy bullet resistant glass with a fantastic *CRACK!* The glass starred so that she became a blur. A second later she punched again, and this time the sound was more of a crunch. The windshield sagged inward with the blow.

Cole yanked the gear into reverse and stamped the gas, throwing everyone forward and almost causing the Dead-eye to lose her one-handed grip. The squad car raced backward down the alley, smashing into mounds of garbage and sending rats squealing out of the way. It jittered and shuddered over potholes and splashed through puddles of city muck a foot deep.

Once again, the Dead-eye smashed the glass and this time her fist came through. "Holy fuck!" the Krupp driver screamed from the back seat, pointing past Cole at the hideous creature.

Cole, who was half-turned back in his seat so that he could see where he was going, knew there was no need to ask what he was screaming about; he could feel the woman's nails trying to get a hold of the slag's shirt he was wearing.

Just as she got her fingers bunched in the material, two things happened almost at once. They emerged from an alley and Cole heaved the wheel over just as fast and hard as he could. A split second later, just as the centrifugal force started to send the Dead-eye flying out and away from the car, Corrina fired the Bulldog.

She had dropped it in the mad scramble to get to the passenger seat seconds earlier, and as they were driving backwards, she and it kept bouncing around. When she finally grabbed it and pulled the trigger, it felt like the gun exploded in her hands. The shock of it ran stingers through her palms and up her arms. The gun jumped on its own as well and banged hard off her forehead.

The explosion was so huge that it seemed to blast away the woman and when she went flying, she took the entire windshield with her.

The squad car spun halfway around and came to a rocking stop in the middle of the street, smoke drifting up from its tires.

"Did you hit it?" Cole asked, staring at the woman lying in the middle of thousands of small cubes of glass.

Corrina looked up from her hands, which were somehow both numb and throbbing. "Yeah, yeah, I think so." It would've been hard to miss as she pulled the trigger from all of a foot away. And yet the woman was already starting to struggle to her feet. "Holy fuck," Corrina whispered. "How is she still alive?"

Cole went to reach for the gun, but Corrina had dropped it. He had to climb over the center console to get it but just as his fingers found the grip, a police siren ripped the air. It was close, maybe all of a block away. The Dead-eye took off running back the way she had come. She was going back to the Krupp factory where a hundred cops wouldn't be able to find her.

"We gotta get out of here," he said, yanking the car into drive and peeling out of there, his horn blaring. Pedestrians dove out of the way as he sped up the block and took the first turn he came to.

"She stood up, Cole," Corrina said, her face slack as if what she had seen had been the equivalent of a punch. "I-I shot her and she got hit by a car and…How? How did she do all that?"

"Drugs," Cole lied as he veered through traffic, heading east with no real destination in mind. His head was spinning nearly as much as Corrina's. After five blocks, he pulled over and fished the handcuff keys from the console cupholder. "Put out your hands," he ordered the Puerto Rican. As he unlocked him, Cole warned, "I wouldn't say anything about this if I were you. If anyone asks, your van broke down in that tunnel after the infinity pit, and I don't know, tell them that you hit your head or something. If you talk about this, it won't be me you're going have to deal with. It's going to be that lady."

The man looked just as stunned as Corrina. "But her eye. Did you see her eye? Does…does she work at Krupp? Will she come after me?"

Cole sighed as he struggled out of the foul-smelling clothes. "First, I said don't talk about it. She doesn't know you exist. Here. Here's five bucks. Keep your mouth shut."

"He gets five bucks?" Corrina asked, her eyes regaining focus. "What the hell for? I'm the one that guarded him. And he talked, Cole. While you were gone, he talked a lot. Like ten. How much is that in nickels?"

"Fifty cents."

"Oh. Well, yeah, he talked more than that. He musta talked at least five dollars worth. So either get punchin' this guy or start paying me what you owe."

Cole was within a word of giving her a twenty and kicking her into the gutter—only he knew if he came back in a week, she'd be face down in that very same gutter, bloated and covered in flies. "He gets the fiver because I might have cost him his job. You have a job, Corrina, and you're going to get paid just as soon as I have time to think."

This quieted her. She remained silent in the hope he would get his thinking done and over with. Instead, he changed back into his fancy suit and drove off, leaving the Puerto Rican on the sidewalk in clothes that stank of shit and death.

They didn't drive far, only a few blocks, before he pulled over again and opened up the file. "Who is that?" Corrina asked, pointing at the picture stapled to the inside of the folder.

"His name is Mike McDonald." The picture had come from a driver's license. He looked like a normal person. Cole was pretty sure that he wasn't, not anymore. "Everyone seems to be after him and a girl named Christina. If we get her before that…" He had been about to say: *that Dead-eye.* "If we can find her before the others do, then we get paid."

"We?" Corrina asked. "I get paid, too, right? And more than just seventeen. I should get that five dollars, too. You took me from my job too, you know. How much is that? Seventeen and five more? Is it thirteen?" Thirteen was a number that just didn't fit anywhere in her mind.

"It's twenty-two. Look, why don't we make it an even fifty dollars? If you stick with me right to the end, I'll make sure you get paid too. Just stop nickel and diming me, okay?"

She knew what fifty dollars was. It was a *gob* of money. It was so much that she didn't think he'd ever pay it. He would dangle it over her head and make her jump through hoop after hoop. That's what he'd been doing so far—but he had given that Puerto Rican five dollars just for keeping quiet. *Shooting him woulda been loads cheaper*, she mused.

"I don't know. You're weird, Cole. And this is all really weird. And that lady...she was no lady, was she?"

"As far as you're concerned, she was," he answered, stiffly.

Corrina struck a defiant pose, crossing her arms and jutting her chin out. "No, not if that lady was what I think it was. Tell me the truth Cole, she was a zombie, right?" Simply nodding could lead to a death sentence. But did it matter? There were zombies running around the streets of New York in the bright light of day. The situation wasn't just getting out of hand, it was spiraling out of control.

Chapter 20

Had it been the Puerto Rican Krupp driver, or pretty much anyone else, Cole would have laughed the question off. With Corrina, it was another story. It wasn't fair to keep her in the dark over something that could very well get her killed. "I'm not allowed to say whether that was a zombie, or not. All I can say is that being with me is dangerous, but I promise I'll do everything I can to keep you safe."

Corrina's mouth suddenly filled with the copper taste of fear. It was true. The lady had been a zombie.

"That's, that's supposed to be impossible, isn't it?" She had heard a hundred stories about the grey plague that had swept over the earth a century and half before. In some stories, the zombies were practically unkillable. Supposedly only nukes or headshots with high-powered rifles had any chance of bringing them down. If you only nicked them, they would heal in a day.

And they were unstoppable when they were on the hunt. They ate human flesh, preferring the flavor of children and babies, and they drank only hot blood straight from the neck.

Everyone knew they still prowled the wastelands outside the cities. It's why it was illegal to cross the river to scavenge and it was why the Carolinas set off nukes every few years along "The 77." It was a stretch of blasted land that ran from Cleveland to Charleston, West Virginia. The sunsets afterward were spectacular to behold.

The idea that there were zombies in New York was too much for a slaggy honey. "Maybe we should tell someone," she suggested, feeling a sudden desire to get out of the car. *It* had touched the hood and maybe germs were crawling around like invisible bugs.

She was on the verge of getting out when he said, "We can't talk. If I say anything, I'll end up dead in a day. And if you say anything, no one will believe you. And if they did…you know what happened in Ottawa, right?"

Other than stories told in the dark, she knew next to nothing about history. "They got nuked right? A whole city was zapped because the zombies invaded. That's what I heard."

"That's partially true. Officially there were only fourteen of them, but in reality their numbers were around two-hundred. Still, it only took those fourteen to start a panic and look where it got them. The League of American States wiped the entire city off the map. And it'll happen here, too, that's why we can never say anything."

"How many of 'em are there here?"

Cole could only shrug. "A dozen or two, it's hard to say. They've gotten smart. They stay hidden and generally feed on stray slags and little honeys like you. It's one of the reasons I haven't given you your money and let you go. You would make a tasty treat for them." This was a lie meant to scare her straight. It was a thousand times more likely that she would get her throat slit by a deep-earth trog than eaten by a Dead-eye.

She put a hand to her throat; it had gone tight. "But…" Being a honey was all she knew how to do. She assumed she was good at it, though she really had nothing to compare her work to. Regardless, she would kill herself before she went back to one of the factories out in Brooklyn. That was a living death in itself. But, staying with Cole seemed impossible no matter what he promised. He could barely keep himself alive. In fact, he would be dead by now if it wasn't for her or in jail, or both.

And what did she get out of the deal? "Fifty dollars doesn't seem like enough," she finally said. "I'm taking almost as many risks as you. That…" She had been about to say zombie, but he gave her a warning look. "That thing almost killed me and it woulda killed you if I hadn't shot it." A shiver went up her spine as she pictured its face. It had been twisted by such pure hatred that it hadn't looked human.

"Fifty dollars is what I'm paying," Cole answered. "Plus food and lodging, and maybe some make-up." Fifty wasn't a lot, that was true, but she was just a kid. What he needed was real backup. Taking on a Dead-eye that knew you were coming was hard enough, but taking on one that was somehow part of Krupp Industries was something akin to insanity. For the hundredth time, or so it felt, he said to himself that if he had another choice he'd walk away.

Fifty seemed like a huge amount of money to Corrina, only, "I can't spend it if I'm dead. How much do I get if I walk away now?"

"Twenty-two. It's what I owe you." He considered for a moment and then dug out her money. "Maybe this is better. Maybe you should take it and go while you can."

Her hand shot out for the money before her mind kicked in. She stopped with her hand on the bills. "Hold on," she whispered to herself. "Can I see what fifty looks like?" He stacked a couple of tens, on a few fives and added all the ones he had left to the pile. In size it was much more striking than the twenty-two dollars. Her grey eyes shifted back and forth from the piles as she tried to come to a decision.

"You ever kill one of them?" she asked without looking up.

"Yeah, a few."

She pulled her hand away; it was shaking as she did. "Okay, I'm in. Fifty to help you. But with what exactly? I'm not quite sure what we're doing."

"Me neither," he admitted. He told her the entire story from start to finish and as he went on, she grew more confused.

"This blonde *person* that the guy in purple killed, was she working for Krupp, too?" Cole gave her a shrug. "Okay, was she trying to kill Santino or was it the other way around?" Cole really didn't know that either. "Jeeze, you don't know nothin'. What about the vamp? She buys you this fancy suit and dinner an' all just so you can find a maid who disappeared? That's weird. Why not let her stay disappeared?"

He didn't know the answer to that either. "You can never know what a vamp is thinking. They're not like us.

At least with a Dead-eye, you know what's going on in their head. It's almost all about feeding and hiding. Though some of them think they're still human. Those are the ones who are most obvious. They can only hold off killing their friends and families for so long, then it's chomp city."

There was a little cube of glass on the sleeve of her red jacket. She gave it a flick and remarked, "So after all we've gone through, you basically know nothing? And we're sitting in a stolen cop car in the middle of the day. Even I know that ain't smart."

He climbed out and gave it a look. There was black blood smeared across the hood. It was diseased, which meant he couldn't leave it sitting out for the locals to pick over. Hamilton's lighter was in the console, along with a pack of Texas Longs. He took both, lighting a cigarette before ripping off a length of the driver's seat cover. He fed one end into the gas tank and lit the other.

"Can I get a smoke?" Corrina asked as they walked down the alley.

"You smoke?"

She forced herself not to glance back, determined to be as unafraid of the coming explosion as Cole. "Oh yeah, all the time. My customers always light up when we're done. They're pretty free with the cigs at that point."

Cole had been about to hand her one, but the image of her skinny, naked body propped up next to some slob turned his stomach. "That's just gross. Tell me you're going to give that up once we..." Behind him the tank exploded with a windy *frump!*

Corrina's shoulders hunched and now she did look back. The squad car was half covered in flames already. "Maybe. We'll see. Now don't be chintzy with the cigs. We should split all the loot fifty-fifty. That means you give me half of everything you steal."

"I wouldn't call it stealing. It was, uh more like I was rescuing them from a fire. It would've been a waste." She wasn't buying the argument and held out her hand until he portioned out five apiece. They strolled along, smoking and not saying much of anything. When they passed an Italian joint with twenty-cent bowls of pasta, Corrina's stomach rumbled. He didn't need to ask if she was hungry.

It was twenty-cents for ten ounces and although the greasy slick behind the counter usually thumbed the scale, he decided against it and not because Cole was a big man with scabbed-over knuckles. Beneath the counter the slick had a scattergun, and behind a curtain that led to a backroom was his brother, sleeping on an old, stained mattress. His brother was a big man, too and liked nothing more than mixing it up.

No, the slick, who was literally greasy with synthetic olive oil from the lunch rush, kept his thumb off the scale because he didn't like the look of Cole's suit. It was clearly expensive which meant he was connected to someone high up the food chain. Guys like that could make trouble with a snap of their fingers. Of course, the girl with him didn't make any sense, unless he was one of those pervs who got off on the kiddies. *Which is none of my business*, the slick thought. "You like. You tell everyone Paulo's is nice, okay?" he said, giving Cole a friendly grin that was as greasy as the rest of him.

"Sure thing, pal." Cole could have done without seeing the days-old spinach in the man's teeth. As always, he chose a seat where he could see the door, and as Corrina began sucking up strand after strand of spaghetti through her puckered lips, he looked into the file on Michael McDonald. There was little to it.

"It says he was a Tier 2 last year and only just became a driver a few months ago. These papers are testimonials from some of his coworkers, this is his Tier 2 test, and his driver's license."

Corrina glanced from her bowl long enough to frown at the papers. "That's it? Does it say anything about him trying to eat anyone?" He grunted a "no" through a mouthful of spaghetti, causing her frown to deepen. "Then what fuckin' good is this? We almost died for nothing."

"Hey! Enough with the cursing. And it isn't all bad. We have an address. Maybe we'll get lucky and he'll be there snoozing."

She snorted at this. By now she was beginning to understand that luck wasn't exactly Cole's strong suit. He made up for it by making sure she was well fed. He didn't blink an eye when she asked for seconds, and she was practically bursting at the seams when she finally pushed the bowl away.

"So we get paid if you get any of *them*? Then why don't we go back to Krupp?" she asked as they headed back out to the street where the day was still bright enough that she had her eyes squinched up. Normally, the air in New York was something that a person struggled to peer through like a neglected fish tank.

"I wish it was that easy. You saw the size of that place. It takes up seven or eight blocks all by itself. There's probably a million places in there she could hide. And I can't officially go in when we got the cops on our ass. And even then…" A shiver ran up his back. Going in without backup and only a six shot revolver would be suicide. "I need a proper gun," he decided.

Six shots, no matter how powerful the round, wasn't going to cut it, not against the thing at Krupp and maybe not even against McDonald. If he was part of a nest, things would get hairy in a hurry. "We gotta make a pitstop," he told her and stuck his hand out.

A two-dollar cab ride got them to the gun shop in midtown where Cole had bought his beloved Crown two years before. Back then it had cost him five large; half the bounty he'd picked up for killing a boy no older than Corrina. The kid had been a Dead-eye and had eaten both his parents, which hadn't made it any easier.

When Corrina got out of the cab and looked through the bars that lay across the thick windows of the building and saw the display guns propped up, her eyes bounced wide open. She began tugging at his sleeve, excitedly. "Can I get a gun, too? You said you wanted to keep me safe. A gun'll do the trick, don'tcha think? Oh man, that would be cool." She put her hands together forming a pistol with her fingers. "Pow! Pow! Got ya, sucka!"

"Stop that," Cole muttered, taking her by the arm and leading her into the antechamber where he had to surrender his Bulldog before being allowed inside the store. "Try to be cool or you'll get us kicked out. Don't say anything and definitely don't touch anything."

The owner was ironically named Tom Storck; not only was he short, barely coming to Cole's shoulder, he was also extremely round through the belly and had become more so every time Cole came in. He was now at the point where Cole had to wonder how he undid his own zipper. Though maybe he didn't have to do it himself; clearly his business was growing even faster than his waistline. The watch on his wrist had been silver the last time Cole had come in. Now it was gold.

He was waiting on a man in a grey suit who stood bent at the waist, three feet from the glass, as if afraid to get any closer. Clutched to his chest was a bowler hat, the brim of which was wilting from sweat.

"Ah, look who it is. Mister 59 Crown High Crest," Storck said, recognizing Cole right off, and waddling away from his first customer. "Don't ask how I got it, but I have the 62 Prototype stashed away in the vault. It looks like you can afford it. I like the Fedora. It's a classic. I have... two myself." He had just seen Corrina and his words faltered.

Storck knew trouble when he saw it, and the honey was trouble. And now that he got a better look at Cole, he saw the bruises and the scabs. And where was the very slight underarm bulge where proper discerning bounty hunters carried their Crowns?

"Did you pawn it?" Storck asked, aghast at the idea.

Cole couldn't meet his eyes. "Worse."

"No! Lost or stolen?"

"Lost in battle," he said. He was not about to mention that he had lost it in a fight with a hundred pound woman. "I'm afraid that I'm not going to be able to replace it just yet. What do you have in the four hundred dollar range that's comparable?"

Storck let out a sarcastic laugh. "Nothing! Nothing's even close. You know what sort of hurdles I have to jump just to keep this inventory available, and you want me to peddle cheap knock-offs? No! I only sell the best. For four hundred, I can show you an array of .38s. The *Lady Eagle* is not bad for the money."

"A *Lady Eagle* sounds cool," Corrina exclaimed, starting towards the glass case on the right. Cole snatched her back.

"No," Cole said. "Sorry. I'm going to need something *more*. Six shots isn't going to cut it."

Storck sighed. It was a sad sound that came from deep within his great girth. "There's always Bingo Max's on Canal, *if* you don't mind taking a chance on your gun blowing up in your face."

"What about for six hundred?"

He puffed out his already round cheeks and blew out a breath that smelled strongly of mint. "Cole, Cole, Cole. I don't think I have what you're looking for. Maybe I can knock a few dollars off a Maltese. Here, take a look. That is real nickel my friend."

Cole tried to hide his disappointment. The Maltese was a very shiny, very pretty gun, but it fired an underpowered 9mm slug that required pinpoint accuracy to bring down a man. Against a Dead-eye, it was almost useless. "Hey, thanks, but no." He turned to leave.

"Tell Mr. Crumb I said hello and good luck, Cole. You're going to need it dealing with him."

The cab was still out front and Cole slid back in. Corrina hesitated before getting inside. "That *Lady Eagle* was choice. Maybe he woulda gone down to three hundred each if we both got one." When it came to haggling, she had innate math skills that were out of proportion to the rest of her knowledge.

"You're not getting a gun and that's final."

In a huff, she climbed into the cab and turned her hard, angry face up at him. "I can shoot, you know. You saw what I did to that zom...that bad guy, I mean." She lowered her voice. "Come on, Cole. Give me one good reason why I can't have a gun."

"You're not trained to use a gun," he answered, sticking out the first of four fingers. "You're not mature enough. You're still hungry for the mule and nothing's more dangerous than that. And, it's not *my* money that you want to spend."

"I said one reason," she muttered.

He ignored her. "Canal Street right where it ends at that bridge mound. Don't take the West Side Highway." He didn't want to get anywhere near the Krupp factory.

Corrina kept quiet on the trip back south. She even made sure to smile pleasantly, hoping that Bingo Max would have a cheap little gun for her and that Cole would see that going after zombies barehanded was just wrong. She stared out the window at the crumbling city. The afternoon was fading and with dark brown clouds growing off to the west, the city was cast in a sepia hue, and looked like an old-time picture. The clouds hinted that the fine day was going to turn into a hellish night.

She had never been to the east end of Canal Street before and didn't ever want to go back.

The sand-crete buildings were crumbling away, making the streets more or less packed sand over piles of trash and crumbling asphalt. The erosion was so bad that windows and doors could no longer be mounted as they had once been. In many places, rusting tin slabs were pounded into the openings and in others odd, makeshift hinges of rope and wood held doors at cockeyed angles.

It was rare that a cab came down that way and whenever they passed a knot of young toughs or old men gathered around a checkerboard, they would stop and give the cab a dull-eyed stare.

"You be wantin' a ride back uptown, right?" the cabbie asked.

To Corrina's shock, Cole said no. "What? We're gonna get killed in this..."

She stopped as he opened the door and the stench in the air hit her full force. The cabby wanted to spit as the stink seemed to settle on his tongue. Cole muttered his usual long, "Fuuuuck," under his breath as his lips twisted. Corrina's mouth came open. Although she had never heard of either chromium or zinc, she knew the smell they gave off when powdered and heated with the catalyzing enzymes found in Rican Mule.

A terrible hunger hit her. It didn't originate in her stomach, but in her bones. Her entire body suddenly ached for it.

"McDonald's place is only a few blocks away. I think we can walk that far. Corrina?" He turned and saw the pain and the need in her eyes. "Aw, crap. Come on. Stay with me. We're just picking up a piece and we'll be moving on. Do you need some calc?" He had hoped that three days without a ride would've made a difference, but she was just as hooked as ever.

She mumbled a "Yeah," and he quickly dug out a pill. She dry-swallowed it and probably would've chewed it if she had to. "It's not working," she said after less than a minute. They were almost to Bingo Max's and he hurried her along, dodging around the slags that walked the filthy sidewalks. Their faces were pocked and scarred where they weren't actively rotting off.

One in particular was as close to being a trog as a person could get. She was hideous to look upon, which made it all the harder as she came right up to Corrina and tried to grab her.

"My chide," she hissed as she reached out a hand that was missing two fingers altogether, while the rest were mere nubs. Cole had his Bulldog out and crammed it into her face.

"Back off!" He shoved her away with the bore of the gun and whisked Corrina through the one door on the block that was hung properly. Just like in the last gunshop there was an antechamber, though this one had a heavy iron door with a slot in front. No light showed through the slot. When no one greeted him, Cole bent to peer inside and saw nothing. "Hey! I need a piece. Anyone home?"

There came a low groan and a stirring from within the darkness. "Who that?" a gravelly voice asked.

"I'm looking for Bingo Max Crumb. I need a piece. He still in business?" Cole had bought his first revolver off of Bingo Max years before. It had been a damn ugly hunk of dubious metal that had held together long enough for him to kill his first Dead-eye.

"Hell yeah, I'm still in business. Let me find my underwear."

A light flicked on and Cole stood, not wanting to see Bingo Max wearing only his ratty socks. "Put on some pants, too. I got a kid with me."

"Pants?" Max muttered. "Fuck, where the hell are my pants? They were right here. I remember I had to piss and then I did. So where are they? Fuck. I don't need pants, buddy. I got a sheet. It'll work. Hey, stand back so I can see you." Part of a face appeared in the slot. Max's bloodshot eyes peered out from folds and bags of deep purple. He looked like he might have been dead for the last few days. "Let's have the Bulldog."

Cole slid it through the slot. They could hear Max give the cylinder a spin. "Not bad. You sellin' it? I'll give you thirty bucks for it."

Even used the gun was worth at least five hundred. "No. I'm buying. I'm looking for a used Crown if you have one." Max snorted. "Okay. What do you have that's close?"

"I got a Maltese. I'll let it go for five hundred."

"Open the door so I can see what you got. I'm a returning customer, Max. I bought a revolver from you four years ago."

Now there was a jingling of keys and metal scraping as locks were turned. Max was slagging badly. Along with several open sores, half his lower lip had been eaten away. His pale blonde hair was wild and greasy, half plastered to his head on one side and going everywhere on the other. "Oh yeah, I remember you. You were wearing a Fedora even back then. The world's moved on, friend." He wore nothing but a stained and frayed sheet which he didn't work too hard to keep closed.

"As much as I appreciate the fashion advice, let's just talk guns. Forget the Maltese. I need something with more stopping power and at least a twelve shot capacity."

"Might as well ask for the damn moon," Max said under his breath. Louder he said, "Okay, let's see what we have."

His "establishment" was nothing more than a two-bedroom apartment that was as bad off as he was. His couch was held up on one side by some books. His table had once been glass; now, there was a square board set over the top of it. The kitchen smelled of sour milk and the one bathroom was worse. Dreadfully worse. The acrid stench cut through Corrina's daze.

"Fuuuck," she whispered. This got her a hard look from Cole, but he held his tongue out of deference to her predicament.

"In here," Max said, heading into one of the bedrooms. There was a single mattress on the floor. It was partially covered in a single blanket. All around it was trash and dirty clothes.

Cole looked around in disgust, thinking that the slag had gotten to Max's head. Either that or he was riding the mule, too. Or both. The last time Cole had been there the room had been stacked with boxes of ammo, magazines, scopes and of course, guns.

"All right, take your pick." Max heaved up the mattress and leaned it against the wall. A shriveled rat darted away as did a hundred or so roaches. "Yeah, don't mind them. So, what do you think?" He gestured to eight handguns and a single scattergun with a broken stock.

"Fuuuuuck," Cole said.

Chapter 21

"What the hell? What kind of stock is this?" Cole demanded, staring at the smattering of weapons with absolute disgust.

Max tried to look offended and nearly lost his sheet. "It's what I got, okay? Everyone wants those stupid Eagle knock-offs. They're the worst guns ever made. I had a few blow-up on some of my customers—through no fault of mine—and after that things sort of dried up. And, AND, the taxmen have been coming down on all of us dealers."

"This sucks," Corrina said. "Maybe we should go somewhere else."

"Go then!" Max practically shrieked. He stomped back toward his living room, losing his sheet in the process. The slag ran up and down his body in ugly grey patches, dripping lesions and mottled scars. He didn't seem to care that his man parts, withered and looking like they belonged on an eighty-year-old, were on display.

Annoyed at the spectacle, Cole snapped his fingers and pointed.

"What?" Bingo Max demanded, looking down at himself. "Don't get your panties in a bunch. I bet your little honey has seen all the dicks in the world by now." Regardless of his protest, he grabbed the sheet and held it in a bundle in front of his crotch. "Happy now?"

"Not particularly," Cole answered, looking back at the handguns sitting among the sprinkles of rat turds.

Max felt some of his anger turn to despair at the sight. "If it's all such shit, then go. What're you waiting for? But trust me, all the little dealers are like this. The fat-cats are on one of their anti-crime kicks. They blame guys like me for the crime rate, as if I'm the one out there shooting anyone. And you know what they'll get in the end, right?"

"More crime?"

"And worse crime. Remember the machete gangs of the 40s? Bah, you were probably just a kid. When the stupid bangers couldn't get guns, they used machetes and chains and anything they could find. If you ever saw the aftermath of one of those battles you woulda puked, let me tell you. Body parts everywhere. Blood running like rivers. And did it reduce crime?"

Cole already knew the answer. "No. But that was old…"

"No, it did not!" Max cried. "It made everything worse. People became like animals. They got a taste for blood and no one was safe. The gangs were like fuckin' barbarians. They would roam unchecked all over the city taking whatever they wanted, killing whoever they wanted. Guns are better. Guns are smarter. You never know who's packing. And they're the great equalizer. With a gun even a little thing like this honey don't need to be afraid."

Corrina was nodding along to this as if Max was the Messiah of the Holy Bullet. "That's why I want one, Mr. Bingo," she said. "I don't want to be afraid no more."

"Of course, you don't," he said, waddling back into the bedroom. When he squatted over the weapons, the splayed crack of his ass was out for all to see. Cole rolled his eyes and moved to the side as Max waved his hand over the guns. "What do you think, honey? You like the .38?"

She liked the *Lady Eagle* back at the other store. Max's .38 was rusty and made a rattling sound when he picked it up. He gave it to Corrina, who tried to dry fire it but the trigger wouldn't give. She went to ask Cole for help, however he shook his head and she read in his face the warning that the gun couldn't be trusted.

He eased down next to Max and picked up a .40 caliber *Ferro* that looked older than he was. He had to fight the slide back and when he looked in at the chamber, he saw that the barrel was corroded and flaking rust. Sighing, he set it down and then picked up the Maltese. Next to him, Max said, "Ooooh. Yeah, she's a beaut. Sure, she's not a Crown but feel how light she is. Think how fast you could draw her. And you know about her precision. You couldn't get a thumbtack any closer to the center of a bullseye."

"How much?"

"Five hundred and that's with two magazines and forty rounds."

Cole shot a side eye at him before jacking the slide back and forth, dropping the empty magazine and inspecting the weapon. It was clean, well-oiled and rust free. "Five hundred? Are you kidding me? It's used."

"Gently used," Max assured. "It's the best gun I've gotten off the street in five years. It's a '59 model and everyone says good things about them." They did, but only in comparison to the disastrous 2155 model, which had a tin firing pin that was so brittle it frequently hadn't lasted ten shots. "Maybe I could go four-ninety," Max said.

"Four hundred," Cole answered, setting it back down. He hated the idea of going even that high, but he knew the market. Semi-automatic pistols had become increasingly hard to find over the years. Compared to revolvers, they were complex and outrageously expensive. Only a few manufacturers made them anymore and if a part was needed, it could be months before it was available. Many times an older gun was made up of scrounged parts which didn't always gel properly.

The Maltese was all original. "Four-seventy," Max countered.

"Four hundred."

Bingo Max glared and, forgetting his sheet, pulled down the mattress. "Four-sixty is a good price. Take it or leave it. That gun's worth it."

"But no one's got that kind of money," Cole replied, "otherwise it woulda been gone by now. The problem is I don't even want a damn Maltese. What did we just turn down at the last place?"

This was directed to Corrina, who pointed at the Maltese. "A better one than that. All their guns were better. I think we should go back." Like most honeys, she knew how to haggle. It was important to let it be known early that she would have no problem walking away from a bad deal. She was halfway to the door and Cole was catching up when Max let out a long weary breath.

"Four twenty-five and that's the best I can do. Damn it. Look at me. I need the money. And it's a fair price."

Cole was stirred by pity and almost agreed. Corrina crossed her arms and appraised the slag with a scornful eye. "We all need the money and a fair price is four-hundred."

Bingo Max's shoulders drooped. "Fine," he sighed. "Four-hundred." He stood dejectedly to the side as Cole rechecked the weapon, dry-fired it a few times, loaded it and strapped it on under his suit coat. Max seemed to perk up once Cole put the money into his palm. "My Bulldog?" Cole held out a hand for the gun that Max had been hoping he'd forget.

Once he had it, he nodded to Max and walked out with it still in his hand. He hadn't liked the feel of the neighborhood going into Bingo Max's and he liked it less coming out. Directly across the street was a small knot of teens, staring at him with hungry eyes. They were at that age where aggressive stupidity was their default setting. Cole saluted them with the massive handgun and turned north.

"I did pretty good, didn't I?" Corrina asked. "How much did I save us? I bet it was a lot."

He grinned. "You did great. I'd say you saved us about thirty dollars. They still back there?"

She punched him playfully on the arm and laughed as if he had told a joke. "Yep. Four of them. Two got guns. You think they're just walkin' us out of their territory?"

"If they keep a steady pace. If not, they mean trouble." A minute later people started to slip away from their side of the street, averting their eyes, and a couple of kids who had been scrounging through the trash in the gutter were called in by their mother. They knew something was about to happen. Cole rubbed his chin on his shoulder and saw that the teens were closer. "I think you should hop down the next alley we come to," he said to Corrina. "Things may get ugly."

"Maybe I should hold the money," she suggested. "You know, just in case. I'm serious."

He was sure she was. "Not with that dope smell in the air. Ah, here you go." To their right was a space between two buildings that had once been wide enough to drive a car down. Now it was something like a mini-landfill. The alley was five feet higher than the street because of the amount of compacted trash that had been hurled down it over the years. On top of this stratus of trash was more trash. To the right and left were ten-foot tall piles that towered over a narrow ragged lane of filth.

Corrina darted up the lane while he spun, switching the Bulldog to his left hand, before drawing the Maltese in a fluid motion and aiming it at the young man in front. He was so tatted-up that his features were unrecognizable.

The teens stopped. The two that held handguns had been carrying them close to their thighs, as if they were pretending to hide them. Cole could easily drill the one in front without being overly worried about return fire. With the second, he'd be on more of an even playing field—of course, he still had his training and experience. Cole liked his odds.

"You kids need something?" he asked, low and slow.

"Nope," the tattooed man answered. "Just walkin.' Ain't no law about walkin' in my own neighborhood."

Cole stared at him down the length of the Maltese. A smile had just started to creep over his features when the first cloud slid across the setting sun. With the Fedora thrown slightly forward, Cole's face was completely shadowed with only a glimpse of his white smile showing through. This unnerved the kid even more than he had been. "Why don't you go walk somewhere else?" Cole suggested.

If he twitched, Cole would've pulled the trigger and if there was anything he liked about the Maltese, it was its light touch. The kid forced out a laugh to hide his fear. One thing he was sure of, if there was going to be a fight, he would be the first to die. "We were crossin' here anyways, old man." Acting as if Cole didn't exist, he turned abruptly to his left and headed across the uneven street, his feet gritting through the sand-crete; it was loud in his ears. His friends followed, each feeling Cole's sights in the center of their backs.

Cole only moved when they were on the other side of the street, lounging on a stoop, pretending to be interested in the picture menu of a mom and pop deli. He went back north, whistling for Corrina, who appeared from the shadows.

"I barely even smell it anymore," she said after a block. She meant the toxic fumes from the mule that was being spun in a dozen places around the neighborhood. On her face was a brittle smile as if they were walking in some green park from out of a book—New York hadn't had parks in a hundred years. From the western edge of Manhattan to the Hempstead Wall out on Long Island, every inch of ground was covered in concrete or asphalt.

"Good," Cole said to the lie. "The longer you're off the mule the better. What do you think? Is that honey behind us working for herself or for the gang that wanted to test out my new gun?" He knew the answer already, but there was now sweat on the young girl's brow from fighting the desire and he wanted to take her mind off of it if he could.

Corrina glanced back at the honey, a stooped, anorexic girl who should have thought twice about wearing fishnet stockings that might have fit her twenty pounds ago; they hung off her legs like black spiderwebs. Corrina stared at her for a long time, so long that she almost forgot the question.

"So?" Cole asked.

"Huh? Oh yeah, she's following us. And there's another one across the street. See that ol' hag with the pink hair? She's been keepin' pace."

He had seen her, too. "It's the suit," he realized. It made him stand out. Everyone else wore tired old blue jeans or worn and patched poly-blend. He looked like a rich man who had foolishly wandered into the wrong area of town—alone. The local street gang assumed correctly that he had cash and although he had scared off four of them, he was sure there were runners darting down every alley, alerting more of them. Four of them he could handle, but not ten or twenty.

Normally, he would've vacated the area as fast as he could, even if it meant running away with his tail between his legs. Things weren't so simple with Corrina around; she wouldn't be able to keep up. And he still had a job to do.

"Which can wait til later," he muttered. "Here's the plan: we're going to get out of here and come back after things calm down a bit." It was a fine plan without a chance of working. They hadn't gone half a block past McDonald's building when five or six men emerged from around the corner. Across the street, three more came stomping down from another building.

"Fuuuck," Corrina said, under her breath.

"Enough of that," Cole barked even though he'd been on the verge of saying the same thing. "Come on." He spun and hurried back to the entrance of McDonald's building. Although the place was crumbling just like so many others around them, its door had been repaired sometime in the last few years and there was even a secondary door of some weight after the usual antechamber.

Cole locked them both. Corrina spun to run. "If we can get to the tunnels…" Cole grabbed her shoulder.

"We'll be trapped if we go down there. They know their own tunnels. We'd just be running in circles. Here, take this." He handed her the Bulldog. She needed two hands to hold it. As she was marveling over it, he pushed her to the side and sat her down in the corner of the antechamber. "Shoot the door if anyone even touches it. Don't waste bullets. Shoot just once every time someone touches the door. Okay? Aim at about the level of the doorknob. And don't talk at all. Say nothing. I'll be right back."

Her mind was still trying to comprehend all of this when he left her, disappearing into the building. She'd been asking for a gun all day and now that she had one, she was regretting it. The gun was too big and she was too small. Worse than that, even with her limited math skills, she knew there were more gangsters outside than there were bullets in the gun.

"Oh crap, I need a hit so bad." If she could have just a whiff of mule, she knew she'd be good to go. She'd be cool and calm. She wouldn't care that there was someone walking towards her, their boots making that gritting sound. But she did care; the gun went slick in her hands as sweat seemed to burst out of every pore of her body.

"Cole?" she whispered over her shoulder. "Cole! Get back here." The boots crunched closer, step by step. "Oh shit!" she hissed and held the gun out toward the door. She tried to sight down its length, only her hands were shaking and the clunky gun seemed to get heavier with every second.

To solve that problem, she kinked her arms and rested the butt of the gun on her knees. Then she waited as the man came slowly up the stairs, and paused for a second at the top before giving the knob a rattle. Corrina struggled the trigger back and fired.

When she had shot the Bulldog in the squad car, it had been easy. The moment had been too filled with chaos for her to feel fear or guilt or the endless hunger for her drug. Now she fired in cold silence. The shot was so loud that it felt as if someone had stabbed a pick in both of her ears. The gun leapt up and out of her hands. It did a flip in the air, banged off her shoulder, and rattled on the floorboards.

Quickly she grabbed it with throbbing hands and aimed at the door again. She had forgotten Cole's order to fire only once and would have emptied the gun if the man she had shot wasn't currently rolling down the stairs screaming in pain. The heavy slug had hit him in the right wrist and had almost torn his hand off.

Cole came racing back from the basement where he'd been boarding over the entrance to the tunnels. "You okay?" She nodded, her grey eyes like half-dollars. "Good. Stay down and remember, only one shot at a time." Once more he left her and hurried back into the dark hallway. The only light came from beneath the doors making ghostly shapes out of the lumps of trash. One of the lumps was a woman in rags. Her clothes had been torn so often that they were tied about her rather than buttoned or zipped. Her skirt was hiked high up her thighs, exposing the hideous grey skin of someone who was slagging out.

As bad as her skin was, her eyes were worse. They were almost devoid of any sentience. She'd been riding the mule for so long that it was now all she cared about.

"Hey baby! Hey, I need a hit. I need a ride. Come on. You can do what you want to me, just give me a ride." She slurred this from the floor. Sitting up was too much of an effort. "Come on, baby. Do your thing if you wan…" A door opened across the hall. Dishwater-grey light spilled onto her and she cringed from it, pain searing in her retinas.

"What did I tell you about turning tricks in the hall, Jean?" It was a pale, slaggy man in dirty boxers. Both his thin hair and his grey-streaked beard hung down past his nipples. In his hand he held a rusty knife. Cole aimed the Maltese at his face. "What?" the man asked, showing three yellow teeth in his mouth. "There shouldn't be no fuckin' in the hall. That's respect."

Behind him were seven other men sitting around a small dank room that smelled of ashtrays and endless disappointment. They had been crowding in front of a dinky seventeen-inch TV, watching Texas League football. A few of the men raised an eyebrow at Cole's gun; none got up.

"Get back inside and lock the door," Cole ordered.

"Ain't got no lock," the man with the knife grumbled as he went back into his apartment.

The woman on the ground grabbed Cole's ankle, but he tore himself loose. He didn't have time for her and even if he did, he was already busy with one charity case. Leaving the girl whining about her "need," he sprinted down the hall and up the stairs for the third floor. He hated the idea of leaving Corrina alone any longer than he had to. Eventually, the two-bit hoodlums would force their way in through the sewers or the back door, and then Corrina would be a sitting duck.

"312," he muttered passing the door. "313. 314. Here we go. 315." He smartly rapped on the door and then stepped back with the gun up.

A long pause, then, "Who is it?" The voice was male, suspicious and unfriendly. It sounded close, perhaps only inches away.

Cole sucked in a breath before launching his foot at the door. He kicked hard enough to smash in a heavy deadbolt with a medium security plate. The door had neither. His foot snapped the cheap lock in two, sending the door into the dark face of the man on the other side.

With a cry, he fell back as Cole stormed inside, his gun out. He pointed it at every corner and behind the old couch. Cole then went to the one bedroom. There was one mattress on the floor and three more stacked against the wall—the man was alone.

"I'm looking for Mike McDonald," he said coming back to where the man was lying on the ground, moaning and holding his face in large brown hands

"You mean Mack-D? I'm not him. You got the wrong guy."

Seeing as this man was black, Cole said, "No shit. Where is he?" Cole leaned over him and pulled his hands away. He was maybe twenty-five, but the grey slag on his scalp was making his afro fall out in patches and that aged him an extra twenty years. He was trying to cover more of it on his cheek with tattoos, though what the artist was going for was lost because of the scars. The blood coming from his nose was properly red, disappointingly so.

"I-I don't know. He just up and left one day. That's all I know, honest."

"That right?" Cole asked, watching him closely. The man wouldn't look up. He nodded, which wasn't good enough. "Get up," Cole growled. When the man was on his feet, Cole hauled him to the one partially opened window and pulled aside the lead shutter so he could look closer into his murky brown eyes. *They could be contacts.*

"Your mother loves you," Cole said, hoping to catch the man off guard with one of his empath statements.

He hesitated, confusion registering. "Yeah, I guess she used to back when she was alive. Did you know my mom?"

It was a proper human reaction, but Cole decided to try the empathy hook with another cast. "Your neighbor had a baby two days ago. She is small and beautiful. Her skin is a delicate pink and her legs are chubby. Now, the mother is boiling her baby for dinner." A failed response would be one showing any interest in the details.

The man looked shocked at first and then both dubious and disgusted. "What the hell are you talking about?"

"Nothing," Cole grumbled, stowing away the Maltese and walking around the apartment a second time. "So, when did your friend Mack-D take off?"

"It's been a few months, I guess."

That was a lie. "And your other roommates? Their mattresses are here and some clothes, but your kitchen has only been used by you lately. One plate in the sink. One cup. A single pan."

"I don't have to answer…" Cole took a quick aggressive step toward him. "Okay. They left at about the same time. They wanted to be closer to work."

On a hunch, Cole asked, "At Krupp?" When he nodded, Cole asked, "What's your name?"

"Bosch Smith."

"Let's see some ID. And I'll need the name of your friends. I'll also need a copy of your lease." As Bosch scurried about, Cole went to the window and saw in the low evening light that there were twelve or thirteen hoodlums out front, most gathered around one of their friends who was lying on the far sidewalk bleeding. They kept casting angry looks up at the building. It wouldn't be long before they made another attempt.

Corrina wouldn't be able to stop them this time, and Cole didn't like his chances in a shootout. When slags wanted revenge, they tended to become fearless; and there were so many of them.

"Son of a bitch," he whispered, realizing that there was only one way out of his predicament and it was a long shot at best. "You got a phone?"

Chapter 22

The phone call was strangely short and to the point. Gavin Baker answered with a simple: "Do you have her?"

"No, but I'm getting closer. I accidentally stirred up some trouble down on Canal and Chrystie."

"I'll send help." That was it. The phone went dead in Cole's hands. "Get away from the window," he barked at Bosch. "Let's have that lease." It was the law that all residents of an apartment be on the lease. This included even temporary residents. It was a law that landlords followed even in poor areas because a building could be seized if it was considered under-utilized.

"This is my only copy," Bosch said, holding the lease close to his body. Cole could read some of the writing on it and there was the name Mike McDonald—Driver, Krupp Metalworks, written on it. "I'm not allowed to give it away. I'll get in troub…" A gunshot from below froze them both in place, but only for a moment. Then there came an entire barrage of shots from the street, which got Cole moving in a blur. He snatched the lease from Bosch's hand and flew from the apartment, racing down the hall to the stairs, which became a blur under his feet. On the first floor he leapt over the mule-honey; she was so out of it that she hadn't noticed the gunshots at all.

"Hey baby," she slurred as he ran by.

The hall seemed to stretch forever as more bullets riddled the front of the building. Cole ran like mad, his heart stuck between beats, afraid that he'd be too late to save Corrina, afraid that by the time he got to her she'd be blasted into red goo.

Ahead of him, the air grew hazy with dust and flying hunks of prefab as bullets from the street tore through the lobby door, blasted through the back wall, zipped across the hall and into the closest apartment. So many holes were appearing in the wall that Cole was sure he'd be hit as he ran through the debris cloud. Foolishly, he threw an arm over his face. The arm wouldn't have stopped a bullet, and it didn't keep him from being sprayed in the face with a storm of fragments from the wall as it came apart.

When he reached the lobby with its little antechamber, the air jumped from the thundering gunshots and vibrated from Corrina's shrill screams. Zipping orange sparks came through the front door from all angles and disappeared into the wall inches above the girl's head. Cole yelled for her to crawl to him, but the noise was so overwhelming she couldn't hear him.

Dropping down to the floor, he dragged himself to her and was shocked when she threw herself on him. "They keep shooting!" she screamed.

"Yeah, I noticed," he said, trying to untangle himself from her. She clung to him with the unnatural desperate strength of a jungle cat. Every time he managed to dislodge one hand, the other would find a new hold until he finally just crawled away with her holding on, bullets smacking the wall inches above his back. She was so terrified that she wouldn't let go of him even when they made it to the hall.

"Corrina, it's okay. You're okay. Calm down, damn it, no one can hurt…" The shadow of a man was just emerging from one of the apartments down the hall.

There was just enough light to cast a single glint from the pistol in the man's hands as he aimed. The gun bloomed with orange fire and a hot sizzle streaked just to the left of Cole's cheek. Corrina screamed again and held on more tightly than before, causing Cole's aim to go awry. Instead of hitting the man in the center of the chest, the bullet hit him in the crook of the arm—his non-shooting arm.

The hit spun him sideways, but did nothing to slow him down, and he and Cole traded shots at a range of twenty-two feet. It was so close that Cole felt the hot air billow out from the bore of the man's huge, ungainly weapon as he fired. The street hood had been turned slightly after being hit, and he missed a second time, even worse than before. His bullet traveled straight down the center of the hallway, crashed through the door at the end, and into the neck of the building's manager, who dropped like a rock.

Cole was slower to fire. He still had the girl clinging to him and had to adjust his aim. For him, twenty-two feet was a gimme and he hit the hood directly in the center of the chest. He collapsed, making a guttering, bubbling sound as he fought to breathe.

Now, the gunfire from the street slacked away to nothing and as it did, Corrina stared at the dying man. "They-wouldn't-stop-shooting," she said, her chest hitching with every word. "I-I tried to give up, but they wouldn't stop shooting."

"Yeah, they do that sometimes. People who aren't trained or experienced rarely know what the hell's going on in a battle. They think everyone's shooting at them."

"Everyone *was* shooting at me."

"So now you know what it feels like and nothing else will ever seem so bad. Wait here," he ordered, dislodging her claws. He slipped back into the lobby to fetch the Bulldog she had dropped. The gang was out on the street discussing who should go in to see if: "Corn Carl had gotten the fucker," as someone put it. Their ears were ringing from the gunfire and none were being particularly quiet. With the front door of the building riddled and looking like a sieve, Cole heard the entire conversation.

"Your friend, Corn Carl is dead," he called out. It wasn't quite true. Corn Carl was still on his back, slowly drowning in blood, proving beyond a doubt the weakness of the Maltese. A bullet from his Crown would've torn the man's heart out of his chest and left it on the wall behind him like some piece of modern art. "I have all night. Keep coming and I'll keep killing you."

Someone fired a couple of shots at the door and someone else yelled for Cole to go fuck himself.

"Yeah, yeah, yeah," Cole muttered, heading back into the hall. He reloaded the Bulldog and handed it back to Corrina. "I want you to watch the stairs leading down into the basement. Shoot at anyone with a gun." What little color in her face drained away. He put a hand on her bony shoulder, saying, "Don't be afraid. It'll be okay." No sooner had he finished the sentence than they heard the first police siren suddenly scream into life. "Fuuuck!" It was the worst time for the cops to decide to actually do their jobs.

They had to get out of there. It didn't matter that Cole was acting in self-defense this time, the cops still had him for the murders at the chop-shop, the arson, the theft of one of their squad cars, more arson, and who knows what else.

"Come on. Let's see if we can get out the same way that guy came in." He made a gesture towards Corn Carl and then went to the door he had come through. It was locked. He hammered on it with the butt of the Maltese. "Open up! Open the door!" There was sly movement in the apartment; the creak of a door, the scrape of a storm shutter. He couldn't tell if someone was coming into the place or leaving it.

He was about to put his shoulder to the door when he happened to glance over and saw Corrina rifling through Corn Carl's pockets. Her hands were shaking and her face was screwed up partially in fright and partially in intense hunger.

"Stop that!" he hissed, furiously, rushing to her. She clung to the dying man much like she had clung to Cole only moments before.

"No. I gotta have it." She practically ripped out the man's pockets searching for mule or anything, really. The shock of being thrown into what felt like a full scale battle had brought back the *need* with driving force. It was inside her and yet it was bigger than her. The need was huge and growing and growing.

Cole grabbed her hands in an iron grip and stared into her eyes. "You don't need this."

"What do you know?" she hissed back savagely, her face suddenly distorted and old. "I never asked for your help. I was doing good on my own."

"Oh yeah? You want to see what you looked like when I found you?" He lifted her to her feet and hauled her down the hall to where the slagged-out woman lay drifting in a haze.

She started right in when she saw Cole. "Hey baby! Hey, I need a hit. I need a ride. Come on. You can do what you want to me, just give me a ride." Her skirt had been up around her thighs before, now she dragged it up, revealing a diseased gash that reeked of corruption.

The sight and smell stunned Corrina and she turned away. Cole grabbed her in his big hands and forced her to look back. "That is going to be you in a couple of months," he said. "Is that what you want?" Corrina shook her head and mouthed the word, no. "Then give it up. Forget the mule. Let it go. Can you try?" She nodded, now unable to look away from the horrible woman.

By then, two more sirens had joined the first. They were very close, racing from three directions, surrounding the building. If there had ever been a chance at escape, it was gone now. Even going out the back wouldn't work. Every eye in the neighborhood was centered on the building and as much as the gangs hated the cops, they hated Cole more.

"Let me have the gun," he said to Corrina. The gun was a forgotten item dangling from the end of one arm. "I want you to go to the stairs. If things go bad, run to the top floor. If the cops search the building, tell them you don't know what was going on. Tell them that you were hiding from me. They'll believe you."

She cast a last look at the slagged-out whore and then walked to the stairs with her head down. When she was gone, Cole went to the dying man and considered putting a bullet in his head. It would've been a mercy. As he was standing over the man, the front door was smashed down. He raised the Maltese, ready to kill the first gangster to show his face.

"Cole, you in here?"

"Son of a bitch," he muttered. He knew the owner of the voice; it was Sergeant Bruce Hamilton. Cole crouched and aimed his gun at the entrance of the lobby. If Hamilton had come for revenge because of what Cole had done to his squad car, he was going to get one between the eyes—which was pretty much the only part of Hamilton that wasn't armored. "Yeah. I'm in the hall. Have you come to arrest all those dumb fucks outside?"

Hamilton snorted. "Where's the profit in that. No, I'm here for you, dickhead."

"You know where to find me." Cole drew in a long breath and gradually became one with the gun. He knew the bullet would go exactly where he wished it would go. Hamilton was a second from death when something suddenly occurred to Cole: Hamilton had known he would be there. How?

His old partner stepped partially around the corner and saw Cole crouched down in the dark. He gave Cole a long look before he shouldered his rifle and moved closer, glancing casually at the dying man. His slow death did not affect Hamilton in the least. "What's with the BB gun?" he asked.

Cole lowered the Maltese, but didn't put it away just yet. "It's just a temp," he lied. "The Crown's getting an inlay. So how did you know I'd be here?"

"I got a call from my L.T. saying that some asshole needed help. The first person I thought of was you."

This was only partially a lie and Cole caught it immediately. He stood and holstered the Maltese, keeping his chin down to hide his surprise. He hadn't known what sort of help Gavin would send, but calling up an entire squad of cops had been the last thing he had expected. It was more than a little frightening. Ashley Tinley's pull must have been enormous and her interest in Christina Grimmett far greater than she was letting on.

"Who you working for?" Hamilton asked, coming even closer and staring into Cole's eyes. He had stepped on Corn Carl's hand and was crushing the bones in his fingers to splinters; Hamilton didn't care. Cole only gave him a shrug. "No," the cop snarled, poking Cole in the chest. "That's not good enough. I got ten warrants out on you. I told my L.T. that and he says forget 'em. The only way that happens is if you're in with a player. Who is it? Tell me and I'll make those warrants go away for good."

This was a lie you told a child. Once Hamilton knew who he was working for, he'd start applying his own sort of pressure until he got a healthy chunk of the action. "It's the King of England," Cole answered.

From the way his armor creaked, Cole knew Hamilton wanted to smash his gloved fist into his face. It was telling that he didn't. "Fuck you, Cole."

"Hmm, yes. So you were *ordered* to help me. I'm going to need a few things. Your radio to start with. And a change of clothes." As much as he loved the suit, it just wasn't the proper thing to wear when tailing a guy through the dregs of New York.

Hamilton demonstrated his jealously over the suit by sneering at it, as if he wouldn't be caught dead in it. He snorted again and turned away. "You're not getting dick from me, Cole, except maybe another bullet. I was told to help and that's what I've done. No one said anything about kissing your ass." He left, going out into the twilight where the street was flooded with lights and squad cars. The neighborhood gang was across the street on their knees, further away were crowds of slags watching carefully, ready to disappear in a flash if the taxmen turned their way.

It was likely Cole could leave at any time, but if he did a hundred eyes would mark where he had come from, where he went and who was with him. People would talk and others would listen, perhaps even someone at Krupp. Cole had no real idea what was going on when it came to the case, still he knew that his life was in danger. His and Corrina's.

Cole needed to disappear. He needed to slip away, and at the same time he needed to keep an eye on Bosch. He hoped to God that Bosch knew where Mack-D was hiding. If not then his case was over. Bosch was his only lead, which meant someone had to tail him. Someone who wasn't quite as conspicuous as Cole, and that left only Corrina. He told himself that it would be good for her. She needed to be moving and thinking to keep her mind off the mule.

He also told himself that it wouldn't be dangerous. It's what he told her as well. "You'll have a radio and I'll be close by. A block away at the most. And he doesn't have a gun." Cole left out the part that Bosch could kill the skinny girl with his bare hands.

She was all over the board at that point. Her aching addiction made her jittery, while her rampant fear made her more so. She was hungry and tired, but would never be able to sleep. Giving up was the easiest thing in the world and yet the slagged-out honey was still down the hall oblivious to everything going on. She had pissed herself and didn't care.

Whenever Corrina looked over at her, she saw herself lying in the stinking wet rags. It scared her, it just didn't scare her straight. Nothing could. You rode the mule until one day the mule rode you, and for Corrina that day had been long ago, lost to her ragged memory. And yet, she wanted to get better. She just didn't know how except perhaps to grab onto something and not let go. For her, it was the loose straggly ends of the case. She grasped it with both hands and held on.

"Now if only everyone would leave," Cole muttered. Bosch wasn't going anywhere with the streets filled with police cars. An hour went by before there was any action and in all that time, Cole had been trying to get Hamilton's attention, only to be studiously ignored.

Finally, a police van pulled right up to the front of the building, grinding trash under its tires. An officer got out and hurried up the stairs. He frowned at Corrina, who was chain-smoking the cigarettes they had gotten from Hamilton's squad car. He then gave Cole a long up and down look. "Cole Younger?" Cole nodded and the man held out his hand. "I'll need your weapons."

"Why?"

"You'll be safe, trust me. Come on. We don't have all night." Cole gave up both guns, and was frisked. "Let's go."

"Hold on. I can't leave just yet. I need a couple of radios and a…"

"A change of clothes, yeah we know." He held out the radios. Cole took them both and gave one to Corrina, causing the officer's frown to deepen. Cole nodded at her and she nodded back. She knew what to do.

He was hurried outside to the van, which pulled away the moment he climbed in. The entire back bench was taken up by one of Ashley Tinsley's immense bodyguards. In the next bench was Gavin Baker, looking dapper in a charcoal grey suit, his brown hair oiled and perfectly parted. As always, his thin lips portrayed inordinate disgust at being in Cole's proximity. Next to him was a metallic silver bag, which he slid over.

"Your belongings. I figured you would make a mess of things and would need them back. I had them cleaned, which feels as though it might have been a waste of time."

Cole didn't bother glaring at the jumped-up waiter. He struggled out of his suit, handing the items, piece by piece to Gavin, who took each using only the very tips of one finger and thumb. "Ugh! Is this blood? Mr. Younger, let me just say how disappointed Miss Tinsley and I are in the way you've handled the investigation. Your results or the lack of…"

The front of the van was divided from the back by a heavy steel door. It slid back and Cole was surprised to see Ashley sitting in the passenger seat. Her eyes were the color of a coral lagoon. They matched her hair perfectly. She was pure vamp from the chin up. Below that she wore the grey armor of a police officer. Cole, who was wearing only his boxers, pulled his old suit coat across himself. She smirked, her eyes roving over his muscled torso without the least restraint. His scars seemed to draw the most attention. They were new to her. The men in her world were utterly unblemished.

"I'd like to speak for myself on this. Let me say, Mr. Younger, when I hired you, I did so thinking that you might show a little more restraint. Remember what I told you about my name. It's not to be dragged through the mud and yet, here you are with a hundred people trying to kill you and the police everywhere. It seems they would like to kill you as well. And for good a reason. You have a laundry list of charges against you; murder, arson, grand theft, et cetera. Please tell me that you've managed to find a lead in the middle of all this."

She was involved with this in some way and although he was technically on her payroll, he didn't trust her one bit. Still, he had to say something. "I have one play," he conceded. "If it works out, I might have some news for you some time tomorrow."

"A play? One?" she asked, and waited for him to go on.

He shrugged. "Yeah, a play. I have one chance and maybe not even that. But I can't make it with this area crawling with cops. So if you wouldn't mind calling the dogs off."

She stared at him, her fake coral-blue eyes narrowed and colder than ever. "Call them off? Just like that. Do you have any idea what it cost to bring them out here to save your hide? And do I get a thank you for my efforts?" She paused, clearly expecting Cole to thank her.

Cole had no intention of doing so. "If you had acted out of the goodness of your heart, I would've thanked you to no end. You're not fooling anyone. You only acted to protect your reputation. To you, I'm only an employee. A valuable one I suppose, at least for the moment."

Her eyes burned hot fire for a second, but then she abruptly smiled. "You are so very cheeky, Cole. It's refreshing. Yes, you are valuable…for the moment. If you become less so, well, remember, those warrants against you? They have only been put on hold. With a word, I can have the entire force hunting you. So, let's try to be a bit more civilized."

"I don't think so. If you wanted civilized, you wouldn't have hired me. I get the feeling that you want me to stir up trouble." Her face froze for an instant too long. He wasn't wrong. She was neck deep in what was going on.

She shrugged, knowing that a lie wouldn't fly just then. "I think it's time you got out. Find Christina Grimmett, Mr. Younger, and find her quickly, for both our sakes."

Chapter 23

The van stopped sharply and a second later the side door was pulled back by the driver, another of Ashley's hulking misshapen bodyguards. "Ge' out," it said in a voice that was just as unnatural as the rest of him. The voice was both deep and gravelly. It was also the voice of an imbecile, though whether this was because the man was stupid or because he was still "muted," Cole didn't know.

"Hold on," Cole groused. "Let me get dressed for fuck's sake."

"Drag him out as is," Ashley ordered. "It'll be a more realistic performance. From what I understand, the police are not the kindest of people."

The bodyguard played his part in the performance as if he was created specifically for the roll of "ugly brute," which in a way he had been. As Cole was mostly naked, the brute grabbed him by the back of the neck and threw him into the gutter. He then threw his clothes out of the van, uncaring that they had been newly cleaned.

"What about my smokes?" He had a hand out, but the brute threw the box at him, blinking it off Cole's head, much to Ashley's amusement. She had the side window rolled down and was laughing behind a small hand that seemed smaller due to the outrageous diamond set on one delicate finger.

"Sorry," she said, still chuckling. "It's just your expression is so precious. It's obvious you've never been this helpless in your life. Perhaps you'll learn from it."

Cole glared up from the gutter. "I've learned a lesson alright. Never trust a vamp. Yeah, I got that one etched for good. Tell your goon, I'm gonna need my guns."

She watched with that perfect little smile of hers as the brute tossed both of the empty guns at Cole at the same time. He only managed to catch one. The other hit his forehead. "Tomorrow, Cole," she said as he rubbed his head. "Give me news tomorrow, or else." She grunted, adding, "I've never said that before; 'or else.' I don't think I like it. It's too dark."

"Then don't say it." Cole knew better than to reload his guns with the guard standing over him. Instead he fished out a smoke and lit up, blowing a grey plume into the grey air.

Ashley wrinkled her pert little nose. She glanced up and down the block, the wrinkle still in place. "I don't like your world very much. It's ugly." That was her goodbye. She rolled the window up and, seconds later, the van left Cole still sitting in the gutter, his ass wet with the city muck. He finished his cigarette before he bothered to get dressed, and while he smoked he tried to concentrate on the case, but instead could only think about Ashley Tinsley.

Although her hair and eyes changed color faster than a chameleon, her face never changed. The tall, thin nose, the full lips, the high cheek bones...a quarter bouncing off his chest broke in on the picture he had formed of Ashley in his mind.

"Get yourself out of the gutter, boy," a man passing by rumbled. The parts of him that wasn't hidden by his long trench coat and the bowler hat that was stuffed down onto his head so low that his ears bent outward, were the color of gravestone.

Cole picked up the quarter. "Yeah, I will, but I don't need this." The man was already lost in the crowd of greying people. Tired and numb, Cole thumbed the edge of the old quarter and found himself entranced by the flow around him. There was nothing special about any of them, just like there was nothing special about him.

"Or Ashley," he muttered. In one very obvious way, she was just like the worst slags walking by covered in their make-up, their tattoos, their high collars and their long hair. None of them were happy with themselves. They at least had a reason. She did not.

It was strange to think that someone so rich was so insecure.

He tried to wrap his mind around the idea as he pulled on his pants, his shirt, his shoes. The radio crackled to life just as he tucked away the now loaded Maltese. "Cole, you there?" It was Corrina. Her voice was a shaky whisper.

"This is Cole. Please tell me he's on the move."

"Yeah. He's going up Bowery. How close do I need to be?"

Cole sagged for a moment in relief. If Bosch had been going to work, he would've been traveling east. He was going north, which hopefully meant he was going to warn Mack-D that people were after him. Cole hopped up, slid the Bulldog into his belt under his torn coat and took off at a fast walk, heading east to get ahead of Bosch. "It depends on how cautious he's being. If he's not looking around a lot, then you can be closer."

"He's kinda looking around."

Kinda wasn't exactly helpful. "I'm in front of you guys. Hang back until you see me." Cole was well ahead of them and had time to kill. He crossed the street to where a man was selling sandwiches out of a cart. The only meat he had was old cod and the new style version of spam which, thankfully, did not list the actual ingredients.

Cole took two of the spam. It had a vague bacon-ish taste…at first. The after taste was not pleasant, which was why it was always served with pickles. Just as he was about to rip into his sandwich a lady in a long, vaguely pink housecoat came by pulling on the hand of what looked like an eight-year-old. The young boy had his other hand pulled by an even smaller boy, who was caught between his older brother and a younger sister. The little girl was wearing the wretched hand-me-downs of her older brothers; her shoes didn't fit and clopped as she walked.

All three of the children were wasted, hollow-cheeked things that stared unabashedly at Cole's sandwich, their mouths hanging open.

"Fuuuck," Cole muttered. Louder he addressed the woman. "Hey lady. Your kids look hungry. I can get them a sandwich if you want."

"No. That's okay. My husband's waiting at home and it's getting late. And I shouldn't. It's kind of you an' all but I shouldn't."

Despite her denials, she had stopped and was looking at the cart with open desire. "How about we get your husband one as well. Does he like fish or spam?" Cole was thinking that as he'd been given a quarter by a nice person, he might as well pass it on to someone who looked like they needed it and this lady was running on empty if anyone was.

"The fish, I think," she answered.

"What about you three?" Cole asked the children. They looked to their mother first before the boys said, "Spam," and the girl answered, "Toast with jelly, please."

The vendor, who'd had a bad night of it so far, and was happy to have so many sales in a row, grinned. "I can do that. And what about you, ma'am?" Cole hadn't mentioned buying her a sandwich, but he didn't think the presumption was overstepping.

Cole nodded encouragement. The sandwiches were a dime a piece and not bad for the price. She decided on the spam and Cole guessed it was just in case her husband didn't like the fish. She thanked Cole, who did his best to downplay the idea of charity. *It's fifty cents*, he thought. Fifty cents was nothing, especially since half of that had been given to him. And he could afford it. As he slid his hand into his pocket for the two quarters, he felt the wad of cash that he had left.

There was over five hundred dollars in the wad. The cash made him feel sudden shame. A moment before he'd been playing the big shot, handing out pennies to the street urchins so he could feel like he was a somebody. It was nice, but then the family would go home to a cold apartment, and no money for real shoes for the girl. And it was obvious the way the mom was wearing her hair pinned that she was deliberately trying to cover the left side of her face. If Cole pulled her hair back he was sure he would see scars and grey flesh, or maybe the lesions of radiation poisoning.

He gave the vendor fifty cents and then folded up a twenty and pushed it into the mom's hands along with the sandwiches. "Go get some shoes for the kid," he said and left, crossing the street, already angry with himself. The part-time Catholic in him knew he should've given more, while the realist knew he had just wasted twenty dollars—the family was doomed no matter what.

Every time he had money, these two sides of him vied for control. James Smith liked to say Cole had a soft spot for orphans and strippers. James wasn't wrong. It was a combination that could make a rich man poor in no time.

True to form, the moment Cole crossed the street and found himself looking through the bars of a tailor's shop. Had he not been on the job, he would've been in there asking to see a Fedora in black felt. He felt somewhat naked without a good hat. When the radio crackled to life in his hand, he jumped. "Where the hell are you?" Corrina hissed. "I'm at Grande and I think he might've spotted me."

"I'm a block north at Broome. Hang back a bit more. It'll be okay." Cole caught sight of Bosch within a minute. The man was hurrying up the block and although he had his head down, he was sneaking quick peeks over his shoulder every minute or so. Thankfully, his gaze never seemed to settle on the girl in red following after him. She was perfect for the job since no one would expect a little street honey like her to be working a case.

Cole stepped into the tailor's and watched Bosch pass. He then waved, Corrina inside. "You're doing great," he said, handing over the sandwich he'd bought her. "He doesn't suspect a thing."

"But what if…"

He stopped her. "Don't worry about what ifs. If he spots you for real, call me on the radio right off and then tell him I'm on my way and I'm pissed. Trust me, he'll run. But that won't happen. I watched him all the way up here. He's not looking for a kid. He's looking for the police or me."

"I'm not a kid," she said around a mouthful of sandwich. She had mayonnaise at the corners of her mouth. She looked like a kid, but one who had seen far too much of a bad world.

"I know. Now get going. I'm going to run ahead again. Let me know if he makes any turns at all."

"Yeah, sure. I could also use a drink, you know. Following people and getting shot at is thirsty work."

He promised her that he would get her a drink and then turned her around and pushed her after Bosch. After watching her for a few seconds, he cut down a side street and pounded the pavement for a few blocks before coming back to Bowery. On the corner was a little catch-all mart which offered fizzes for a dime and, as they were all out of lemon, he bought one that was green. What flavor that would be was something of a mystery.

Bosch came into view not long after and Cole made sure to keep out of sight until he had passed. Corrina took the green fizz and chugged it down before proclaiming it to be awful. "I think that was kale-flavored." Even Cole would've turned his nose up to that.

It wasn't long after when Bosch left Bowery. He headed down into one of the tunnels. There was a good deal less foot traffic down there, which worried Cole until he saw Corrina start to meander oddly along the sidewalk. At first, he thought that she had gotten drunk off the fizz, but then he saw that she was play acting. To anyone else, she looked like a strung out kid-honey.

But she could take the act only so far. The tunnels beneath the city were a maze and eventually they became mere dark holes carpeted in trash where rats ran underfoot. Cole stopped Corrina when Bosch turned into one of these. "Stay here and keep out of sight," he told her. He started to follow after Bosch when he hurried back to her. "You did great, by the way. And I'm going to still need you, so don't take off."

Her brow creased. "Why would I do that? You still owe me money." He grinned, knowing she was back from the edge.

"Yeah, I do."

Bosch had a flashlight and used it to pick his way along the tunnel. Cole had to slip along in the dark and hope not to kick over anything. Thankfully all the cans and bottles had been scavenged already and there was plenty of ambient noise to mask what sound he was making. The sound of cars rumbled along the tunnel, and there were odd screams that came and went without reason. Once there was a giggle of laughter that had Bosch shining his light back and forth.

Cole slunk low and waited until Bosch went on. Twice he seemed to disappear, but both times the light gave him away and Cole was able to track him deep underground to a metal door. Bosch tried to knock with his fist, but swore and shook his hand. He thought about using the flashlight, but worried that it would break the bulb. With little subtlety, he kicked the metal door; *boom, boom, boom!*

The sound of his kicks echoed up the tunnel, which made Cole wonder why he whispered, "Mack? Mack?"

It took a minute before the door slid back and there was a version of Mike McDonald that had Bosch stepping back. "Mack? Jesus, your, your, your…" He trailed off, pointing at Mack-D's hideous black eyes.

"What d'ya want? Did you change your mind about joining us?" He started to slide the door further open causing Bosch to take another step back. "Don't be afraid, man. We're all friends here. Come in."

"Naw, I don't think so. I just wanted to tell you that some guy came asking for you. He asked me all sorts of questions. He knows, Mack. He knows what you are. I could tell."

Rage swept over the zombie and he had to hold onto the door to keep from leaping on Bosch and screaming: *What did you tell him!* Instead he asked the question in a choked voice.

Bosch took another step back. He looked like he was about to take off running. "Nothing, I swear. The good news is that the guy got nabbed by the cops. Yeah, yeah, the taxmen were everywhere up and down the block. They took him off about an hour ago. That's why I'm here. To warn you, Mack. And I did. So, what do you think that's worth? A couple of bucks, right? I mean I coulda ratted you out, but I got beat up and I still didn't talk. See?"

He pointed at the mark left by the door on his face. Mack-D stepped closer, squinting his black beetle eyes at him.

"And you didn't talk?"

"He might next time," someone croaked from the doorway. Even Mack-D seemed unnerved by the owner of the voice. He jerked a little and scooted outside, keeping his eyes on the doorway. The croaking voice went on, "They'll be back. The hunters are relentless. They'll be back and next time your little human friend will squeal."

"I won't, I swear." Bosch's face went dusky grey. He was rooted in place by the creature hovering in the shadow of the door.

Cole couldn't see it, but guessed that it had to be a Dead-eye and one that couldn't hide what it really was anymore. He'd heard that if a zombie lived long enough, the radiation that killed normal people would turn them into demon-like creatures with skin like an alligator. Whatever Bosch was looking at was far worse than even Mack-D, and that was saying something.

"Should we believe him?" the thing croaked, addressing Mack-D. "Do we stake our lives by trusting a man?" Mack-D seemed uncertain and so the creature answered for him. "Of course we don't. Remember the old adage: dead men tell no tales. Besides, I'm hungry."

By the time Bosch realized that the creature really meant to eat him, it was too late. Mack-D might have been a moron in all other respects, but when it came to feeding, his mind was a spring ready to go. It didn't matter that he and Bosch had been friends since childhood, the hunger had a hold of Mack-D and it was greater than any addiction. He launched himself on his onetime friend who screamed high and shrill.

"Inside with him!" the thing croaked from the doorway. A scaly arm waved out of the darkness.

Bosch tried to fight back, but he was weak and unskilled. Although Mack-D seemed no bigger than his friend, he was able to grab him by the back of his coat and haul him to the door as if he were made of straw. When

Bosch grabbed the side of the door, Mack-D snapped both bones in his forearm with just a flick of his wrist.

The screams were now deafening. They were loud enough that Cole's running steps went unheard as he charged for the door, a gun in both hands. He wished he had a third pistol, if not a fourth. He was going against a nest of the undead. There was no telling how many of them would be behind the door, however it was a harsh fact that if there were more than two, he probably wouldn't be coming out again.

Chapter 24

The blood pumping from Bosch's wrist wasn't the purest. They could smell the corruption, the impurities, the toxins. Not that it mattered. The four Dead-eyes were starving. They were always starving. Even with their outrageous doses of syn-ope dousing their hunger, the need to feed was constantly with them, gnawing at their insides.

Before the door was even closed, Mack-D was on his friend, his teeth biting down on the torn flesh and crushing the bone jutting from Bosch's forearm. He sucked the rich blood straight from the pumping artery. As much in horror as in pain, Bosch shrieked at the top of his lungs. It was a terrified, pitiful sound that evoked no pity from the creatures. Instead, it drove them into a blood lust.

The four of them attacked, three going for the tender throat. There was a shout of anger and a scream of rage. In seconds, the zombies were fighting like lions above Bosch. For a moment, as they tore into each other, shredding clothes as well as flesh, he was forgotten. As black blood rained down on Bosch, he tried to make a break for freedom. He leapt up and ran, but in the wrong direction. The room was something of a cavern. There were no walls except the dirt and stone, and there was no light except that coming from a smoldering tire fire that filled the air with choking black smoke.

The orange glow of the fire drew his dark eyes and he ran for it, stumbling over old boxes, and mounds of trash, and flung-about bloody clothing. Something caught his foot and he fell into a pile of old bones that had been gnawed at by small teeth. A new horrified scream welled up in his throat at the sight of them, but it was cut off when he saw the creatures disentangling themselves. They weren't human. He had known that about Mack-D and their roommate Billy Fish. They had come back from work one night changed. They stank of old meat and their eyes had gone black and their skin had turned grey. Still, they had been *close* to human and he had been able to deal with it.

But the other two…one was a creature of bone. It barely had enough muscle left on it to hold it upright and what flesh it did have hung off of it like old rags. Its face had been torn off so that Bosch could see the bones beneath. And yet it was still "alive." It was a living scarecrow that looked as if it had crawled out of the pile of bones and had knit itself together with thread.

In a way, the other creature was worse. It was tall and lean, wasted appearing but with a demonic vitality that made it greater than the other three combined. It did not have skin, but instead was covered in the grey scales of a diseased lizard. Its eyes were huge, black and wet. Its fingers ended in long ragged claws, while its teeth were broken and sharp. They looked like they belonged in the mouth of a barracuda. It exuded evil with every foul breath it took.

The four separated, Mack-D and the bone-creature moving to his right, Billy slipping to his left and the scaled monster coming straight at Bosch.

His heart seized in his chest as he screamed like a child and turned to run. There was an alcove and what looked like a broken sewer pipe running from it. He made it three steps before the scaled creature was on him, tripping him from behind and slamming a fist down into his spine, snapping four vertebrae.

This was the scene playing out in front of Cole after he hauled the heavy door back. He paused, uncertainty and fear freezing his bones. He had never gone against four Dead-eyes at once. It was too many. One could be bad enough. They could eat bullet after bullet and still come on. Before this case, he had never fought more than one at a time, but he had heard the stories of hunters who had gone up against two or more. These stories were rarely told by the hunters themselves since they rarely lived to tell them.

I can just leave.

It was a weak thought for a weak man. Bosch was a weak man as was Santino before him. The world chewed up the weak and spat them into the gutter. Cole gripped the Bulldog even tighter. It was in his right hand. He second guessed using it first and stuck it back into his belt.

The Maltese was wimpy but more accurate at this distance. Cole settled in behind his gun, aimed, overthought the moment and fired, skipping the puny round off the top of Mack-D's head. It cut a groove through his lank, greasy hair, but didn't do more than crease his skull.

With the sound of the gun, the feast in front of the Dead-eyes was immediately forgotten. Hatred and rage were more of a driving force in them than feeding, and as one they turned and charged at Cole. There was thirty-four feet between them, and they were shockingly, dreadfully fast. Billy Fish was closest and was on him in four seconds, just enough time for Cole to rip off five shots.

The first two hit low; one striking him just below the chin and the next splitting his jaw dead center and cracking it in two. His next three shots stitched little black holes in Billy's face. One got through and hit something vital, spilling Billy Fish to the ground eight feet in front of Cole.

Mack-D tripped over him and the howling bone-crow fell over Mack-D. There was no respite from the danger, however. The scaled thing leapt over all three with surprising grace. Cole was dialed in and hot. He fired knowing he was going to hit the thing's forehead dead center, but it jerked in anticipation at the last second and the bullet snapped off the top of its scaled right ear.

"Fuuuuck!" Cole cried, knowing he had bitten off far more than he could chew. He fled back into the tunnel and heaved his shoulder into the door, sliding it almost shut. A scaled hand stopped it. Even with Cole straining with all his might, the creature pushed the door back using just its one arm. Cole stuck the Maltese around the side of the door and fired blindly, pulling the trigger as fast as he could. He had a good estimate of where the creature's head was and after four shots, the door suddenly slid forward and banged shut.

So far, he had fired eleven shots and had only one left in the Maltese. It wasn't quite time to panic. He still had another mag in his pocket and the Bulldog in his belt. With only seconds before the door would be tested again, Cole thumbed the magazine release button as he dug for the extra magazine. His hands worked almost without him needing to direct them and with practiced ease, he had the second magazine in hand and was ready to slide it into place when he realized that the old magazine hadn't jettisoned like it should have.

It was still lodged in the grip. Cole thumbed the release a second time and shook the gun frantically. It wouldn't drop and now the door was creaking back again! He leaned into the doorway and found himself face-to-face with Billy Fish. Billy's face was streaming black blood.

"I killed you!" Cole growled, as he stuck the Maltese right to the zombie's head and pulled the trigger, sending the last bullet in the gun hammering home. This time, there was no doubt. Billy Fish went stiff and then fell back like a statue being thrown over.

In a blur, Cole dropped the Maltese and pulled the Bulldog just as the bone creature rushed the door. Up close he saw that half her scalp had been torn off and he could see white bone that was mostly covered in what looked like black mold. Long dark hair that was matted with dried blood hung from the other side of her skull and Cole was suddenly struck by the thought: *This is Christina Grimmett.*

Maybe it had been Christina once. Now it was a Dead-eye that was hell bent on eating him and yet, Cole hesitated. He fired late and low, hitting her square in the sternum. The power behind the Bulldog sent her flying back, though he doubted that she died—a second time, that is.

He aimed with more determination and just as he did, he saw Mack-D coming at him low and fast. With his face covered in a curtain of blood and his yellowed teeth opened wider than humanly possible, he looked like a demon coming to drag Cole down to hell. He was so terribly fast that Cole had no time to aim as he fired. Mack-D took the huge hunk of lead in the shoulder and didn't even blink. The impact didn't slow him a bit and he struck Cole square-on with a great crash, bowling him over.

The air whooshed out of Cole as he wound up on his back with the creature on top of him. He tried to bring the Bulldog around, but it wouldn't be enough to hit the Dead-eye in the side or the neck. It had to be a head shot. Before he could line one up, Mack-D grabbed his wrists in an iron grip and, as if Cole was as weak as a child, he bent his arms back until they were pinned to the ground.

Desperate, Cole twisted his hand as far as he could and fired the Bulldog at an extreme angle, missing badly, the bullet caroming off the rock ceiling and clanging off the metal door with a deep lasting note, as if an out of tune church bell had been rung. The note was awful.

The post-apocalyptic Catholic church preached heavily about the influence of demons and the fiery pits of Gehenna. To Cole that sound was what he imagined the tolling bell before the gates of Hell would be like.

The sound had an odd effect on him. Instead of going crazy and thrashing in panic, he felt sudden calm. In fact, he felt detached from his body, as if it was someone else a second from having their throat torn out. From this odd perspective he could see Mack-D's black eyes go wide in anticipation, and saw his mouth gape wider, showing rotting diseased gums, and he smelled the sickening stench coming from his mouth.

This detachment allowed him to think clearly, and he realized that fighting the horrid creature with its animal ferocity was useless. He could not match its strength, but he was quicker and smarter.

Cole could not lift his hands, but he could shift them. As Mack-D hunched forward to bite, Cole yanked both of his hands in closer to his thighs which brought Mack-D's hands in toward him while transferring more of his weight forward. At the same time, Cole slammed his right knee upward. He had no intention of trying for a crotch shot. It would be wasted on a zombie. Instead he used the pistoning knee to assist Mack's momentum forward.

The Dead-eye was strong but relatively light and Cole was able to launch him over the top of his chest. In a flash, the two had changed positions. Cole was on top and again, instead of trying to press down with his arms, pitting his strength against Mack-D's, he pulled back and to the left, bringing the barrel of the Bulldog in line with Mack-D's face.

He fired the gun, *BAM! BAM! BAM!*

Each bullet struck home like a sledgehammer and Mack-D's head came apart like an over-ripe melon.

Cole's first thought was not one of victory. The first thing that flashed through his mind as he straddled Mack-D's chest was: *I'm out of bullets!* It was a terrifying thought. He had no idea if Christina or the lizard thing were still alive, but he *felt* it in his bones that they were only wounded.

"Come on, motherfucker!" Cole screamed, attempting a bluff to get more time. "Come get yours." As he waited for an answer, he dug in his pocket with shaking hands for more bullets. He had only two left; they clinked in his palm. "Jesus Christ," he hissed.

"Jesus won't help you down here." It was the creature. His words were wet and soft, weaker than they had been. Cole had hurt him, but hurting a Dead-eye only meant so much.

"What do you know about Jesus?" Cole asked, stalling for time. The calm he had felt a minute before had deserted him and now his hands were shaking so badly that he could barely fumble open the cylinder and as he did, he dropped one of the bullets.

Movement in front of him. It was the creature. The lizard-like grey scales that covered him head to toe were glistening with what looked like motor oil. Half its jaw was missing and more of the oil leaked from the open wound. "All I know is you better start praying to him. You only have one bullet in that gun."

He wasn't wrong, but before he could begin praying, a disembodied voice called out to him. "Cole! Cole, can you hear me?" It was Corrina, though with the radio static worse than ever, it came across like a person speaking from the dark side of the moon.

She had been crouched near the tunnel entrance, her shoulders hunching further with every gunshot that echoed up from below. The sound of battle made her shiver and she'd had to fight the urge to call to him, but just then a long black car had taken the turn down the tunnel. Its front windows had been rolled down and inside were two of the giant goons. Although they could've been Ashley Tinsley's guards, Corrina didn't think they were. They hadn't blinked at seeing her. The closest one had sneered, seeing only a slag-whore.

"A car's coming, Cole. It's one of them big black ones."

This made the lizard creature pause. He was stuck between his desire to feed on Cole and the need to stay hidden.

Cole, too, was in an unusual position. He wanted to believe it was Ashley coming to the rescue. The reason he didn't: that would've been lucky. And when had he ever been lucky? If it wasn't Ashley, then it could only be "someone" from Krupp, or, more than likely, some*thing*. Taking his eye from the zombie, he stooped and picked up the bullet that had fallen.

"Afraid are you?" the creature asked. It took a limping step from the doorway. One of Cole's bullets had shattered its kneecap. "What does a hunter fear? The mouse wonders what the cat fears, but we know. He fears the fox. And what does the fox fear? A wolf, maybe? I thought I smelled the wolf on you, earlier."

"What are you talking about?" Cole asked as the tunnel filled with light. The car was getting closer.

The creature laughed at him, enjoying the fresh scent of fear. "You know. You know what's coming for you. Or should I say, *who* is coming for you. You know who I'm talking about, don't you?"

Cole knew. It wasn't Ashley Tinsley. It was the Deadeye that had been hounding him for days. And now she had him trapped. Cole was no longer the hunter. He was the mouse.

Chapter 25

Cole wanted to ask how the creature knew about the Dead-eye working for Krupp. Through Mack-D? No, he said he had smelled her before, which meant he knew her personally. He highly doubted that the brunette was the sort to hang around in the sewers. But it was even more farfetched to think that the lizard-thing ever came out into the sun.

Light slashed into his face, breaking in on his thoughts. The car was there, filling the tunnel. As it came closer, Cole edged toward the creature. If there was trouble, he planned on killing it and locking himself in the cavern.

The fact that the driver kept the lights blaring in their faces spelled all sorts of trouble, and it didn't take long to show itself. The doors opened and the two mountainous men stepped out. Cole had never seen them before. He took another sliding step toward the creature who had moved forward and was glaring into the light. It wasn't an angry glare or even a hungry one. It was defiant.

Which made absolutely no sense to Cole. If the brunette Dead-eye was there, why would another Dead-eye feel the need to...the back door of the limo opened.

"Fuuuuck," Cole said, under his breath. She was right there, a smile playing on her cold lips.

"Terri Rush," the lizard said. He said her name as if he were spitting out poison.

The smile was the only acknowledgment she gave him. She looked past him at the bodies. Nodding approval, she said to Cole. "I see McDonald and Fish; did you get the girl as well?"

He hadn't. A moment before he had heard something moving away beyond the door. It hadn't been Bosch. With his broken back, he wasn't going anywhere. Cole wanted to give her a smart-ass answer, however none came to him. He was very aware of the Bulldog. Despite having only two bullets in it, it felt very heavy.

"No? Ashley is going to be so disappointed in you. I tried to warn…"

Who or what she had tried to warn remained a mystery as just then Corrina whispered over the radio, "What's going on Cole?" Her voice came to him from two places at once.

Rush held up her own radio. It was an exact match to Cole's. "Courtesy of your friend, Hamilton. He sold you out for five dollars." She put the radio to her mouth. "Sorry, darling but your friend Cole is hurt. You better get down here in a hurry or…"

"No!" Cole roared, bringing up his gun. Rush was fast and before he could line up a shot, she ducked behind the car door, which was undoubtedly bullet proof. He couldn't waste a bullet testing it, not when he had five enemies and only two shots left. He could only run. Just as the men pulled shining pistols from their coats, he took off.

For all their size, the giants were fast, much faster than Cole expected. He was four steps from the door when they fired. One had a bead on him and the bullet whizzed past the back of his neck. The other was going for the lizardish Dead-eye, who hadn't reacted at all. As Cole swept behind him, he spun backwards, blood erupting from a new hole that had appeared above his right brow.

Shocked, Cole spared a look to his right as he ran and saw both men pivoting their pistols in his direction. He dove for the doorway like he was going headfirst into second base. The wet trash that carpeted the ground made it slick and fast, and Cole was only hit once before sliding into the room.

The back of his right thigh felt as though a red-hot poker had been ripped across it. There was no time to check how badly he was hurt. He scrambled for the heavy metal door, slamming it shut and locking it as bullets smacked into it, making it sound as though men with hammers were banging on it.

"Corrina!" he yelled into the radio. "Run! Head for that motel we stayed in last night!" As he shut off the radio, he realized that the gunshots had stopped. There was a brief silence and then: *Thoom!* Something huge had hit the door. The giants were heaving themselves against it.

The door wouldn't last. Already the hinges were giving way. Cole pushed himself up, wincing as much in anger as in pain. A bullet had taken a thumb-sized chunk of meat from his hamstring. He was sure worse things were in store for him if he didn't get out of there. And he knew there was another exit because the ragged skin and bone Dead-eye had disappeared. No, *Christina* had disappeared. That had been her, after all.

Cole hurried to where Bosch was lying, staring up at the ceiling. "Where'd she go?" It was a credit to Bosch that he didn't whine or beg. He had no hope whatsoever. Hospitals only existed for vamps. Everyday people called in a sawbones for maladies that wouldn't go away on their own. A street doc could pull a tooth or stitch an ear back on. They could dose you if your cock had begun to drip green, and they could set a bone and bind it up, but there wasn't jack they could do about a broken back except maybe slit your throat for you.

Bosch lifted a shaking hand and pointed through the haze from the tire fire at the broken sewer pipe. "Thanks," Cole said, patting his shoulder.

Before he could dash for the pipe, Bosch said in a hoarse whisper, "I wasn't a part of any of this. I said no."

Thoom! There were now gaps around the edges of the door. One or two more hits and it would come down. *A part of what?* Cole wanted to ask, but there was no time left. He ran to the pipe and right away saw it was going to be a tight fit. In fact, a dreadfully tight fit, and if his life wasn't on the line, he wouldn't have gone in that pipe on a bet. What if the pipe got smaller and he got stuck, trapped eighty feet below the ground, swallowed in darkness? What if the rain came in a deluge and filled the pipe completely? What if it ended at a grate and Christina was there waiting for him? Or he came on a nest of rats each the size of a terrier and each famished and unafraid in their black world? A shiver racked him as he paused in front of the ragged-edged opening. Desperation drove him on and he had just crawled inside when the door to the cavern came down with a rolling boom.

He squirmed forward through a sick dark sludge that dribbled down toward him. *I'm going up*, he told himself. When it came to waste sewers, up was better than down. Ahead of him was darkness, behind him was a dull orange glow. He figured he had about a minute before one of the guards would find the pipe and start shooting up it. There was no way he could out-crawl a bullet, but he was determined to try. Thankfully he came to a smaller pipe that branched up and to the left at an angle. It took some squirming, but he managed to back into it. Both shoulders wouldn't fit at once so he was forced to leave his head and arm dangling out.

The Bulldog was out as well of course. He sighted down its length hoping that Rush would be the first to stick her head up into the pipe. Instead, it was one of her guards. His head was so large that it took up a third of the pipe. Cole couldn't miss. The Bulldog went off, sounding like a grenade in the close tunnel. Cole's ears felt like spears had been driven into them.

As bad as they hurt, he was doing better than the guard who was slumped face first in the oozing muck. Cole's bullet had turned his brain into little more than grey snot, which was currently leaking from his nose. Seconds later, the guard was pulled away and a gun was stuck in the opening.

Bullets started racing up the tunnel. Cole sucked himself into the side tunnel as far as he could which still left five inches of his shoulder, part of his head and all of his arm exposed. By a miracle, the whining bullets sang past him. Eight shots had missed him!

He aimed the gun a second time, but the guard didn't give him a good enough target as he poked his head into the pipe for a quick look. Rush gave muffled orders and the next thing Cole saw was trash being thrown into opening. "Ah, holy crap!" he hissed, knowing right away what they were planning. He squirmed back into the main pipe and started crawling up as fast as he could.

As he knew they would, they set fire to the trash. As most of it had been sitting in and over a layer of old zombie piss it stank horribly, but still it went roaring up in flames. Like the tire fire, the trash smoldered, puffing out a rancid stench that turned his stomach, but wasn't enough to kill him especially as he came to more of the branching pipes. Each stole a bit of the smoke.

Cole was dizzy and sick by the time he saw a dim light ahead. There had been a grate over the pipe. Its hinges had been twisted off by Christina and now Cole climbed out into a subbasement of some unknown building. He gazed blearily around with the gun pointed outward. She had run off, her muddy prints headed for a real tunnel.

For all of a second, he considered going after her. Then the gun seemed to multiply in weight and he dropped his arm, letting it swing. He was too tired to go chasing a creature that could run forever. Besides, he had his bounties. There was thirty grand worth of dead bodies somewhere below him, and for now that was good enough.

"Ashley can go fuck herself," he muttered and started limping for the stairs, hoping that there was a deluge outside. He was covered in filth and though the rain itself was suspect, it was better than the crap that had been worked deep into the material of his ratty suit. Unfortunately, the sky was dark but clear, showing off a single dull star; the rain was still far off.

A haze of vile-smelling smoke vented upward through the cracks in the street, but this was nothing new and no one seemed to notice it. Cole's presence was another thing altogether. People walked in wide arcs around him, most muttering things like, "Fuckin' trogs." Or, "Get back below where you belong."

There was no sense trying to tell them he wasn't a trog or even a slag. Besides, it was good cover. If Rush was still hunting him, she probably wouldn't be able to look past the facade and see the hunter beneath, and she certainly wouldn't be able to smell him, the real him that is.

Still, he didn't think he should press his luck. He kept to the darkest part of the street as he hunted down a working phone. Someone had destroyed every phone in a two-block radius and his leg was beginning to gripe when he found one off the main street. The call was short and not at all sweet. The recovery team wasn't exactly happy to hear from him. They considered his Santino call to have been nothing short of a prank and if they'd had a reason to delay his call they would have.

"Yeah, we'll get a team right over," the operator drawled, suggesting that they would get there, but they weren't going to run any red lights in the process.

This was fine with Cole, who felt the need to get to Corrina before anything happened to her. He normally liked to babysit his bounties, but this case was far from normal. If Rush was really hunting him then she would know that he liked to stick around. There was a good chance that she was lurking somewhere nearby hoping to take him out.

Besides, he told himself, the bodies were safe. The only people that lived down there were trogs, and slags on the verge. They wouldn't care about the bodies. They'd rifle through the clothes of the dead and leave happy with a few nickels, not realizing that they were leaving behind the true fortune.

Cole cut through an alley where three toughs in the faux-leather vest of the Red Dogs lounged against a wet brick wall. They would've jumped him if it wasn't for the smell. None wanted to touch him. He ignored them and their stupid trog jokes, and went limping on, thinking what he would do with his bounty money.

With thirty grand in his pocket, he could retire. "Or buy a boat," he said, picturing himself standing at the rail of a white trawler with blue trim. "Yeah, a boat."

He still had the image in his head when he came to the tunnel entrance he had taken two nights before. The underground motel wasn't more than a mile away, but it felt like ten with the pain in his leg. The idea of the boat helped take his mind off the wound. Nothing could keep him from worrying about Rush and her giant of a bodyguard. Although he had only one bullet left, he slunk along the tunnel holding the Bulldog under his coat, ready to pull it at the first sign of trouble.

When he reached the motel Rush wasn't in sight and, at first, neither was Corrina. Cole stumped up to the office and was about to go inside with gun drawn, when a little shadow detached itself from behind an old battered cab. It was Corrina, her green hair looking blue under the neon light.

"Did you get the *you know what?*" she asked, stopping ten feet from him. "Are we done now?" She seemed smaller than ever and she was shaking in her red coat. She had run in a sprint all the way to the motel, constantly looking over her shoulder, sure that a Dead-eye was hot on her heels. And then had come the wait. With every passing second, her fear left her only to be replaced by the pressing voracious hunger of the mule. It started telling her lies: Cole was dead. The monsters that were loose in the city were coming for her. The only safe place to hide was in a little hit. She could close her eyes and all the bad in the world would pass over her and leave her alone in her bliss.

Just one hit would do it.

The need grew inside her until she couldn't take it anymore and had gone inside the motel and propositioned the counter man, giving him her most alluring look. The most alluring look from a twelve-year-old was the saddest thing imaginable and he had yelled at her to leave. She had begged him for fifty cents or a hit of something. It didn't matter what.

He had kicked her out only a minute before Cole had shown up and now she was wracked with shame and fear and her hated need. She hated that it owned her. She was a slave to the mule. It had an iron collar around her throat.

Cole could see that the stress of what was going on was getting to her, and he went to hug her because it seemed like the thing to do just then. She might have even let him, however his stench preceded him by a few feet and she went as green as her hair. "Oh my God! What is that stink? Is that you?"

"Don't be a pain," he grumbled turning away and sticking a hand out. He wasn't about to walk back to the building.

She shook her head. "You didn't get her? That's just great. What about the guy? Did you get him? Hey, what do you think you're doing? No cabby is going to pick you up. You got blood all over you. You look like a trog for fuck's..." He glared as much because of the curse as the fact that he knew what he looked like. "Ooooh, I'm so fucking sorry. I meant you look like a trog for *goodness* sakes."

Furious as his glare was, she secretly reveled in it. If there was one thing she could count on it, was a glare from Cole Younger. It was oddly reassuring, even if the rest of him looked as though it had gotten the shit kicked out of it. "You know that doesn't sound right," she went on. "Goodness sakes. What does that even mean?"

"It means..." He paused for a moment as an empty cab drove right past him. His arm fell to his side with a slap. "It means you should try to be good."

That felt like a put-down to Corrina. She had been trying to be good—right up until she had begged the counterman to fuck her, that is. Before that, she had done everything Cole had asked. "I am trying. You don't have any idea how hard it is to be good when you're me. I coulda left you, Cole. I coulda sold you out. But I didn't, did I. You said come here and now here I am, and all you got to say is 'be good?' Fuck that. I bet I saved you again, and you got the fuckin' balls to tell me to be good. No way! Gimme my money."

"I didn't mean it like..."

"Gimme my fuckin' money!" she screamed. She was going to show him just how good she could be. She would take the fifty and get a fat bag of mule and suck it all down at once. That would show him. That's what he deserved for treating her like a worthless whore. Her mind was filled with the idea. She was practically bursting with excitement at the idea.

"How would you like to buy a boat with me?" he asked, softly, deflating the brittle manic energy inside of her.

He was serious. "A boat?"

"A fishing boat."

The ocean's unending vastness scared her, while at the same time the freedom of a boat enthralled her. A boat meant escape. It meant leaving this shit life of hers far behind. "Yeah. I could be a boat girl. So, does that mean you got her? The one with black eyes?"

"I got three of them," he said, grinning broadly, boasting and not caring. "It's enough to get a boat and maybe have a little left over for gas and stuff."

He had started walking back up the tunnel and she followed after, forgetting the need that had been gripping her only seconds before. "Like what kind of stuff? Fishing poles?" She had seen pictures of people fishing from bridges, casting lines into beautiful clean rivers. In those pictures, it was always sunny and the people were always pretty and perfect. It was the sort of thing that seemed like a fantasy.

"I guess, but nets, too. With nets you can catch a hundred at a time. That's where the real money is." They strolled down the street, both lost in their imagination, dreaming about the perfect rather than the realistic. Neither gave a thought about the union dock thugs they'd have to bribe to offload their catches, or the pirates that lurked just over the horizon, or the Cat-3 radiation storms that came and went without the usual warnings.

There was nothing to break in on their thoughts. Certainly there were no sirens. Gunfire in the city was considered mundane and no one bothered calling the cops anymore to report a body unless it was a relative. The recovery team never made a big fuss when they came on the scene since secrecy was what they aimed for.

In fact there was nothing about the scene that gave Cole any reason to feel the gnaw of worry that erupted in his gut when he and Corrina made it back to the building he had crawled from forty minutes earlier. The dark street had just as much traffic as before, the same star sat casting its dull light out to an uncaring universe, and the same people gave him the same ugly looks. Even the air was filled with that same vile haze of smoke.

Still Cole worried. He and Corrina hunted for an access to the tunnels that would take him down to where he had left the bodies.

"Ask him," Corrina suggested, pointing at a shambling mound of rags and filth. It was a trog. Its greasy, unwashed hair hung down past its waist. Its face was covered in open sores and so many layers of dirt that his race was unguessable. Not that it mattered. He was an untouchable. None would claim him as one of their own.

"Hey, pal," Cole said, waving a hand in front of the man's face. "How do we get down?"

The trog regarded Cole through the vines of its hair. He must've seen something of himself in Cole and he grinned, showing off a few black teeth erupting from black gums. "Ya caint, pal. The wolds on far."

"On fire?" Cole's stomach began to ache.

"Ita bunnin' from da inside."

Corrina leaned back from the trog. "Did he say it was burning from the inside?" The trog nodded and pointed at her, letting out a mad cackle. He wanted the world to burn and a part of Cole did too. But he knew it wasn't all burning. It was just the part of it that mattered to him.

Chapter 26

Cole sat on the curb, his feet in the gutter and stared at the building across the street. Supposedly, its foundation was on fire, but you wouldn't know it from the lack of panic. People came and went, most without realizing there was a fire at all. Things burned in the tunnel all the time and it rarely affected the outer world.

Without much hope, Cole called the local fire department and was told that it would cost a thousand dollars just to scramble a pair of trucks; paid up front.

It was a few hours before the recovery team went down. They were back again in fifteen minutes. The lead investigator tore off his hood and stared down at Cole. "Are you sure you want your name attached to this? Because I got five bodies down there, burned beyond all recognition. Five *human* bodies."

"They were not human!" Cole cried, scrambling to his feet. "Well, two were, but I only killed one and it was in self-defense. Their blood should…"

"Their blood boiled away. Those are charred corpses; there's nothing left to test. Now, I'm going to ask you again, do you want your name associated with this mess? This is the second one of these you have on your head in the last week. It's more than just a career killer. They'll hang you for this."

Cole sat back down before he had a chance to collapse. The truth didn't matter. Once someone was accused of a crime, they had to prove their innocence and there was no way Cole could. He had no eyewitnesses, and by his own admission he had killed three of the five people in the cavern, only one of whom was armed.

"No…I guess I don't," he said.

"Then it'll cost you," the investigator replied, squatting down next to Cole. "Two-grand."

The Bulldog tucked beneath his coat seemed to pulse with malignant heat. It might've only held one bullet, but one was all he needed to kill this blackmailing asshole. Of course, if he did, he would be set upon by the rest of his team. And then what would happen to Corrina?

"I don't have anywhere near two-grand. I might be able to scrounge up four hundred." *And that's if I steal from Ashley Tinsley.*

"I'll take your apartment."

Cole couldn't believe what he was hearing. "I don't own it. Jesus! What sort of man tries to take someone's apartment?"

"Don't play dumb with me, Cole. I remember when you were hot, you crowed to anyone who'd listen that you signed a three-year lease for some fancy midtown pad, and that you paid it all up front. By my calculation, you have another year and a half of free living. Hand over the key and I'll see that this fiasco never sees the light of day."

He had no choice. He gave up his key without looking up. "Thanks, Cole," the investigator said, suddenly all smiles. "Hey, you should have that leg looked at. An open wound around Dead-eyes is a bad combo. You got a booster, right?"

"Go fuck yourself."

The investigator looked hurt. "Don't be like that. I saved your ass. You should be grateful. Here. This is the number to my doc. He doesn't do house calls, but he isn't too far. Good luck."

The recovery team picked up and left as quietly as they arrived, leaving Cole with his feet in the gutter and blood trickling from the back of his leg. Corrina sat next to him, her hands stuffed into her pockets. "At least you know where that jerk lives," she said.

In spite of the indignant fury roaring through his veins, Cole couldn't help laughing. It lasted about ten seconds before it transitioned into a screamed, "Fuck!"

Corrina nodded in agreement. "I know a guy who can get us some mule, cheap. It'll take the edge right off. Look at me. I'm homeless and I couldn't care less." He glared, but this time she only felt sorry for him. "I know you were hoping I would kinda end up being more like you the longer we hung out, but I don't think the world works that way."

"Yeah? How does it work?" It was a real question and he wanted a real answer because just then he didn't have the answer to anything.

She was cold and leaned against him, putting her head on his shoulder. "The world wears you down. It's supposed to be great when you're born. Everyone gets all excited and everything's great for a while but then with every year you get older, the world tries to crush out that happiness. Then you die. The slag gets you or you get the blood fever or a cabby runs you down. And that's it."

"Sounds depressing."

"Oh, it is. Unless you're a vamp, life sucks. That's what the mule is for. You just get on and…" Her eyes turned dreamy as she leaned back and stared at nothing. "You just ride away into sweet bliss. That's how I'm gonna go out. I'm just gonna ride the mule out into space and never come back." She turned to him and grabbed his arm, her fingers digging in, her eyes alight with sudden fervor. "That's what we should do. You and me. You got enough cash to get us gone; enough for us to never have to come back."

Cole was so tired and depressed that he actually considered her plan for a long time. Nothing he could think of spoke against the idea of just letting go. Other than Corrina, he had nothing tying him to the earth. It seemed he had come without attachments and there was nothing stopping him from leaving in the same way.

Then the rain came. The first drops arrived before the clouds. They appeared out of nowhere, the lone star still ineffectively conveying its light to earth. It was a cold, stinging rain that drove the two out of the gutter. They wandered north until Cole realized they were only a block or two from the office of "Doctor Ben Kraus MD, PhD."

Corrina sniffed at the card. It wasn't a part of her plan. Then again, neither was the rain or the late hour, or the growl in her stomach. All three pushed the idea out of her head. They found Kraus's office on a dark side street. In front of the barred door was a wide puddle that jumped with rain. The place was dark as the night.

Undeterred, Cole rapped on the door as Corrina stood to the side, yawning over and over again, one on top of the other. "We'll get you to bed in a bit," he told her as a pale, amber light came on above them. "I need a doc, open up."

"Lemme see your cash," a woman demanded from the other side of the door. "It's one-fitty at this time of night. Put the money in the slot."

The door had a letter slot, dead center. Cole reached through the bars and dropped the money inside. There was a long moment as it was counted. As he waited, Cole flung his coat in the puddle and tried to wash the now muddy crap out of it. The woman caught him squatting in the rain.

"I'll wash that for an exter five bucks." She had the look of an old whore about her. She was braless in a man's undershirt, her nipples jutting out just above the level of her bellybutton. Her face was worn and wrinkled; every other tooth was missing so that they resembled the keys of a piano when she smiled.

It was an outrageous fee, but Cole only said, "Yeah. And do hers, too." He was too tired to haggle. The woman's keyboard grin widened and she unlocked the door

"Come in. The doctor'll be right witchu. If I could get that five bucks, I'll go get a wrap for you and your…your little friend." Cole fished out a five with the woman on tiptoe trying to see into his wallet. She took the bill and left them in a rundown waiting room; the threadbare carpet was stained with blood and what was likely urine. The desk near the door leading inside was missing a leg and was propped up on a small stack of medical books that might have been published in the previous century.

The woman was not quiet and the walls were not thick. They heard her plainly as she hissed, "You got a couple of slags out here who wanna see you."

A groggy male voice mumbled, "What am I supposed to do with slags?"

"Hell if I know. You're the doc and they's paying customers, so go do some-tin. Give 'em a dram of some-tin. Make it 'spensive. The guy's loaded."

"A dram? I'm a real doc, Cloe. I don't just give out drams willy-nilly. Now do me a favor and send them packing. You know I just started a ride. No, don't give me that look. Have them come back in the morning."

"They paid already. Take a hit of zap or some-tin. Gawd." She came back with a reassuring smile and a pair of sheets. "Come on back. You can change in the exam room."

The exam room consisted of a dresser with half-open drawers, a folding chair, a bench-like table and a flickering overhead light. They took turns changing in the room and then waited for the doctor wearing nothing but the thin, unpatterned sheets. When Kraus, MD, PhD came in he was nothing like Cole had pictured him. He had sounded old and bent.

Although he had only a ring of thin hair around the crown of his peeling head, Kraus couldn't have been over forty. He was middling in height but so great was his girth that his shirt barely contained his belly. His cheeks were large and sagging toward soft jowls. His eyes were unnaturally bright and he couldn't seem to stop touching his nose as he came in filled with energy.

"What seems to be the problem that couldn't wait until morning? Huh. You know I can't treat the slag. It is what it is, sorry. Your best bet is to stay indoors during the cat-storms. That's what the alarms are for. Also if you work in one of those factories out in Brooklyn, it's going to catch up to you sooner or later. So, maybe find a new line of work."

"I'm not here about slag. I got shot." Cole pulled his sheet back far enough for Kraus to see the wound.

Kraus squinted in at the crease in the back of Cole's leg. "Oh, well that's different. Still, it could've waited until morning. That's hardly a reason to wake a man in the middle of the night."

"I'm also going to need a booster." At this the doctor made a sound like a curious owl. "Semi-vax," Cole explained. "Larson sent me."

This caused Kraus to lean back away from him. "Semi-vax?" he asked, touching his nose again. He glanced over at Corrina as if she had just sprouted fangs. His fever-bright eyes then slid over the different items on the bench next to Cole, finally noticing the Bulldog, looking huge and menacing an inch from Cole's hand.

"Yes, semi-vax," Cole repeated, satisfied with the reaction. It meant that the doc knew the score; there'd be no reason to come up with a lie. "And it better be covered by what I paid. One-fifty for a few stitches is crap." It was easier to haggle now that he was inside the office. Undoubtedly, the Bulldog helped and Cole exuded such menace that Kraus quavered and didn't argue.

The doctor started with the shot and then moved on to the wound, which he cleaned with the knowledge of where it might have come from. He was quick and thorough, wanting Cole out of his office as fast as possible. When he was done, he hurried from the room, saying, "I'll be back with your clothes when they're dry."

"He knows, don't he?" Corrina asked. "I thought it was supposed to be a big secret."

"I think it's okay that a doctor knows. Besides I didn't tell him, so I'm in the clear." At her confused look, he explained, "It's a death sentence to ever let out the secret."

"I'm so happy I know," she said, glumly. She was on the floor with her knees tucked up to her pointy little chin. When she yawned, her eyes crinkled completely shut and leaked little tears. After her fifth yawn, she asked, "What are we going to do? A boat's out of the question, ain't it?"

He grunted a, "Yeah," and went back to staring past the edge of the table at the old linoleum. His leads had all dried up. Yes, he was pretty sure that Rush was holed up in the Krupp building, but he wasn't going to make it inside now. They'd have every entrance double-guarded with his picture hung everywhere. And even if he managed to get inside, it wasn't like he could just wander around armed to the teeth, hoping to come across her.

A boat was out of the question. He didn't even have a lead on Christina. She was long gone. When a Dead-eye was flushed out of their nest, they tended to put as much distance between themselves and the hunter as possible. By then she could be in Queens, slunk down in the deepest tunnels feeding on trogs until she got her strength back.

"Fuck," he whispered and put his head down on his folded arms. He was suddenly too tired to worry just how fucked he was. While they waited for their clothes to be washed, they both fell asleep, him on the bench and Corrina in the corner. She was used to sleeping without a bed and slept just as soundly as Cole, who didn't budge until the sun cracked the sky.

The woman woke them, her voice braying like a donkey. "Git up! Come on. This ain't no flop house. Here's yer clothes. Let's go. We got real customers lining up outside."

They dressed in front of each other, both a little too groggy to care what the other looked like. Corrina was thin, her bones looking as though they were on the verge of erupting from her pale flesh. Cole was bruised, cut, scraped and shot. He winced with every motion.

"You need help with them pants, sugar?" the woman asked. She didn't mind a few bruises, not when they were on a big swinging man.

"No, thank you. I'm just a little stiff. I'll warm up here in a minute." Once he was dressed, she lost interest in him, and they were shooed out the door with indecent haste, especially since the "line" of customers consisted solely of one bundled-up woman and her croupy baby. They needed the layers because of the rain that was coming down sideways.

Cole and Corrina were immediately soaked.

"Fuuu…" Corrina began.

He cut her off midway. "Don't say it."

"Why? You say it all the time." She looked up at him, squinting against the rain. "So, about my plan. Do you want to get breakfast first? I could kill for some eggs. And maybe some French toast. Also some sausage. We should go all out because it's not like we can take it with us, right? Do you think we could get into one of them swanky vamp places?"

"Yeah, I think we can." He pulled her away from the curb as a big black limo slid silently up from behind.

It stopped next to them and the rear window came down. Cole had his hand an inch from the grip of his Bulldog. If it was Terri Rush, he would shoot first and to hell with any questions. But it was not her. It was a man, thirty-ish, with studiously bland features and oiled hair that was precisely parted. He was someone's servant.

"Mr. Younger?" His voice, like his face had a submissive vanilla quality to it. "Miss Tinsley would like to have a word with you. If you'd be so kind as to accompany me."

"The girl comes, too," Cole said, making no move for the door. He nodded curtly as if he'd been expecting the request and then tapped the glass divider that separated him from the driver area. One of Ashley's giants pulled his bulk from the front seat, nearly splitting the seams of his black suit in the process. Cole recognized the man from one of his earlier encounters with Ashley; he seemed to have gotten even larger, if that was possible.

The frisking was thorough and somewhat embarrassing. From him they took the one bullet and gun, the radio and the folded-up lease. The guard even took Cole's wallet, which was much thinner than it had been. Most of Ashley's thousand dollars was gone and what did he have to show for it? Nothing. They then moved onto Corrina, confiscating her last two cigarettes, a rubber band, a nickel she had kept squirreled away from Cole and her radio. All of this went into a zippered bag.

"You gonna give that stuff back, right?" she demanded. The giant opened the door and stuffed the girl inside. Without hesitating, Cole got in after her. He had read the implication in the giant's eyes. He would shove Cole in as well if he had to.

At least the young servant was less condescending than the last one. He pretended not to notice the fresh bruises on Cole's face, some of which even Cole couldn't remember how he got. "Would you care for some water? I also have a cherry fizz for the young miss."

"Yeah, the young miss would like that," Corrina answered. "You got any booze in this thing? You know, just a little pick me up to get my day going."

"I'm sorry, no. Miss Tinsley is particular about certain things."

"Yeah, me too," agreed Corrina, casting one leg over the other and placing her small fingers on her knee in imitation of a picture she'd seen once. Relaxed, she sipped her cherry fizz with a pinky cocked outward, enjoying the ride.

The limo took a tunnel and slid smoothly underground. Two turns later, they came to a reinforced steel door that slid back at their approach. Minutes later, they entered onto vamp street, passing the restaurant Cole had eaten at, and Miss Bobby's salon, before coming to the lower entrance of Ashley's building. Everything was shining brass and spotless crystal. The carpet in front was deep and so perfectly golden that it looked like it was replaced any time a vamp crossed it.

They slowed as they came up to it, but they did not stop. Instead the car went around the building to the back, passing the dumpsters and heading down to the garage. There'd be no fancy dinner this time. They were coming in through the servant's entrance. It was Ashley's way of putting Cole in his place and, he was sure, this was just the start. He had failed her time and again, and he fully expected her to not just scream into his face, she would do her best to humiliate him.

And she had every right to since he was just as much a servant as the vanilla-looking man across from him.

At that moment, a long ride on the mule seemed quite appealing.

Chapter 27

Ashley's majordomo stood with the same pair of guards as last time. The two guards were so devoid of emotion that they may as well have been faceless. Gavin, on the other hand, gazed on Cole without amusement. "It's a little too early for games, and yet, here you are."

Cole was not in the mood to be lectured to by the likes of Gavin. "Save it. I'm not here to see you."

Gavin only hummed disapproval in his throat. He snapped his fingers and the cloth bag that held their possessions was handed to him by the younger servant. Then, without a glance at either Cole or Corrina, he turned to the elevator which opened in front of his nose. They went down seven levels, past a hundred feet of rock and dirt, where the strongest beam of radiation could never pierce. The guards were silent, muted.

When Cole explained what that meant to Corrina, a shiver went up her spine. She thought she had known what rich was: the flashy cars, the good food, the perfect teeth, but this was rich on a level that was deeply unsettling. She stuck close to Cole as they stepped off the elevator and into the black and white entrance to Ashley's home. The stark contrasting colors only made Corrina, with her green hair and her mismatched red outfit, stand out even more.

"Don't touch anything," Gavin warned her. He had not stepped off the elevator, but watched from the steel chamber.

She wasn't about to. Everything in the room was worth more than her entire life. She even tried to walk lightly, hoping her old, second-hand sneakers would make only a tenuous contact with the floor and thus not leave a mark.

The entrance way was intimidating enough, but the long parlor that Ashley used to greet guests was enough to steal the bravado right out of the girl. She gaped at the two fireplaces, the gold-framed pictures, the lion skin rug, and the long piano. She was stunned speechless by the opulence and then stunned again by Ashley Tinsley herself.

Her hair was now a pale, Nordic blonde. Her eyes were blue in the center, surrounded by what looked like liquid gold. The blue matched her gown which was deep cut in front, sharply narrow at the waist and then flowed down and out like a waterfall.

In comparison, Cole looked like a disheveled, beat-up slag standing there with his mouth open and closing like a landed trout. Her beauty was such a force that he found himself speechless.

"You have certainly made a mess of things," she declared. "To use a turn of phrase that you might understand better: you've fucked things to pieces. And what in God's name is that smell?" Her perfect nose wrinkled in disgust. Cole's clothes might have been clean, but he wasn't.

And this was why Cole knew he'd never be able to "bliss out," as overdosing on mule was called. He had too much anger inside him for that. "That's the smell of someone who's been around one too many vamps. You guys are so full of shit it's amazing."

Her brows, a pale blonde to match her current hair color, came down sharply, nearly forming a perfect V. "I am full of shit? How so? Please tell me what I have done in all of this? All I asked you to do is take care of one simple problem and you can't even seem to do that right."

"Actually, I can. Christina Grimmett is dead. She died days ago. In fact it was the very night she went to *Leather Lounge*, but I think you knew that all along." As he spoke, strange pieces of a distorted puzzle were suddenly falling into place. "You don't care one whit about your servants. I bet you don't even know their names. And yet you knew all about Christina. You knew where she was last seen and you even knew the fake name she'd been using."

Ashley's blue and gold eyes flicked away, confirming to Cole that he was on the right track.

"The question is why?" Her face went stone still. It was a perfect statue. She was afraid to give anything away.

Would she be afraid that her fellow vamps knew a servant had stolen from her? No. Vamps looked down their noses at everyone. It wouldn't be a surprise to them that a half-slag servant was stealing. And there was no way a person like Ashley Tinsley would be upset that someone dropped her name in some dive like the *Leather Lounge*.

No, this was far bigger.

It was big enough to include a Dead-eye hunter. Cole suddenly felt very stupid. "You already knew Christina was dead or had *changed*." A single muscle next to Ashley's lip twitched—he had struck home.

"Perhaps we should continue this conversation in private." As her guards were already "muted" she meant Corrina. When Cole hesitated, she added, "For her sake." It was a strange thing for a vamp to say and Cole wondered if she really meant it.

"What do you think?" Cole asked Corrina. "You want to see what they have to eat in this place?"

Ashley's smile twitched again. She had been thinking the kid could wait in the garage or out in the rain. Corrina saw the twitch and guessed correctly what it meant. "We're in this together," she said to Cole, taking a possessive grip on his arm. She didn't like the struck-by-a-hammer look he had gotten when he had first caught sight of the vamp.

"It's your funeral," Ashley replied. "So, Cole what do you know?"

"I know Christina showed up at the *Leather Lounge* and was taken by a Dead-eye named Mike McDonald. He just happened to work for Krupp Metalworks, which I'm guessing is owned by the Tinsley family?"

"We own a controlling interest," she admitted.

Cole hoped that she would share more information, but when she didn't, he went on, "Two other Dead-eyes also worked there. Billy Fish and a woman named Terri Rush. She mentioned you by name." Ashley drew in a long, slow breath and again Cole waited for her to fill in some of the many blanks in his narrative, and again she remained silent. "McDonald, Fish, and another very odd-looking Dead-eye died last night, but Christina managed to get away. As did Rush. But once more, you know all this."

She shrugged. "I knew most of it. The important parts, I should say."

By that she meant she really didn't care about McDonald or Billy Fish. But she did care about Christina, or rather, she cared that she was connected to Christina and Cole guessed that hadn't happened by accident. "You were being blackmailed, weren't you? By your brother?" During their dinner together, she had mentioned that her family was "broken" and the first time he had met her, Ashley had let slip that her brother's home was twice the size of her own. Was he twice as rich, as well?

"In a way, yes." She went tight-lipped, but Cole was tired of doing all the talking. He stared at her, perfectly comfortable with stony silence. She gave in when Corrina decided to take a seat on one of the soft couches. Ashley's upper lip drew back. "Fine. He was counter-blackmailing me. I had found out about Rush and the others. He was using them to do his dirty work for him, and I threatened to let it get out. He retaliated by trying to turn Christina."

"And you stuck me right in the middle of your little war. Nice," he added sarcastically. "You and your brother aren't twins, are you?"

Anger flared like a volcano inside her and her eyes flicked to one of her bodyguards. Cole guessed that she was contemplating having him beaten. Perhaps the idea of him bleeding on her carpet made her second-guess herself. "I paid you extra to do your job," she spat. "You should be thanking me. If you hadn't screwed up, you could've been thirty-grand richer."

She wasn't done venting. She turned to Corrina. "And you. What's with the hair? You could be pretty if you tried."

"It was supposed to be blue but cuz my hair is the same color as yours, it went green."

Ashley rubbed her temples. "Does it even matter?" she asked, looking into Corrina's face. She wasn't talking to Corrina, however. "You cleaned up my brother's problem for him. McDonald or whoever it was, tried to get cute and took Christina, thinking they could double blackmail both of us. It's why Rush was out there searching for her at the same time you were. But then you went and killed off the riffraff and left Rush alive. Now there's no way we'll be able to get to her. She's almost certainly back at Krupp and she knows that factory inside and out. She knows the tunnels. She knows everything. I can't go to my father with tales of a ghost. Besides, my brother says he has Christina and if I go to our father he'll bring her out. It'll be tit for tat in my father's eyes. Chances are he'll turn the company over to one of our cousins."

"Tit for tat?" Cole asked in shock. "These are Deadeyes you're talking about. Harboring one is a capital offense. They'll string you and your brother up by the neck."

She laughed at this, waving a hand. "*Who* will? The governor? Don't you realize who runs this city? My family and families like ours. We put the governor in place and we tell him what to say and how to act. He's a puppet. You all are." She turned and waved a hand. "You can go."

Cole didn't budge. "I don't think so. You owe me a thousand dollars. I found Christina and for all intents and purposes, she has disappeared. Trust me on this. Even if your brother has her, which I highly doubt, she looks nothing like she used to. Someone screwed up and they fed on her and she died. What came back isn't her."

Ashley looked over her shoulder at him. To Cole it looked like a practiced pose, but practiced or not, she was breathtakingly beautiful and he had to pretend her beauty didn't affect him—her words helped. "When you show me her dead body, I'll give you a thousand. Until then, leave. And I'd think really hard about telling anyone anything about this. I like you, Cole. I really do. But I will have you killed if I have to. That goes double for you, sweetie," she said to Corrina.

Ashley turned and walked away. Cole took one step to follow when a huge hand clapped down on his shoulder. It was the guard. He dug his fingers into Cole's flesh. They were irresistible, like the roots of an oak. Cole's teeth clamped together in pain. "Wait! I can get Rush. I can kill her."

This stopped Ashley. She stood next to the piano, her blue lacquered nails tapping gently, all five on her left hand going up and down as one, like blue teeth. "How?"

"If you can get me into the factory, I can make her come to me. You said there were tunnels? Get me inside and I'll take care of the rest. There's just one thing I need." In truth, there were a dozen things he needed, but the first and foremost was a new gun. He couldn't go up against Rush with only the Bulldog. "I need a Crown '61. Really, any Crown will do, but if I…"

Ashley turned away. With her back to him, she said. "No. I don't throw good money after bad. I bet on you and lost. Slink back into your dirty world and give this up. Or go and die. I really don't care which." She walked away, leaving Cole fuming and Corrina feeling vindicated.

She did not like Ashley Tinsley one bit, except her hair that is. Corrina had already decided to grow hers out before she remembered that she and Cole had already made a suicide pact. They were supposed to be blissing out. "Come on, Cole. We don't need her."

She had been watching Ashley and didn't realize that the guards were already "assisting" Cole to the elevators. She ran to catch up and considered kicking one of them in the shins, but thought better of it. It would be like kicking a tree-trunk. She was almost an afterthought and slipped into the elevators just as the doors were closing.

The ride was quick and silent. The guards were still muted and Cole stood between them in tight-lipped fury. Corrina expected them to be let out in the servants' area, but they went all the way to street level where Gavin waited. "I trust this will be the last we see of you, Mr. Younger."

When Cole said nothing to this, Gavin shrugged and lifted the zippered bag with their belongings. Instead of handing it to them, he opened it and fished out Cole's wallet. He held it by the edge. "As your services are no longer needed." He slipped out the remaining cash, a wad of over three hundred dollars.

"Hey! That's…" A giant hand came down on each of his shoulders, buckling his knees.

"You did not fulfill your end of the contract and deserve nothing. Luckily for you, Miss Tinsley is not petty." Stepping closer, he took a twenty from the stack and stuffed it into Cole's pocket. "For services rendered." He then handed Cole the bag.

"Services rendered," Cole muttered, looking through the bag. "That's complete bullshit. Hey, where's my bullet?" He felt utterly stupid asking for the single bullet; stupid and weak. There was the Bulldog but no bullet.

Gavin held up the last bullet. "Take my advice, Cole. Forget the bullet and pawn the gun. You aren't made for this type of work."

Cole only held out his hand. He wasn't cut out for any work as far as he could tell. He would never enslave himself to a heartless corporation like Krupp, and he didn't have the imbecilic patience to be a bodyguard for some preening vamp. Retail was out of the question, as was anything to do with food, except fishing that is.

He had a fleeting image of a thirty-two foot sailing vessel in his mind when he was unexpectedly shoved from behind. When one of the giants shoved someone they tended to go airborne. Cole was a little too big for that; still, he would've gone face first onto the marble floor, if he hadn't been caught by the building guard in the blue suit. Somehow this giant managed to be even less sympathetic than the other two and in seconds, Cole was thrown out of the building.

Once more, he found himself sitting in a gutter. It was a cleaner gutter than the last one he'd been in. "At least it's an uptown gutter," he muttered as Corrina came to sit beside him. They were quiet as the rain pelted them until Cole groaned. "I'm such an idiot! Now I know why she had dinner with me. She didn't think I was interesting. She was trying to send a message to her brother that she had a bought and paid for hunter going after Christina. God, I hate vamps."

"Everyone does, but it's okay. Twenty will still get us there," she told him.

"Get us where? Oh, the mule." He grimaced. "I'm sorry, but I can't. It's wrong. And I'm not done with this. There are still two of them out there. If I can get into Krupp one more time..." He sighed, the rain in his hair was coming down in little rivers. "Twenty grand will still get us a boat. Maybe not the best one, but we'll make do."

Deep down, she didn't believe there would ever be a boat. He would have to get incredibly lucky just to get inside the Krupp place, and when had Cole ever been lucky? Never as far as she knew. She glanced up at him. His battered face was turned out, but he saw none of the rainy city. His eyes were unfocused, his mind elsewhere. She found herself staring at him and decided that even with his battered face, he was handsome. She liked him. He was always trying to do the right thing. It was weird.

"How you gonna get in?"

He stood, seeming as tall as the giants. "I'll go through the front door. It'll work. I know the place now. I know how everything works."

She wanted to believe him, but she was afraid. This was Cole's last chance and maybe hers as well. A part of her that had been growing larger over the last few days didn't want to bliss out. It wanted to buy a boat with him and explore to the edge of the world where the sun lifted every morning. It wanted to do something besides ride the mule and spread her legs. That part of her was afraid. For the first time in a long time, she had something to be afraid for.

Of course, with that fear came the desire to hide, to run, to smother herself in a vague drug haze. Her leg started bouncing up and down.

"It'll be okay," Cole told her. He put out his hand and helped her up. "Come on. I can't go in looking like this."

She took him in from top to bottom. "You look like shi…crap. You look like crap." He had shot a glare her way.

"Yeah, I'm sure. Still, I don't look crappy enough." They headed for the nearest subway and took it south. They were still damp when they were let out a block from Tom Storck's and soaked again by the time he let them in.

"Change your mind on that *Lady Eagle*?" he asked, grinning up at Cole. "She's a beaut."

Cole wished he could afford a backup, even one as tiny as a *Lady Eagle*. "No, I need some ammo for the Bulldog."

Storck's round face fell inward in disappointment. It lasted only a second and then he was off, grinning again, rambling that: "A sale was a sale," and that, "A gun needs bullets. Isn't much good without them. Am I right?" He was very eager to sell ammo, but only at his price. He would not budge from a dozen rounds for fifteen dollars. Not even when Cole begged him. Cole even tried to bring patriotism into it, which only confused Storck.

"Patriotism? I don't follow you. Like patriotism from the old days? If so, don't be vulgar."

As Cole couldn't mention the word zombies, he gave in and accepted the dozen bullets. He walked out into the rain, down to his last five dollars and even that was soon gone as he dragged Corrina to a tattoo parlor. It was located in the backroom of a very questionable wig shop. On the way through, they passed a pair of tiny Mandarin ladies shaving an old corpse right down to its pubes.

"Fuuu…" Corrina started to say, only to be elbowed by Cole.

"We're in Dragon territory, so be careful what you say," he warned. "They can be touchy."

Corrina didn't just hold her tongue, she held her throat, afraid that she would puke. The back room doubled as a bedroom. At Cole's knock, a beautiful, deeply tan woman of unknown heritage opened the door. She had huge dark eyes and waves of luxurious black hair that hung down to her waist.

"Mr. Cole! What have you done with my favorite face? You are supposed to come in handsome and leave a slag. I cannot do the other way around."

"It's nothing, Anuba. And I don't want to be handsome. I need you to make me more of a slag than ever."

Wrinkles appeared around her mouth as she pursed her lips. "If you say so, Mr. Cole. Do you want me to butch your hair as well? A couple of hunks out will change your appearance very much."

Corrina shook her head, however Cole sighed and said, "Do what you got to do."

Much to Corrina's annoyance, Anuba sat Cole in a chair and straddled him, staring at his face. "You're halfway there already." She ran her fingers through his short hair, frowning harder than before. With a flourish she produced a pair of scissors and began hacking away indiscriminately. Next she used foul-smelling yellowed lard from an old jar to spike up what remained of his hair.

Once he looked as though he had missed his annual bath for the last three years, she brought out a long needle. It was very much like a knitting needle, but instead of stabbing him with it as Corrina figured she might, Anuba began to draw on his face and neck.

The drawings were crude: a naked woman took up one side of his face; her right breast centered on his left eye while her other breast was only hinted at, disappearing into his hairline. Across his left cheek she drew a pair of dice showing a five and a two. On one side of his throat were five playing cards, all aces, and on the other, a pile of cash. All of this was done while incorporating his cuts and bruises, making it seem as if the tats had been there first. It was crude but also incredibly deft.

When Anuba was done, Cole barely looked like himself.

"What kind of Puerto Rican are you?" Corrina asked, while staring in wonder at Cole.

"I'm not a Puerto Rican, thank you very much," Anuba replied, indignantly. "I am Indian and I can trace my lineage back fifteen generations to the Governor of Raigad who served at the pleasure of Queen Victoria. What Puerto Rican can say that?"

As Corrina couldn't even remember her mother's real name and Cole was an orphan, neither could comment on what Puerto Ricans could or could not say. "A real queen. Like with a crown and all?" Corrina asked. "That must have been awesome."

The haughty, imperious look on Anuba's face melted away. It was wrong to boast when she was living only slightly better than the average slag. "For them I'm sure it was. Mr. Cole, I thank you for your business and I wish you the best."

With the five dollars gone, they were down to Corrina's last nickel.

It sat in her palm, all but useless. "This had better work," she told Cole, handing it to him. He had no need for it, but took it for luck. He was once more walking into the lion's den; he needed all the luck he could get.

Chapter 28

Corrina had one job: she was to linger within eyesight of the main entrance to the Krupp factory and watch for anything out of the ordinary, like the police. Cole thought he had a better than even chance if he was just going up against Rush. If she brought in security guards, his chances dropped dramatically to maybe one in four.

If the police were called in, all bets were off.

As Cole meandered down the block toward the end of the line of slags waiting to get inside the factory, he huddled in his ratty coat, shoulders hunched up around his ears. Although his chin was down, he kept his eyes up, shifting them right and left, looking for his old partner, Bruce Hamilton. The fact that Bruce had been bought off by Rush for five dollars spoke volumes. He didn't want money, he wanted Cole dead.

It seemed a lot of people did.

He caught sight of Corrina "pretending" to be a honey, soliciting the men walking by. For both their sakes, he hoped she was pretending. "What if they take me up on it?" she had asked around the ragged end of a thumbnail she'd been chewing on. He didn't think she'd have a nail left with her nerves jacked up like they were. "Men do want me, you know."

Sadly, he knew they did, and for the right price she could have them lined up around the block. It's why he told her to keep her rate high. She was to start at two dollars, an unheard of price for a girl who was little more than gristle and bone.

As he walked by she keyed her radio and his crackled softly in his pocket. He nodded, but left his untouched. No matter what, he couldn't call attention to himself. He had to look and act like every other down on his luck slag standing in the line. Other than his height and his broad shoulders, he blended in perfectly.

A man in a suit walked by, his nose in the air, his right arm cocked at a ninety-degree angle, an umbrella in his hand. He kept his eyes straight ahead, and to him, Cole was just part of the background scenery that set the stage for his life. To him, Cole was no more alive than the sidewalk under his feet.

Perfect, Cole thought. It was his first test. The second was how he was accepted by his fellow slags. There were three types. The first and most prevalent was the quiet, staring loner who was only taking up space on the sidewalk. If there had ever been magic in their lives, it was long gone and now they were simply accumulating minutes and seconds, stacking them up like casino chips; worthless casino chips. None of these men bothered to focus on anything short of a five-alarm fire and to them, Cole was a faceless shadow.

The second type were the talkers. These were men who still had a touch more spark than the rest. The fact that they had nothing of importance to say did not deter them. In the long line there were easily a dozen of them talking about the rain. Maybe another half dozen were talking about their endlessly bitching, plain-faced wives. A few talked sports, though there were very few sports left to talk about.

The last group were the listeners. These tended to lack the wit to reply to the talkers, but they appreciated the constant flow of words, nonetheless. They came at a fixed rate and that was good. They ate up time in line, time on the job and the worn-out minutes during the long walk home.

Cole acted the part of a mute, drenched to the bone shambler and was accepted. He was just another worker. Standing on the various stoops, the neighborhood men advertised their disregard for him and the others in line by the way they wore their old and frayed wire-stiffened wool Fedoras low on their brow. It made them eyeless and, eyeless, they judged the Krupp slags and found them wanting.

Half the slags in line sipped from discrete thermoses and by the time they cleared the Krupp gates, they had trouble standing straight. The Tier 3s didn't care how drunk they were. If a slag fell into a blast furnace, that was their too bad; Krupp didn't pay the dead.

Except it turns out that they did.

The thought almost made Cole chuckle, but he held back as he made his way through the gates and into the Charging Room, where the one line branched out. He chose a center line so he could better blend in and, like everyone else, he shuffled along in a puddle of his own making under the watchful eyes of the Krupp guards. It was not just his imagination, they were far more vigilant than they had been. Here and there, men were pulled out of line and dragged away.

Cole forced his eyes down and slouched further into himself, praying that the bulge made by the Bulldog beneath his coat wasn't obvious. It seemed like forever before he found himself in front of a desk, trying to look small. Behind it was a Tier 3 in the usual one-piece green overalls. He took a long weary breath before sliding over a pin. "You're gonna be 5229. Where you been working?" At the question, Cole felt his throat clench—the words and the voice were the exact same as the last time he'd come through the Krupp gates. Cole stole a quick peek at the man behind the desk and yes, he saw the same big head and the same sparse, weedy hair. The same dark eyes sat over the same cracked bloodshot mesh of a nose regarded him with practiced indifference.

Unbelievably it was the same Tier 3 who had in-processed him only a few days before.

"Da pit," Cole said, dropping his eyes before the Tier 3 could see the intelligence in them. "Da in-fin...da in-trin..."

"The infinity pit. Good. We'll get you back there. Sign here. The pay is five cents 'n hour. You get two fifteen-minute bathroom breaks every shift and a thirty-minute lunch. Once you change into your uni, take this form down the stairs as far as they'll go. Next!"

Almost in.

The last hurdle was a stern-faced Tier 4 in white. He was not taking any chances and he made a study of every man who went past him. His look was one of angry suspicion and when he looked into his face, Cole felt his mouth go dry. Anuba's artwork fooled the man. He saw only a slag and grunted for Cole to go on to the locker rooms. From there his infiltration took on a more normal routine. As before, the Tier 2s directed him to his locker and then, when he was draped in brown, to the stairs.

"All the way to the bottom," the last said, with a touch of sympathy in his voice.

Cole limped his way down. The Bulldog was too much metal to try to hide beneath the form-fitting material and so he had it strapped to his ankle. It wobbled there, threatening to spill out onto the stairs.

He didn't have to go deep into the earth. The second level down was dedicated to a vast subterranean machine shop that ran the entire length of the enormous building above. The noise inside was shocking to the ears. Metal was being ground, filed, drilled, pounded, heated and then pounded some more. Machines whirred, stamped, screeched and rumbled. The noise would've drowned out a dozen jackhammers. Krupp not only refined scrap, it also churned out thousands of items from forks to the fine springs found in the internal workings of the Crown semiautomatic handguns.

For the most part, the workers here wore Tier 2 blue overalls. Even though most of them were slags, they were still considered skilled labor and many of them could command wages north of a dollar an hour.

In his brown overalls, Cole stood out, and within seconds a Tier 3 accosted him, screaming at the top of his lungs to be heard. "You! You tryin' to get yourself killed? Where's your friggin' hardhat? Who the hell let this fuck-face on the floor like this?"

"I'm a runner from Finance," Cole cried, producing a piece of paper that he had brought with him. He had done his best to make it look official. "Is there someone named Don Tate here? It says Don Tate, machinist." It was the fourth name on McDonald's lease. As Cole had no idea if he still worked at Krupp, it was a bit of a Hail Mary.

The Tier 3 looked at the paper, his eyes hopping bird-like to land on the words he knew. "It says just machinist? It doesn't say what section he's in?"

"No. They said the Finance Division has back pay for him. You ever heard anything like that? Back pay; that's when they owe him money, right?"

"I think so," the Tier 3 agreed, but only half-heartedly. He had never heard of Krupp forking over extra money in all the time he'd been there.

Cole pulled him aside and spoke directly into his ear. "You think Tate might give us a finder's fee? You know, if we help him get his money, we get like a dollar or a quarter or something." The man had never heard of that either, but he jumped at the idea. Together they went to the various sections and asked around until they got a nibble. A finger was pointed and by process of elimination, they found Tate hunched over a complicated-looking hunk of machinery that was spinning and whirring, shooting sparks in a golden fountain.

Tate was taller than Cole had expected. When he unfolded from the lathe, he was Cole's height. Although he had broad shoulders, he was not particularly thick. His dull brown eyes peered out from a face that was even more covered in tattoos than Cole's. The tats were themeless, representing a shifty mind. Like his mind, his eyes were shifty as well. This was expected. A no-one like Tate had every right to be nervous when a Tier 3 stopped him in the middle of a job.

But those eyes were also nervous and shifty when they took in Cole's large form.

Who would be nervous of a slag? As far as Tate was concerned, Cole was a nobody runner whose only job was to convey messages. So why the look? Why did he continually touch his oily hair? Did he think Cole cared that the part in it wasn't exact?

"It may be your lucky day, Tate," the Tier 3 yelled, clapping him on the shoulder. "I had to hunt you down because Finance owes you some money. When you come back we're going to have to talk."

Tate sent another glance Cole's way before asking, "Coming back? Where am I going?"

"Finance," Cole told him. "Come on." He wasn't about to walk in front of Tate. Cole kept to his left as they snaked their way through the level. Instead of going to the stairs, Cole directed him to a suite of offices he had noticed during the convoluted path the Tier 3 had led him on.

The doors bore the owl eye emblem of Hooty's Bikes, a company that had gone out of business when Cole was a kid. Despite transportation of all sorts being overly expensive, bicycles had never been a hot commodity in New York. They were easily stolen and, for the most part, people lived, worked, and shopped all within the same ten blocks.

One of the doors into that part of the factory was leaning, cockeyed and drunk. Its hinges had been stolen or "re-appropriated" as it was termed on the second level down. "In there," Cole said, taking Tate by the elbow in a fierce grip. "We have to talk about some of your old friends."

It was a strange thing with Dead-eyes; put a gun in their face and they were fearless; dangle them over a fire and they'd spit on you, threaten to unmask them and they became weak. They want to blend in. They want to be people.

The pair moved deep into the dark offices until Cole found an interior one where the light wouldn't slip out to the rest of the level. Not that anyone would care. Everyone on the floor had been toiling like ants since the moment they had arrived. They didn't have time to worry about what someone else might be doing.

As the cacophony had faded to an ever-present background thrum, Cole was able to use his normal voice. Though his normal voice when dealing with what might be a Dead-eye was edgy and fast. There was nothing friendly about it. "Tell me about your friends Mack-D and Billy Fish." He pushed Tate down into a chair in front of a conference room table. Cole sat opposite from him, facing the door. "What happened to them? And don't play coy. You see this?" Cole took out his hunter's license. "It means as far as you are concerned, I am the police." To further make his point, Cole pulled the Bulldog and laid it on the table, without taking his hand from the grip.

The blood drained from Tate's face as he stared at the gun. It took him three tries to begin and then he couldn't finish. "They…they, uh…they, uh, they got bit. By, by, by, by…" He choked and sobbed, and to Cole's amazement, he started to cry.

"Enough!" Cole snapped. He was beginning to fear the worst: Tate wasn't a zombie. "Look at me. Look in my eyes. Your mother loves you."

It wasn't right to ask the question while Tate was crying. It would most certainly mess up the response. Or so Cole thought. Tate seemed to latch onto the statement. "Yes. Yes, she does. She's a good woman and she did her best with me and my sister…"

"Shut up. Only answer the questions I put before you. You are outside your apartment and you find a litter of puppies beneath a…"

Tate raised his hand. "What's a litter? And I don't wanna be mean or anything, but puppies are extinct."

Cole bunched a fist and nearly pounded the table. "Don't interrupt. Forget the puppies, okay? Let's talk about your neighbor. She had a baby two days ago. The baby is small and beautiful. Her skin is a delicate pink and her legs are chubby. Now, the mother is boiling her baby for dinner."

His face devolved into lines; some crossed his forehead, some made deep parentheses on either side of his mouth, making folds in his tattoos. "Who? I-I mean, why? I don't understand. I don't know any of my neighbors. Why would they do that?"

"Perhaps she was hungry," Cole said calmly. Tate's response had been uneven at best.

"Well, that's stupid. You don't eat a baby. It's wrong and gross."

Cole took a deep breath, not liking his answer as it was too human. "You're out by the Hempstead Wall and you come across a turtle that's on its back with its four legs kicking feebly. There's a big hole in the wall, big enough to crawl through. Rats are coming in to eat the turtle. The rats are starving. On the ground next to the wall is a pile of bricks which you can use to either close up the wall or kill the rats."

Dead-eyes are invariably confused by the question. To them the main feature of the story is the hole in the wall. It represents a way into society. But a hole in the wall was also wrong. It could mean that worse things than rats could get in. The Dead-eye feared that by not choosing to fix the hole, the questioner would assume that he would want things to come in.

"I'd kill the rats," Tate said quickly. "Look, I don't know what they told you, but I'm not one of *them*. I know I should've gone to the police, but they warned…no they threatened me and said that if I went to the police, they would kill me and I…"

"Shut up," Cole ordered, blowing hot air from his nostrils in a quick burst, like a bull. Tate wasn't a Dead-eye. It had been a long shot to begin with. In truth, Cole hadn't expected to even find Tate. He had expected to simply grab the first slag he came to and fake it. There was no way Rush or anyone at Krupp really knew who was who on this level.

On the table in front of Cole, sitting primly, despite the fine particles of dust across it, was a black phone. He dialed his boss. Ms. Foller was cool to him, but not hostile. She was adopting a wait and see approach to hating him.

Lieutenant Lloyd had the same idea. His tone was conversational, but leery. "Whatcha up to, Cole? Making more trouble for the department?"

"I'm doing my job. I'm at Krupp staring at a probable Dead-eye." Tate started to gather himself, preparing to release a new round of proclamations of innocence. Cole pointed the Bulldog at him. "Yeah, I got a guy here named,

Don Tate. He was the fourth roommate on McDonald's lease."

Lloyd didn't ask who McDonald was. He knew the players, which meant he wasn't just keeping tabs on the case, he was neck deep in it. Cole was counting on this.

"Yeah? Don Tate?" Lloyd said distractedly. The sound of a pen scritching was loud in Cole's ear.

"Yeah, he just told me that two of his roommates had a run-in with a chick here at Krupp named Terri Rush. They came away zombies. She's connected. She's working with the Tinsleys, so we better tread carefully on this one."

"Of course. That's always been the policy. You should keep that in mind. Take your time with this one. You hear me? Before you even think about plugging anyone, I want you to give this guy the full empathy test. No shortcuts, do you hear me? I'm going to head over and make sure you don't fuck this up."

You mean you'll make sure you can profit from this, Cole thought. "Sure. Just make sure you bring plenty of backup. We don't know if it's just the two of them." Lloyd said that he would and hung up without another word. Cole didn't hang up the phone, he set it aside where it buzzed softly, as if it were alive.

Tate sat shaking his head. "I'm not one of them. They wanted to turn me but I ran. You gotta believe me."

"I do."

"Then, then I can go?" He started to stand, but stopped as Cole aimed the Bulldog once again.

"Sorry, no. I need you. What's a trap without bait?"

Chapter 29

Strictly speaking, Cole was the actual bait. No one cared about Tate. He was the excuse. He was the trail of breadcrumbs.

Lloyd was probably already on the phone seeing who would pay the most to know that Cole was once again in the Krupp factory. Would his first call be to Ashley Tinsley? Cole pictured her in all her many forms. She was a chameleon. She could be anyone. "Except for her ears," Cole muttered. He would know her by her ears.

Tate looked like he wanted to ask what Cole had said. His mouth came open crookedly, his jaw not quite under his control.

"Just sit there and try not to move," Cole told him, his mind slipping back to Ashley. A call to her would be a waste of time. There was a reason he had been tossed out on the street in front of her building. Just as with the dinner, she had been sending a public message. This time she had announced that she was done with Cole Younger.

Feeling the sting of rejection made him think of Corrina. He reached into his pocket for the radio. "You there?"

Static hissed at him in reply; then there was a moment of jumbled scraping sounds before Corrina got on, whispering, "Yeah."

"I just made the call, so be on the lookout. We should expect some sort of response in the next ten minutes or so."

"Okay. Be careful, alright? Everyone around this place is extra jumpy." She was afraid. He could picture her slunk down in the doorway of the building across the street, looking like just another orphan hiding from the rain and scratching for a nickel. The reality of her situation was far more precarious and it struck him that he had been wrong not to buy her the *Lady Eagle*. She deserved to be able to protect herself.

"Remember, you're just eyeballing things. We'll meet up at that gin-joint after, okay?"

"Okay." She sounded small and far away.

He was just thinking that he should say something else to reassure her when he caught Tate looking at him. "Those aren't real tattoos," Tate said, grinning. "They're fantastic. Who did them?"

Before Cole could answer, he heard a metallic *thunk* from somewhere in the maze of offices. "That was fast." In fact, it was way too fast. He had left clues for Terri Rush. Tate's name was obvious, but he had also told him he was a machinist, which would narrow the search to the second level, down. It was still an enormous area. And he had left the phone off the hook, which would clue in the company's phone operators,

Cole had figured he would have fifteen minutes, not two. Whoever was out there had zeroed in on him…him or Tate. "They told you I was coming, didn't they?"

He looked startled, too startled to think up a quick enough lie. "Yeah," he admitted. "It was a woman. She said she worked for the boss. The *big* boss. I had to do it. Don't shoot me, okay."

"Shut up," Cole growled, slipping from his chair. "Come over here and lie down. Don't move and don't call out. She's after me, but that doesn't mean she won't want to clean house. If you get a chance, run and don't look back. I'm going to try to draw her away."

"You're leaving me?"

Cole slammed a hand down on his mouth. "Shut up! They can hear just fine. Listen for the gunfire. If I take her down, I'll call out. If I don't, then run, and for fuck's sakes keep quiet." Cole gave his face an extra hard shove before getting up. A part of him wanted to let Darwin take care of Tate. He looked like the kind of guy who would run at the exact wrong moment anyway.

Why not let that moment work for me? Cole shook off the evil thought and headed for the door. He didn't want to head out into the hallway—he was afraid to. That was the truth. He wanted the Dead-eye to come to him. He wanted her to open the door to the conference room and eat half a dozen bullets. At the same time, he felt trapped in the room. What if she brought two other Dead-eyes with her? Or three or five? They could overwhelm him with sheer numbers.

No, it felt better to be moving in the semi-dark where he could hide in the shadows. And there were a lot of shadows on the deserted factory floor, all bizarre, angular and alien. Machines that Cole had never heard of stood like hulking menacing statues. In a way, they resembled an unknown metal race. They were alive. For now, they slept, but with a flick of a switch they would roar into motion, their mouths filled with razored edges, their arms protruding foot-long spinning spikes.

Cole slipped between them, his head jutting up high on his extended neck, a strange sensation coming over him. He was being hunted. He could feel it; he could feel *her*. He could feel Rush's animal presence looming, growing larger. She was the lion and he was the mouse, small and weak. It was a sickening feeling.

His entire body was stiff and straight as he listened, straining to catch the slightest sound. There were a thousand sounds pulsing through the walls and up through the floor. They were the backdrop. What he needed was one close by.

The first sound that came to him was a tin *pkank*. His elbow had hit an oil can and knocked it off a squat little iron machine and onto the cement floor. Cole came close to shooting himself in the foot as he spun and pointed the Bulldog down at the can.

"Is that you, Mr. Younger?" Rush called out, playfully.

Goosebumps flared across his arms and down his right leg as he shrunk down next to the closest hunk of rusting iron, his gun pointed outward; he had to will it to stop shaking.

A shadow flitted from one machine to another. Rush moved with feline stealth while at the same time, she wanted her shadow seen. She was toying with him.

"Do you know who I work for?" she asked. Now he saw her. Rush stood, partially entwined in an upright knee miller. She was slim and athletic, only slightly wider than the miller. He could take a shot at her, but his chance of hitting her was less than fifty-fifty. And even if he hit her, what good would it do? He needed a headshot, a clean one. She knew this and was offering him just enough of herself for him to waste a bullet.

Did she know that he only had the Bulldog? Six shots and then came the slow process of reloading.

She knew. "Cat got your tongue, Mr. Younger? I see you. I could kill you, if I wanted. Or should I say, I could kill you if Dennis Tinsley wanted me to. He's the only reason you're still alive."

Was that Ashley's brother?

"Is that so?" Cole finally answered, easing behind the machine, careful not to touch any of the buttons or switches. He was sure that if he accidentally turned it on, it would snatch him up and turn him inside out in seconds. "I thought it was because I was killing off Dead-eyes faster than you could make them. How many have I got so far? Five, six?"

"But you haven't got me yet," she said, swinging out from the miller, one leg kicking high, like a pole dancer. She was baiting him to shoot. "McDonald and Fish? They were dim bulbs to begin with. You know that. You know that a Dead-eye slag is still just a slag."

Cole edged to his left behind a line of hydraulic presses and for a moment, he lost sight of her, but then she changed position as well and for a fraction of a second he had her in his sights. He didn't waste the opportunity. From twenty-six feet he fired twice and once more, the Bulldog pulled down and to the right. Instead of blasting out the back of her head, his first shot missed altogether, passing just below her ear. The second slug went into her shoulder and threw her backward.

She went with the momentum of the shot and turned a neat somersault, disappearing behind another hunk of metal.

"What kind of shooting is that, Mr. Younger? You had me dead to rights and you missed. Maybe Mr. Tinsley is wrong about you."

"What's he know about…" A booming, thunderous gunshot rang out and the air in front of Cole's face roiled with the heat of a passing hunk of metal. When the slug struck one of the machines, it didn't whine away. There was a huge *Krraang!!* sound as if someone had smacked it with a cast-iron frying pan. "Christ!"

Rush laughed. "You like that? It's the latest model Eagle. It's the .70 caliber *Screaming Eagle*, Mr. Younger. The damn thing is a cannon. It makes your Bulldog look like a water pistol."

It also only has five shots, Cole thought. They were even. Four apiece. This was the only thing that kept him from running out of there at full speed. Just getting clipped by a .70 cal could be enough to put him on his back. He decided to switch positions and dashed from behind his machine. Three long strides took him across a short walkway. He wasn't fast enough. The head-ringing thunder again was followed by a harsh burning pain across his back as he dove behind a many-armed metal creature.

She was faster than he had expected and her aim, even with a gun that was far too large for her hands, was shocking. He felt blood trickle down his sides even before his slide stopped. Above him on the machine was a switch that was pointed down toward a tiny red "STOP" sign. He snapped it up and began rolling to his left just as the Eagle roared again. Another *Krraang!!* cut the air, only now it was muffled as the machine came to life with a high, fierce whine.

The machine was possessed. As two of its robotic arms went up and down in unison, a third began jabbing out at nothing. At the end of the arm was a stunted, blunt spear that spun into a blur; it could go through flesh in an instant.

From beneath it, Cole could see Rush's running legs. She was heading for him in a dead sprint. He jerked over, bringing the Bulldog around. From beneath the machine, he aimed high and left of his target and managed to put a bullet into her knee. She stumbled, but managed to throw herself to the side. For the time it took for the whirring metal arm to nearly cut his head in half, Cole had a shot at her. He could have holed her heart, which might have slowed her down for a few minutes, but it wouldn't have killed her.

"Another miss," she said, laughing, pulling herself behind another of the hydraulic presses. "Your job interview isn't going very well."

He stole a peek to his left, the Bulldog up and ready despite the pain in his back. That he could move at all told him that the heavy slug had only grazed him. "What are you talking about?"

"For some reason, Mr. Tinsley likes you. He likes your integrity. If you live, he's going to offer you a job."

"If I live, he'll be going to jail."

She laughed, the sound edging to Cole's left. "That's cute. Dennis Tinsley is the seventh richest man in New York. When his father dies, he'll be the richest. When you have that kind of money, you don't go to prison. People who even talk like that disappear. You should keep that in…"

"Cole!" It was Corrina speaking through Cole's radio. "It's me. A vamp car just showed up. I don't know whose it is. Cole? Cole? Can you hear me? Damn it, Cole. I think you should get out of there."

He could hear her just fine. Even from across the room, her tinny voice was clear. At the first "Cole," he had pulled the radio from his pocket with an idea already formed in his mind. Setting it on the machine, he had slithered backwards and then crawled behind a long, waist-high die-press.

Rush would be listening to Corrina. Was it her boss coming? Was it Ashley looking to take advantage of the situation? Cole couldn't care less who it was. He had a Dead-eye on the hook and if he could land her, he would be legally untouchable.

Corrina's voice cut off and now there was movement among the machines. Rush was in a crouch, limping forward. With the news, she was throwing caution to the wind and was advancing toward where Cole had been seconds before. He lined up a shot just as she saw the radio sitting on the edge of the machine.

Even with two bullets in her, she was terrifyingly fast. Cole fired just as she spun away. There was no dodging a bullet from this distance. Black blood, like a thousand tiny, glistening drops of tar, exploded out of her head and rained down over the equipment. The force of the impact continued her spin so that it looked as though she were screwing herself into the floor as she crumpled.

He stared for three seconds, the gun held out, ready to fire, then, "Oh, thank God," he whispered, his shoulders slumping, his back bending, making it seem as though he had suddenly aged forty years. Days of built-up exhaustion were hitting him hard. Pain was as well. It wasn't just the latest wound, which had been only a distant sting. It was his leg, his face, the side of his head, and, "What's with my shoulder?" There was a deep ache in it that he hadn't noticed before.

Grimacing, he took a limping step forward to pump the last two bullets in his gun into her head. It was out of habit only. Half of her head was a black gory mess. Black blood was everywhere. Thinking of the recovery team, he muttered, "It's gonna be a hell of a clean…"

From fifteen feet away, he saw her chest rise and fall. *She isn't dead*; the thought was just crossing over the sluggish synapses in his brain when her hand seemed to float up on its own. She still held the monster gun. As he stared in shock, it bloomed with a gout of orange flame. The thunderclap that came with it got him moving a hair too late, and if her vision hadn't been compromised, he would've lost his head from his eyebrows on up.

She missed and it was no wonder. The huge hunk of lead from his Bulldog had struck her just as she had spun away, hitting the outer corner of her left eye. The black goo in the orb had instantly vaporized as her eye socket exploded, sending out splinters of needle-sharp bone. The bullet had then run a divot an inch deep through the side of her head, shearing off half her face.

Cole's battered body acted on its own. Without thought, he fired his gun as he dove once more for cover behind some iron machine. He missed badly, the bullet shrieking away.

Now he was down to one shot. He could reload, but if he took the time to, she would either escape out into the factory or she would also reload. The idea of Rush with five more chances to kill him had his heart cranking out heavy, unsteady beats like an old jackhammer.

"Make it count," he whispered to himself before he came up out of his crouch with the Bulldog aimed. He was a second too late. The Dead-eye was already running away, lurching heavily because of her destroyed kneecap. Cole ducked around the machine he'd been hiding behind and started to run after her. He had taken three strides when she hit an upright jig saw. Her leg buckled and she fell. It looked like she was dancing with the man-sized machine as she held on with one hand and pirouetted around it, bringing the gun up and firing in one motion.

He ducked away as the bullet tore through the air with a ripping sound.

Grinning, he was up in a flash. She was out of bullets! He had to get to her before she had a chance to reload. He limped after her, following the blood trail. She was leaking like a sieve. It wasn't just drops he was following, there was an unbroken line of black blood that meandered through the maze of machinery. At one point he came to a bizarre Rorschach-looking splash of black on the floor.

"Musta fell," he said, his grin stretching wider.

Then he saw her. The factory floor had never been bright. The only light came from a few dim overhead bulbs. She was in the deeper shadows near one corner. Cole hoisted the Bulldog and advanced. There was no need to talk. He would kill her and call in the recovery team, and maybe someone from the Governor's office, as well.

It wouldn't do to wound a vamp like Dennis Tinsley. Like Dead-eyes, it only made them more dangerous.

At eight paces, Cole stopped. He was close enough to kill her, although that wasn't why he had stopped. She wasn't alone. Unbelievably, she had Tate by the throat with a grip so tight it looked as though she were stretching and smearing his tattoos. In her other hand she held a knife, the point touching the soft flesh below his ear.

"Don't!" Tate said in a strangled voiced.

"Sorry. You know what she is. I can't let her live." *And you are too stupid to live*, he wanted to add. He should've been long gone by then. "Sorry," Cole said again and sighted down the length of the gun, aiming high and left of Rush's forehead.

In response, she slid further behind Tate. It made little difference. She wouldn't be able to hide behind him much longer. Cole took a step forward and she dragged him back, saying, "I thought you were a Jesus freak. Shouldn't you care about the innocent and the meek? Or is all that horse-shit to you?"

"I do care. It's why I haven't pulled the trigger yet. You aren't getting out of this alive. Let him go and I'll make it quick. Piss me off and this may take a while. I have more ammo and all the time in the world."

She shuffled a little further away. "How about this, Mr. Younger, turn around and walk away and I'll see that there's something in it for you. How does twenty-thousand sound? It's twice what you'd make for me." He shook his head, and she bumped up the bribe, "Thirty-thousand then."

The glib way in which she said this made him hesitate; she smiled through the ruin of her face. "So, there is a price that'll bend you. It turns out that even the White Knight of the 7th Precinct can be bought."

"Not for thirty-thousand, I can't. Try a hundred large." She scoffed and at the same time her one eye slipped to Tate, as if considering his worth. His ten-year contract as a machinist was probably worth sixteen-hundred dollars. His price as a slag was maybe three dollars and just then his value was only that of a human shield.

Oddly, he wasn't trying to help his case. In fact, he seemed more like a spectator than a hostage to a zombie. "What do you think, Tate?" Cole asked. "Is your life worth a hundred thousand dollars?"

"Yeah," he answered, readjusting the loose grip he had on her arm. His hands seemed to be simply hanging there. With a sudden jerk, he could pull away. "That's a lot, right? I'm worth a lot, so don't shoot."

Just like before in the conference room, his reply was strange. It was almost as if he was having trouble being normal. In the conference room, he sometimes seemed to be a slag acting like a Dead-eye and sometimes like a Dead-eye acting like a slag. It was as if he didn't know how to be either one, which made no sense to Cole.

You were either a slag or a Dead-eye...unless. Cole suddenly pivoted his gun so that it pointed at Tate. "Damn, I should've seen it. The henna tattoos, the soft hands for a machinist, the words. What slag says, 'fantastic?' Let me guess. You're a Tinsley."

"Dennis Tinsley." He bowed his head and as he did, he ducked under Rush's arm and switched places with her. It was a smooth move, but what was more so was the way a gun suddenly appeared in his right hand. It was pointed at Cole.

Cole thumbed back the hammer on his Bulldog. "Put down the gun, jackass. You're interfering with a bounty hunter during a Class 1 arrest. It's a felony and besides, I'd hate to kill you by accident."

"If you weren't grinning, I'd believe you. All the same, it's your neck you should be worried about. If you shoot me, she'll kill you. If you shoot her, well, let's just say, I don't miss."

"This is a big bad gun, one bullet might take care of both of you." At this range a round from the Bulldog would pass through her throat, blast out her spinal column and still have enough striking power to penetrate his heart.

Dennis grinned at the idea. "You might be right, but you'll still be dead. Even if I don't get you, I have guards all over the building. Your life won't be worth a nickel."

"Is that a joke? My life isn't worth a nickel now. You have made my life unlivable. I'm completely broke, I'm homeless, and I have who knows how many warrants hanging over my head. Hell, death doesn't seem so bad."

Cole took another step forward. Even with the pull of the Bulldog he couldn't miss now. "Your one chance is to drop that gun."

"Are you sure? You seem to have forgotten one tiny little thing. What's the name of the girl who hangs out with you?"

Cole's stomach dropped at the question. "No. You wouldn't."

"Her name is Corrina," Rush answered.

"Yes, that was it," Dennis said. His confident smile did not seem to go with his slagged face. It made him seem like two different people sharing the same body. "Just because I don't understand a man's fetish doesn't mean I can't profit from it. You will lower your gun, or she dies."

Chapter 30

Cole's chest began to thrum. He was ready to die, but he wasn't ready for Corrina to. Still, his gun didn't budge. "You're making a mistake. I'm still rational, but if you bring her into this all bets are off. And if you hurt her, you *will* die."

"Hmm, interesting," Dennis said, appraising Cole. "The White Knight is willing to risk everything for a child. Very interesting. Noble, even. I was serious about offering you a job. I need men of integrity around me. My father always said that you can tell a man by the company he keeps."

"And you hang around a Dead-eye assassin. It says a lot about you."

The vamp smirked, making the blue-green naked lady on his cheek swing her hip suggestively. "What it says is that one way or another, I get what I want, and what I want is someone I can trust in your department. Someone loyal. Someone who knows that I would never do anything to endanger the city. Trust me, Cole, my Dead-eyes know their place. The ones you were tracking down were temps who were supposed to do a job and then disappear."

"Disappear?"

Dennis ignored the question. "So, what do you think? A thousand dollars a month and I steer you toward those assets that need to be removed from circulation. This way we both win. It's either that or we both lose and little, sweet Corrina loses, too. And yes, this is a very limited time offer and I'm only asking once. I don't beg."

I say no and Corrina dies, Cole thought. *But if I say yes, I sell my soul and become nothing more than a hired gun.* He found himself at the top of a slippery slope where the promises seemed bright and shiny, and the corruption that would eventually rot him away from the inside out was hidden from him. He was sure Rush never expected to be standing where she was; a mutilated human shield. Where were her promises now?

"No," Cole decided. "Here's what's going to happen. I'm going to kill this Dead-eye and then I'm going to arrest you. From there, who knows? I suspect your money will get you off, but that's not something I can control so I'm not going to worry about it."

Dennis stared at him, his fake slag eyes unreadable. "What you're saying is non-negotiable and here's why." On cue a door opened to their right and in walked four hulking bodyguards. They were so large that at first Cole didn't see that Lieutenant Lloyd was among them. He had Corrina by the back of her jacket, like she was a dog on a very short leash. She was tightlipped and fuming, however, Cole knew this was her way of masking her fear.

"Those guards are some of my best negotiators," Dennis said in what sounded like an aroused whisper. "They can break every bone in her body without killing her. In about five minutes, she'll be begging to die. What are you going to do then? Kill me? Do you think that'll help her in any way? It's time to put the gun down, Cole. Then we can talk like civilized..."

He was interrupted as another door on the floor opened and in walked Ashley Tinsley and four of her own bodyguards. They moved through the machines, dwarfing them. At twenty paces, someone twitched and, in a blur, guns were drawn on both sides, the bodyguards pointing them at each other. The guards were so fast that Lloyd only had his hand in his coat and was now too afraid to pull his piece.

"I love it!" Dennis cried, smiling at his sister. "Beautiful moves, sis, bursting in here like that. I had no idea that you cared so much. Either way, I think you are a little too late. You seem to be a pawn down. Do you understand chess, Cole?"

"Well enough, I guess."

"Then you see how my sister has been out maneuvered. Look at the board. Our pawns cancel themselves out and what does that leave her? Yes, you are threatening me, but I have a firm checkmate on her. She can't make a move without losing. Her only option is to concede defeat." Ashley eyed the room angrily, with an especially malevolent glance at Lloyd. "What do you say we clear the pawns, sis? We wouldn't want anyone to get hurt."

Ashley had on skin-tight black leggings and a black leather biker's jacket with gold zippers and buttons. Her hair was like jet as were her lips and nails. Her eyes were golden once again. "Agreed." She snapped her fingers and her four guards holstered their weapons, turned and marched out of the room. Dennis' guards did the same, leaving just the six of them.

Now came an odd strained moment for Cole, Corrina and Lloyd. They glanced around, not sure what was going to happen next as the two siblings stood in strained silence; Ashley in between a pair of jig saws, Dennis, crouched down behind Rush, his gun pointed at Cole.

"I guess I don't understand chess as well as I'd like to think," Cole said. "I don't see how your sister is losing this. As far as I can tell, she hasn't done anything illegal. She isn't the one breaking the law by harboring Dead-eyes. Lieutenant Lloyd, this isn't our game. We have a Dead-eye right here. We need to take her out and we'll let the authorities worry about the rest."

Dennis' tattooed lips broke into a wide smile. "I thought you were the authorities." He laughed at this. It bubbled up out of him like a spring. It was a mad sound that made no sense with the gun in his hand and Rush's black blood pattering around his feet. The laughter was far from infectious. In fact, it made the moment worse as the tension in the air built up, thrumming in tune with the sound of the factory. Finally, he sobered and looked past Cole. "Do you give up, Ash? The game is over and you lost, fair and square."

"This isn't a game!" Cole barked from behind his revolver.

"Of course it is," Dennis replied. "We've all been neck deep in it for days now. I played the part of the king. Rush, here roamed the board as my queen. Belinda Ryan was my knight until you took her out. Mack-D and Billy Fish were some of my many pawns. Hell, I even had a bishop in your little friend Father James. Perhaps he played the part unwittingly, but that's neither here nor there. He still forced your moves and kept you from getting too close."

Belinda Ryan? Was that the blonde who had nearly killed me? And who was the scaled creature? Did it really matter? In the end, Cole didn't think so. His finger tightened on the trigger. "And what part did I play?"

He expected Dennis to say something like: *The fool*, however, he answered, "You were my sister's white knight and she played you superbly." He bowed his head towards Ashley. "By using you, she managed to take out more pieces than I would've guessed possible. And now we're down to the end game, waiting for our rook, Lieutenant Lloyd to make his move. I generally dislike the rook because it lacks imagination, but it can be devastating in the latter stages of the game, when the board is clear."

A prickle of fear crept up Cole's spine. If Lloyd decided to shoot him in the back he wouldn't be able to do anything about it, except pull his own trigger. Cole was surprised to find that he was buying into Dennis' analogy. They *were* in a chess game and he was basically out of moves.

It seemed the only one that could move was Ashley. She was tense, her golden eyes hard on Lloyd as if judging him and his loyalties. "Yes. The rook can be devastating, depending on whose side he's on." She said this flatly, devoid of emotion.

Cole was only just then realizing that Lloyd had been on the take from both of the Tinsleys and now he was being forced to make a choice between them. One thing was clear, if he chose to side with Dennis, Cole was a dead man.

Lloyd looked back and forth from the siblings, eyebrows raised as if expecting one of them to put out a new bribe.

They weren't about to get into a bidding war over a schlub like Lloyd. When he realized this he shrugged and said, "I'll go with Mr. Tinsley, I guess."

"What a heartfelt pledge of loyalty," Dennis drawled, rolling his eyes. "But weak as it was, it still represents a win. Sorry Ash. That is check and mate. Cole, you can't say I didn't give you a chance, but the charade is over. I understand that you have a gun and it's pointed at me, but let's be adult about this. I'll have my sister take little Caroline…"

"Corrina," Cole whispered. He could no longer feel his feet. His legs just seemed to ghost away somewhere below his knees.

"Corrina, of course. I'll have Ash send her to one of our factories out in Queens. It'll be a two-year indentureship, but after that she'll be free to leave and do whatever. Except mention what went on here that is. I think that's eminently fair of me, seeing as I could just as easily kill her."

Ashley slid her eyes from Lloyd long enough to glare at her brother. "First, I don't work for you, and second I haven't conceded anything. I'm not nearly so helpless as you think." She slipped her hand into her jacket; as she did, Lloyd partially pulled his gun. The shining aluminum could be seen winking just on the edge of his jacket.

The tension mounted even higher as Dennis turned cold, "All I have to do is say the word and the cop will kill you. Trust me, you're not that fast." When she didn't take her hand from her coat, he spat, "You tried to destroy me and you've failed. The price you'll pay will be steep and your penance will be long, but in the end we'll still be family. Or you can die here. The choice is yours."

Her eyes narrowed so that only two slivers of gold could be seen. Before she could answer, Corrina spat out, "I ain't goin' anywhere without Cole." She had her hands firmly planted on her non-hips. "And I ain't goin' to no factory. I'd rather die first."

Dennis was no longer laughing. "Then you will die. I don't really care a whit about you. I care that my own flesh and blood is willing to die over this bit of trash and his ragtag whore. Ash, I'm going to count to three. One!"

Lloyd slid his gun out another two inches. His jaw was clenched and there was a cold look in his eye that Cole had never seen before. He might have been something of a slouch now, but he had been a hard man at one time and the feel of a gun never quite left a man. Lloyd also knew that when you got in bed with a vamp, you couldn't keep one toe on the floor. You were all in or you were just another forgotten corpse lying in the gutter. He would kill Ashley if that's what his new boss asked of him.

"Don't do it, Lloyd!" Cole barked, his eyes flicking back and forth from the Dead-eye who was inching forward, to Lloyd who was a blink from killing Ashley. There was no way she'd be fast enough to draw her gun in time.

"That's up to Miss Tinsley," Lloyd said. "Take your hand off your gun or I will shoot."

She didn't budge, except to glare furiously at him, her black eyebrows pointing sharply down. "Don't try to turn this on me, Dennis. We both know you orchestrated all of this so you could put me under your thumb. I will not be one of your slaves."

"Two," Dennis answered simply. "Play time is over, sis. You know the alternatives. It's time for you to make a decision."

"You can go fuck your decision, Dennis. I won't be one of…"

In the middle of her sentence, Dennis shoved Rush right at Cole. The Dead-eye not only seemed to be expecting the move, she was *eagerly* expecting it. Her one eye glittered with hunger and her mouth gaped.

Taken by surprise, Cole fired the Bulldog by reflex alone. The gun went off with a thunderclap. A huge chunk of Rush's throat disappeared in a black cloud and even as she reached Cole, her limbs were failing. His aim had been perfect. The bullet pierced flesh, muscle and just enough of her C-4 vertebra to explode the bone, which in turn pierced her spinal column. She was going numb in mid-lunge. He caught her, pivoted in a short, fast circle and threw her bodily at Dennis, who had been staggered by the same bullet.

It had mushroomed on impact with Rush, and when it blasted out the back of her neck and struck Dennis in the shoulder, it hit him like a sledgehammer. The impact spun him halfway around and by the time he turned back, Rush was flying at him. In the dark he mistook her for Cole. His reactions and his aim were better than his eyesight and the bullet he ripped off smashed into her sternum and lodged in her heart—her fifth gunshot wound in the last ten minutes and yet, she was still alive.

At Cole's gunshot, Lloyd pulled his gun and aimed down the length as he had done a thousand times in the basement range at the police headquarters. Had Ashley simply put her hands up, he wouldn't have fired, but she slid a subcompact Crown from her coat in one fluid motion.

"Damn," he whispered and pulled the trigger just as a wild cat in red attacked him. Corrina had been watching the entire conversation in a growing fury. Her need for a ride on the mule was making her crazy and seeing Cole bleeding and caught in the vamp's trap had her mind tipping. But it was the idea of being sent back to one of the factories that made her attack a man three times her size.

She went for his gun arm a half second before he fired and instead of Ashley being shot through the forehead, she was hit in the thigh. She collapsed under her own weight, her pistol going off. The slug sang off four or five different machines, but not no one noticed.

Lloyd hollered as Corrina sank her teeth into his arm. She was no one's idea of a fighter, but she was a survivor and she knew she had a tiger by the tail. There was no letting go. The moment she did, he would turn the gun on her.

Cole saw this out of the corner of his eye, and desperation drove him to launch himself on Dennis just as he threw Rush off him. Dennis fired before he could line up his shot properly and the bullet drew a hot, fierce red line across Cole's side. The pain wasn't even worth a curse. Cole was too focused on getting the gun to care about a flesh wound, or even to worry about the niceties of civilized combat. He grabbed the gun in both hands and wrenched it up and around with all his strength, twisting Dennis' elbow at an obscene angle which should have broken it, however, Dennis was much stronger than he looked and stopped the twist, even though his own body was torqued back so that his chest was facing the ceiling.

He was so strong that he started to bend Cole back the other way. "Jesus!" Cole cried. Even with a hole in his shoulder, Dennis was unbelievably strong. Still, there was more to fighting than just strength. Cole kicked Dennis' legs out from under him and when he fell, Cole stepped around and used the entire strength of his upper body to twist the gun out of Dennis' grip. Bones snapped and the gun came free.

Cole's mind was filled with fear for Corrina. A justified fear. Even as he turned, he saw Lloyd slam the little girl into one of the machines. The back of her head *cracked!* against metal and her grip loosened enough for Lloyd to get his hand free. Despite the blood and her vision going in and out, there was still fight in Corrina and she lunged forward like a rabid dog, and like one, Lloyd aimed to put her down.

His gun came up, but so did Cole's. Cole had to rush his shots and didn't know if he had hit anything. He got off two rounds before Rush slammed into his leg, her teeth ripping through his brown overalls and going into his calf.

The pain was immediate and shocking. Nothing else mattered except ending the pain. He screamed and pointed the gun into what was left of her face and pulled the trigger. A great black hole appeared above her one good eye. It was a hideous dark tunnel that ran right through her head. In a blink, she dropped and Cole was allowed one breath before Dennis was on him. A hole in one shoulder and broken fingers on the opposite hand didn't stop him from slamming Cole back into one of the hydraulic presses. The gun went flying out of his hand as Dennis pushed Cole down on the receiving plate, a mad gleam in his fake brown eyes.

He slammed a green button and the machine hissed, coming alive. Above Cole's face was a grey metal cylinder, eight inches across; at fifty tons of force per square inch, it would flatten his head like a grape. All Dennis had to do was pull a long-armed lever, which he was reaching for even then.

At first, Cole heaved against the hand holding him down, but it felt like it too was attached to a hydraulic machine. He couldn't budge it. The cylinder began to descend. "Fuuuuuck," Cole whispered, hypnotized by it. That cylinder was an unrelenting, unforgiving force and he froze beneath it, his mind vapor-locked, his body suddenly uselessly weak.

Across the room, Ashley began ripping off a string of bullets, causing Dennis's attention to shift. When it did, Cole slammed his fist into the crook of his arm and, just like that, the shocking power that was holding him down was gone. Cole went for the gun. It had bounced off one machine and was practically at his feet. Dennis didn't seem to notice it. All he cared about was crushing Cole. He grabbed Cole once more and drove him back down onto the press.

By then, there was very little room between him and the cylinder. Cole couldn't see where he was aiming as he shoved the gun up into Dennis' chest and fired. There was a muffled boom and Dennis flinched—and still the cylinder came down and Dennis was still above him, holding him down as though he were a child.

Misfire? Cole wondered, bringing the gun up, his mind slow once more. It wasn't a misfire. His hand was covered in blood. It was black blood. Realization crept over him and as it did, Cole brought the gun up again, higher this time until it was pointed beneath Dennis' chin.

He pulled the trigger. There was a wet explosion as the crown of Dennis' head shot up into the air along with a fountain of black blood. *Dead-eye*, Cole thought in wonder. *He had been a Dead-eye this entire time.* Now his answers made sense and his utter lack of fear and his...the cylinder was still coming down. Dennis had toppled partially on Cole and partially on the lever. "Fuuuck!" he cried as he flailed desperately for the red *Stop* button. He smacked at it three times and on two of them he hit the green *Go* button. On the third, he hit red and the cylinder whispered to a stop an inch from his nose.

He wiggled free and stood in time to see Lloyd aiming his gun at Ashley Tinsley. She was glaring up at him from her knees. In her hand was the subcompact Crown, which she was desperately trying to reload with fingers that lacked the muscle memory of long practice. She was too slow and even as Cole sucked in a breath to scream: *NO!* Lloyd fired. From twelve feet, the impact sent her flying back.

Cole choked on his breath and his chest started to spasm as if he'd been the one shot. He was amazed at the pain, and the rush of anger, and the sudden, sharp feeling of emptiness. He hadn't realized that he cared, or at least that much. Since he'd met her, Cole had been telling himself that Ashley Tinsley was only a cold-hearted vamp and barely a real person. And yet, she wouldn't stop sneaking into his thoughts.

She was beautiful in a world without beauty, and she was headstrong in a world where moping obedience was the norm. She was graceful in motion as if she were drawn onto every backdrop. And her laugh, her real laugh, the one she kept hidden from the other vamps, redeemed her quick anger. And she...

Lloyd turned his smoking gun on Corrina. The girl was a tiny bloody bundle of rags on the floor.

Although Cole's feeling for Ashley had been a mystery even to himself, his feelings for Corrina were crystal clear. Like a knife, they cut through the sudden fugue that Ashley's death had thrown over him.

"Don't," Cole said. He was in a crouch on the floor, his bloody calf wouldn't hold his weight. "Don't do it."

Lloyd didn't budge. The gun was still pointed at the girl. "You fucked up, Cole. I'm just cleaning up your mess."

"I said don't! If you shoot, you're a dead man."

Slowly, Lloyd glanced over at Cole. There was blood in his thin hair. "And if she lives and talks? What then? I'm pretty sure my life won't be worth a damn. You know who these people are. They're the fucking Tinsleys, Cole, and we killed two of their kids. You think they're going to take that lying down? No. We need to clean up this shit now. No witnesses."

"Does that include me?" Lloyd hesitated a second too long before opening his mouth. Cole grunted out a laugh. He would be the fall guy. Lloyd would blame everything on him. It wouldn't be hard. Cole forced himself to his feet, fighting a wave of dizziness. "Not this time, Lloyd."

"What's that supposed to mean? We're cops, Cole. We're brothers in arms…" Cole pulled the trigger. He had a perfect bead on Lloyd and he couldn't miss, and if there had been any bullets left in his gun, he would've killed Lloyd. Instead, the trigger refused to budge. Goosebumps flared as he turned the gun sideways and saw that the slide was back.

With the dark, Lloyd hadn't seen that the gun was empty, but now that Cole had turned the gun, he saw that he was the last man standing and the last man armed. It felt like fate was justifying murder and he was cool with that. He turned his gun on Cole.

When the last gunshot roiled across the room, Cole didn't even jump. He was too tired and in too much pain to care anymore. Death would've been something of a relief. But he did not die. The gun that went off was Ashley's. She stood sagged against one of the machines as Lloyd clutched at his chest and stared at her in shocked confusion. He was still staring when his legs gave out and he fell, dead by the time he hit the floor.

Cole was also mired in confusion and relief and a wave of happiness that crested and fell just as quickly as Lloyd had. Then he was tossing aside Dennis' empty gun and scrambling for the Bulldog he had let drop earlier. His hands knew exactly what to do and in seconds, it was loaded and pointed at Ashley.

"Cole. Wh-what are you doing?"

"I know what you are," he said. She had taken at least one bullet straight to the chest. By the laws of nature, she should've been dead. She should've been lying in a pool of red blood like Lloyd. "You're one of them." He should've shot her. He should've pulled the trigger without pausing to think, let alone talk. *It's my job. Killing her is my job*, he tried to tell himself and yet his trigger finger felt frozen. He took his eyes from his target and stared at his finger and tried to will it to move.

"Are you sure?" she asked. She glanced over at the body of her brother and her golden eyes suddenly began to blur. "I warned him. I told him it was a stupid, stupid idea, but would he listen? No. He wanted it all. He said he would live forever and now look at him." She gestured with her pistol.

Cole didn't have to look. "You don't live as a Dead-eye. You simply exist. It's not living, Ash. Now…now turn around." He didn't think he'd be able to shoot her in the face. Hers was too beautiful to damage.

"I'm no Dead-eye, Cole." She dropped her pistol. It rattled on the cement. She faced him and unzipped her coat, grimacing as she did. "Would one of them need a bulletproof vest?" Beneath the jacket was a Kev-6 vest, the best vest on the market.

"Jesus," he whispered in shock. Before it could accidentally go off on its own, he swung the revolver away. "Jesus, Ashley I almost shot you. I almost…" Forgetting the gun, he limped to her and took her arms in his large hands and would've kissed her if Corrina hadn't moaned. He spouted a third, "Jesus!" as he went to the girl, his eyes raced over her body, afraid he would see half a dozen gaping bloody holes in her.

"She got conked pretty good but I think she'll be okay," Ashley said. "She's a fighter. You're lucky to have her."

"Lucky?" Since when had he ever been lucky? He pushed himself up and stared into Ashley's face, her ever-changing beautiful face. "I have a question. What color are your eyes?"

She grinned. "Blue, if I can remember right. I haven't seen them in years, but I think that they were blue at one time." Those eyes were golden orbs. They accented the touches of gold on her jacket and the single earring. She was wearing the earring Cole had brought to her days before.

Ashley was far too deliberate for that to have been an accident.

"I'd like to see them blue one day," he told her. As she opened her mouth to answer, he leaned in and kissed her.

It was a deep, warm, passionate kiss that lasted forever and at the same time, ended all too soon. She broke away and took a long shuddering breath. "I can't. This, us, we… I can't. I can't be seen with you. It's my family, Cole. They're…difficult people. Lloyd was right. They're going to want revenge and if they think you were involved at all, they'll kill you. And I can't have that."

"I'll risk it." Just then, he'd risk everything for her. In fact, he had been risking everything for her all along. He could've set aside the hunt from the very beginning, but he had held on long after honor had been satisfied. And that was the problem and the greatness about love; it was never satisfied.

"Huh? Cole?" It was Corrina. She tried to sit up but when she tried to push herself to a sitting position, she couldn't get her arm to work right. It hung loosely and she couldn't lift it. "What happened? What are we doing?"

He glanced up at Ashley and saw that she was barely holding on to her resolution. If he pressed it, she would weaken. If he kissed her again, she would relent. If he asked to stay with her for Corrina's sake, she would agree.

"We're leaving," he said, scooping her up. He would risk everything for Ashley, everything except Corrina.

"Did we win?" she asked, whispering hot breath onto his neck.

"Yeah. We got lucky."

Epilogue

"I'm bored," Corrina said for the tenth time. Cole knew what was coming next, and after a slight pause it came. "And I'm hungry."

"Me too." He hadn't eaten in two days. They'd been two very long days. Two days of pain and very little sleep. Two days of wondering if the next breath would be his last. Two days waiting for the police to snatch him up and beat him down.

Two days before, he had carried Corrina through one of the secret tunnels that led from the Krupp factory. He'd had to walk through knee-deep sludge that smelled like it had only been recently been expelled from the bowels of a million trogs. He thanked God for the rain that pelted him when he finally made his way out into the new morning.

He had decided not to go into hiding. If the Tinsleys were after him, hiding would only put off the end for a matter of days. If the police were after him, he'd have a week or two longer. But no one had come for him.

Of course, he had played the "innocence" game. While he was still bleeding, Cole had called his office and had casually asked for Lloyd.

"He's not in yet," Ms. Foller answered as cold as always. She hung up without waiting for him to leave a message.

The next time he called, there was a new receptionist. "Mr. Shamus McGuigan's office, this is Jenny speaking." She sounded exceptionally perky.

"McGuigan? Where's Lloyd?"

"He's passed on. With whom do I have the pleasure of speaking to?"

As much as Cole appreciated the polite talk, he knew it wouldn't last. Anything new and refreshing never did. Cole stayed on the line long enough to find out that any past "indiscretions" on Cole's part were being considered a problem stemming from the previous administration.

"All I care about is numbers, Cole and yours have not been very good lately," McGuigan said. "So, let's get out there and make some money."

His blatant greed made Cole's stomach turn. Still, Cole had promised his new boss that he was a "team player" with his eye on the "prize." He had limped from the phone booth and headed to the nearest pawnshop, where he brought out a single gold earring. Just before he had plunged down into the horror of a tunnel, Ashley had given it to him along with a kiss on the cheek which he still felt two days later. The rest of him was a colossal bruise, but that one spot was warm.

"What if she never shows up?" Corrina asked, eyeballing the jar of blood sitting by the front door. The top had skimmed over again and was beginning to harden. "Hey, it's getting hard again." The only good that had come from wasting all the money they had received from pawning Ashley's earring was the cast on Corrina's arm. She couldn't stir the ugly looking blood with one hand.

Cole groaned his way to his feet and gimped to the door. As he stirred the jar of blood—his own blood to be exact—he reminded her, "Zombies are like cats used to be back before when there were cats. I told you this already." Of course, she might have been high on syn-ope at the time. Her broken arm was like fire sometimes and when it wasn't, her head would pound like she was back down in the factory.

"I don't think you did. But one way or another it doesn't mean jack to me, Cole. I never saw no cat in my life." She rubbed her head asking, "Is it time for my pain meds yet?"

"It's time you stopped asking. I'm not getting you hooked on a new drug when you're almost over your craving for mule." He sneered at his own blood as he stirred. He would have to add a little more soon and he was already light-headed. "Back when there were cats, if you fed a stray, they'd keep coming back. Christina had been feeding on her mom."

Although Corrina had heard this before, she made the same face. "Gross. I would never do that. Sorry, Cole not even for you."

"That's probably a good idea. A Dead-eye will drain you down to the last ounce. I think that's what happened to her mom, then dad didn't know what to do with the body and so he chopped her up and put her in the freezer."

"But if dad's dead, why would she come back?"

The answer wasn't easy to admit even to himself: on some level, zombies were still people. If they could set aside their cravings and their rage, they still had feelings and desires. They held grudges, they could laugh, they could maybe even cry. As a hunter, it wasn't something he cared to think about.

And yet, he was there, penniless, hungry and homeless, betting that Christina had some shred of humanity left so he could snuff it out and make a little cash.

"It's a sad fucking world," he muttered and went back to the wall and slid down it.

Corrina was sleeping on his thigh when Christina finally showed up. Cole heard the shuffling outside the door. It came and went indecisively. He put a finger to Corrina's lips. When she cracked her eyes, he whispered, "It's time."

It was time to fight a Dead-eye with only a six-shot revolver and a shattered kid as backup. She nodded and lifted off of him just as the front door came open. In the dark, Christina Grimmett was a fiend with black eyes, staring out of a bone face. She saw Cole and half-turned as if she was going to take off. If she ran, he wouldn't be able to catch up. She didn't run. She sucked air in through the holes above her leering teeth. The need for blood was on her. It raved like a monster inside her. It was a raging scream that drowned out the idea of survival.

"Have some," Cole said, gesturing to the jar. Half a tongue slid from her mouth and wetted the remains of her lips. She couldn't stop herself and when she dropped to her knees and grabbed the jar, he stood in a fluid motion, barely feeling the pain. The Bulldog was out and pointed at her. Only it could have stopped her. She watched him from above the edge of the jar.

"I won't shoot until you're done. It wouldn't be right to let blood go to waste."

She nodded and lifted the jar, holding it sideways so she could watch him and drink at the same time. Even when it was empty, she didn't pull it away from her mouth. Like everyone else, she wanted to live.

"Sorry," Cole whispered. He didn't miss and it was the only thing that allowed him to sleep that night.

The End.

Author's Note:

Thank you all for taking the time to read my stories. I certainly hope you've enjoyed this one. Dead-eye Hunt is actually a spin off of The Apocalypse Crusade series.

If you would like to read along chapter by chapter as I write book two all you have to do is go to my Patreon page (**Here**) and support my writing. The tier levels are exceedingly generous with freebies, running from autographed books, video podcasts, free Audible books, signed T-shirts, and swag of all sorts. At a high enough tier you will even get to meet me in person as I take you and three friends out to dinner.

Patreon a great way to help support me so I don't have to go back into the coal mines…back into the dark.

Another way is to write a review of this book on Amazon and/or on your own Facebook page. The review is the most practical and inexpensive form of advertisement an independent author has available to get his work known. I would greatly appreciate it.

Now, that you've gone to my Patreon page and left your review—thank you very much—I would love for you to take a look at the series that is the genesis of the new story: **The Apocalypse Crusade**.

Forget what you think you know about zombies...

Forget the poorly acted movies and the comic books. Forget the endless debates over fast and slow walkers. From this day on, all that crap will fade away to nothing. America is on the precipice of hell and not for a moment do you believe it. You have your cable and your smartphone and your take-out twice a week and your vacation to Disney Land all planned, and you tell yourself you'll drop those ten pounds before you go.

But you aren't going anywhere.

In one horrible day your world collapses into nothing but a spitting, cursing, bleeding fight for survival. For some, the descent into hell is a long, slow, painful process of going at it tooth and nail, while for others it's over in a scream that's choked off when the blood pours down their windpipe. Those are the lucky ones.

But you will live, somehow, and you'll remember day one of the apocalypse where there was a chance, in fact there were plenty of chances for someone to stop it in its tracks and you'll wonder why the hell nobody did anything.

At first light on that first morning, Dr. Lee steps into the Walton facility on the initial day of human trials for the cure she's devoted her life to; she can barely contain her excitement. The labs are brand spanking new and everything is sharp and clean. They've been built to her specifications and are, without a doubt, a scientist's dream. Yet even better than the gleaming instruments is the fact that Walton is where cancer is going to be cured once and for all. It's where Dr. Lee is going to become world famous...only she doesn't realize what she's going to be famous for.

By midnight of that first day, Walton is a place of fire, of blood and of death, a death that, like the Apocalypse, is just the beginning.

What readers say about The Apocalypse Crusades:
"DO NOT pick this up until you are ready to commit to an all-night sleep-defying read!"
"WAY OUT WICKED"
"...full of suspense and intrigue, love, both innocent and romantic, hate, both blinding and unnatural, non-stop action, and a very real gripping and palpable fear."

PS: If you are interested in autographed copies of my books, souvenir posters of the covers, Apocalypse T-shirts and other awesome Swag, please visit my website at
<https://www.petemeredith1.com>

PPS: I need to thank a number of people for their help in bringing you this book. My beta readers: Joanna Niederer, Kari-Lyn Rakestraw, Annette Harvey, Doni Battenburg, Monica Turner, Shamus McGuigan, Victoria Graves Haugen, Ginger Dailey, Corrina Marie, Kim Phillips, Roseann Powell, Amanda Peterman, Chris Beckmann, Steffi Foller, Mindy Grindstaff, and Michelle Miller—Thanks so much!

Fictional works by Peter Meredith:

A Perfect America
Infinite Reality: Daggerland Online Novel 1
Infinite Assassins: Daggerland Online Novel 2
Dead Eye Hunt
Generation Z
Generation Z: The Queen of the Dead
Generation Z: The Queen of War
Generation Z: The Queen Unthroned
Generation Z: The Queen Enslaved
Generation Z: The Queen Unchained
The Sacrificial Daughter
The Apocalypse Crusade War of the Undead: Day One
The Apocalypse Crusade War of the Undead: Day Two
The Apocalypse Crusade War of the Undead Day Three
The Apocalypse Crusade War of the Undead Day Four
The Apocalypse Crusade War of the Undead Day Five
The Horror of the Shade: Trilogy of the Void 1
An Illusion of Hell: Trilogy of the Void 2
Hell Blade: Trilogy of the Void 3
The Punished
Sprite
The Blood Lure The Hidden Land Novel 1
The King's Trap The Hidden Land Novel 2
To Ensnare a Queen The Hidden Land Novel 3
The Apocalypse: The Undead World Novel 1
The Apocalypse Survivors: The Undead World Novel 2
The Apocalypse Outcasts: The Undead World Novel 3
The Apocalypse Fugitives: The Undead World Novel 4
The Apocalypse Renegades: The Undead World Novel 5
The Apocalypse Exile: The Undead World Novel 6
The Apocalypse War: The Undead World Novel 7
The Apocalypse Executioner: The Undead World Novel 8
The Apocalypse Revenge: The Undead World Novel 9
The Apocalypse Sacrifice: The Undead World 10
The Edge of Hell: Gods of the Undead Book One
The Edge of Temptation: Gods of the Undead Book Two
The Witch: Jillybean in the Undead World
Jillybean's First Adventure: An Undead World Expansion
Tales from the Butcher's Block

Printed in Great Britain
by Amazon